# ANCIENT GUARDIANS

## The Awakening

## S. L. MORGAN

x

Pasidian Press 2012

**ISBN-13: 978-0578159195**
**ISBN-10: 0578159198**
(Pasidian Press)

The Ancient Guardians novel
Series is Dedicated to

My sister, Amanda.

# *Introduction*

Harrison leaned an elbow on the windowsill of the carriage and rested his chin on his fist. He closed his eyes and struggled to fight back the grief he was feeling. Looking at his father, who was also overwhelmed with sorrow, was another daunting reminder of the great loss Pemdas had endured. *This should have never happened!* he thought in frustration. *If my men and I had only arrived moments earlier, none of this would have ever taken place.* Harrison was suffering from guilt over the loss of the emperor and the many warriors who had lost their lives; however, he maintained his composure because he knew the constant risks that the Guardians were up against while they protected Reece, The Key.

Hundreds of carriages followed Navarre's riderless stallion as it led the procession to the personal burial grounds of the Oxley family. Six Guardian horses, including Areion, were harnessed to the shiny black carriage that followed directly behind Navarre's stallion. Levi, Allestaine, Elizabeth, and Reece were in that carriage, while Harrison and his family followed closely behind.

Harrison said nothing in the carriage as the processional followed the riderless stallion to the final resting place of Emperor Navarre. Harrison's heart wrenched for Levi, his aunt, and his cousin. Until now, everyone appeared to be holding themselves together very well, but the hillside that overlooked the graves of many loved ones began to make the situation feel unbearably real again.

Navarre's stallion sprang into a ceremonial trot as he approached the flower-covered burial site of the emperor. Six Guardian warriors and imperial guards stood in proper formation around the immaculately decorated grave. The carriages encircled the area as Navarre's stallion halted and lowered himself onto one knee in front of the grave of his master. Harrison cleared his throat as he stepped out of the carriage and turned to assist his sister.

After King Nathaniel, Queen Madeline, and Lillian descended from the carriage, Harrison left both his mother and sister in his father's care in order to be of assistance to Reece. Harrison promptly strode to where Levi stood, assisting the ladies out of the carriage. Reece's eyes were filled with tears as Levi kindly handed his intended wife's hand to his cousin.

After all of the families took their places around Navarre's grave, Levi began the ceremony with the final parting words for his father, the emperor. Harrison felt

Reece grip the bend of his arm tightly while she blotted her eyes with her delicate handkerchief. Harrison instinctively brought his hand up to cover Reece's as he felt his own tears surfacing. Harrison glanced over at his aunt, who was now in care of his father, King Nathaniel, and her expression remained solemn.

Once Levi took the emperor's shield from Navarre's stallion and placed it over the flowers on the grave, the Guardian warriors approached where Lady Allestaine stood and bowed before her. They offered her Navarre's sword, which was placed on his neatly folded cloak. A tear slipped down Lady Allestaine's cheek as she took the articles from the men. She ran her fingers over the engraved handle of her husband's sword and clutched his cloak close to her heart.

After all of the ceremonial protocols had concluded, Harrison and Reece followed Levi, Lady Allestaine, and Elizabeth to their carriage. Reece remained quiet but leaned into Harrison affectionately, showing him her appreciation for his care of her.

"Thank you, Harrison," Levi said somberly as Harrison escorted Reece to his side.

Harrison nodded, "It is my honor."

Harrison climbed into the carriage behind theirs, expecting this to be as silent of a ride back to the palace as it was when they traveled to Navarre's grave site. Unfortunately, his sister felt it was time she vocalized her opinions about the events that surrounded the death of the emperor.

"It is such a misfortune that we have lost our dear uncle," she started. "I may never understand why he died in such a manner," Lillian said as she blotted her eyes.

Harrison refrained from commenting, but he did not hesitate to show his disapproval by turning his back to where she sat at his side.

"It is a tragic loss, Lillian," King Nathaniel answered, "and you may, in fact, never understand it. However, it will serve you well to learn about the honorable reasons for the loss of not only your uncle, but also the loss of Samuel and the many other brave Pemdai warriors."

She sniffed, "How does understanding the reasons why our men were slain in a thoughtless battle bring them any honor?"

Harrison began to feel the blood boiling beneath his skin. "You would be wise to vocalize your senselessness elsewhere," he answered curtly.

"Harrison, I mean no disrespect by my words."

Harrison looked at her with disgust. "Are you so mindless that you cannot understand why we battled Armedias? You dishonor all of Pemdas and each of the Guardians with your ignorance. It is a disgrace to hear such words come from the mouth of a daughter of a Pemdai king!"

"Harrison, enough!" his mother ordered. "We have just laid our beloved emperor to rest. I will hear none of this quarreling from either of my children."

Lillian sighed, "So once Levi and Reece are married, she will stand in my aunt's place?"

*I swear, if she doesn't shut up we shall be attending her funeral,* Harrison thought as he bit down hard on his bottom lip, refraining himself from lashing out at his sister.

"Rightfully so, Lillian," King Nathaniel answered.

Lillian exhaled loudly enough for Harrison to glare back at her.

"Are you against the emperor's choice of wife as well?" he asked sternly.

Lillian's eyes narrowed at Harrison's expression. "I believe I am. She is not a natural resident of Pemdas, and she is the reason we have lost our emperor."

"You will join your friend Simone in the Isle Dungeons should you or anyone else plan to conspire against her or Levi's wishes," Harrison retorted.

"There is no need for threats, son."

Harrison ignored his father. "Lillian, you are a foolish, spiteful woman, and I am ashamed to be known as your brother. You blame Reece for the emperor's death, but you are wrong to do so. The reason our warriors and the emperor are dead is because of people who have held the same opinions you so freely vocalize. You would be wise to keep your treasonous thoughts to yourself and not disgrace our family with them."

Lillian went into hysterics, forcing Harrison to close his eyes in frustration. Fortunately, they were arriving at the palace and Harrison wouldn't have to speak another word to his sister. He was the first one out of the carriage, and he could not get away from his family fast enough. His father gently grasped his arm, forcing Harrison to stop.

"Father, I am in no mood to listen to you defend Lillian at this time."

"I am not here to defend her words," King Nathaniel said. "Your mother has already decided it is best that she return to our estate with Lillian. The Oxleys should not be subjected to any such nonsense after what has happened."

"Very well," Harrison answered. "I believe that Levi will be detained for most of the evening, and I must report to the command center."

King Nathaniel stretched his arm out in the direction of a secluded entrance to the palace. "Let us have a drink first. I think it would be wise to unwind our nerves before returning to our duties."

Harrison nodded. "I will gladly join you."

# Chapter 1

evi had been in constant meetings with the kings of Pemdas since performing his father's burial ceremony, and this meeting seemed to be the most exhausting of them all. It had become pressing that the leaders of Pemdas meet with the Council of Worlds in regard to the war they had engaged in with Armedias. Levi planned to have Harrison accompany him to the council meeting, as Harrison had assumed the position of Commander of the Guardians after Samuel was killed in battle.

A number of the kings of Pemdas had expressed their concern about Levi and Harrison representing the Guardians on their own. Many felt that since both men were new in their respective positions that it might be prudent to bring additional counsel to accompany them to the council meeting. However, Levi remained inflexible on his final decision. He had learned from his father that he was to maintain his confidence at all times once he assumed the throne, and this meeting was undoubtedly putting that ability to the test.

Without warning, Levi stood and interrupted the kings as they bickered about arranging for a more mature king to join the men at the Council of Worlds.

"I appreciate each and every one of your concerns; however, my decision has been made. When I arranged this meeting, I did not do so in order for you to debate my competence amongst yourselves. I do not seek your permission or approval, nor do I require it," Levi announced in an authoritative tone that resonated in the room.

Harrison remained silent, sitting to Levi's right. Levi glanced at him before adding his final thoughts on the matter at hand.

"My commander and I will handle the Council of Worlds, and we will report back to all of you when we return. Whether or not they agree with how the Pemdai handled the recovery of The Key or how we have avenged our emperor's death, I will be the one to answer for those actions, as I am the one who commanded the land to be laid to waste." Levi nodded. "Gentlemen, this meeting is adjourned," he said dismissively.

King Hamilton and King Nathaniel approached Harrison where he stood next to Levi as the other kings left the room with concerned, yet humbled expressions.

King Nathaniel gripped Levi's shoulder. "They mean no insult to you, nephew. You must understand that. Each king understands how the majority of the Council of Worlds feels about our people and the protection of The Key."

Levi gazed somberly at his uncle. "If I should show weakness as their new emperor, I will never gain their respect. I will deal with the Council of Worlds. Harrison and I will represent Pemdas and our cause, as my father and Samuel have done so many times in the past. I have no fear of the Council, and I am prepared for their ignorant words."

King Hamilton unexpectedly let out a soft laugh. "You do remind me of your father; I only wish I could be in attendance to watch you and Harrison deal with those simpleminded leaders."

Harrison crossed his arms and grinned subtly. "Rest assured, Your Majesty, you won't be disappointed with our report."

King Nathaniel grinned. "I expect that you will not taunt our greatest enemy; you know Movac is anticipating this event like none other."

"Taunt?" Harrison asked with an arch of his brow. "I would never consider such a thing."

"Gentlemen, I believe it is nearing the hour, and I know that the rest of the kings are eagerly awaiting your return and your report," King Nathaniel said as he turned with the men to exit the room.

"We will arrange for a meeting as soon as we return," Levi announced as the men walked out of the command center.

"Make it quick!" King Hamilton said with a laugh. "My tolerance with the rest of these kings only goes so far."

With that, Levi and Harrison went their separate ways to change into their Guardian regalia. Once they were ready, Levi met Harrison in the courtyard.

"Forgive me, but I believe I have not had the opportunity to thank you for all you have done in my place while I have been attending to my duties," Levi said as he descended the steps.

Harrison nodded. "Think nothing of it. I only wish I could do more to give you additional time with Reece, your mother, and Lizzy. These kings are starting to get on my last nerve. Their relentless requests for meetings have me utterly exhausted. We need to move forward, and they need to leave."

Levi's lips tightened. "In time, I believe everything will settle down in the palace. I am confident they all will leave soon for their respective kingdoms, especially after we return from this meeting with our report." Levi sighed. "That is my hope, anyway. I would appreciate some solitude with Reece and my family."

Harrison swallowed hard as he looked at Levi. "I do not wish to intrude, but I worry over you. I am well aware that we all grieve differently; however, I am unsure if you have had any time to deal with your great loss and the profound responsibility placed on you overnight as emperor. I believe it would serve you well to spend more time with your mother, Lizzy, and Reece, instead of remaining in constant meetings."

Levi faintly smiled at his cousin's sympathy. "My father and I have had many discussions about what would be required of me should this day come. Do not worry over me."

Harrison shrugged. "I simply want to ensure that you are not taking on too much at once. It might have been best to have King Hamilton join us today."

Levi gazed sternly at Harrison. "Do you not trust that I can deal with the Council?" he questioned curtly.

"It is not that I do not trust you. I do, however, feel that you have overextended yourself already. After all, it is your *father* who was lost, and no one has given you a moment's reprieve from the drastic changes that our world has suffered."

Levi tilted his head to the side. "Unfortunately, it is my responsibility to ensure Pemdas recovers from that. Taking personal time for my own selfish emotions is not a privilege I am afforded." Levi pulled Areion's reins over the horse's head. "Now, let us get this meeting over with," he said as he hoisted himself onto Areion.

The men raced their horses to where the black Pemdai car awaited their arrival. Once the men were seated in the car, Harrison wasted no time bringing the vehicle up to top speed toward the vortex that led into the dimension of Faylein.

As the car traveled through the vortex, the vehicle audibly alerted that it had transitioned into flight mode. The car gained speed as it flew through the dark green sky of the dimension. "I must admit," Harrison said, "it will be difficult for me to listen to anything negative said about our warriors today. I am in no mood to tolerate the usual ignorance from these council leaders."

Levi glanced out his side window, studying the ominous sky the car was soaring through. "I will handle that. I understand how you are feeling, as I am in no mood to deal with accusations at this time either." Levi turned to Harrison. "However, do not forget that Jie Seintra was close to my father. I believe that is the reason he has arranged for the meeting to take place in his realm. I am confident he will keep things in order."

Harrison guided the car toward an illuminated road that led into a dark structure. They followed a small spacecraft through the structure's entrance. *Movac,* Levi thought in annoyance as the circular ship hovered over to a corner and disappeared before their eyes, cloaking itself.

"Of all the beings we have the privilege to encounter first," Harrison grumbled while he parked the Pemdai vehicle purposefully in front of Movac's ship, blocking it in its place.

"Why is it that you choose to provoke him already?" Levi asked in humor.

Harrison swung his door open. "How is it that you believe I am provoking him? This is the only place to park our vehicle," Harrison replied flippantly.

*Yeah, right!* Levi thought. As he got out of the car and joined his cousin, Movac's ship let down its platform. The tall, gangly creature walked out of the ship, along with six Ciatron guards. Levi stood tall and unyielding as Movac and his guards approached where he and Harrison stood.

"Guardians," Movac acknowledged both men in a grave tone.

Levi nodded. "Movac."

Movac stopped and stood, towering over Levi and Harrison. "Is there a problem?" Levi inquired authoritatively.

Movac narrowed his black, almond eyes. "Once again, the Guardians have proven they are not to be trusted. It is a shame that Emperor Navarre has met his demise due to your persistent cause of protecting The Key. He sacrificed his life by taking such power into his own possession. Foolish emperor, your father was."

Levi swallowed hard as he gazed into Movac's eyes threateningly. He started to answer the Ciatron leader, but Harrison stepped forward abruptly. "You are right about one thing, Movac," Harrison said with an edge to his voice. "Our kind is *not* to be trusted, especially where your kind is concerned!"

Movac stepped back, while his guards stepped forward. "However," Levi interrupted his cousin, "we will let the Council of Worlds make that determination, not you."

Movac stretched out a long arm. "After you, Guardians," he returned mockingly.

Levi restrained himself from rolling his eyes as he and Harrison walked toward the entrance of the steel building.

Large windows lined the chamber walls, displaying the green atmosphere of this dimension. All of the leaders representing every dimension were present, watching Levi and Harrison skeptically. Levi had no desire to read into the minds of those that could be read, as the expressions on their faces showed him what they had already concluded.

"Emperor Levi," Jie Seintra, the leader of this domain, announced as he stood to greet the men.

Movac walked over to an empty chair and sat slowly. He clasped his long fingers together and watched as Jie Seintra addressed Levi and Harrison.

*Why do I get the feeling we are suddenly on trial?* Harrison asked Levi telepathically.

Levi ignored his cousin and stepped forward to address the group, breaking the awkward silence. "Leaders of the Unification, we are here to seek your opinions as to what should be done with the prisoners from Armedias."

"Firstly, allow us to convey our deepest sympathies for the loss of Pemdas' emperor," Jie Seintra responded. "Emperor Navarre was a most excellent man."

Levi nodded toward the transparent being. "Your sympathies are appreciated."

"Do you not believe the emperor of Pemdas died in vain?" Movac asked the council leader.

Harrison turned sharply and glared at the waxy, gray being. Levi spoke up in order to keep Harrison from lashing out at the gangly creature. He brought his solemn gaze to Movac. "Emperor Navarre's death was most certainly not in vain. You all are well aware that the Guardians will fight to the death to protect The Key. Had Lucas not successfully lured The Key out of the protective dimension of Pemdas and enslaved her, we would have had no reason to go to war in order to protect her and all of you. He died honorably in pursuit of The Key. If it were not for his valor, all of our worlds would have seen their enslavement or demise if Lucas was successful in retrieving the map to the stone."

Movac's thin lips tightened as he brought his long fingers together into tight fists.

"We understand the Guardians' cause, and after The Key was presented to Council of Worlds, our respect for the Pemdai was restored," Jie Seintra started. "However, this council stands in question as to why the dimension of Armedias suffered absolute destruction in order for the Guardians to retrieve The Key. Do you believe this was necessary, Emperor Levi?"

Levi stood tall. "Allow me to remind the leaders of this council, as Emperor Navarre did when he presented The Key before all of you, that we will uphold our responsibility to protect her, and we will let it be known to all worlds what their fate will be should they choose to pursue her. Armedias serves as an example to all of you who may consider testing our duty to protect The Key, the map to the stone, and all of our worlds."

"Your point is clear to all of us," another spoke out. "Now we must decide if the Guardians believe themselves to have authority above the Council of Worlds to destroy any world for their cause."

Levi studied the fiery red being, but before he could respond, Harrison interjected.

"Is this why we are here, then, to justify our actions? This is the gratitude we receive for saving all worlds and dimensions from Lucas' attempts to rule over or destroy them?" Harrison continued brazenly. "Will you cowards always find a way to dishonor our duty as protectors of The Key and of *your* worlds? You all know what would happen to your realms should the stone be recovered by someone with the will to have total domination, yet you continually make us defend the cause that keeps you all free. You should be thanking us instead of putting us on trial!"

"Enough!" Movac said. He stood up and narrowed his almond eyes at Harrison. "I will not sit in a room and be referred to as a coward. Right now, this council must decide together if The Key should be removed from your protection. The Guardians have violated laws by taking it upon themselves to go to war with another domain in order to sustain their cause."

Levi's jaw tightened as he brought his deadly expression toward the leader of the council. "My commander is correct." He stepped forward as Jie Seintra rose up and watched Levi with an expression of sympathy. Levi let out a dark laugh of disbelief. "Once again, this council has lured us here under false pretenses. We came out of respect to all of you, yet you accuse us blindly."

"Emperor—"

"I have heard enough!" Levi snapped, cutting off Jie Seintra. "The Key will remain in the protective lands of Pemdas. My commander and the kings of our realm have already decided upon helping to rebuild the land of Armedias, and we no longer seek advice or help from any being in this room in regard to that land. We will also deal with the prisoners as we feel is just, and they will stand trial for their actions against Pemdas. Armedias was once a very close ally to our people. The Pemdai will work to help rebuild and restore Armedias to what she once was before Lucas took over the throne."

Movac laughed mockingly. "The young emperor believes himself above the council." He brought his long fingers to his elongated chin. "How interesting. Council leaders, this is why I have always held the position that the Guardians are not to be trusted. When will they invade our lands and rebuild them as their own?"

"If The Key had never been revealed to all council leaders, then Lucas would have never attempted to pursue her, and his priestesses with their dark powers would never have persuaded The Key to leave Pemdas. If one should place blame on any being in this room, let it fall upon Movac and his constant scheming and pursuit to take possession of The Key." Levi pointed toward Movac. "If this being had not been so desperate for the map within her mind, Emperor Navarre would still be alive, and The Key would still be living on Earth with her life unaltered."

"Can you contemptible Pemdai see that none of us will ever trust the Guardians or their word?" Movac looked over at Jie Seintra. "What say the council? I stand in opposition of their cause. I believe they will find a reason to destroy any domain, and they use the protection of The Key as their justification. They must be reprimanded in some manner. The Key must be removed from their dimension at once!"

Levi stared at Jie Seintra. "I will not allow my people to stand trial for what all of you have created in the first place. Leaders of the Unification, as Emperor Navarre made you all aware before leaving the last council meeting, We. Are.

Pemdai. We answer to no one. We will turn The Key over to no one, at any cost. If I were you, I would not take these words lightly. We served to protect, guard, and keep harmony not only in our land, but in yours as well. If there be any world that should attempt to challenge our protection of The Key, then you and your world will represent everything Armedias signified on the day the Guardians left her in ruins. That is all." Levi spun on his heel and turned to leave the room.

With that, Levi and Harrison marched briskly out of the room to their car. Levi glanced back when he heard the clatter of footsteps approaching hastily behind them.

*Please, Levi! Let us leave. I am in no mood for this. I fear I may end Jie Seintra's life if he questions us one more time,* Harrison said to Levi telepathically.

*Just get in the vehicle,* Levi returned.

"Emperor," Jie Seintra said with relief in his voice. "Please know that not all worlds are in agreement with Movac."

"Is this the reason you followed us out?" Levi returned in a low voice.

"No." He reached for Levi's shoulder. "Our kind will always be indebted to the Pemdai and their cause. I apologize for the speculation that took place during this meeting. Your people and your land are continuing to grieve a great loss."

Levi nodded in response.

Jie Seintra looked at Levi sorrowfully. "I was deeply saddened when I heard of Emperor Navarre's demise. My people are grateful to the Pemdai for their sacrifice to protect all of our worlds." He grinned at Levi proudly. "Emperor Levi, today you have shown me that you are as bold as your father, and I will rest at ease with the knowledge that our worlds remain under your supreme protection."

Levi cleared his throat, repressing the emotions that were beginning to surface. "I will never be the man my father was; nonetheless, I appreciate your words."

Jie Seintra nodded with a pleasant smile. "Forgive the council, Emperor Levi."

Levi studied the being for a moment before asking, "May I inquire something of you?"

"Anything."

"I have gone through my father's notes. After he was made aware that The Key was removed from Pemdas, I saw that he sought out all world leaders for immediate assistance in recovering The Key, as our men were few at the time." Levi's gaze bore into Jie Seintra's now guilty eyes. "Answer me this: why is it that the beings of Briedirken were the only ones to respond to him in our time of need?"

"Emperor Levi—" Jie Seintra stammered.

"I have no desire to listen to any excuses," Levi responded, cutting him off. "The trembling in your voice has given answer to the question I have asked." Levi shrugged the man's hand off his shoulder. "Go!" he ordered the being sternly. "It is evident to me that my father's blood is no longer on my hands alone. All of you have always been quick to condemn the Guardians, and frankly, I have grown weary of your interrogations. Be sure to relay my warning to the others. We will destroy any being and their land should they choose to pursue The Key as Lucas so foolishly did." Levi turned to open the passenger's side door of his car. "I do hope one day all of you will cease the questioning of our motives."

The man nodded humbly as Levi sat in the car and closed the door. Harrison sped out of the structure and brought the car up to top speed. The vehicle engaged flight mode and sent them soaring out and away from the structure. Both men remained silent as they re-entered the vortex to Pemdas.

As they parked the car in the stone structure and exited the vehicle to retrieve their horses, Levi clasped his hand on Harrison's shoulder. Harrison exhaled and glanced at Levi with a stern gaze.

"It is over, and we shall deal with Armedias alone," Levi told him reassuringly.

Harrison's eyes narrowed at Levi. "It is over?" he responded in a tone of disgust. "Levi, unless you are as blind as the rest of the fools in that room, you should understand completely that it will *never* be over."

Levi shrugged. "Very true," he returned, "but we waste our energy worrying over their opinions. In time, they will understand. Let us return to the palace and put this behind us."

"Agreed!" Harrison said as he wheeled his horse.

When they reached the palace, they made their way to the command center where the kings of Pemdas awaited their report. Once the report was concluded, the kings expressed their apologies for questioning whether or not Levi and Harrison were prepared to handle the Council of Worlds on their own. The kings agreed to help rebuild Armedias and offered their assistance as it was needed.

Harrison was assigned to head up the task alongside Vincent, his second-in-command. With the pressing issue of the Council of Worlds now behind him, Levi made it his first priority to search out Reece's whereabouts.

# Chapter 2

eece, Elizabeth, and Allestaine walked leisurely through the palace gardens. The fragrance of the fresh blooms and the soft breeze wafting across Reece's face complemented the nature of the soothing environment around her.

Reece was grateful that Allestaine had suggested that the three women spend this time outside and away from the palace. She would have never believed that a building as monumental as the palace could make her feel so claustrophobic. Kings and their families had filled every part of the massive structure, and there seemed to be no way of avoiding them.

Since her return from Armedias, the treatment she received from the physicians in Pemdas helped promote her rapid recovery. She was thrilled when Allestaine suggested they spend their afternoon outdoors in order to retreat from the activity in the palace. The fresh air was exhilarating, and the warmth of the sun on Reece's skin was calming.

The ladies strolled through the palace gardens. "It is truly amazing how a beautiful day can lift even the lowest of spirits," Elizabeth observed as they walked along the path.

Allestaine turned to face Elizabeth but stopped suddenly when she saw a visitor approaching from behind. Unexpectedly, her face radiated with excitement when she acknowledged who was nearing them. Reece turned. *Levi!* she thought as her eyes locked for a moment with his weary ones. As Allestaine approached her son, Reece studied his appearance. He had been so occupied with the responsibilities of assuming his new position as emperor that Reece was fortunate if she had five minutes alone with him. It felt as if she hadn't seen him in nearly a month. She longed to have him embrace her wholeheartedly, to have more time with him, and most of all to ensure that he was coping with everything well.

Levi's face was worn, and Reece's heart ached for him. Behind the faint smile he offered her, she saw the grief in his jewel-like blue eyes. It was obvious he was trying to cover his anguish and his weariness, and because of that Reece became all the more concerned for him. She stood patiently at Elizabeth's side as Allestaine addressed her son.

"Levi, this is a wonderful surprise indeed!" Allestaine greeted him cheerfully. "I trust everything is settled with the Council of Worlds after your visit with them today."

"There is no need to bore you with the details, mother; they reacted no differently than was expected," Levi answered her formally. "To their credit, they did express their sympathy for the loss of our emperor."

Allestaine gazed purposefully into her son's eyes. "My son, you have no need to be reserved with me. Your father and I have had many discussions about how those leaders truly feel about the Guardians' responsibilities." She smiled faintly. "I have spoken with your uncle and King Hamilton, and I have no doubt your father would have been proud of you today."

Levi bit down hard on his bottom lip and gazed out into the shrubbery behind his mother. Reece quickly picked up on his emotions, knowing he was suppressing thoughts of his father. His expression changed drastically, and Reece saw the pain he was trying to hide in his piercing blue eyes. She felt an overwhelming desire at that moment to hold him and bring him comfort.

Levi brought his attention back to his mother and cleared his throat. "I do hope the leaders took my words as seriously as they would have his," he answered in a low voice.

"I am certain they did," Allestaine answered proudly. She exhaled softly. "Son, you appear quite exhausted. You must find time to rest, my darling." She tenderly caressed his cheek. "Until then, I believe it will serve you well to have some time alone with Reece, as I know that neither of you have had the pleasure of each other's company in quite some time." She glanced at Reece with an affectionate smile, and then back to Levi. "I will see to it that you and Reece are not interrupted for the rest of the afternoon. If you will excuse Lizzy and me, I believe it will serve as a very entertaining distraction for us to hear Harrison's animated narrative of today's events." She laughed softly as she nodded toward Elizabeth.

Elizabeth embraced her brother with a hug. "Please heed Mother's advice. You and Reece should enjoy the solitude of your afternoon, and we shall see you both at dinner tonight."

Elizabeth stepped toward her mother while Levi nodded in response. "Harrison is with King Hamilton and Uncle Nathaniel."

Allestaine smiled. "Well then, it would seem that our afternoon promises to be more and more amusing," she murmured with a soft laugh before turning with Elizabeth to walk back toward the palace.

Reece wasted no time approaching Levi and wrapping her arms tightly around his waist. "You have no idea how much I've missed you!"

Levi brushed his hand over Reece's hair and rested his chin on her head. "I have missed you as well, my love," he said as she felt him place a soft kiss on her head.

Reece stepped back and ran her fingers under his eyes as she gazed into them. "You look so exhausted. You should—"

Levi grabbed her hand and kissed it tenderly before he scooped her into his arms and carried her over a small bridge to where stone benches surrounded one of the large fountains in the palace gardens. "I should," he kissed her lips, "be with you," he said as he sat on a bench, still cradling her in his arms.

Reece traced her fingers along the distressed lines of his forehead. "It seems like the only times I've seen you lately are when you have snuck out of your meetings to work with Arrow." She smiled at his guilty expression.

He sighed in return. "I intended to surprise you with that." He kissed her forehead. "It looks like you have uncovered my secret. Forgive me for spending so much time apart from you; I wanted to have him fully trained for you to ride as a wedding gift."

Were it not for the seamstress delivering and altering her wedding dress, the last thing on Reece's mind would have been her and Levi's wedding. The atmosphere of the palace was far too chaotic with the death of the emperor for her to concentrate on wedding arrangements.

Reece smiled sympathetically at him. "I'm teasing you," she answered with a laugh. "From what I can tell, it seems like working with Arrow has been therapeutic for you. It's not healthy for you to be stuck indoors and in meetings all day."

"Therapy is one word for it. Your horse has quite the spirit." Reece laughed as Levi nuzzled his lips on her neck. "For now, I wish to speak no more about anything and simply enjoy our solitude together," he said as he trailed a line of kisses along her neck.

"That sounds wonderful to me," she shivered as she tilted her head back to expose more of her neckline to him.

Levi happily accepted her gesture, and soon after his lips seized hers in an overwhelming kiss. Reece ran her fingers through his hair, grateful to be in his arms again. They stayed this way for a long while before Levi gently withdrew from her.

Reece sat there catching her breath as Levi continued to bestow soft kisses across her face and jawline.

He ran his sturdy hand along her arm. "Are you feeling well today, my love?" he asked as he leaned back. He gazed into her eyes. "You, my mother, and Lizzy appear to be coping well."

"I'm feeling wonderful, especially now that I am here with you. In regard to your mother and Lizzy, they do seem to be managing well enough. Elizabeth has had her moments of sadness, but Lady Allestaine has been a constant support to both of us while you've been away. She is dealing with the loss of her husband so differently than I would ever have imagined. She is a very strong woman."

"She is, indeed," Levi grinned. "Either way, I cannot thank you enough for being by her and my sister's side during my absence." He caressed her cheek as he studied her face. "Are you sure you are feeling okay? The physician has reported that you are completely healed; however, I want to be sure the busy atmosphere of the palace is not too overwhelming for you."

Reece tilted her head to the side. "Yes, trust me. Jasmeen fusses over me like a mother hen each morning and ensures that I am feeling well before she lets me out of her sight. I have enjoyed being with your mother and sister," she ran her fingers through his thick, wavy hair, "and it has served to pass the time while you've been busy. I'm perfectly fine; I'm only worried about you." She gazed into his fatigued eyes. "You look very tired. How are *you* coping with all of this?" she asked, hoping he would open up to her.

"There is no need to worry about me," he said as his lips claimed the side of her neck. "Everything I should desire is in my arms. I am perfectly well now." He returned his eyes to hers and tucked a stray lock of hair behind her ear. "I love you," he said earnestly.

\*\*\*

The next morning, Reece walked out of her dressing room and clasped her bracelet around her wrist. She absently rubbed the slender arrow, feeling overcome by concern for Levi. She wandered over to her divan and sat for a moment to enjoy a cup of tea.

She was up earlier than usual, and she sighed in relief when she learned that most of the kings and their families were already departing the palace to return to their respective kingdoms.

Reece desperately hoped Levi would not be detained by any business today, and she hoped that perhaps they could enjoy some time alone to talk about how Levi was handling the passing of his father and his new role as emperor.

"Reece, Master Harrison is here for you," Jasmeen announced.

*Harrison?* Reece thought in disbelief. He was the last person she expected to arrive at her room this early. She stood to greet him. "This is a surprise," she said as she walked over to Harrison. "Is everything okay?"

Harrison smiled faintly. "Forgive me if I have intruded on you, Reece, but I wanted a moment alone to speak with you about Levi."

Reece smiled sympathetically at Harrison's apologetic expression. She took a seat on the sofa across from him. "First of all, when have you ever asked *anyone* to forgive you for anything?" She laughed. "You don't need to use the Pemdai formalities with me; you're going to make me uneasy. I'm already worried about Levi, and I don't have the energy to worry about you, too," she teased.

Harrison laughed. "You are correct. The meeting I have just come from with Levi seems to have put me off of my game." His face grew somber as he stared into the teacup Jasmeen handed him.

Reece watched him with trepidation. "What's going on? What happened?"

Harrison swallowed a sip of his tea. "Levi left the palace abruptly after an unexpected outburst this morning. I have been quite bothered about how he has been dealing with everything, but he will not open up to me." Harrison looked at Reece. "I am hoping you might be able to talk with Levi. If there is anyone that may be able to get through to him, it's you!"

Reece's heart began to race, and the expression on Harrison's face wasn't helping. This was exactly what she was worried about. "Do you have any idea where he went?"

Harrison shook his head. "I have no clue. He apologized for his outburst, then told me he needed to get away. He has always been the type to take a ride to ease his tensions, but I became even more concerned when he requested that I tell no one that he was leaving...especially you." Harrison looked at her genuinely. "You know I am not one to violate someone's trust, but I feel there is much more going on within Levi than he would have us believe. I am uncertain about why he was adamant I not tell you he was leaving the palace, but I knew I needed to let you know."

Reece thought for a moment before an idea as to where he may have gone came to her. "I think I know exactly where he is, but I need you to ride there with me."

Harrison's face lit up. "Your carriage should be ready to go within the hour."

"Then we won't go by carriage. I don't want to waste any time," she stated simply.

Harrison looked at Reece quizzically. "Well, the Guardian horses are the only horses currently at the palace, and—"

"Perfect. I'll meet you at the stables. Please have Javian saddle Arrow for me," Reece responded determinedly.

Harrison chuckled in disbelief. "Arrow? Absolutely not! Have you lost your mind as well?"

Reece grinned. "Yes, *Arrow;* and no, I haven't lost my mind. Over the last two weeks, I've been watching Levi work with him. I can see that he's ready to ride now."

"Reece, do you realize the stubbornness of that young horse? The trouble he is giving Levi? He's worse than Areion ever was. There is no way—"

"Harrison," Reece interrupted, "if you don't tell Javian to saddle Arrow for me, I will find a way to do it myself."

Harrison's eyes narrowed as he groused, "You sound like your intended husband." He brought both hands to his hips and grinned. "I will meet you at the stables, and then I will face my cousin's wrath when and if we encounter him."

Reece walked to where Jasmeen was organizing the clothes in her closet. "I need to change," she said as she plucked her riding jacket off its hanger. Jasmeen located the rest of the riding ensemble and quickly helped Reece change into it.

Once she was dressed and ready to ride, Reece walked to the stables where Harrison waited with Javian. "Miss Bryant, please. I have already sent for another horse," Javian pleaded. "The horse should be here within the next ten minutes. I am uncomfortable with you riding Arrow; Master Levi needs more time to guarantee that you will be safe with him."

Reece smiled as she pet Arrow on his muscular neck. "I appreciate your concern, Javian, but Arrow and I will be perfectly fine," Reece answered as she noticed the new black saddle strapped to her stallion. "Besides, he's already saddled."

Harrison crossed his arms and leaned against the fence. "Javian, you waste your time attempting to convince her otherwise. Don't worry, my friend," he clapped Javian on the shoulder, "Levi will have both our heads if anything were to happen to Reece. Nevertheless, she will not budge from her demands." He pushed himself off the fence. "I, myself, should like to see how this stallion responds to her mastering him," he said with a smirk.

Reece exhaled. "I'll be fine, and I will personally take the blame if anything happens." She looked at Javian. "Harrison will be with me for the entire ride. I am sure Saracen will help to keep Arrow in line as well."

She grabbed Arrow's reins, but before she could step into the stirrup, Harrison stopped her.

"Reece, before you mount up, you need to know that Guardian horses are much different than the others you have ridden."

"I have already gone through this with Levi," she stated confidently, "and I've already ridden, or should I say *mastered*, Areion."

"Alone?" Harrison questioned.

"No, Levi was with me."

"There is a monumental difference, Reece: Levi was with you." Harrison rested his arm over Arrow's saddle. "Now, from the moment you step into that stirrup, you must mentally give yourself over to Arrow. If he approves of you mastering him, well, then Javian and I will not have to worry about Levi's condemnation this evening. If not—"

"If not? Maybe you shouldn't put those thoughts in my head right before I get on the horse, Harrison." Reece arched her brow at him.

Harrison sighed. "Good point."

Reece turned and without hesitation stepped into the stirrup and swung her leg over the massive stallion's back before settling into the saddle. She reached for the reins and leaned over to pet Arrow's firm neck.

It appeared as if everyone had frozen in place except for Arrow, who immediately raised and turned his head to study Reece. Harrison's eyes were intense as he stared at the young horse, and Reece could feel the tension radiating like heat from Javian as he watched Arrow. The men stood at either side of the horse, ready and waiting for whatever Arrow's response might be to Reece wanting to master him.

"Hello, Arrow. How's my boy? I've missed you!" Reece greeted the stallion cheerfully.

Arrow jerked his head out, stomped his feet, and grunted in response. Harrison sighed in relief while Javian reached out to a fence post for support.

Reece could not help but burst into laughter at the sight of the two men. She reached out and patted Arrow on his strong, powerful shoulder. "These men stress out way too much, don't you think? Now, let's go find your dad!" Reece said as she directed the horse away from the stables.

Harrison shook his head. "You have got to be kidding me."

Javian chuckled. "I have never seen anything like it. This horse has always been fond of Miss Bryant in a way Master Levi and I could never understand."

Harrison hoisted himself up on Saracen. "Well, Arrow," he said as he directed Saracen over to where Arrow stood gallantly, "show me what you've got, boy!"

With that, both stallions set out at rapidly away from the palace grounds.

Harrison and Reece slowed their horses as they rode along the tree-covered road that led to the stately home Levi had purchased for him and Reece.

"Thank you for riding with me. If Levi is here, it's probably best that I speak with him alone," Reece said.

Harrison grinned, "Allow me to be certain he is here; then believe me, I will leave directly." He nodded toward Arrow, who was trotting briskly on the road. "If he is still in the same mood he left me in, I do not wish to be anywhere near him when he sees that you have ridden Arrow here on your own."

"I'm not worried about that. If he's in the state of mind that I think he's in, I highly doubt he'll notice that I rode here on Arrow."

As the road opened out from under the trees, the imposing house was the first sight to greet them. Reece looked around for a moment before she spotted Areion grazing by the large pond to the right of the house, and then she saw Levi sitting on the stone bench that faced their small lake.

Both horses halted. "Are you sure you want me to leave?" Harrison asked. His tone was sincere as he stared somberly to where Levi sat alone.

Reece smiled at Harrison reassuringly. "We'll be fine." She reached over and patted his arm. "Thank you again for coming with me."

Harrison nodded. Reece could tell that seeing his cousin in this state troubled Harrison immensely.

Harrison turned Saracen. "I will see you back at the palace."

"Harrison," Reece softly called out. "I'm sure he'll want to talk to you when we return; either to yell at you or something else of that nature." She offered him an encouraging smile.

Harrison chuckled. "I am quite certain you are correct about that," he said while directing Saracen back down the road.

Reece guided Arrow toward the pond where Levi sat. It was quite a distance from their stately home, and as such, Levi had no idea Reece and Harrison had shown up. Once close enough, Reece dismounted from Arrow and left the stallion to wander over to Areion. She slowly and quietly made her way to where Levi sat leaning forward, resting his elbows on both knees.

"Levi," she called out to him softly.

Levi's head snapped up, and when Reece saw his face and looked into his eyes, it took every ounce of strength within her to restrain her tears.

# Chapter 3

Anguish, grief, and sorrow dulled Levi's usually vibrant sapphire eyes. For the first time since Reece learned Navarre was no longer alive, she saw Levi's face show his suffering and utter distress.

Reece plucked a glistening pink flower from the grass, held it to her nose, and inhaled. "It's a lovely day to be out at our house, don't you think?" she asked, smiling down at him.

Levi quickly recovered his composure and stood. He said nothing as he brought her into a tight embrace before guiding her to sit on the stone bench next to him. "It is a pleasant day, yes," he responded. He looked over at her. "I had no intention of leaving without seeing you first; however, I desperately needed some time away from the palace," Levi said as he turned his attention out to the water before him.

"I understand. I feel the same way," Reece responded, studying his sorrowful demeanor.

Levi leaned forward, rested his elbows on his knees, and ran his hands through his hair. He softly exhaled, clasped his hands together, and stared down at them. His cheek fluttered with a twitch, showing he was holding back his emotions.

It was agonizing for Reece to watch him in this state. *How long has he been out here alone like this?* she wondered before Levi finally spoke again.

"My father promised me—" Levi's voice cracked. He cleared his throat. "He promised me that he would allow me to live the normal life I had always wanted. That he would not—"

Levi ran his hands through his hair again and hung his head. He closed his eyes. "Why?" he whispered painfully.

He looked at Reece. His eyes filled with tears as his lips twisted in sadness, and though he tried not to cry, he suddenly lost the battle. She reached out for him, and at first Levi mouthed the words *"Please don't"* while he pressed his hand into her chest softly, preventing her from embracing him.

Reece ignored him and brushed a tear from his jaw. She pulled him close, and Levi collapsed into her embrace. Her lips tightened as tears filled her eyes while he wept in her arms. They sat this way for a few moments before Levi gathered himself and slowly withdrew from her embrace.

Levi looked at Reece and shook his head, upset, as he wiped the tears away from her eyes. "Please forgive—"

"Don't," Reece said sternly. "Don't you dare apologize to me for anything."

She reached up and swept more tears from his cheeks. His eyes were glossy, but there was a hint of vibrancy returning to them. His mouth twisted up, forcing a smile. He returned his gaze to the water, reached over, and took her hand into his. His strong hand covered hers, and he began to rub the back of it absently with his thumb.

"You need to talk to me." She looked at him purposefully.

"My love, please, I will get through this. There is nothing to talk about."

"Levi, you can't run away from it."

Levi cleared his throat and glanced away from her. "I cannot talk about this. Not right now."

"Yes, you can." She reached for his arm, bringing his attention back to her. "Talk to me. You have been there for me when I've needed you. You've always played *my* hero, now it's time for me to be there for you."

"I will not burden you with my sorrow, my love." His eyes pooled with tears again. "This is not your burden to bear. As I said, I simply need time alone, and I shall get through this."

Reece gazed at him sternly and gripped his hand. "So this is how our relationship will be, then? You give everything, and I get to receive? Your feelings are a burden that you must bear alone?"

"Reece—"

"No, Levi. This isn't right, and it isn't healthy. Don't you understand that I can't be happy when I know you're suffering on the inside? You need to know that I want to help you as much as you've always wanted to help me."

Levi's eyes penetrated her soul as he contemplated his response. His jaw clenched tightly, and his eyes seemed to beg her to give in to his wishes.

"Talk to me, my love," she whispered softly as she caressed his cheek.

Levi finally spoke, sighing. "It is my fault." He pulled his hand from Reece's, stood up, and walked a few steps toward the lake. "All of it. If I had never left you alone with Simone, we would not have had to go to war with a fraction of our warriors. I should have been stealthier in that battle when we were overtaken, but I wasn't, and my father met his death because of my lack of skill."

Reece followed, walked up beside him, and intertwined her fingers through his. Levi looked down at her sadly.

Reece maintained her composure. "You can't blame yourself for what has already been done, something that you're powerless to change. You only left me alone with Simone because I demanded you do so while the priestess was manipulating my thoughts." She smiled sympathetically at his saddened expression. "And being the gentleman you have always been, you respected my wishes and did what I asked of you without questioning me or my sanity at the time."

Levi shook his head. "There are so many things I wish I had been wise enough to prevent." He withdrew his hand from hers and crossed his arms. "If I was more furtive, that soldier would have never pinned me to the ground, and my father would have had no need to rescue me." He glanced at Reece. "It is why he is dead," he said flatly. "Our line broke, and utter chaos ensued. My father sacrificed his life to save mine." He gripped his head. "It is an image that will never leave my mind."

"It sounds to me like you both might have been killed," she said softly.

Levi glanced at her in confusion. "My father died because I failed."

Reece gazed out at the lake as a soft breeze came up and blew across her face. "You are a Guardian warrior, are you not?"

"Yes." He sighed.

"I've heard you say countless times that the Guardians are fearless warriors who aren't afraid to die honorably fighting for their cause. None of you knew what you were heading into, but you went in despite being outnumbered. You are all lucky to be alive, considering your odds, and I think deep down you know that."

"Reece, you do not understand..." He trailed off softly.

"No, I may not understand. I may never understand. What I do know is that you are not the reason your father is gone. Do you think he would want you to bear guilt for his death?"

Levi exhaled and shook his head subtly in response as Reece continued.

"Do you think that you weren't the most important person to him on that battlefield, or that he would regret giving his life to save yours? Your father died so that you might live, and he would not want you to live with the constant guilt that you could've done something different to prevent his death," she said meaningfully. "You cannot dwell on that which you cannot change. To do so is to rob yourself of the life that your father would want you to wholly embrace."

Levi let out a long sigh before he looked at her. "You are right," he said with relief. "The loss of my father has had me reliving that moment over and over, and I suppose it is difficult to move forward and heal when you are constantly living in the past." He pulled her close and rested his chin on her head. "My father would be the first to tell me to let it go and move on, if only for the sake of you, my mother, and sister, so I must." He stepped back and cupped her chin with his hand. "Thank you," he said purposefully. "You have no idea what your words have freed me from."

She smiled up into his sapphire eyes. "There is no need to thank me for being there for you. I know what it is like to grieve the loss of a father, and I also know that people grieve differently. You were placed in a position of great responsibility at the same time that you should have been trying to process his death," she added as she reached for his hand. "I think what is important now is that you let go of your guilt and start to move forward as best you can. It won't happen overnight, but I promise it will get easier, and I'll be here to listen and talk with you whenever you need me."

Levi gazed intently into her eyes. "I love you," he said as they walked over to the bench and sat together.

Levi brought his arm around her shoulders, and Reece leaned into his embrace. "I love being at our home together," she said contentedly. "It's so peaceful here."

Levi turned to face her, and then stared at her in puzzlement. He looked back to where the house was, and when he brought his gaze down to Reece, his eyes narrowed.

"Reece?"

"Yes?" She smiled up at him.

"Where is your carriage? How did you—"

"Arrow," Reece returned with a smug grin.

Levi's expression caused her to laugh. He sat there motionless as his eye caught Arrow grazing next to Areion. Reece sat perfectly straight, ready to react to whatever scolding she might receive from him.

When Levi looked back at her, Reece brought her hand up to cover her smile as she watched the many different expressions cross Levi's face.

Levi finally broke the silence as he cleared his throat. "My love, forgive me if I seem upset; I am only concerned about your safety in this situation. Firstly, please tell me you saddled Arrow on your own, as Javian will soon be—"

"You know I don't know how to saddle a horse," she interrupted. "Javian saddled him, and you will absolutely not blame him for anything. I didn't give him a choice. He and Harrison both—"

Levi's eyes widened. "Harrison? Do not tell me my cousin allowed you upon that horse's back with the knowledge of what Arrow has put me through while trying to train him?"

Reece exhaled. "You need to calm down. Harrison and Javian had no say in the matter. Apparently, the carriage was going to take too long to prepare, and I wasn't going to wait," she simply stated. "I needed a horse, and the only horse I trust is Arrow. I refused to let them convince me otherwise."

Levi's eyes grew stern. "That horse could have severely injured you, or worse. He could have—"

"I know, believe me," Reece said, interrupting him. "Harrison and Javian both nearly had heart attacks waiting for his response to my climbing on his back."

"I am amazed both men allowed this. As I was saying, that stallion could have taken your life, or at least injured you greatly.

"Well, he didn't." She lifted her chin. "Do I look injured to you?" she said as she sat back and smiled.

Levi's eyes scrutinized the frame of her body, and he struggled to hide a slight grin. "No, my love." His hand rubbed tenderly along the outside of her thigh. "You are perfect, stunning, and as always, breathtakingly beautiful."

Before she could respond, Levi pulled her onto his lap, facing him, and cradled her neck in his hands. His mouth captured hers in a passionate kiss, which Reece welcomed enthusiastically. Finally, and for the first time since their return from Armedias, Reece felt like the man she loved was back with her again.

After too few moments of being lost in their overwhelming kiss, Levi slowly withdrew from Reece and finished with a soft brush of his lips to her nose. He gazed adoringly into her vibrant eyes. "May I request something of you?" he smiled.

Reece traced his lips with a delicate fingertip. "Request?" she returned with a laugh. She ran her hands through his hair. "Yes, you may *request* anything of me."

Levi's grin broadened as he ran his hands along her hips. "With an eye toward moving forward, I believe Pemdas has mourned long enough, and I am ready to resume the plans for our wedding."

Reece tilted her head to the side. "Will this result in all of the kings and their families returning to the palace, or will we go ahead with the private Pemdai ceremony instead?"

Levi offered Reece a mischievous grin. "Allow me two weeks so that we can honor both ceremonies in a special way."

Reece's eyes narrowed. "What exactly do you have in mind, Levi?"

He laughed softly in return. "It is true that all of the kings and their families will have a strong desire to take part in the celebration of our union. However, we will be on our vacation during that time." He kissed her chin. "We will still honor a traditional wedding ceremony as performed on

Earth, but our wedding will only consist of close friends and family."

"Close friends and family?" Reece eyed him skeptically. "I can only imagine how many *close friends and family* the emperor's family has," she teased.

Levi laughed. "I will not lie, there will be quite a few in attendance, but the number of guests at our wedding will not compare to those who will show up for the celebration after we have left." His gaze drifted toward the lake, and he laughed.

"Am I missing something?" Reece answered, confused as to what could be going on in his mind.

Levi brought his attention back to Reece. "No." He laughed again. "I am only imagining our leaving Harrison alone to deal with a palace filled with guests for a celebration."

"I'm sure he'll enjoy the company."

Levi exhaled with a laugh. "Oh, indeed. I am confident he will." He kissed her chin. "Enough of Harrison's future problems. We need to bring our focus back to you and me and the thrilling idea that we will be husband and wife within two weeks."

"Wonderful idea." Reece smiled as she ran her hands along his sturdy arms. "I do wonder, though, is it going to be awkward for the guests if we don't attend our own Pemdai celebration party? Not only for the guests, but I am concerned about your mother. Will she be comfortable with us leaving her alone to deal with a palace full of guests?"

"My mother has conveyed to me numerous times that she is eagerly anticipating hosting this event. She does not need us in attendance in order to enjoy herself."

"Two weeks?" Reece answered with a glint in her eyes. "You really think you can arrange all of this in two weeks?"

"I am confident I can, and with my mother's assistance, I will." He pressed his lips against her throat. "We have waited longer than I would have liked, anyway."

Reece framed Levi's face in her hands. "After everything we have been through, I couldn't agree with you more."

"Then it is settled!" Levi said as he scooped her into his arms and stood. He spun around with her in his arms as he nuzzled her neck, causing Reece to squeal with delight. He gently let her down and offered his arm. "Shall we return to Pasidian? I believe we have exciting news to share," he said proudly.

Reece placed her hand in the bend of his arm. "Yes, we shall," she answered as they walked to where Arrow and Areion were grazing.

Levi softly exhaled, compelling Reece to glance at him. "Is something wrong?" she asked, noticing his demeanor had changed to a more serious one.

Levi gazed intently at Arrow. "Everything is perfectly fine. Remind me when we return to the palace to reprimand my cousin for allowing you to ride this horse." He was baffled that the horse had carried her safely to this location. He understood Arrow was taken with Reece, but for her to master a Guardian horse in less than a day? That was unheard of.

"How did you manage that horse anyway?" he asked as they leisurely strolled towards the horses.

"Like I said, he was wonderful. He didn't fight me at all."

Levi couldn't fathom why Arrow trusted Reece the way that he did. Guardian horses in their maturity did not naturally take to one who was not a Guardian, and during the time Levi had spent working with him, Arrow seemed as though he would be the type of horse that would never allow anyone to be his master. Levi was resigned to the fact that Arrow was the most fierce and stubborn horse he had ever encountered.

He stopped and observed as Arrow grazed. "Arrow!" he bellowed.

The horse's head instantly shot up. *The only call he ever seems to respond to,* Levi thought.

"Arrow, come here, boy," Levi commanded.

Areion and Arrow both responded to Levi's orders and walked in his direction. When Arrow looked over at Reece as she stood at Levi's side, he stopped, grunted, and returned to grazing.

Levi then commanded the horse again. "Arrow!" he said as Areion approached his side.

Arrow began to walk slowly in their direction, as though he was inconvenienced by having to listen to Levi. *Could he be any more arrogant? I swear. That obstinate horse,* Levi thought as he watched the young horse meander in their direction.

"See, Levi, he's perfect!" Reece exclaimed happily, and Arrow stopped again.

Levi folded his arms, stared intently at the horse, and shook his head. Arrow watched Levi for a moment before he brought his attention to Reece, obviously waiting for her command.

"My love, I fear you have indeed ruined that horse." Levi laughed as he looked at Reece and leaned down to kiss her.

"I didn't ruin him."

Levi cocked his head to the side. "You are correct, love; he has been enamored with you from the first day he saw you, just as I have been." He leaned over and kissed the top of her head. "It appears he will only heed your commands, and none other's." He reached down, took Reece's hand, and started walking toward the horses. "Arrow is perfectly fine and has proven he is most definitely *your* horse."

Levi helped Reece onto Arrow and watched the horse willfully give her control over him; control that, despite his greatest efforts while working with Arrow, Levi struggled to achieve. Reece laughed softly as Levi studied Arrow's response to her. Before he turned to Areion, Levi took Arrow's halter with both hands and studied the horse's vibrant, golden eyes.

Arrow let out a grunt and tried to jerk his head free from Levi's grip. Levi ignored his response and continued to stare into Arrow's eyes. *What do you sense in her, boy?* As soon as the thought absently came into Levi's mind, Arrow nudged Levi in his chest and pawed the ground with his massive hoof. Levi smiled knowingly. *There is something unique about her, isn't there? Something more—*

Arrow jerked his head back, prompting Levi to let his halter loose. He laughed in astonishment. *You may be able to read into my mind, young friend—I only wish I could read into yours.*

"What are you doing? Are you giving him a telepathic Pemdai lecture or something?"

Levi grinned, turned, and hoisted himself up onto Areion. "Absolutely not. I believe Arrow is as protective of you as I."

Reece laughed and guided Arrow alongside Areion. She stopped the horse and looked over to Levi. "Want to race?" she asked with a playful wink.

Levi reached out, gently gripped Reece around her slender neck, and leaned over to secure an enthusiastic kiss. When he released her, Reece's eyes dazzled as she searched for air, inspiring Levi to laugh aloud. "A race between these two stallions sounds intriguing!" He watched as Reece regained her composure.

"That was cheating," she teased.

"Indeed, it was." Levi nodded, and then looked toward the tree-covered road that exited their estate. Before he could turn back to Reece, the loud clatter of Arrow's hooves thundered past him. Areion immediately became impatient, forcing Levi to hold a tighter rein. He watched in astonishment and with great pride at the beauty of Reece riding Arrow so gallantly. His heart swelled with love for her while adrenaline began to course through every fiber of his body. Reece was nearly out of his sight when he loosed the reins on Areion and allowed the horse to find his stride. Areion let out a loud whinny as he gained more speed, catching up to where Reece and Arrow were swiftly galloping down the cobblestone road. Reece glanced back with a brilliant smile and called out loudly to Arrow, resulting in Areion being challenged further in their race back to the palace.

# Chapter 4

The following day, Levi and Lady Allestaine left the palace before daybreak. Levi advised Reece they would be gone for close to a week as they made preparations for the ceremony and celebration party. As much as Reece didn't want to be apart from Levi for that long, she knew she would need that amount of time in order to arrange the wedding gift she had planned for him. Once she was clad in the exquisite red dress that Levi had admired so greatly in Greece, she quickly left her bedchambers in search of Elizabeth.

"Are you ready?" Elizabeth asked in excitement as they met in the corridor.

Reece hooked her arm through her future sister-in-law's slender one. "I am," she responded gleefully.

"You look radiant, Reece. I am truly confident that this is going to turn out perfect," Elizabeth said as they shuffled past the servants in the corridors.

"Whoa!" Harrison called out as he approached them in the grand foyer. He looked down at Reece's shimmering red gown. "Is there an event I should be aware of? I believe this is the first time I have seen you wear a gown from Earth rather than a Pemdai-styled dress. I must admit, I admire your boldness, Miss Bryant. That is quite the fashion statement," Harrison said with a wink.

Reece laughed. "Thank you. And yes, there is an event you should be aware of, because we might need your help."

Harrison shoved both hands into his pockets and narrowed his eyes at Reece questioningly. "What exactly are you young ladies up to?"

Elizabeth's cheeks colored lightly while Reece lifted her chin. "You'll see. Now, we need to leave before all of the servants start wondering why their emperor's future wife is dressed like this."

Harrison sighed, spun on his heel, and followed Reece and Elizabeth as they walked swiftly out of the palace's back doors.

As the three made their way down to the stables, Harrison noticed that Javian had Areion and Arrow harnessed, yet Areion was the only one saddled.

Javian looked at Reece somberly. "Miss Bryant, remember what we discussed. I am aware that Areion approves of you; however, Emperor Levi is away from the palace, and Areion has never allowed—"

"Wait just a minute, Javian," Harrison said as he looked down at Reece. "What *exactly* are you planning to do with Areion?" His eyes locked sternly onto hers. "I am in no mood to go through this with you again."

Reece tilted her head to the side and exhaled. "Harrison, please don't start with me. I need to use Areion for the gift that I have planned for Levi. I know he will be—"

"Reece!" Harrison interrupted with a soft boom in his voice. He cleared his throat. "I was lucky that my cousin was deeply remorseful for his rude behavior toward me yesterday, which is the only reason I didn't receive an hour-long lecture from him for allowing you to pull your little stunt with Arrow yesterday. Now he charges me to watch over the lady he loves while he is away, and you expect me to allow you to try to work your magic with Areion in some way? Absolutely not. *You*, my lady, have lost your mind."

Reece laughed, "Harrison, please relax. I understand that Areion may not be as accepting as Arrow, but I have a feeling that he'll let me do this."

Harrison closed his eyes and inhaled deeply. When they reopened, he stared intently into her eyes. "Reece, this horse has accepted me as well as he has you, but he only did so in the company of Levi. Forgive me when I say that you do not fully understand the connection between a Guardian horse and his master, and especially the bond between Areion and Levi. I cannot and will not allow this."

Reece looked past Harrison and softly sighed. When she looked back at his silvery-blue eyes, which were set with absolute purpose, she gazed at him in discomfiture. "I understand that this is putting everyone on edge again, but please let me have an opportunity to try." She watched as Harrison's stern expression toward her began to fade. "Please, Harrison, I really want to do this for Levi."

Harrison looked over to where Areion and Arrow stood patiently waiting next to Javian. Reece let out a breath of relief when Harrison surprisingly grinned in response. "My cousin will definitely have his work cut out for him in marriage." He turned toward Areion and gripped the horse's reins under his chin. "Now, what exactly do you have planned for this beast?"

Harrison led Areion with a firm grip on his halter, and Arrow followed closely behind Reece as the entire group walked into the forest behind the palace. They soon ended their walk when they arrived at the same location where Levi first avowed his love for Reece. They positioned the horses in such a way that the palace was visible in the distance through the foliage behind them. Elizabeth had her painting supplies and a canvas set up, and she was prepared to paint an enormous portrait for Levi's office. Now it was time to find out whether or not Areion would cooperate with Reece's plans.

Harrison stood, holding onto Areion's harness. Arrow watched Reece as she approached. As Reece advanced toward Areion, Arrow turned his attention to the massive horse. Javian stood at Areion's hindquarters, and he and Harrison waited silently to take action if Areion reacted harshly. Areion seemed agitated, and Reece began to second-guess her idea.

She walked over and took the formidable stallion's face in her hands. "Areion, we're doing this for Levi. Now, if we don't want to be in trouble when he returns, you need to cooperate. I'm not riding you; I'm only going to sit on your back for a while. Will you be okay with that?"

Areion's golden eyes stared down at her solemnly. He stood perfectly still as he locked his gaze on Reece, forcing a shiver to run down her spine. This horse was definitely intimidating, but she had witnessed a different side to him as well. She couldn't give up now.

Reece rubbed him on the nose. "Don't forget that I'm the one who offers you treats, Areion," she said to persuade him. "You will have to watch Arrow receive them from here on out if you're going to be stubborn."

Everyone quietly waited for the horse's response. Areion glanced past Reece and looked at Arrow standing protectively behind her before he grunted and nuzzled Reece in her chest.

"That's a good boy!" Reece said gleefully as she rubbed the silky coat of his face.

Harrison, still gripping Areion's reins under his chin, stood in shock. "Are you kidding me? *Treats*, Areion? Really?" Harrison was in complete disbelief.

The horse brought his head back and bumped Harrison with his snout, as if to brush off the comment.

Harrison pushed Areion's face away from him playfully. "Knock it off, boy, or I'll tell Saracen about your weakness for women and treats. Unbelievable."

Harrison walked toward Reece in order to help her onto the horse. He let out a sigh that was more resignation than resistance. "Now for the interesting part."

"What's that?" Reece queried with a confident smile.

"Getting you on this stallion without destroying your dress."

Reece gripped Harrison's shoulder. "I knew you had a little romance buried deep inside you."

Harrison smirked. "Nothing romantic about it, my lady," he said, gripping her waist and hoisting her up onto the horse. "My only wish is to ensure that this portrait will take my cousin's mind off the fact that I, once again, was responsible for allowing his wife to test death." He ran his hand along Areion's muscular shoulder, studying his current response.

"Areion appears to have accepted Miss Bryant without any reservation," Javian noted.

Harrison looked up at Reece. "Make sure you give him that treat you promised," he said with a laugh as Elizabeth joined Harrison to arrange Reece's crimson dress to cascade in an elegant fashion along Areion's side.

Reece reached for an apple she had hidden in the saddlebag and chucked it directly at Harrison's chest. "I'll allow you to give him his first treat for being so cooperative and as an apology for insulting him," she smiled, raising both her eyebrows.

They laughed in unison as Elizabeth sat down and began to sketch the large portrait she would paint for Levi.

All during the week, Reece and Elizabeth spent their time discreetly working on the portrait while Levi and Lady Allestaine were away from the palace. When the portrait was finished, Reece was awestricken by Elizabeth's talents.

"This is absolutely amazing, Elizabeth," she declared.

Both massive stallions stood magnificently with the glowing foliage of Pemdas surrounding them. Reece sat properly on Areion's back while her long gown shimmered like diamonds as it cascaded down Areion's side. Reece's golden hair flowed neatly in large curls over her shoulder, and the vibrancy of her blue eyes added a flawless definition to her face. The details of color that Elizabeth brought to the portrait were breathtaking.

"Levi will love it, Reece."

Reece's eyes brightened. "Do you think we can have it hung in his office in the palace after we leave for our honeymoon? I want him to surprise him with it when we return."

Elizabeth smiled. "Of course. It will allow me even more time to add appropriate enhancements to the scenery."

Reece returned her attention to the massive portrait and shook her head. "Lizzy, there is nothing more to add. It's perfect."

# Chapter 5

The day that Levi and Reece were set to be married had finally arrived. Reece had hardly slept a wink the previous evening, riddled with excitement about what Levi was planning for their ceremony.

Jasmeen and three maidens had spent hours that morning on Reece's hair, makeup, and dress fitting. When they were assured every last detail was attended to, they left the vanity room. Reece stood in front of the large mirrors of the room, spellbound by the final result.

The gown she wore was stunning, yet simple in its appearance, and Reece could not have been more impressed with the final result. The silky white dress accentuated her slender frame and flowed gracefully down before it swept into a short train behind her. The bodice front was cut square and lined with a jeweled sapphire trim that was highlighted with vibrant, miniature diamonds. Three slender strands with the same diamond and sapphire stones swept over her shoulders, glistening brightly under the lights of her dressing room.

Reece turned slightly to glance at the back of her gown again. A silk material was attached by jewels to the top of her shoulders, sweeping into a swag pattern that framed the shimmering lace material covering her back. A large sapphire jewel gathered the satin material into an intricate style at her lower back before flowing onto the floor behind her. It fit her flawlessly and framed her body beautifully.

Reece stood in astonishment as she watched the numerous diamonds and sapphires sparkle against her creamy skin. She laughed softly with excitement as she gave a small twirl. The finished product of what she and Lady Allestaine had designed together was much more than elegant—it was enchanting.

Three slender bands embellished with tiny diamonds and sapphires sparkled against Reece's honey-blonde curls, which Jasmeen had arranged meticulously on the top of her head. *You look like you fell out of a fairy tale,* Reece thought in humor.

She smiled brilliantly at her reflection in the mirror, excitement radiating through her as she held up the front of her dress to examine the sapphire blue heels that were designed to match the blue details of her dress. They were coated in an array of glittery diamonds, adding a distinctive quality to them.

"You, my darling Reece, are a sight to behold. You look unquestionably astonishing," Lady Allestaine proclaimed as she entered the dressing room.

Reece turned and walked over to embrace the empress. "Thank you so much. The dress is so much more amazing than I thought it would be. I'm in awe of it."

Lady Allestaine stepped back, took both Reece's hands into hers, and examined the beautiful gown with pride. "My dear, you are the reason this dress is a portrait of loveliness." She looked into Reece's eyes. "I could not have dreamt of a more perfect and strong woman for my son. I am honored to have you as my daughter."

Lady Allestaine released Reece's hands and walked over to a table where a black velvet box sat next to the dozens of glimmering blue roses Levi had sent to her room that morning. She picked up the box and walked back toward Reece, beaming as she faced the box toward Reece and opened it. Inside the velvet box sat a silver tiara lying delicately on a satin material. It was crafted with bold blue stones set in a pattern with a multitude of glistening diamonds. Reece held her hand over her heart as she studied the exquisite piece.

Lady Allestaine laughed softly as she gently turned Reece to face the enormous mirrors in front of them. She walked in front of Reece and gazed lovingly into her eyes. "This was Navarre's mother's tiara. It was created for her to match the ring you wear, which shows your commitment to Levi. These magnificent stones are from Earth as well. At the time Navarre's father acquired these jewels, they were the only stones of this color and were extremely rare. The headdress was designed for Elisia to wear during her marriage celebration to the emperor, because she loved the jewels immensely," Lady Allestaine said as she placed the tiara on the crown of Reece's head. "It now belongs to you. You are a rare gem for this family, and you are loved beyond measure by all of us," she said as she positioned the ringlets of Reece's hair to gather around the glistening crown.

"Lady Allestaine," Reece inhaled deeply, "this is more than I could ever ask for. Please—"

Before Reece could finish her sentence, a gasp from the doorway caused both women to turn. Elizabeth stood in the opening with a bright smile on her face. "Reece, you look absolutely sensational. I am speechless," she said as she approached Reece with a decorative gift box.

Elizabeth carefully embraced Reece and offered the gift to her. "Levi has instructed me to offer you this as a gift from all of us."

Reece smiled as she opened the box to find the earrings and necklace that matched the gemstone of her ring. Lady Allestaine pulled the jewels from the box as Reece stood frozen and at a loss for words. She gently clasped a strand of diamonds that held a deep blue gemstone around Reece's neck. The gemstone fell perfectly in place, covering the center of her décolletage. Gemstones fashioned as tear drops hung neatly on each of her ears, and the deep blue color of the jewels glistened in the light as they dangled.

Tears welled up in Elizabeth's eyes as she stood admiring Reece's final appearance. Then she softly laughed. "My brother is likely to sweep you off your feet and carry you away before any words are spoken in the ceremony when he sets his eyes upon you." She stepped forward and embraced Reece once more. "It is truly an honor for me to call you my sister on this day. I am overwhelmed with joy."

Reece tightly embraced Elizabeth. "I feel the same way," she softly returned, overwhelmed by the emotions filling the room. "Now, let's hope I don't trip with these heels I'm wearing, and I might just pull all of this off."

Elizabeth stepped back and laughed. "You will be marvelous; I have no doubt of that." She glanced over at Lady Allestaine who was standing still, admiring both young women. "King Hamilton is awaiting me in the carriage to escort me to my seat." Elizabeth smiled at Reece. "This will be a marvelous ceremony indeed, and one I shall never forget."

Reece embraced Elizabeth once more. "I am highly anticipating it as well." Reece stepped back and smiled at Elizabeth. "I'm also looking forward to hearing all of the music you have composed for our wedding. I can't thank you enough for everything, Elizabeth."

Elizabeth smiled mischievously and offered Reece a small curtsey. "I must say, after you witness the décor of your wedding location, I doubt you will hear a sound coming from the piano." She gathered her dress with her hands. "Now, if you will excuse me, the piano awaits," Elizabeth said with a laugh and left the room.

Lady Allestaine continued to make small adjustments to Reece's dress. When she finished, she stood back and smiled. "I must say, you will steal everyone's hearts today, this I know for certain."

"Lady Allestaine?" Reece questioned in a solemn voice. "May I speak with you for a moment?"

Lady Allestaine's expression grew serious. "Of course."

Reece took her hand and led her over to a private chaise in the vanity room. "I'm not sure if right now is the time to bring this up, and I really should have asked Levi first, because I don't want to offend or burden you in any way."

Lady Allestaine brushed her hand over Reece's cheek. "Do not concern yourself with overburdening me. What is it that is bothering you?"

"I really shouldn't be thinking about any of this on my wedding day, but then again, I never thought I'd be marrying an *emperor*." Reece laughed nervously.

Lady Allestaine laughed as well. "I agree." She smiled warmly. "The only thing that should be on your mind is becoming the wife of Emperor Levi Oxley," she said with excitement.

"Exactly. But this is why I am feeling a little overwhelmed at the moment," Reece said as she exhaled.

Lady Allestaine grew more serious. "Reece, what is overwhelming you?"

Reece's lips twisted as she shuffled her thoughts. "Bear with me, because I'm not sure if I can properly put into words what I am feeling. You giving me this tiara and these jewels has brought something to my attention that I hadn't been considering at all." Reece glanced past Lady Allestaine, and then stared intently into her warm green eyes. "I have to admit, I always have trouble remembering Levi's position in this world. I never gave much thought to him being the son of the emperor, because he is so much more than that to me, and now he has become the emperor. I guess what I am trying to say is that after Levi and I are married, am I supposed to be the new empress? Is that how it works in Pemdas?"

"This is what you are so troubled about?" Lady Allestaine laughed softly. "Indeed, this is one of the reasons my son is profoundly in love with you. Do not concern yourself over your duties as empress. Yes, marrying the Emperor of Pemdas will give you not only his name, but you will also share his station in our world. A coronation ceremony will eventually take place, but that only serves to honor you as our new empress."

Reece's heart beat rapidly. "I'm not sure I'm prepared to become the empress so soon, Lady Allestaine. Pemdas has already grieved the loss of Emperor Navarre; if I could wish anything, it would be that they won't lose the empress they also love so much."

Lady Allestaine tilted her head to the side and smiled sympathetically. "That is the very reason you will make a most gracious empress and will be adored by our people. Your humility in this matter will shine through, and they will see it."

"I will confidently stand at Levi's side and assume my rightful place, not only as his wife, but as the empress as well," she shifted in her seat, "but I humbly request that you will be at my side during this transition."

Lady Allestaine offered Reece a warm smile. "I will gladly be at your side so long as you desire it."

Reece nodded. "You cannot imagine my relief to hear that, not only for me, but for all of Pemdas."

Both women stood when Jasmeen entered the room. "Lady Allestaine, King Nathaniel is here to escort you to the ceremony location."

Lady Allestaine leaned in to place a soft kiss on Reece's cheek. "It is time, my darling. Harrison should be here momentarily to retrieve you." She stepped back and took in the image of Reece once more. "Your beauty is immeasurable. I eagerly await your arrival, and I am confident our guests do as well," she said with a broad grin before turning to exit the vanity room.

"Reece, would you care for a cup of tea to help you relax before your departure?" Jasmeen offered as she arranged more curls to accentuate Reece's tiara. "You appear quite frazzled."

"Frazzled? That's one way to put it." Reece laughed. "No, thank you. In my current state, I'd most likely spill it down the center of this dress," she answered.

"Very well, then. I will see you when you arrive at the ceremony location," the maiden responded before leaving the room.

One last glance in the mirror, and Reece walked out to her sitting room to await Harrison's arrival. To her surprise, he was already there. He stood sipping a glass of wine in front of the fireplace and turned as soon as she entered the sitting room.

Harrison set his wine glass on the elaborate mantle before walking over to Reece and extending his gloved hand to her. Reece smiled as she placed her hand in his, and Harrison bowed formally over it. He gently brushed his lips over her knuckles and straightened. "Reece, you are an exquisite sight to behold. My cousin is a lucky man, indeed."

Reece smiled. "Thanks, Harrison. Please, don't be so formal; you're making me nervous. Besides, you look pretty handsome yourself! Gray tailcoat *and* a top hat? I'm speechless," she teased.

"Oh, do not be ridiculous. As you should know very well by now, my handsome features know no bounds," Harrison playfully returned as he drew her arm up into the bend of his. "However, it is not often that a woman takes my breath away, such as you have done just now." He winked at her. "It is truly an honor to be the one to escort my cousin's bride to him," he said, becoming more serious.

Reece recalled the absence of her father and the realization that Harrison was standing in his place. She fought back her tears, knowing that in her heart he was there with her, whether in person or not.

She looked somberly at Harrison. "Thank you," she returned, "your friendship means a lot to me, and I know my father would approve of you being the one giving his only daughter away."

She felt the tears well up in her eyes. Harrison bent down and kissed her tenderly on her cheek. "As I said, it is my honor. Now, before you start shedding tears and ruining your makeup," he smiled, "let us get you to the man who eagerly awaits your arrival."

Harrison led Reece out into a different courtyard in the palace where a white, luxurious carriage awaited them. It had an opened top with plush blue velvet seats that shimmered in the light of the afternoon sun. Two footmen were polished in their royal regalia, standing perfectly straight on the back of the carriage. The coachman and an imperial guard were dressed identically, and Reece felt her heart start hammering against her chest as the importance of this day began to sink in.

Fortunately as they approached, one of the well-dressed palace guards walked over to open the door for Reece and Harrison.

Harrison dismissed the footman with a grin. "Until Miss Bryant has been delivered in impeccable condition, I believe it is my responsibility to keep the bride in my care until the emperor receives her."

The guard smiled faintly and stepped back. He glanced at Reece, offered her a formal nod before clasping his hands behind his back, and stood properly next to the carriage. Glistening ivy and a multitude of vibrant, multicolored flowers ran along the top of the carriage and matched the decor of the four white horses that patiently waited for the coachman to guide them out of the courtyard.

Once Harrison guided Reece up into the carriage and she was settled in the seat behind the coachman, Harrison hopped into the carriage and sat in the seat across from her. He smiled amusingly at Reece as he glanced down at her fidgeting hands.

"Nervous?" he asked as he adjusted his top hat and sunk back into the comfort of his seat.

"Excited would be a more accurate term," Reece answered in a soft voice.

Harrison knowingly grinned as he glanced down at her fidgeting hands. "Ah, I stand corrected. My observational skills must be somewhat off today."

Reece exhaled. "All right, I'm a little nervous. Who wouldn't be?" she said as she glanced at the beauty that surrounded them.

Harrison laughed. "Well, you have no need to be. Levi is anxiously awaiting your arrival." He glanced up at the scenery they were slowly traveling through. "And I must admit, everything you are about to witness was all his doing. Your soon-to-be husband has astounded me with his creativity, of which I would have never assumed he possessed."

Reece glanced up as the sun dimmed in the archway of flowering and glowing bushes they were traveling through.

"Where are we?" Reece asked as she gazed up at the twinkling flowers streaming down from above.

"We are in the palace gardens," Harrison simply answered.

The beauty of the scenery and Harrison's calm demeanor began to fade all of Reece's anxiety. This magical land would never cease to amaze her. "Levi did all of this?"

Harrison choked on his laughter. "Absolutely not, but he orchestrated the staff to do so. He had the gardens turned into quite the enchanting venue, knowing that you are taken with the beauty of Pemdas' evenings."

Reece softly sighed as they traveled slowly through the captivating world Levi had created for their ceremony. She was at an absolute loss for words. The darker the environment became, the more the blooms and greenery around the carriage began to glow. She glanced down at her dress, and the shimmering stones took on a fascinating appearance of their own. She looked as though a bright light were cast upon her gown, and the stones glittered in a rainbow of colors in return. All that was left now was to see the area that Levi had designed with his mother for the ceremony.

"Do *you* know where we are going?"

Harrison grinned. "Of course I do. I left your intended husband only moments ago to retrieve you. We are almost there. Are you ready for this?"

Reece spread her hands across her shimmering gown. "More than ready. I can't wait to see him. I can't wait to thank him for all of this."

As the carriage slowed, Reece looked around for a hint as to where Levi waited for her. She saw nothing but forestry and vividly glowing flowers. Once the carriage had stopped, she heard piano music softly playing in the distance. *Elizabeth*! she thought in amazement. The soothing sound of a cello played along with the piano, and Reece knew they had reached their destination.

Harrison stepped out of the carriage and offered his hand. Surprisingly, Jasmeen was there to ensure that Reece's dress and hair were in their proper places before Harrison led Reece onto a wooden walkway, which was complemented by more radiant flowers. The rich aroma from all of the blooms was as intoxicating as the enchanting environment itself. Reece gripped the inside of Harrison's arm as she started to see familiarity in this location.

They followed along the wooden path, leading them deeper into the majestic forest. They crossed over a small, arched bridge with a shimmering creek below them. Reece studied her surroundings as the piano music grew louder.

Without noticing, she froze in place, forcing Harrison to halt with her. In that moment, the piano music and cello accompaniment flowed into a different melody. Reece looked straight ahead but could only see a few of the guests that had turned at the sound of her and Harrison's arrival.

Reece knew exactly where they were. It was where Levi first swore his love for her and asked her not to leave Pemdas, and the same place where she had Elizabeth paint the portrait of her on Areion as a reminder to Levi of that day.

Harrison bent over and whispered in her ear, "It seems as though you are not the only one who cherishes this special location."

She fought back her tears with all her strength. She held her hand over her heart, trying to gather herself.

"Are you ready?" Harrison asked as he looked down at her.

"More than I have ever been, Harrison. Take me to him," she managed.

They walked under a canopy of golden, shimmering blooms before it opened up to an area with thousands of different dangling blossoms, glistening and shimmering throughout. There were close to a hundred guests standing for her entrance, mostly family and the close friends of the Oxley's. Reece was holding up excellently, until she spotted Levi waiting for her at the end of the walkway. Her heart seemed to stop, and the whimsical atmosphere of their wedding location disappeared as the sound of Elizabeth's piano music faded away. Her entire being was captivated when her eyes met his.

Levi stood imperially with both arms behind his back and waited properly to receive her. He was a faultless picture of royalty. He wore the attire of the Pemdai Emperor, and he was an intimidating, yet magnificent portrait of a nobleman. His black tailcoat was embellished with silver accents and complemented with a sapphire blue scarf, which swept over his right shoulder, crossing his chest and ending just below his waist.

Levi's eyes glistened like gemstones when they met hers. His smile was subtle as his gaze locked intently and exclusively onto her. She felt the heat in her cheeks from his penetrating gaze. Reece never took her eyes off him, loving him more with every step she took closer to him. His smile, even though faint, was radiant, and his eyes were entrancing.

Finally they reached him, and Harrison formally placed Reece's hand into Levi's. Levi stared down at her, and she felt nothing but love and admiration emanating from him as he gracefully placed her hand in the bend of his arm. He brought his other hand up to cover hers and gently guided her to face King Nathaniel, who waited to perform their ceremony. As King Nathanial spoke, Reece and Levi both stole glances at each other. He smiled as he continued to lovingly rub the back of her hand in the bend of his arm with his thumb.

Their moment had arrived, and soon Reece and Levi would declare their love for one another in front of all of their guests and become husband and wife. Reece's smile broadened as she gazed intently at King Nathaniel, greatly anticipating the moment when he would pronounce Levi and Reece husband and wife.

# Chapter 6

Levi stood in admiration of how Pasidian's staff and the hired decorators orchestrated such a majestic scene for his and Reece's wedding. He had personally gone to great effort to hire the proper professionals to bring to life what he had envisioned. Not only did they surpass all of his expectations, they also managed to create all of this overnight while Reece slept. Now he waited to see the expression on his bride-to-be's face as she walked down the shimmering walkway toward him.

Levi surreptitiously watched the guests, studying their expressions of amazement as they entered the lavishly appointed area. To Levi's knowledge, nothing so resplendent had ever been created in Pemdas. For Levi, it had to be done for reasons only he and Reece would truly understand. From the first evening Reece spent in Pemdas, Levi had paid particular attention to Reece's reactions as the glistening lands transformed into an array of gleaming colors in the evening. Having already been in love with her at the time, he could not help but be entranced by the many expressions on her face as she beheld the enchanting transformation of Pemdas in the evening. It was very clear to Levi that their wedding location and ceremony should represent everything that fascinated Reece about Pemdas. The ceremony, without question, would take place in the same location they first spoke of their love for each other.

Levi clasped his hands behind his back and gazed around the glowing scenery, waiting patiently for Reece to arrive with Harrison. He allowed the dulcet melodies of Elizabeth's piano compositions, complemented by the palace's finest cellist, to calm his racing heart. A subtle sound in the distance brought his attention back to the guests who quietly awaited the bride.

Lady Allestaine wore a proud smile as she sat next to Harrison's mother, Levi's aunt Madeleine, and the Hamilton family. He smiled kindly toward Lady Allestaine but did not fail to notice King Hamilton holding back a laugh. King Hamilton, much like Harrison, never failed to find something humorous about any occasion. It was obvious that the king had received word that the enchanting environment they sat in was all Levi's doing, and Levi would need to prepare himself for the relentless teasing at the small reception which was to take place after this ceremony. A small arch of his eyebrow toward King

Hamilton nearly sent the king bursting into laughter. Before Levi could glance away, he was distracted by the clattering of horses' hooves announcing the arrival of Reece's carriage.

Levi's heart jolted with anticipation when everything grew silent. The only visible movement was that of the flowering blooms illuminating all around them. The sound of the spring that trickled over the smooth stones surrounding the area melded perfectly with the music. Levi's lips tightened in anticipation as Elizabeth's playing transitioned to a song announcing Reece's arrival. The guests remained seated, while Levi's eyes were intently focused on the entrance that Reece would appear through. Once she and Harrison stepped onto the opalescent, velvet covered runner and into their secluded location, Levi locked his gaze with Reece's dazzling eyes.

The world around Levi simply vanished from his attention in that moment. It took everything within him to restrain himself from approaching her as his cousin escorted his intended wife to him.

The guests stood to honor the bride entering the ceremonial area, obstructing Levi's view of Reece. He stepped to the right in order to savor the moment he had longed for. When he did, he noticed Harrison's grin broaden as he walked Reece along the velvet runway to him. Levi's emotions calmed as his eyes continued to take in the beauty of Reece approaching him. This day, *their day,* had finally come. He simply could not take it all in. His grandmother's tiara was sitting in its rightful place upon the crown of her head, the Oxley family jewels highlighted the radiant tone of her skin, and her flawless figure was outlined perfectly in her brilliant dress. Her cheeks colored lightly as she continued to gaze into Levi's eyes, enhancing the brilliance of her light blue eyes. Levi finally let out the breath he held and returned her warm smile, his senses recovering as he basked in the allure of the woman he loved with all of his heart.

As Harrison approached, King Nathaniel instructed the guests to be seated.

"As you are all aware, Emperor Levi and Miss Reece Bryant have chosen to unite the traditional ceremonies of marriage on Earth and in Pemdas. It is quite obvious," King Nathaniel said with a soft laugh, "that most of the ceremony you will witness today is how many on Earth, protected by our Guardians, choose to celebrate the unification of a couple."

As King Nathaniel's voice trailed off, Levi glanced down to find Reece looking up at him. He was transfixed by her gaze, and it took Harrison softly clearing his throat to snap Levi out of his daze so as to take Reece's offered hand.

Levi smiled at Reece again and brought her delicate hand to rest in the bend of his arm. Levi stood tall at Reece's side, proud and honored to take her as his wife on this day. King Nathaniel formally nodded once the couple turned together to face him.

"It is my privilege to commence this unprecedented ceremony by announcing on the behalf of the bride and groom that we are honored to have you amongst us to bear witness to the exchange of matrimonial vows," King Nathaniel spoke boldly. "There is no greater distinction than to stand in the place of my brother, the late Emperor Navarre, and perform this ceremony. Knowing my brother well, I can say this is a day that would have made him proud beyond measure. He was, indeed, quite fond of his son's choice for his wife. Having been your leader for many years, Emperor Navarre knew that in order to live his life as ruler over all of Pemdas, he needed stability more than anything. That stability included a strong and encouraging woman to stand by his side."

King Nathaniel glanced over at Lady Allestaine, who was blotting her eyes with her white handkerchief. She nodded in agreement with King Nathaniel, who went on, "The late emperor shared with me on more than one occasion that, in his opinion, Miss Bryant carried within her those qualities and much more. It was extremely important to the emperor that his only son find a woman of this nature, and one that he truly loved in order to be happy and contented should the day come that his son stood in his place as Emperor of Pemdas. Today that day has come, friends and family, and we are all invited to bear witness to a marriage of true love, honor, chivalry, and most of all, a demonstration of our world moving forward with courage."

Levi felt Reece grip his arm tightly, forcing him to glance down at her. He saw her glittering eyes filled with tears, prompting him to discreetly offer her his handkerchief. He tenderly touched her hand, hoping to soothe her.

"At this time, His Imperial Majesty and Miss Reece Bryant will declare to each other their vows of commitment in marriage."

Reece sniffed softly, maintaining her composure as Levi turned, took both her hands into his, and gazed intently into her eyes.

Levi softly exhaled, gathering his thoughts as the brilliance of Reece's expression played across every emotion within him. "My only love," he began, "I believe you have a perfect understanding of my devoted love for you, and now I can share it with those who are in attendance this day." He tilted his head as he gazed into her brilliant blue eyes. "Never in my life have I encountered a woman such as you. From the moment I became your guardian, I was intrigued by everything about you. Your enthusiasm, your compassion towards others, your inner strength, and your appreciation for all things were mesmerizing to me. It was not long before you truly and completely captivated my heart," Levi cleared his throat.

"Reece Bryant, I vow to you on this day that you, my love, will be the only woman who will forever hold my heart, and today I shall commit my entire life to you. Your love reigns more supreme to me than anything else, and I will not only ensure that you shall be loved every day beyond measure, but I will forever protect your life with my own, as my life is now yours. I humbly ask that you accept my vow of love and commitment to you, as I am honored to accept yours. Reece Marian Oxley, will you have me as your husband?"

Reece's smiled broadened as a tear slipped down her cheek. Levi brushed it away as Reece nodded in return before murmuring, "Yes." She sniffed. "I will wholeheartedly accept you as my husband."

Reece exhaled softly before lifting her chin. She gazed intently into his eyes and gripped his hands tightly. "You, too, know how much I love you with everything that I am, and I am grateful to be able to share it with those in attendance.

"To say that you have completely changed my life would be an understatement. Never in my wildest dreams would I have imagined that my life would end up where it is at this moment, and never could I have imagined that a man like you would love me as you do. You have filled a void within my heart and soul that I didn't know existed. The unconditional love and support you have given me since the day I met you have saved me in so many ways. You have inspired me to be a better woman, and you have shown me what it is like to truly love and be loved.

"Levi Oxley, I commit every part of my heart, soul, and entire being to you as your wife. I will stand at your side through whatever difficult times we may encounter, and I will happily walk arm-in-arm with you wherever our lives' paths may lead us. I stand here today proud to be loved by such a humble, selfless, and honorable man. I commit myself wholly to you in front of all our guests, and I vow that I will forever love only you, my one true love. Will you, Levi Alexander Oxley, accept me as your wife?"

"Without any reservation, I humbly accept you as my wife," Levi said as an array of emotions flooded through him after hearing Reece's words of devotion to him.

Levi turned and plucked a slender platinum band from King Nathanial's outstretched hand and slipped it onto her slender finger. Levi had the band designed to match the ring he gave her after his proposal of marriage. A single row of tiny aquamarine stones, which matched the center stone of her engagement ring, was cushioned on either side by rows of tiny black diamonds.

To his surprise, the ring that Reece had slipped onto his finger nearly matched hers. The ring she designed was a brushed platinum band in an onyx hue with a brilliant swath of dark aquamarine stones set into it.

"And now, Your Royal Majesty," King Nathaniel announced, "you and your bride may seal your consecration of love with a kiss."

Without hesitation, Levi cupped Reece's face in his hands, stepped forward, and placed his lips on hers. Levi tenderly caressed Reece's cheekbones as the audience applauded their approval. Reece gracefully smoothed her hand over his cheek, and Levi's lips turned up into a smile matching hers. With one more kiss to her soft lips, he withdrew, never once removing his eyes from hers.

Reece's expression was radiant as Levi silently mouthed the words *"I love you"* to her before turning to face the happy crowd.

"All guests, please stand in honor of your emperor, the new Empress of Pemdas, and their commitment to one another," King Nathaniel announced.

The guests stood in unison. "Until death shall part them, Levi and Reece are now one. It is my distinct honor and privilege to present to you His Imperial Majesty, Emperor Levi Oxley; and Her Imperial Majesty, Reece Oxley; Emperor and Empress of Pasidian and the Empire of Pemdas," King Nathanial proclaimed, concluding their ceremony.

Levi led Reece down through the guests and along the velvet aisle to the carriage that awaited them. Once at the carriage, he helped Reece into it before taking his seat next to her. The horses energetically carried them out of the enchanted clearing and back to the palace. When the carriage halted in the courtyard at the back of the palace, Levi smartly stepped out and offered his hand to his bride. He wasted no time in finding a secluded entrance, and he led Reece into one of the private libraries on the first floor.

After he pulled the large ornate door closed, he paused to take in her beauty once more before he offered her a simple kiss.

Reece giggled in response. "We did it! No backing out now, Emperor Levi Oxley," she teased.

Levi remained captivated by his new wife. He brushed his hand along her delicate jawline. "My love, there are no words to describe how I am feeling at this moment." He exhaled. "You, Empress Oxley, have stolen my heart in its entirety. You are so profoundly and utterly, breathtakingly beautiful. I have—"

"Levi," she interrupted him with a dazzling smile. She gave him a mischievous grin, and his heart fell out of its normal rhythm at her expression. She stared into his eyes provocatively, halting his breath. "*Kiss* me!"

His lips were on hers at that moment, absorbing her essence into every cell of his body. He reveled in their kiss for many moments before he slowly withdrew.

He traced her luscious, rosy lips with his fingers. He looked down and brushed his hands over the jewels that shone beautifully against her décolletage. "You are the first to wear these since my grandmother was alive. You, my love, outshine every ounce of their beauty."

Reece sighed softly. "You are always too generous to me. I am honored to wear them." She ran her fingers through his hair as her eyes gazed into his fixedly. "This is the best day of my life. I love you so much."

Levi grasped her hand and brought it to his lips. "I promise you, my beautiful wife, this is only the start of our best days together. I give you my word that from this day forward—"

Her lips were on his, and he was more than happy to be silenced by them. Would they ever make it to the reception of guests waiting for them? *Do I care?* Levi thought as he drew her in closer, feeling the perfect lines of her slender body through the silky fabric of her gown. *Why did I agree to a wedding reception?* Somehow, his mind managed to remind him that it was for Reece. She was the only reason he was able to end this satiating moment between them.

He gradually withdrew from her kiss and rested his chin atop her head, inhaling the fragrant aroma that enhanced her immaculately styled hair. "Mrs. Oxley, I must admit, I regret arranging this small luncheon with our wedding guests. Right now, I selfishly have no desire to share your company with anyone. I do not know if I can last these next few hours without showing you how much I ardently love you and proving my love to you in other ways."

Reece stepped back and widened her eyes playfully at him. "Oh, really? Well, Mr. Oxley, you must. And you are right; everyone is probably looking for us right now. Tonight," she lifted her chin and tugged on his cravat, "I will hold you to your promise of showing me your ardent love through other methods. For now, you must be a patient and proper gentleman," she teased with a flirtatious wink.

As Reece brushed past him, Levi gently clasped his sturdy hand around the bend of her arm. He bent down and brought his lips to her ear. "My love, you should know that I shall be tortured during these next few hours."

Reece turned seductively to face him. "Good! That will make for more of an exciting time when we are alone tonight," she said as she ran a fingertip along his jawline.

Levi gazed intently into her eyes. "Mrs. Oxley, you are teasing me?" he asked in a low, raspy voice.

"Indeed, I am."

Levi shook his head. "Allow me to escort my lovely bride to our awaiting guests before my passions overrule my better judgment," he said, raising an eyebrow at her while pulling his white dress gloves back on and offering his arm.

Reece smiled widely as she reached to accept his support. Together, they strolled out of the library and toward another enchanting area in the palace gardens.

# Chapter 7

When they entered the reception area, Reece gripped the bend of Levi's arm tightly as the guests stood to acknowledge their arrival. She glanced up and around at the magically illuminated area and was again at a loss for words. She had strolled through the well-manicured gardens of Pasidian Palace numerous times, yet it was decorated in a way that was almost unrecognizable, and Reece could hardly tell what part of the palace they were in.

Iridescent white blossoms glistened like diamonds strung intertwined with the glowing, green ivy that hung over the open reception area. Blue, yellow, and cherry colored blooms were placed meticulously throughout all of the dark green topiary bushes. She realized they were in the back of the palace when Levi led her over a familiar bridge that brought them to a large, ornate fountain. It was the fountain where Levi and Reece had shared their first private moments together on her first night in Pemdas, and it was where they shared their first moment of solitude on the evening they professed their love for each other. That Levi had planned this day to be celebrated at some of the places where they had their most special moments together made the day all the more memorable for Reece.

Long tables, surrounded by guests who were standing and applauding, were decorated with shimmering ivory fabric. On the fabric were crystal flutes and goblets, which were arranged around shiny silver place settings. Enormous vases filled with brilliant blue roses were garnished with more glistening white blossoms that reached up and cascaded down to the tabletop.

Reece glanced up at Levi, who was standing tall at her side and formally, yet cheerfully acknowledging their wedding guests. She smiled as Harrison approached and turned to address the crowd to announce the bride and groom.

While Harrison spoke, Levi leaned down toward Reece and whispered in her ear, "My love, you appear quite shocked by the décor. I do hope these arrangements are to your liking."

Reece glanced up at Levi and smiled brilliantly into his jewel-like eyes. "I have no words to express how much I love what you've done for us today. Everything you have planned has been so thoughtfully orchestrated, and I couldn't have imagined a more perfect ceremony or reception. I don't think you will ever cease to amaze me."

After Harrison finished his announcement, of which Reece heard nothing, he winked at them, prompting Levi to guide Reece to a table facing their guests. Levi, as he had always done, gently pulled out her chair and helped guide her to sit before he took his place at her side. The distraction of servants dressed in outlandish regalia walking out to serve the guests gave Reece the opportunity to speak to Levi without causing a scene.

"Is it just me, or did we get *crashed* by more wedding guests?" she whispered.

Levi brought a fist to his mouth and gently coughed out a laugh at Reece's Earthly reference to guests showing up unannounced. He shifted somewhat to face her. "This is only a few of the guests that are to arrive for the celebratory event that will take place after we depart." He brought his lips close to Reece's ear, his warm breath causing a brief shiver down her spine. "It appears as though guests are arriving much sooner than anticipated in order to steal a glimpse of their future empress," he said with humor in his voice.

"Well, don't ask me to do any speeches, and I'll be right as rain," Reece teased.

Levi chuckled and nodded. "All that is required of you is to enjoy the festivities that we will be a part of for the next hour or so. I have no intention of staying at this palace and entertaining guests for very long." He gently took her hand into his. "My intentions on this day are to entertain only you." He reached for the chalice that a servant had filled with sparkling wine and handed it to her. "And that is after we have left the palace for our wedding night location," he said with a wink.

Before Reece could respond, her heart pounding in her chest with anticipation for what Levi was implying, he stood up. He reached for his chalice while the area grew silent to recognize their emperor.

Reece watched with admiration as Levi addressed their guests, "It is my honor and pleasure to have our close family and friends in attendance on one of the most important days of my and Reece's lives. Today is not only the day that I commit my life to the most endearing woman in all of my acquaintance," he glanced down at Reece with adoring eyes, and then brought his attention back to their guests, "but this is also a day for you all to acknowledge Mrs. Reece Oxley as your new empress. Now, I humbly request you all to raise your glasses to my bride, Reece Marian Oxley, Empress of Pemdas."

Reece stood gracefully as she gripped Levi's offered hand. He brought his chalice to hers, and with the harmonic sound of their glass rims tapping, they sealed Levi's words with a sip of their sparkling wine.

After they were seated, the staff began serving their meals. She gazed out at the candlelit tables and the enormous crystal chandeliers that were hung in the area and let the soothing sounds of the water flowing out of the fountains calm her unnecessary nervousness.

"Reece?" Levi's low, smooth voice questioned softly.

She glanced at Levi, spellbound by his vivid blue eyes. She smiled in relief, finding security in them. "Sorry, I'm just a little overwhelmed by everything," she responded.

Levi studied her eyes for a moment. "Do eat," he grinned mischievously at her. "I will not have my lovely bride starving on her wedding night."

After the second course was finished and taken from them, an enormous, opulently decorated cake was brought out by six of the palace's staff members.

*When is the rest of the kingdom showing up to eat all of that?* Reece wondered in disbelief. The colossal cake was adorned in silver colored floral patterns, and blue accent roses braided on vibrant gold vines glistened all over it. At the top of the cake sat a crystal figurine of a bride and a groom.

King Hamilton stood and crossed the open area in front of Reece and Levi's table. He stood in front of the cake that was situated perfectly across from the garden fountain and nodded toward Levi and Reece.

"If our beautiful empress, Lady Reece, will snatch up her husband, who seems to be unable to peel his eyes away from her for less than a moment today, I will gladly commence the cake ceremony," King Hamilton cheerily proclaimed.

Reece laughed as she noticed a light blush color Levi's cheeks. He faintly rolled his eyes, stood, and helped Reece to her feet. "Well, Emperor Oxley," she said with a smile, "let us eat cake."

Levi offered his arm, smiling. "As you wish, my lady."

King Hamilton extended an arm to receive Reece as she and Levi approached. "Along with the ceremony of the cake, Levi and Reece will entertain all of you with their first and only dance of the evening, as they will be departing shortly thereafter. As you are all aware, this ceremony has been to honor the traditions of Earth for the lovely new empress. I speak on behalf of the royal family when I say that the festivities of the Pemdai Commitment Ceremony will commence after we wish our emperor and new empress off on their vacation. It is the family's greatest wish that you stay and celebrate their union, whether or not they are present during this time. Now," King Hamilton gazed at Reece and Levi with a playful smile, "please stand as we commence the cake ceremony and as Levi and Reece dance in celebration of their union."

As elaborate as King Hamilton made it seem, the cake ceremony for Reece and Levi was no different than from any usual reception on Earth. They carefully cut into the base of the cake together, Levi's strong hand gently guiding Reece's. Levi held the crystal plate with one hand and very delicately placed a piece of the sumptuous cake in Reece's mouth. As a mélange of sweet and succulent flavors satisfied Reece's every taste bud, she carefully placed a piece of cake in Levi's mouth. Although his always enticing lips were tempting her to kiss them, she took a small piece of icing and placed it on the tip of his nose instead. Levi's eyebrows shot up in surprise and humor. He softly chuckled as Reece grinned at his reaction. After taking the offered napkin from King Hamilton, he brought Reece into his arms and stared adoringly into her eyes.

"I love you," he whispered before carefully placing his lips on hers.

"The dance, and then we're out of here, right?" Reece teased.

Levi nodded. "Indeed. I will have the staff send a portion of our cake to our location, along with other varieties of food and wine." He grinned and offered his arm. "Shall we dance, Mrs. Oxley?"

Reece gathered her dress up with her other hand and walked at Levi's side as he led her to the glistening dance floor.

Levi brought Reece into a proper dance form, and without warning he placed his hand on her lower back and pulled her in close to him. Elizabeth joined the palace's orchestra and began playing a new melody she had composed for Reece and Levi's first dance. There was nothing more enchanting than being in Levi's arms and staring into each other's eyes lovingly and longingly. Levi led their dance flawlessly as the guests stood in silent awe, allowing the musical medley to fill the atmosphere. Impulsively, Reece pulled her hands from his and tenderly ran them along his cheeks. Their dance slowed, and her eyes left his questioning ones as she gazed longingly at his lips. What she felt in her heart for him, and her need for his love, was so great that she stopped dancing, even though the music played on.

Levi's head tilted to the side as he smiled down at her. "My love? Is everything—"

She silenced him with a consuming kiss without a care as to what anyone might have thought. Levi never once tensed or pushed her away in embarrassment; instead, he clinched her tighter to him and returned her loving kiss as everyone else in the room began to fade away from them.

As the music played, petals began to fall from the trees above like tiny snowflakes showering them in a crystal globe. The moment was so surreal that Reece longed to be in her husband's arms and far from a palace full of guests.

"I knew you both would be unable to wait until this reception was over," Harrison said in a low, humored voice.

Levi slowly withdrew and brought his arm securely around Reece's waist. Even though the orchestra played on, the melody was new, and the guests stood and applauded. "Sweetheart, let us bid our guests adieu, and I will escort you to your room so that Jasmeen can prepare you for our departure."

Reece's heart raced as she reached up to caress Levi's cheek. "Do I even get a hint as to where we are going?"

A proud grin stretched across Levi's face. "Our wedding night destination will include only you and me. No servants or maidens will attend to us until we are ready to depart for our vacation."

"Will I have an opportunity to dance with my cousin?" Harrison asked with a mischievous grin.

Levi drew Reece's arm up into his. "Unfortunately, even though we are honoring the traditions of Earth and Pemdas, we are also honoring our own wishes. A short reception was planned, and in my opinion, it has already exceeded that."

Harrison laughed as he glanced knowingly into Levi's eyes. "I cannot say that I fault you." He stepped back and extended his arm toward the waiting guests. "You two lovebirds enjoy your vacation; I will delay you no longer."

"We will see you upon our return, Harrison."

After Levi and Reece thanked the guests, Levi escorted Reece to her room where Jasmeen awaited.

An ivory satin corset dress embellished with pearls was what Reece had planned to wear to depart to Levi's private destination. After she was fully dressed, Reece pulled on her elbow-length gloves as Lady Allestaine and Elizabeth entered her dressing room.

"This has been the most enchanting and wonderful day, my beautiful daughter," Lady Allestaine said as she approached Reece and hugged her delicately. She handed Reece a box. "I do wish Navarre would have been here to witness this wonderful occasion. Nevertheless, this gift is something special that he wished for you to have."

Reece tilted her head to the side, studying Lady Allestaine's tear-filled eyes in confusion. She took the box and embraced her new mother. Reece's eyes filled with tears, and she was overwhelmed with gratitude for the love she continually received from this family.

"Open the box before we all turn into sobbing messes," Elizabeth said with a laugh.

Reece opened the box to find a dazzling tiara garnished with teardrop pearls that shone in opalescent colors. It was encrusted with diamond-like crystals and was more ornate than any she had seen before.

Reece stared at the opulent tiara, mesmerized by its beauty. She was startled when Allestaine chuckled. "Allow me to put it on you, my darling." She gracefully removed the head piece that Reece wore for her wedding and placed the new tiara on Reece's head. "This tiara was worn by Navarre's mother as well. It is known in Pemdas as the empress' tiara. It is also what you will wear during your formal coronation ceremony, whenever Levi and you decide upon when that grand event shall take place."

"I can't accept this now. Until the ceremony takes place, it's yours!" Reece stammered.

Lady Allestaine smiled. "Reece, please do not frazzle yourself over this symbolic piece. Whether or not you have had your coronation ceremony, you are married to the emperor now. As I mentioned earlier, that makes you the empress."

Reece gazed into Lady Allestaine's eyes, struggling to find the right words.

Lady Allestaine smiled knowingly in return. "As I told you before, I plan to stand by your side and help in every way that I can."

"You must believe her, Reece. My mother will not let one ounce of stress befall you over your new position. Surely, you understand that."

Reece sniffed as tears streamed down her face.

"Darling, do not start to cry." Lady Allestaine blotted Reece's tears with a lace handkerchief. "Your husband anxiously awaits you in the courtyard, and seeing tears in your eyes might distract him from the evening he has planned for both of you."

Reece laughed. "True." She shook her head and forced herself to focus on the wonderful evening she and Levi were about to share.

"Now, let us get you down to him."

With that, the three woman left the room and walked nobly through the corridors of the palace and out to the courtyard, where an elaborately decorated coach awaited them.

The courtyard and cobblestone drive were filled with the guests from the ceremony. Levi stood formally at the door and offered his arm. "Once again," he addressed those filling the area, "my bride and I are honored that you chose to witness our commitment toward one another. It is our hope that you will enjoy the festivities that await you during the next few weeks."

The crowd cheered as Levi escorted Reece to the waiting carriage. Reece glanced over at Levi as soon as they were seated, his brilliant eyes shimmering. She reached for his hand, gripping it tightly. "I couldn't be more excited to leave," she said enthusiastically.

Levi brought his lips to her neck and placed a small bouquet of flowers in on her lap. "There is only one last tradition to uphold. Toss the flowers and allow us to see who will be next amongst our guests to have a wedding ceremony in their near future."

Reece laughed, placed a quick kiss on Levi's cheek, and eyed the audience. *There could be no one better,* Reece thought as she eyed Harrison's mischievous grin. As the carriage started past him, Reece tossed the flowers directly into his chest, leaving him no other option but to reflexively catch the bouquet. Levi laughed aloud before pulling Reece into his embrace and covering her lips with his. The driver called out loudly, and the horses gained more speed, carrying Levi and Reece rapidly to their wedding night destination.

# Chapter 8

Once the palace was no longer in sight and they were steadily on their way, Levi stretched out his long legs and relaxed into the plush seats of their carriage. With the subtle rocking, the clicking of the horses' hooves, and Levi absently playing with a loose strand of her hair, Reece found herself in perfect tranquility. She leaned into his sturdy embrace, resting her head against his chest.

"This was such a beautiful day," she said as she ran her fingers along his ivory waistcoat. "I can't thank you enough for everything you've done to make it so special for us."

Levi placed a small kiss on her forehead. "First of all, your beauty far outshines any of the décor that was designed for our wedding." He reached down to Reece's hands and began to remove her gloves. "You know how desperately I love you; therefore, there is no need for you to vocalize your gratitude toward me."

As Levi proceeded to remove Reece's other elbow-length glove, she sat up and eyed him skeptically. She sighed softly as Levi's eyebrow shot up, and his piercing blue eyes were already challenging her retort.

"I will always *vocalize my gratitude* toward you," she said, mimicking him.

Levi ran his fingers along the inside of her arm and very gently began to distribute soft kisses along it, his eyes never leaving hers. "If you insist, my love," he said in a lower voice. "But if you choose to do so, I believe those will be the only words I shall hear out of your mouth from now until we both meet our demise." He laughed before kissing the inside of her wrist. He inhaled deeply. "And, my wife, you should know that I intend to give you all that your heart desires until that time."

Goosebumps covered Reece's arm, and an unexpected shiver shot through her body. "What am I going to do with you?" she responded, trying to keep her voice from showing her overwhelming emotions for him at the moment.

The back of Levi's fingers gently ran along Reece's cheek as he stared purposefully into her eyes. "I believe that is the very question I am pondering at the moment." His hand gripped the back of her neck, bringing her lips to his. He hesitated for a moment before placing a small kiss on her bottom lip. "I love you, Mrs. Oxley."

"We need to get to our destination soon!" Reece said with a laugh. "This is almost torture!"

"Soon," he simply stated.

Reece glanced out of the window, knowing that if they didn't change the subject, she would likely succumb to her desires and an unexpected change of plans would occur. This carriage ride was turning out to be longer than she could stand. "So will you at least tell me where it is we are going?" she asked as her eyes pleaded with his.

Levi smiled contentedly at her. "That would ruin the surprise. You must wait."

They reached their destination as the sun slid behind the horizon and the foliage began to glow. Once the carriage turned onto a long, tree-lined driveway, Reece knew exactly where their destination was. She sat up as they rode through the illuminating blossoms cascading from the trees. The forest around them was glowing vibrantly, and the massive home that Levi purchased for them was well-lit even from the moderate distance they were away from it.

Reece gripped Levi's hand. "You planned for us to spend our wedding night in our home?"

Levi smiled brightly. "Indeed, I have, and it appears as though you approve," he answered, brushing his fingers over the top of her nose.

The carriage rounded the circular driveway and stopped in front of the house. "This is perfect! We could spend our entire honeymoon here, and I would be elated."

"I couldn't agree with you more, though I have already made other arrangements for our honeymoon," he answered. "But I assure you that you shall not be found wanting after our evening here, and I believe you will enjoy the next journey I have arranged for us even more."

The footman opened their carriage door, and Levi was the first to step out. He dismissed the footman and turned to offer his hand to help Reece out of the carriage. Before her feet could touch the ground, he swept her into his arms and seized her lips.

Levi withdrew and smiled adoringly into her eyes. "Shall we, Mrs. Oxley?"

Reece wrapped her arms tightly around his neck and kissed him enthusiastically on his cheek. "Yes, we shall!"

As Levi carried her up the steps and through the entrance, he whispered into her ear, "Another surprise awaits you. It is what you may call a gift from Elizabeth and my mother."

Reece stared into his sparkling eyes as he carried her into the large manor and she gasped at the elaborately furnished foyer. She looked back at Levi, who continued to walk toward the grand staircase in front of them.

As they began their ascent to the third floor, Levi looked over at her and grinned. "Do you approve of the furnishings?"

"I don't know what to say. When did anyone have time to arrange all of this?"

Levi laughed. "Have you forgotten that the former Empress of Pemdas has a flair for getting these sorts of things taken care of in record-breaking time? She and Elizabeth worked together, paying close attention to what your personal preferences might be. I plan to give you a tour, though that will have to wait."

He winked as he opened the door to their personal sitting room. He wasted no time in carrying Reece past the elaborately decorated foyer and into their bedroom. A healthy fire was lit in the fireplace, flickering candles were arranged throughout, and an enormous four-poster bed sat imposingly on the elevated floor of the room. The large windows that curved around the mahogany bed were framed with rich burgundy drapes. The drapes were designed to match the lavish comforter and the abundance of decorative pillows arranged stylishly on their bed. Even considering the sumptuously appointed rooms in the palace, this room was decorated so beautifully, it took Reece's breath away.

Levi gently set Reece down on her feet and wrapped his arms around her from behind. "Do you like it? With this particular room, I personally opted to advise the designers about your preference of colors and how our room should be arranged."

Reece twisted in his arms, turning to face him. "*Like* it? I love it. I really feel like a true princess," she smiled, "married to the perfect prince."

Levi's lips twisted up into her favorite grin. "Well, you are certainly not a princess. You are the Empress of Pemdas, and as to whether or not I am the perfect emperor in your eyes, only time will tell."

Reece wrapped her arms around his neck and stood on her toes to kiss him on his lips. "I love you so much."

"I love you, too. Now, I have a few more arrangements to make with the staff before they are to be dismissed. Through those doors, you will find everything you need. Are you hungry at all?"

Reece's heart rate began to increase, and even if she was hungry, food was the last thing on her mind. "I'm perfectly fine for now."

Levi bent to kiss her on her cheek, and then whispered into her ear, "I will only be a few moments, but please take all of the time you need. There is a bath drawn for you as well, if you so desire."

Reece nodded and reached up to caress his cheek. "Don't take too long."

"You will hardly notice my absence," he answered with a mischievous grin as he briskly exited their bedchamber.

Whatever he was planning with the servants, Reece didn't care. She was enthusiastic to prepare herself for the rest of their evening together.

When Reece walked into the enormous bathroom, the large tub was extremely inviting. Her hair was still pulled up from the style Jasmeen had arranged it in for the wedding, so without hesitation, she slipped into the tub and used this quiet and relaxing moment to gather her racing thoughts.

After a short soak in the tub, Reece stepped out and walked into her large closet to locate the gown she had planned to wear for this night. As soon as she found it, she dried off and plucked the long, sheer gown off its hanger. She slipped it on, pulled on the matching silk robe, and tied the ribbon into a bow at her waist. After a glance in the mirror, she debated on whether to take her hair down or leave it as it was. Without another thought, she began taking the pins out, allowing it to flow freely down her back. Reece studied her appearance in the mirror and instantly regretted pulling her hair out of the extravagant style Jasmeen had arranged it in.

*Definitely a bad idea, Reece! You look like an idiot.* Her lips twisted in frustration as she started to gather it again. She successfully brought her hair back up, and it would have to do. She could no longer stand there and stare at herself in the mirror; she knew Levi would be back in their room soon, and she did not want to waste another minute away from him.

Once she returned to their bedchamber, her heart reacted wildly at the sight of her husband. He stood gazing out of the open doors to their balcony, wearing only long, tan trousers and sipping on a glass of wine. The sheer curtains danced in the soft breeze that gently blew in. It was a dreamlike image that Reece would never forget, nor ever allow to leave her mind.

Levi turned at the sound of the door closing behind her, and she could feel his smoldering eyes as they seemed to bore through her as he set his chalice on the table next to him. Reece felt the heat rushing to her cheeks, being under his passionate gaze. As he walked toward her, a smile drew upon his face when half of Reece's hair fell out of its style and down her back. Reece had to fight to keep from pulling her hair back up, and she desperately hoped she still looked presentable for this moment with Levi.

Levi approached and brought his hands up to stop her from nervously fixing her hair. He leisurely lowered her hands and tenderly kissed each of her palms. Reece remained perfectly still as Levi gently raised his hands up to her hair. He bent to plant soft kisses along the base of her neck. He brought his lips to her ear as he started pulling out the pins that held her hair up. "My stunning wife," he said in a low, husky voice, "I have always preferred your hair down." He kissed the soft and tender skin just beneath her ear. As the last pin came out, her hair cascaded down her back.

Reece steadied her breathing, although that was getting more and more difficult to do. Levi gently guided her robe off one shoulder, and his soft lips pressed firmly along the delicate flesh exposed to him. When his lips withdrew, he quietly spoke, "If you wish, we can relax with a glass of sparkling wine in front of the fireplace."

Reece couldn't answer, as Levi was now affectionately placing kisses along her collarbone and onto her other shoulder. Reece's legs became weak, and her heart was fluttering rapidly as she ached for more from her husband. She inhaled deeply, trying to steady her breathing and calm herself. She had longed for this moment with him, and the anticipation of it was taking over every steady nerve in her body. She exhaled and succeeded in calming her anxiety.

All she felt now was her strong desire to indulge herself in every part of the passionate night that she and Levi would share.

Longing for more, Reece ran her hands through Levi's hair, prompting him to moan in response. She kissed the top of his head, absorbing the rich aroma of him that she loved as Levi successfully removed her robe.

Levi exhaled gently, his mouth first at the base of her throat, now along her jawline, then her chin, before pulling away. He stood up, and his vivid eyes stared deeply into hers. "It appears as though relaxing with a glass of wine can wait," he muttered hoarsely with a kiss to her forehead.

"I completely agree." Reece reached out and traced along his flawless, muscular chest. "All I want is you."

Levi brought his lips to hers, securing a passionate kiss. Reece returned the kiss with as much enthusiasm as she ran her hands along the firm lines of his sides and slowly up his back.

As Levi's lips left hers, he gently removed one strap of her sheer gown from her shoulder. Reece sighed in utter satisfaction, willing and more than ready to fulfill her every desire of being with her husband. *I love you*, she thought as his soft lips claimed the bare skin of her side. Slowly her gown was being removed, revealing more to Levi than ever before.

"And I love you, Reece," he breathlessly answered her.

The gown she wore fell freely to the ground, and Reece became confused when Levi's mouth froze in place against her burning flesh. Without a word, he rose up, brought her robe up around her, and pulled her into a tight embrace. He was breathing heavily as he slowly leaned back and gazed into her eyes. Reece's heart raced as she stared into his shimmering sapphire blue eyes. They were so beautiful, and they glistened unlike she had ever seen them before.

"What's wrong?" Reece asked, confused and somewhat embarrassed that he so abruptly stopped himself from going any farther.

He cradled her face in his hands. His gaze returned her confidence, prompting the desire for him to take her as his own in that instant.

Levi exhaled vigorously and closed his eyes, seemingly trying to calm himself. "My love?" His eyes reopened, now dark, and studied hers.

"Yes?" she answered, suddenly feeling vulnerable and timid due to the strange way he was acting.

Levi's head tilted to the side. "Please understand. I am trying everything in my power to prevent this."

"Prevent what?" Reece's brow furrowed in question as she traced his tightened lips. "The next step?" she asked, trying to ease the tension of this unexpected moment.

Levi exhaled with a sympathetic grin. "Did you not notice that a moment ago, I answered—" He paused and studied her. "I *answered* your thought?"

Her eyes widened at the realization that she had never spoke the words aloud that she loved him before he answered her in return.

She looked into his apologetic eyes. "You were able to read my mind?"

"I not only read your mind, I felt your emotions, your thoughts, and the sensations of everything you were experiencing. I tried to block it, but I couldn't. It seems as though you are projecting—forcing them into my mind." He ran the back of his knuckles along her cheek. "I am so sorry for this. I don't know if I can block it if it happens again."

Reece leaned into his chest. "It's not happening anymore?"

"No. It stopped when you asked me what was wrong. It is as if our minds were connected in some way, or yours connected to mine. I am unsure; I cannot explain it." He stepped back and studied her. "I feel as though I am intruding on your personal thoughts and emotions."

Whatever was happening, Reece trusted Levi with every part of herself, including her thoughts and emotions. While Levi expressed remorse that he was able to read into her mind, Reece felt the opposite. *If there was any time that I wish you could read my mind, it would be now.*

Levi's eyes became vibrant again. He looked at her as if she spoke these thoughts aloud. "Love—"

"Is it happening again?"

Levi nodded.

Reece smiled, "Then you should know that whatever is happening between my mind and yours, it is an amazing gift." She gently unlatched his belt, slid it out from the loops, and tossed it away.

Reece ran her hands along the sides of his faultless, brawny frame and stared into his shimmering eyes. She removed her robe and molded her body tightly against his. Everything within her ached with the need for him to love her. *Don't make me wait any longer.*

In that moment, his eyes shimmered brilliantly. He answered her thought as he instantly cradled her in his arms. She brought her lips to the side of his neck as he walked them briskly to their bed. As he gently laid her on the plush bed, she relaxed into the pillows while Levi covered her body with his own.

He softly kissed her, and his eyes met hers. "Reece Marian Oxley," he sighed, "my one and only love."

\*\*\*

Levi maintained superior discipline as his mind and body continued to respond to Reece's every thought and emotion being as they were projected into his mind. Every nerve in his body was ignited and fueled by her reactions of utter bliss as he slowly lavished her soft, delicate frame with lush kisses.

The warm room was filled with the sweet aroma of her body, which was so tantalizing that it was nearly impossible not to claim her as his own right then and there. The crackling of the fire in the fireplace, combined with her soft, sweet moans, helped to keep the adrenaline coursing through his veins at bay. With every kiss, he explored her alluring body. He sipped of her delicious fragrance, and he hungered for more. Reece's every thought and desire as he indulged himself was aggressively consuming his mind and guiding his every move. This, coupled with his own emotions in this sensual moment, created an atmosphere of absolute euphoria.

Reece's slender fingers ran through his hair as he affectionately and slowly ran his lips along the impeccable curves of her body. As his lips brushed along her lower abdomen, he felt her anxiety increase. In that instant, every thought and emotion that she had left his mind. It seemed that when she became hesitant with him, her mind would no longer share anything with his.

Reece's hands continued to massage through his hair, and yet he could feel the tension in them, the anticipation. He offered a reassuring kiss to her side and was relieved when her anxieties vanished. Her emotions and thoughts returned to him, and Levi pressed on. Goosebumps covered her firm legs as he ran his fingers along them. Her hands tensed more, and she softly called out. Before he could do anything else, she gripped his hair tightly, encouraging him to bring his mouth back to hers. Levi's heart beat with anticipation, feeling her great desire for more. Levi's calm demeanor disappeared, and his desire to fulfill her aching need for this moment exceeded hers.

Her eyes were wild with hunger and passion for him. Finally, the moment had come, and Levi could not hesitate any longer. He put his energy into an aggressive kiss so that he would not easily succumb to his own desire for the passionate moment they both so desperately waited for.

As soon as their bodies followed their mental state of becoming one, Reece gasped and her hands dug into his back. "I love you," she whispered.

"My love," he managed in return.

Reece's grip softened, and she softly moaned in satisfaction as her hands massaged into his back, wanting more of him. Levi brought his face to hers, needing to see the passion in her eyes. He loved this woman beyond what he could ever put into words. The gratification of sharing this moment with his one true love was indescribable. To have their bodies, hearts, and minds joined together as one was more pleasurable than he imagined it could be. Her normally crystal blue eyes were dark with passion, almost hypnotic. He was sure that after seeing her look at him in such a way, there would be no other expression she held for him that could surpass it.

It was a look that made his heart halt with love for her, one that proved he was giving her everything she could ever need from him in this moment: love, protection, satisfaction, and ultimate pleasure.

Reece's hands firmly gripped each side of his face, forcing his lips back onto hers. She proceeded to kiss him with more power than she had ever done before, and he returned this kiss with the same desire as they had enjoyed in the ultimate pleasure of their unity.

Their kissing slowed, along with their movements. Levi opened his eyes as he ended their kiss. He rested his forehead against hers, allowing them both an opportunity to catch their breath. As their bodies remained lovingly intertwined, Levi stared into his beautiful wife's utterly fulfilled eyes.

They sparkled as they gazed back into his. She smiled and ran her hands tenderly up his sturdy arms, and then to each side of his face. She said no words; she simply looked into his eyes and smiled one of the most dazzling smiles he had ever seen her wear.

"I love you," he said with a kiss to her nose.

She exhaled. "You're amazing," she said with a laugh.

Levi chuckled as her hands returned to massage along his sides and back. She locked her legs around him, forcing him to bring his eyes back to hers.

"Something every man desires to hear from his wife," he said as he exhaled. "However, I must say that *you*," he brushed a loose strand of hair from her forehead, "are the one that exceeded any expectation I could have ever dreamed of."

Reece brought her lips to his for a kiss and relaxed further into the pillows. Her brow furrowed. "Why is it that the most remarkable and beautiful moments have to come to an end?"

Levi brought his lips to her neck as her hands pressed firmly into his back. "They don't," he whispered as he clasped her hands and brought them up into the pillows above her head.

As Levi interlaced his fingers with hers, his lips found hers in a wild and hungry kiss, which Reece accepted fully. Filled with more love for Reece than he could have ever imagined, Levi was in utter bliss. Their wedding day had exceeded all of his expectations, and now being able to enjoy the pleasure of being married to the love of his life was gratifying in every way. A shiver of excitement rushed through his entire being, knowing that this day was only the beginning of their new journey together as husband and wife.

# Chapter 9

The glow of the flames in the fireplace was the only illumination in the room when Reece's eyes opened from a dreamless sleep. She watched as the flames flickered and danced around the wood they were slowly consuming. The room was filled with warmth, and her heart was brimming with love and contentment as she lay in this bed with Levi at her side. As she began to recall their evening, something strange began to unfold.

Even though the room was warm, she became extremely cold. Suddenly, she saw her breath in the chilled air, and she felt as though she had been instantly transported to another place. She was in a dark, bitterly cold cave, and the only warmth she felt was that from Levi's sturdy hand as it gripped hers tightly. The air was extremely damp, and her hair and clothes were soaking wet. The cold began to sting, and she felt overly tired. She let out a sigh of absolute exhaustion, believing it might be her last.

"We are close, my love," Levi said. "Our destination is not far from here."

She struggled to see where Levi was taking her in this vision. She glanced up at him. "I'm so cold and tired," she responded through chattering teeth.

Levi squeezed her hand, and she looked up at him. He smiled while his eyes glowed vividly. "Focus on what you learned, my love."

The moment he said that, the icy pain of her cold, aching body vanished, along with her bizarre vision, and her view was that of their fireplace again.

Reece bolted upright, startled by what had occurred. Levi, who had been in a sound sleep with Reece securely in his arms, leaned up and ran his hand along Reece's back. "Is everything okay?"

Reece glanced over to find him watching her in confusion. She looked back to the fireplace and rubbed her forehead. "The strangest thing happened," she answered as she tried to comprehend what had transpired.

Levi sat upright. "Reece, you're trembling," he said as he brought his arms around her. "Was it a nightmare?"

"No," she leaned into him for support, "at least I don't think it was. I know that I woke up, and I was staring into the fire. Then out of nowhere, the room was freezing." She looked up at him to find him studying the surroundings of their room. "Right after that, you and I were in a cave, and it was freezing cold." She shook her head. "Saying it out loud makes it seems like I've lost my mind."

"You have not lost your mind," he said as he ran his fingers through her hair. "Was that all that occurred?"

Her forehead crinkled in confusion. "You were with me and telling me to focus on what I learned," she exhaled, "But I had no idea what you were talking about. Then the next thing I know, I snapped out of it. I was back in bed in this warm room, staring at the fireplace again."

Levi studied her for a moment before he spoke. "I am highly attuned to any sounds or changes in my surroundings, even as I sleep. If I felt the climate of the room change drastically, I would have awoken as well."

Reece shrugged. "So it must have been a dream? I swear, I've never felt anything more real," she questioned. "I must be on my way to losing my mind completely."

"I must ask," Levi started, "as it was not long ago when the priestess invaded your dreams, and also your mind. Was this experience, be it a dream or not, anything like what she did to you?"

Reece pulled up and out of his embrace. "Nothing like that. I swear, I felt like I was transported somewhere else."

Levi nodded. "A vision, perhaps?"

"Exactly," Reece answered. "Is that even possible?"

Levi brought his lips to her shoulder. "I am still struggling to accept the realization that your mind was able to force your thoughts and emotions into mine earlier. I believe for now we should take note of what happened, and if it happens again, you must tell me. Do you believe yourself to be in danger in any way?"

"No," Reece answered. "Do you think Galleta could tell me what that could have been?"

"If you are comfortable with waiting until we return from our vacation, she shall be the first person we seek out to counsel us about this." He lifted her chin with his finger. "But only if you do not feel threatened by this occurrence; we cannot put ourselves in a position to be taken off guard, as we were by that priestess."

"I feel normal," Reece answered. "Confused that it happened, but I feel completely fine."

"Very well," Levi answered. "We will make it our first priority to consult with Galleta upon our return, unless these visions become harmful."

Reece brought her lips to his, knowing that whatever had happened to her, she was safe. Levi was at her side, and she was in his arms. She leaned into him, encouraging him to lie back. He snaked his arms around her and deepened their kiss. Reece gladly accepted the comfort of Levi's loving embrace and ran her hands along his firm sides, molding her body tightly against his. Levi groaned in response, and her heart reacted as he tightened his hold on her and brought her to lie beneath him. For every advance he made, Reece responded with as much enthusiasm, thankful to partake in the luxury of being married to the man she loved so greatly.

The next morning, Reece was peacefully awakened by the morning light peeking through the drapes. She stretched in contentment and turned to find that Levi was gone. *What time is it?* she wondered with a light yawn. The room was a perfect temperature. She snuggled deeper into the soft comforter and looked over to see that a new log had been placed on the fire. She closed her eyes, lost in the bliss of the passionate night she shared with Levi. She held up her left hand and studied the brilliant gemstone of her wedding ring. *I can't believe we're actually married.* She rubbed her hand across his pillow, and she smiled at the thought that she would have the luxury of him sleeping at her side every night and waking up next to him every day. "Well, every day except today. Where did he go?" she muttered aloud.

Before she could call out for him, the door to their room opened. As Levi entered carrying a tray of food, the aroma of fresh bacon and toast filled the room.

"Good morning, Mrs. Oxley," Levi said with a brilliant smile stretching across his face. "I trust you slept well after what occurred earlier this morning?"

"Good morning!" Reece sat up and smiled at him. "Yes, I slept extremely well," she continued, stuffing pillows behind her back and leaning into them. "Sorry I woke you up last night."

"Do not apologize. As we discussed, it was out of the ordinary, and we will not dismiss what happened. Now," Levi set the tray of food on her lap and kissed her tenderly on her forehead, "here is a gift for you—breakfast prepared by your favorite cook."

Reece returned his humored expression with a playful smile. "Oh? I didn't realize I had a favorite!"

She brought her attention to the tray of food resting on her lap. The breakfast he prepared for her looked delicious: a bowl of fresh fruit, thick slices of crispy bacon, fluffy scrambled eggs, and waffles topped with sliced strawberries and blueberries.

Levi reached over, picked up a perfectly ripened strawberry, and brought it to her lips. "You have one now, as I have spent the last three mornings in the kitchens of Pasidian training in the art of cooking for my wife."

Reece took a bite of the strawberry he held to her lips and smiled. She swallowed. "Levi, I love you. You didn't have to learn how to cook on my account, you know. I hope you're planning on sharing this with me, because there is no way I can eat all of this by myself."

"I had indeed planned to share breakfast with you, but after spending my morning tasting and preparing your meal, I became quite full." He lay on his side, facing Reece as she began to eat. "And yes, I did need to learn how to cook. It was worth the effort, as I had instructed our staff to return only to help prepare for our departure late this morning."

Reece took healthy bites of each item prepared on her plate. "This is so delicious—and it appears that you are, in fact, my new favorite cook," she said with a kiss to his forehead. She took a sip of her tea. "When should we expect the staff to arrive?"

Levi's fingers grazed tenderly along her arm. "They will be arriving in a few hours. Jasmeen will be with them and will help you prepare for the journey to our destination."

Goosebumps covered Reece's arm, and eating breakfast instantly became an afterthought. "What time is it, anyway?"

Levi grinned. "It is only 7:30," he answered with a small kiss to her shoulder.

Setting the tray aside, Reece softly sighed and glanced down into his eyes.

Levi took the tray and placed it on a side table. He smiled innocently at her. "Sorry, love, I did not intend to distract you from your breakfast."

"I was full anyway."

Their gazes locked, and Levi's eyes darkened as he stared intently into hers. Without looking away, he leaned over and kissed her again. "Is there anything else I can get for you?" he asked as he placed lingering kisses first on her chin, and then on her lips.

The tone of his voice and the passion in his eyes made Reece's heart flutter in anticipation. She ran her hands through his thick, wavy hair. "I think it's time that you stop doing things exclusively for me and give me an opportunity to repay the surprise breakfast you made."

Levi's eyebrows shot up, and he grinned playfully. "Sounds perfectly fair to me!"

Reece laughed. "Let me freshen up some. I'll be right back."

Levi dropped his long legs over the side of the bed and turned to face Reece. "Take your time," he said as he reached for the tray of food on the table. "Give me a moment to take this back to the kitchen, and I will eagerly await your return to our bedchamber."

Levi placed her silky robe on the bed before he disappeared from the room. Reece pulled the robe on, shoved the blankets off her, and quickly walked toward the doors that led to their dressing rooms and bathing area. When she approached the sink to brush her teeth, she stopped at the sight before her. *Should have known. What am I going to do with this man?* He had already drawn a steaming bath for her, with the aromas of vanilla and lavender filling the room. The enormous bathing area was filled with sparkling bubbles nearly spilling over the side, and lit candles lined the marble steps that led to the inviting bath.

The lights in the room suddenly dimmed, and two sturdy hands brushed along her shoulders, removing her robe. "You are more than welcome to enjoy this alone, though I would be more than willing join you."

A shiver ran down Reece's spine as Levi slid his hand down her back. "That was a quick trip to the kitchen," she teased.

Levi ran his fingers down the center of her back, "Indeed." He softly laughed. "A thought entered my mind as I exited our bed chambers: should I do dishes, or take advantage of every moment spent with my wife? I would much rather wash your hair." He said as he swept her hair over one shoulder and brought his lips to her neck.

"I'll take you up on that offer," she said breathlessly.

Reece sauntered up the steps, and she sank into the warm bath. Her entire body was enveloped with the warm, silky water as she turned to see Levi intently watching her. After a quick dunk and smoothing back her long hair, she turned to find Levi unfastening the buttons on his shirt without any hesitation. "Hurry, I need someone to wash my hair," she teased.

Levi softly laughed. "As you wish, my love."

After their long, rejuvenating bath, Reece lounged on the chaise in her warm bathrobe. In absolute contentment, she sat taking in the beautiful views that the expansive windows of their bedroom offered her. She took a sip of the fresh cup of tea that Levi poured for her before he left the room, impeccably dressed, to meet the servants that were starting to arrive at their estate. Her eyes wandered around the lavish room, and her heart beat rapidly, filled with both gratitude that Levi came into her life and anticipation for what their future would hold.

Her thoughts were interrupted when Levi placed a soft kiss on the side of her neck. Normally she would have been startled, but her body responded to his warm kiss. He ran his hands through her hair and brought his lips to her ear. "My love, we must have a portrait of you sitting like this. Do you realize how exceedingly divine you appear at this moment?"

Reece turned to face him, and her lips met his in that instant, securing a desiring kiss. She ran her hand along the side of his face and back through his hair. "We're never going to leave this room," she muttered against his lips.

Levi softly laughed and gently cupped her chin. "You, Mrs. Oxley, are going to have a very upset handmaiden soon if you are not careful."

Reece laughed and stood up. She wrapped her arms tightly around his waist and stared up into his eyes. "Really? How's that?"

He brought his hands to her face and sighed as his lips curved up on one side. "Because she is on the brink of having to wait alone in her chambers for quite some time until I have finished abundantly devoting myself to your flawless and appealing body again."

Reece brought her arms around his neck. "We probably shouldn't be so rude to her, should we?"

Levi stared longingly into her eyes. He brought his hand up to tenderly caress her face, while his thumb absently ran up her chin and slowly reached her lips. He traced her mouth with his thumb and sighed. "You are correct. I fear Jasmeen will be suffering enough while assisting you on our vacation." He grinned and bent to kiss her. After the brief kiss, he slowly rose up. "Allow me to retrieve her for you. Once I have finished going over the details with the attendants, I will return."

He brushed his finger over the tip of her nose and turned to leave. Reece watched in pleasure as her handsome husband took his usual, confident strides across the room. Reece walked toward her dressing rooms, and a moment later Jasmeen was in the expansive vanity area with a large trunk.

When she noticed Reece's entrance, Jasmeen smiled. "Good morning, Reece. I do not think I shall require anything to help with your complexion today; you are glowing radiantly already."

"Good morning, Jasmeen." Reece laughed. "So what's the outfit for today?"

Jasmeen motioned for Reece to sit in the chair. She started laying out all of Reece's makeup and styling tools. "That will come momentarily."

Jasmeen went through her normal routine and began applying Reece's makeup before she examined Reece's hair. "Wow. You dried it yourself? Was it any trouble?"

"Do you really think that I am *that* helpless, Jasmeen? I didn't walk around Earth my entire life with wet hair, you know," Reece said with a laugh.

"Well, of course not." Jasmeen flushed.

"You are the one who insists upon doing everything for me. I'm pleased to announce that I even made our bed."

Jasmeen giggled as she began curling Reece's hair. "If you keep this up, I will soon find myself working in the kitchens."

"I don't think that will be happening anytime soon. Now, how are we *lavishly* styling the hair today?" Reece mocked with a wink.

"Emperor Levi has made a simple request to have your hair up for this first destination. You will be wearing the crown of the Empress."

After Jasmeen finished styling Reece's hair in an exquisite manner, she placed a rectangular, velvet box into Reece's hand. Reece stared up at her. "Another request from the emperor," Jasmeen said.

When Reece opened the crimson velvet box, she gasped in astonishment. A slender platinum chain held a multicolored, shimmering stone. As she studied the exquisiteness of this particular jewel, she noticed that the brilliant sapphire would cast off a silver glow, then deep purple, then gold, then blue. All of these different colors twinkled with the light of the room and constantly shifted in patterns. It was more beautiful than any exquisite piece of jewelry she'd seen in the land thus far. In the middle of the necklace lay the matching, delicate bracelet. It was filled with these same unique stones and created to fit her slender wrist perfectly. The jewelry set was complete with matching drop earrings, and Reece was so stunned by the beauty of the pieces that she hardly noticed a tiny white card, penned by Levi.

*My Love,*
*The beauty you might find in these stones will*
*never compare to yours.*
*– L. Oxley*

"This is extraordinary!" she said with tears filling her eyes.

"It is exquisite," Jasmeen said as she clasped the necklace around Reece's neck. "Now, if you will follow me," the maiden beckoned as she turned to walk into Reece's grand closet.

Once inside, Jasmine motioned over to where a black garment bag hung alone in front of Reece's oversized dressing mirror, and a matching black box sat beneath it.

Jasmeen turned to Reece. "Well, open them. Let us see if our emperor can match up jewelry and clothing, shall we?"

Reece was speechless as she walked toward the garment bag. She took another small white card that was pinned to the bag and read it.

*I am highly anticipating how your*
*beauty will embellish this dress.*
*–L*

Reece slowly unbuttoned the closure and stepped back to admire the gown Levi had chosen for her to wear. She was speechless as she stared at the sublime beauty before her. The extravagant red gown had every quality that an empress would require to be in her wardrobe. *Where is he planning on taking us today?* she wondered, somewhat intimidated by the lavish design. The material was rich in texture, tempting Reece to draw her hand out and run her fingers along it to feel its opulence. There were deep red, almost black jewels creating intricate patterns along the material. The bodice of the dress was a black lace and ended where the crimson capped sleeves began. More dark jewels lined the top of the bodice and along the top of the sleeves.

"He wasn't lying when he said I should get used to him consistently giving me gifts," Reece said with a laugh. *I love this man more than he will ever know,* she inwardly thought, being at a loss for words in regard to the beauty of the gifts he had given her.

"Shall we see what is in the other box?" Jasmeen asked excitedly.

Reece bent down, opened the box, and found the shoes that were created to match the dress perfectly. Before she could say anything more, Jasmeen went to work.

"Today you will be wearing two separate underskirts with this dress to enhance its fullness."

"Are we going to a ball?" Reece asked, recalling that was the only time she had worn duplicate underskirts in Pemdas.

Jasmeen smiled. "I am not to say a word. Our emperor has made plans that only he wishes to make known. It is solely my job to prepare you for them."

Reece laughed. "Then we'd better get moving on the transformation."

Wherever they were going, or whatever Levi had planned, Reece couldn't wait to experience it with him. She was elated to start their first day together as husband and wife, and she couldn't be back in Levi's arms fast enough to thank him for the unexpected gifts.

# Chapter 10

Levi hopped up the entryway stairs and back into the large manor after he had finalized the arrangements to leave for their next destination. Upon reaching the third floor, he made his way into the bedroom to find Reece. The sounds of Reece and Jasmeen's excited squeals came from the dressing room and put a tiny grin on Levi's face.

He absently tapped his fingers on the box that he held and meandered down the hall toward Reece's dressing room. His heart and footsteps halted as he took in the perfection that was Reece, fully dressed in the gown he had purchased for this occasion. He leaned against the doorway, crossed his arms and legs, and admired his attractive wife in her dressing room.

Neither woman noticed his presence as he discreetly watched their interactions from the doorway. Reece seemed stunned by her reflection in the mirror, and he was grateful he had shown up at this exact moment. Her expression showed him more than any words she could speak in gratitude for him.

"I will return in a moment. One thing remains to complete the ensemble," Jasmeen said when she noticed Levi in the doorway.

Reece looked at her handmaiden. "Jasmeen, how could anything else possibly be added?" She brushed her fingers over the glistening stone in the center of her chest. "Levi's already outdone himself. I'm trying to figure out how I am going to thank him for all of this."

"Oh, I am certain you shall find a way," Jasmeen answered as she offered Levi a quick curtsy before leaving the room.

Levi crossed the room and stood behind Reece as she sat in her vanity chair. She was fiddling with a small, dangling curl when Levi appeared in the mirror behind her. She turned and stared lovingly up into his eyes. "I don't even know where to begin to thank you for all this. I really need to get started on some surprises for you. I have nothing to offer you in return—well, there is something, but it's at the palace. I—"

"Reece Oxley." Levi's deep voice halted her from saying anything more. He cupped her chin with his hand. "You must already know that you have given me my greatest desire, and that is to be loved by you."

She faintly smiled in return. "You are truly the most wonderful man that any woman could ever have."

"And you, Mrs. Oxley," he said as he kissed her on her forehead, "are the most amazing woman that any man could ever have the pleasure of being in the company of." He placed the gift box onto her lap.

Reece opened the box and gasped at the gleaming tiara that was displayed on a black velvet cushion. Levi reached down and lifted the tiara from the box that rested in Reece's now-paralyzed hands.

"I had this designed to match the rest of your jewelry for our next destination." He placed the tiara atop her head and watched as her eyes fill with tears.

"I'm speechless, Levi."

He looked at her in the mirror. "It is exactly how I felt when I first walked into this room and saw you."

"Well, there is one thing I know for sure. At the rate I've been gifted priceless tiaras lately, I think we might have to build an extra closet to house them if it keeps up," she teased.

Levi laughed loudly as he reached for her hand to help her rise. "Perhaps we can just dedicate a wing of the palace to your tiaras instead of a closet. It seems more reasonable," he said sarcastically with a wink as Reece stood. Levi brought her hand to his lips for a kiss.

"In that case, make it two wings: one for the tiaras, and one for the jewels. I'll let you know if I can think of any other wings that can be dedicated to my things," she said, feigning superiority before she nudged him in his side playfully.

"As you wish, Empress Reece." Levi bowed dramatically. "Now, my wife, your carriage awaits. Is there anything else you may need before our departure?"

Reece laughed aloud. "I think you pretty much covered all of the necessary details."

She stood on her toes and wrapped her arms around his neck. Her eyes gleamed as they stared into his. "Will you give me a hint as to where we are going?"

Levi turned her to face the mirror, resting his sturdy hands on her shoulders. "The jewels you wear now were created from the same location we will be residing at for the duration of our vacation—" He stopped himself. "Forgive me, *honeymoon*," he finished with a knowing grin.

"Well, if that is the case, maybe I have yet to see all of the beauty this dimension has to offer."

"I believe you will enjoy it," Levi said with a wink.

Levi drew her arm into the bend of his and led her down the grand staircase and out to the waiting carriage. Imperial guards were mounted on their horses and waited patiently for their emperor and empress. The coaches carrying their luggage, along with Reece and Levi's personal attendants, had already started the journey to the large city they would be staying in on the way to their designated location.

Once Reece and Levi were settled into the luxurious carriage, Levi gave a rap to the top and they were off. He brought an arm around Reece and lifted her legs to rest across his lap. She reclined against the soft pillow that was provided to enhance the comfort of the long ride. Knowing that they had at least six hours in the carriage, Levi used the time to prepare Reece for their first visit to this particular city as a couple.

Levi softly brushed against her arm. "Today we will journey to the city of Braymese. It is a very lavish city, one that my parents frequently enjoyed visiting. The sights along the way are magnificent as well."

Reece smiled. "Braymese?" She twisted in his arms. "Is this where we're spending our honeymoon?"

"No, this is merely a stop before our final destination."
He smiled at her confused expression before he went on.
"I arranged for the attire you are wearing specifically, as the
city is expectantly awaiting the arrival of their new
empress."

Reece's eyes widened. "First big event as your wife!" She
relaxed and smiled. "Let's hope I don't trip."

Levi laughed. "Love, you are like a gazelle on your feet,
and tripping is not a concern you should ever have." He
kissed her cheek. "You shall shine and steal all of their
hearts, as you did mine. Of this, I have no doubt."

Close to an hour later, the sounds of the horses' hooves
gave notification that the carriage was stopping at a
location that Levi had previously arranged with the driver.
Once out of the carriage, they strolled together in the shade
of large trees, relishing in the serenity of their surroundings.
Levi grinned when they walked into a darkened area of the
forest and a swarm of tenillians fluttered all around them.
Reece stood in astonishment as she admired the many
different illuminating colors.

Levi smiled when Reece walked over to the fluttering
insects and held out her finger, hoping one would take
interest in her. He watched in amusement, just as he did on
her first night in Pemdas when she did the same. It was
enjoyable to see her sweet spirit delight in things he had
always taken for granted in his world. A yellow tenillian
accepted her invitation and landed on her outstretched
finger. She carefully turned her finger so that she could
study it. She looked up at Levi and smiled proudly.

Levi shook his head. "Well, well, well. It looks as though
you have found yourself a little friend."

"They are so beautiful. I haven't seen one since my first
night at the palace. What are they called again?"

"Tenillians," Levi responded, "and you haven't encountered them lately, as they tend to migrate to warmer climates during cooler temperatures."

They spent some time walking through the area before Reece's stomach alerted Levi to her hunger.

"How embarrassing," Reece demurred as she gripped her stomach tightly.

Levi laughed in amusement. "Let us return to the carriage and be on our way. I have some fruit that will help ease your hunger until we reach the next village."

The village that Levi had arranged for them to have lunch in was quite small, and even though the people in the community were thrilled to see their emperor and empress, Levi and Reece were left to dine without any interruptions. Once the convoy was on its way, Levi informed Reece that they would soon be arriving in Braymese for that evening's stay. The journey to the city was a lot more entertaining than Reece had imagined it would be, as short stops along the way and exploring numerous sites made for an adventurous day.

The sun had just slipped behind the large stone buildings on the cobblestone streets they were following, and Reece watched as the lanterns lining the boulevards began to glow brightly. The ivy foliage covering the tall edifices began to glisten as the wonder of Pemdas came to life, as it did each and every night.

With the large convoy of imperial guards leading and following Levi and Reece's carriage, the empty streets soon filled with civilians waving them on. "We still have some time until we reach the inn we will be staying at," Levi noted as he kindly acknowledged the civilians lining the streets.

"Looks like we've already attracted a crowd," Reece said with a laugh.

Levi brought his arm around Reece and pressed his lips to her forehead. "It appears that they are already accepting of you as their empress."

Reece tucked a piece of hair behind her ear. "Nice try. I'm fully aware that I need to prove myself to the people in your land." She sat up and took Levi's hand. "I'm prepared to start doing that tonight."

Levi cracked a smile at Reece's confident expression. "Is that so?"

"Yes," she lifted her chin, "so get ready."

Levi laughed and ran the back of his fingers along her cheek. "I am more than ready."

The imperial entourage followed the carriage to the front steps of the inn they were expected to arrive at. The hotel's staff had been alerted to their arrival and was formally standing on the steps to greet them. Large crowds lined the streets, shouting and waving.

As the carriage completely halted, Levi gazed into Reece's eyes. "Shall we?"

She smiled brightly. "Let's do this."

Levi brushed his finger over the tip of her nose before he stepped out of the carriage and turned to offer his hand. Reece gripped his arm tightly, as the crowds lining the streets were larger than she realized. *Now I know how celebrities feel,* she thought, having never been in the spotlight like this before. Reece girded herself to overcome her insecurity and followed Levi's lead as he graciously waved to the civilians and kindly interacted with the crowd. After addressing the gathering and formally introducing Reece as the empress, Levi turned to walk past the hotel staff who lined the steps into the inn.

Once inside the grand atrium, other guests of the inn were the ones now lining the lobby as they walked through. Both Levi and Reece acknowledged the guests in the same manner as they did the civilians outside. Soon they were in the private wing of the massive hotel, and the only ones surrounding them were the imperial guards stationed on either side of two extravagant wooden doors.

The doors opened, and Levi led Reece into an enormous foyer where another grand staircase awaited them.

"This is our room?" Reece asked in amazement.

They began to ascend the stairs. "Yes. We will most assuredly have our privacy here."

"Sounds wonderful to me."

At the top of the staircase, Levi guided Reece to the large doors that led to their bedchambers. He opened them, and before Reece could absorb the grandeur of the room, Levi scooped her into his arms and carried her into the luxurious space that awaited them.

Reece tightened her embrace around Levi's neck. "I should probably admit that even with all of the time I've spent at the palace, I am still so easily awed by the magnificence of everywhere we go. This room is gorgeous. I don't think I will ever be able to thank you enough for all you have done for our honeymoon."

"I am happy you approve," he returned, gently letting her alight to the floor. "Now, I would like to show you the room in which we will be sleeping, but after our journey here, I am confident you would prefer some time to freshen up." He nodded in the direction of two double doors to the side of them. "Inside you will find that Jasmeen has drawn a bath for you."

"You won't be joining me?" she teased.

"If you intend to have dinner tonight, I believe it would be best that I pass on your desirable offer this time." He bent to kiss her. "You probably should not tempt me."

Reece stood on her toes and kissed Levi in the tiny cleft on his chin. "True. Maybe later, when no one is around."

After their long journey, she was looking forward to a hot meal; and Levi was right, a soothing bath sounded more than inviting. "Since you won't be joining me, what other plans do you have?"

"I must go over my arrangements for this evening with the guards. It appears we've attracted a larger crowd than I was expecting. I must be certain that we can get through our evening without too many interruptions." With his finger, he lifted her chin and brought a quick kiss to her lips. "I will be back in a short while. For now, please relax, as I need my enchanting wife feeling refreshed for the special evening I have planned for her."

Reece returned his mischievous smirk. "Don't take too long," she answered as she turned and sauntered toward the doors.

As soon as Reece walked into the large vanity and bathing room, she was greeted by Jasmeen.

Jasmeen carried towels in her arms and smiled warmly at Reece. "After the long journey, I am astounded to find you are still glowing."

Reece crossed her arms and laughed. "It's nice to see you again, Jasmeen," she responded.

"You as well! It appears as though your journey was remarkable. It is thrilling to see you looking so radiant." Jasmeen giggled, and Reece inwardly questioned her handmaiden's excitement. Something was different. Reece wondered why she seemed so sensitive to Jasmeen's emotions, but she couldn't help it—something was different about her. She shook off the feeling, knowing what she really needed was a nice, hot bath. "It was a wonderful journey, and now I'm really looking forward to relaxing for a bit before Levi and I have to go back out and face those crowds again."

Jasmeen smiled. "Right this way; your bath is prepared for you. The emperor—"

"Jasmeen," Reece interrupted her as they walked into another room where an enormous bathtub awaited her, "please call him Levi when you and I are alone. I'm fine with that, and it would make me more comfortable, too."

"As you wish," Jasmeen responded. "I shall remember that. Now, he gave me strict orders to let you know that you are to take your time relaxing. When you are finished, I will have a hot cup of refreshing tea waiting for you."

Reece smiled. "That all sounds wonderful, thank you."

"You are very welcome," Jasmeen said as she turned to leave Reece to her privacy.

Reece sank into the hot, steamy bath, and she glanced up at the ornate carvings in the marble ceilings. Suddenly, the heat from the silky water of her bath was replaced with the feeling of sweat covering her entire body. Her bathing room surroundings had vanished, and she was now face-to-face with Harrison.

They were together in a room with other Guardians surrounding them. *Why are we in the training center?* The other men were fighting each other, going through various moves and practicing striking routines on the punching bags. She had no idea where Levi was and why he wasn't in this vision with her.

"Reece, remember what we have been working on. You can do this. Levi will be here at any moment. I want him to see this."

"Okay, but what have we been working on?" she asked him in confusion.

Harrison laughed. "Very funny." He looked past her. "Ah, he has arrived. Wait here," he said with eagerness.

She turned and saw Levi dressed in slacks, a shirt, and his waistcoat, the opposite of Harrison and the others in the training unit. The Guardians and Reece were wearing their black training clothes. Levi's expression was somber as Harrison approached him in conversation. He glanced briefly at his cousin before he directed his very grave expression toward Reece. He nodded, stood back, and crossed his arms. In that moment, Harrison turned again toward Reece, his expression radiant with excitement.

Reece stared at him in total confusion. "Harrison, what are we doing? Why is Levi upset?"

Harrison arched his eyebrow at her. "Reece, quit worrying about Levi. I need you to focus." He squared up into a combat position. "Now, we will start slow, but when you feel your body taking over, just go with it like you did before Levi arrived. Do not forget that if you let your emotions guide you, you *will* fail against me!"

*Emotions guide me? What exactly are we doing?* Suddenly, Harrison thrust his fist at her, and without thinking she deflected the powerful man's strike. His grin widened, and before she could question how she countered him, she was sparring with Harrison, defending herself against his every rapid advance toward her in the fight. She felt her mind reading his every move before he made it, and she was quicker to respond because of it. The faster Harrison became in his attack, the more she countered back without thinking. Harrison continued to challenge her. *What am I, one of them now?*

Harrison caught her arm, and Reece instantly responded by manipulating it in such a way that she brought Harrison to the ground. Instinctively, Reece brought her knee to his throat, forcing Harrison to laugh aloud. Reece immediately stood and watched Harrison spring up in absolute satisfaction. She stared at Harrison, amazed and wondering what this entire exchange between them was about. The entire match between her and Harrison was real. The strength and power she felt radiating through her entire body proved that.

As Levi approached, his smile broadened. "Truly amazing!" Levi said as he took Reece's hand into his own.

"Beyond amazing, cousin," Harrison returned with a clap to Levi's shoulder. He nodded toward Reece. "Now you can see with your own eyes that she is ready. She will be perfectly fine."

"Earth to Reece," a voice spoke distantly.

A gentle hand brushed over her hair, bringing Reece back into the warm, silky bath she was immersed in. *Levi,* she thought as her vision disappeared.

Her mind became clearer. "Earth to Reece?" she asked with a laugh. "Very funny."

Levi took the large sponge and began to lather it with soap. "It appeared as though you were somewhere on Earth when I walked in." He chuckled as he began to run the soapy sponge over her shoulders.

Reece sat up and rubbed her forehead. "Well, it definitely was not on Earth."

"Care to inform me of your daydream? Or shall I assume it was recalling the events of our time shared together thus far?"

"Harrison," Reece muttered absently as Levi continued to massage along her back and sides.

"Harrison?" Levi returned in a humorous voice. "I had no idea that you have already grown weary of your husband's passion for you. I must make improvements," he teased.

Reece turned to face him. "Believe me, no improvements are needed." She lifted her chin for a kiss. "How long until we leave? Where's Jasmeen?"

"We will depart when you are fully prepared, and I dismissed your maiden until you are ready for her."

Reece's eyebrows shot up, and she folded her arms over the ledge of the porcelain bath. "There's room for two in here. Would you care to join your wife? I think dinner can wait a little longer, don't you?"

Levi studied her for a moment. "If that is your desire, I will happily agree. Dining can wait."

Reece watched as Levi prepared to join her. "Yes, dining can definitely wait."

As Levi slipped into the steamy bath, Reece reclined back into his embrace. "I have to tell you that when you thought I was daydreaming, I wasn't. It was another vision, like before."

Levi brought his arms around her, kissing the side of her face. "Are you confident they were the same feelings you encountered on our wedding night?"

"Yes. Everything was so real," she said, rubbing along his arm. "I was sparring with Harrison and defeated him in every way possible. Strange as it may sound, he was happy about it, and more than that, happy to show *you* that I could defeat him."

Levi laughed aloud. "Having visions of beating up our cousin? I must admit that if Harrison hears of this, it will not rest easy with him."

Reece laughed. It did sound awkward the more she thought about it. "You're right. I'm sure that wouldn't sit well with his ego."

Levi rubbed his hand over her arm. "Was it frightening in any way?"

"No, just strange. It definitely helps to talk it all out with you, though."

Levi touched her chin, bringing her eyes to meet his. "You are confident that these visions are nothing in comparison to your thoughts being controlled by that priestess before we destroyed her?"

Reece laughed softly. "You mean before *you* destroyed her and taught Simone a lesson."

Levi nodded. "Indeed. I must know if you are experiencing the same thing. Are you certain that there is not something controlling your mind?"

"Quite the opposite," she said, running her fingers along Levi's creased brow. "With the mind control I fell victim to, I had no command over my thoughts or actions. But this is entirely different. I feel like I am fully in control, and the visions—or whatever it is that I am experiencing—are not clouding my rational thoughts. I just don't know why all of a sudden I'm having them."

Levi brought his hands up to massage her shoulders. "When we return to Pasidian, I will send for Queen Galleta. I am fairly confident that this has to do with your being Paul Xylander's descendant. Until then, please keep me informed of any other visions you may have."

Reece sighed. "I promise that I will keep you entertained, or should I say *informed*, if another vision creeps up on me." She twisted in his arms. "For now," she kissed his chin, "let's make the best of our time before we leave for dinner."

After their rejuvenating bath, Levi left to meet with his butler and called for Jasmeen to assist Reece in preparing for their evening out in the city together.

Reece was sitting in her robe facing the large mirror when Jasmeen returned. Her maiden handed her a cup of hot tea and immediately went to work drying Reece's hair. Once finished, she applied Reece's makeup, and then began to style her hair. Reece watched in contemplation as Jasmeen had a particular grin on her face that Reece had never seen. Reece tried to shake off the feeling that she felt compelled to believe something was different with the maiden, but she couldn't. She could sense the maiden's excitement, and more than that. *No,* Reece thought. *There is no way.* Reece absently laughed aloud.

"It appears that you are fully rejuvenated from your trip," Jasmeen observed. "You are positively radiant, and I see little need to embellish your cheeks with color."

Reece watched Jasmeen as she continued to style her hair. Jasmeen's thoughts were elsewhere. Reece could sense that Jasmeen was feeling giddy.

"Jasmeen, something's different about you," she blurted out.

Jasmeen stared at Reece in the mirror, and her cheeks tinted red. *Who's the one who doesn't need blush now? I knew it!* Reece thought.

"Well?" Reece inquired in amusement.

"Well, what?" Jasmeen answered her, trying to avoid the question.

Reece turned to face her.

"Reece! I cannot do your—"

"Jasmeen? Who is he?" Reece asked with humor in her voice.

"He?" Jasmeen asked back.

"There is someone who has captured your interest, Jasmeen. Who is he?"

Jasmeen shook her head. "I have no idea what you are talking about," she said, shrugging off the question. "Levi will return at any moment, and I must have you dressed and ready for him. He has a lovely evening prepared for you both."

Reece shook her head. *I'll figure this out,* she thought in amusement. Jasmeen went on about her duties, keeping Reece's mind busy with other things. The deep red gown she was to wear that night served to fade the emotions that were radiating from Jasmeen, and Reece was grateful for it. Red gemstones fashioned into a necklace, and earrings were designed specifically to match her dress. The last item to complete her first appearance in the large city was the ornate tiara Lady Allestaine passed down to her, arranged magnificently on her head. After pulling on her long, black gloves, Reece turned, fully prepared to leave for dinner with Levi.

"Thank you, Jasmeen."

"You are most welcome. You look beautiful," Jasmeen said. "Now, I believe Levi is waiting for you in the sitting room, and I will see you tomorrow morning. Have a wonderful evening," she said, quickly making her exit.

As soon as Reece walked into the sitting room where Levi awaited her, she stopped to take in his fine image. Her heart was amplified with love when she saw him standing across the way in a dark black tailcoat and a rich, crimson waistcoat to match her dress.

Levi crossed the room. "Mrs. Oxley, you are a portrait of absolute enchantment."

"I was thinking the same about you."

"Come," he pulled her arm into his, "let us leave immediately, or we never shall."

Reece laughed. "True."

They had their dinner at a most extravagant restaurant. They were situated at a table that was isolated from most of the other patrons in the restaurant and in front of large windows. After Reece was seated, she couldn't pry her eyes away from the view outside. The courtyard below the restaurant exhibited couples walking arm-in-arm past glowing, multicolored foliage that surrounded large, sculpted fountains. Iridescent water spilled from tops of the ornate fountains, reflecting the shimmering foliage in an array of different colors. Its enchantment was similar to that of Pasidian Palace's gardens, but the architecture of this enormous courtyard and the views from where they sat gave it an appeal that was exceptionally fascinating for Reece to behold.

"After we have finished our meal," Levi said, bringing Reece's attention back to him, "I had planned to walk with you through the gardens, if that is agreeable to you?"

Reece took a sip of her wine. "That sounds wonderful."

As they started on the first course of their meal, Reece was reminded of the strange intuition she felt about Jasmeen.

"Is everything okay?" Levi asked.

"Oh. Yes, of course. I was just thinking that something's different about Jasmeen."

Levi grinned and took a sip of his wine. "May I ask why you would be consumed by the behavior of your handmaiden at our dinner?" he asked in amusement. "Is this another vision you may have had?"

"No," she smiled, "this is completely different."

"Completely different?" Levi questioned. "Then I must know what my intuitive wife has discovered about her maiden."

"Intuition!" Reece's eyes widened. "I think that's it. Not only am I having visions, but for some strange reason I am picking up on the emotions of people without even trying."

Levi buttered a slice of hot bread and handed it to her. "This is interesting, indeed. It appears that your mind must be opening up in numerous different ways. My lovely wife is now having visions and possibly able to read into the mind of a Pemdai."

"You told me it is impossible for the Pemdai mind to be read."

Levi swallowed a bite of his bread, and Reece could tell that Levi was forcing back a laugh. He cleared his throat. "It is impossible, my love. There has never been a single being capable of reading our minds. They are protected, just as yours."

Reece's eyebrows narrowed. "Are you mocking me, *Emperor Oxley?*

"I would never consider such a thing, *Empress Oxley.*"

Reece's eyes met Levi's in a challenge before she laughed. "All right. No more formalities. And I never said I read her mind. It's more like I can feel her emotions. Go with me on this, will you?"

Levi nodded. "Very well, then, what is bothering you about your maiden?" he asked as he took another sip of wine.

She sat in thought for a moment, contemplating how she would tell Levi without this seeming like girly gossip.

"Reece," he prompted, "do go on."

She sighed. "All right. I'm just going to come out and say this, no matter how trivial it will probably sound to you." She took another sip of her wine. "Jasmeen may have feelings for someone." She laughed. "I know this is none of our business, but I can't help but wonder who it is!"

"You are correct. It truly is not our place to involve ourselves in Jasmeen's affairs. But you seem so strongly convicted about this that I find it somewhat amusing."

"Could it be someone we know?"

Levi laughed. "Well, she traveled here with three other attendants. Maybe she is fond of one of them."

"Which attendants?" Reece sat up.

Levi sat back and smiled at Reece in amusement. "I will never understand women."

"I'm not asking you to understand women, just tell me who the lucky guy is that may have caught Jasmeen's attention."

"If this is such a great concern for you, allow me to ease it." Levi leaned across the table, his eyes dancing with amusement as he forced a serious expression onto his face. He spoke in a low, mysterious voice, "Your maiden traveled with my butler, Henry, and two other servants, Richard and Brianna."

Levi laughed, seeing the expression on Reece's face.

She narrowed her eyes. "Do you think...?"

Levi shook his head. "My adorable wife, you truly enchant me." He reached across the table and took her hand. "Jasmeen may be taken with either man she traveled with today. However, it also may be that she is merely excited, as this is her first trip and partial vacation away from Pasidian."

Reece sighed. "You're probably right."

Levi brought her hands to his lips. "Case solved," Levi chuckled. "Now, shall we enjoy our fine dining atmosphere?"

Before Reece could respond, a staff member approached their table with a note in his hand. He bowed and handed the letter to Levi. "Forgive me for the interruption, sir, but this is from King Gadieus."

Levi took the offered note. "Thank you," he said, and the staff member quickly turned to leave.

Reece watched as Levi opened the note with a serious expression on his face. She remained quiet as his eyes quickly scanned the contents, after which he tucked the note away in the pocket of his coat.

He looked back at her. "Forgive me. That was an invitation from the ruler of this kingdom. He would like us to join him for lunch if we return through this location on our way back to Pasidian."

"Oh," Reece answered. "Well?"

Levi sighed. "He wants to meet the new empress; however, I have my reservations about his request. We can decide upon this later. For now, I wish to enjoy our evening."

For the remainder of their dinner, their conversation changed entirely. Both enjoyed their food and spoke about their excitement of what was to come for their honeymoon that Levi had arranged. Without revealing much, Levi had Reece more than excited to reach their final destination. Once they were finished with their meals, Levi escorted Reece down the streets toward the courtyard Reece had marveled at.

Along the way, they were brought up short when a young girl with brilliant blue eyes and golden hair ran out to Reece and wrapped her arms tightly around Reece's waist without warning.

"Forgive us, Empress Oxley," said an elderly woman with a young boy at her side.

Reece was taken aback for a moment when she gazed into the woman's turquoise eyes. "Have we met before?" she asked, wondering why this woman looked so familiar.

"Not that I can recall, Your Royal Majesty," the woman answered with a warm smile.

The young girl released her hold on Reece when Levi spoke out. "It appears as though you approve of your new empress, young lady," he said with a soft laugh.

Reece knelt down, bringing her eyes to meet the young girl's gaze. "What is your name?" she asked brightly.

"Aria," the girl said with a beaming smile, igniting the vivid blue color of her eyes.

"You have beautiful eyes, Aria." She glanced up at Levi. "They are very similar to the emperor's."

"We really must be getting along now," the elderly lady spoke out. "We are aware that this is your vacation, and we will not burden you any longer."

Reece stood up. "It was lovely to meet you, Aria," she said as she looked toward the lady who held on to the timid young boy's hand. "And to meet all of you."

The boy's eyes widened. "You really are Empress Reece from Earth?"

Reece laughed. "As of a few days ago, yes; I became empress, but not of Earth."

"Oh, yes, please forgive me. It is a great honor to see you face-to-face. We've heard so many stories that it was hard to determine whether or not they are true," the boy said, obviously taken with Levi and Reece.

"I hope the stories that you have heard are good," Reece commented with a laugh.

"Of course they are. You will be a wonderful empress, you should know that."

"Enough, Jeremy," the lady said, cutting the boy off abruptly. "Once again, please forgive our intrusion. We must be getting along now." She reached for the young girl's hand and offered a small curtsy. "We hope you enjoy your evening."

The woman scurried past Reece and Levi before they could wish her well, forcing Reece to glance back. "Something seems so familiar about them," she quietly mused.

Levi brought his arm back into hers. "Maybe it is that strong intuition you have started to experience," he teased.

Reece leaned into him. "Could be," she said proudly.

"They do bear an uncanny resemblance to someone we may have encountered before, as I feel the same way," Levi offered.

Reece sighed. "Interesting."

Levi leaned closer into Reece. "I must admit that you are dealing extremely well with all of the attention that has come your way."

Reece squeezed his arm. "It's definitely overwhelming to have people you have never met take a great interest in you," she smiled up at him, "but it is also thrilling at the same time."

Levi nodded. "Since we started protecting you on Earth, I became extremely intrigued by your outgoing personality. I found it an undeniably attractive feature that you possessed. I truly had no reservations about how you would interact with those in Pemdas who seek to make your acquaintance."

"I'm sure any other person of royalty in Pemdas would feel just as humbled that people would be thrilled to see them. You know, that's when I started having feelings toward you. The day you took me to Casititor, I watched in amazement the generosity and humbleness you possessed while you were constantly being approached."

"I believe I feel the same as you. In truth, I have never felt above any of those in Pemdas. It is truly an honor to be well received as their emperor. However, you should know that there are many in royalty who are so arrogant that they would have instantly dismissed that woman with her children."

Reece looked at Levi questionably. "That is a shame."

"In my personal opinion, they are so distracted with themselves to see the wonder of the world around them."

"I couldn't agree—" They entered into the large courtyard, and Reece became so entranced by the vivid beauty of their surroundings that her response was cut short. "This is so beautiful," she said distractedly.

They strolled through the gardens alongside other couples who were also admiring the beauty of the location. The couples around them took notice of Levi and Reece, yet none approached them, leaving them to enjoy their stroll in peace.

Reece leaned into Levi, staring up at the majesty of the glowing trees. The trees and the surrounding shrubbery illuminated in an array of colors: pinks, violets, and some even appeared to have crystals sparkling in them. Reece studied the fountains she had viewed from their dining table, watching as the water pouring out of them yielded a rainbow of different colors.

"This is all so beautiful," Reece said as she squeezed Levi's arm.

"Isn't it fascinating?"

It was strange to hear the appreciation of such beauty in Levi's voice as well, but these gardens were extraordinary. The buildings lining the location were equally as magnificent. The ivy and the blooms that covered the walls shimmered, completing the feel of absolute enchantment.

Levi guided Reece over to a stone sitting area, and she happily sat staring into the courtyard. He took a seat next to her and brought his arm around her. She leaned further into his embrace, letting the sights relax her.

"We should make it a point to visit this area again. I love it here."

Levi pressed a kiss to the top of her head. "I had planned for us to attend a theatrical performance tonight, but the guards and hotel staff informed me that we would be fortunate if we had any privacy there. It appears as though that is where most are expecting us to go."

Reece chuckled. "That makes perfect sense as to why the crowds disappeared."

Levi squeezed her arm. "Yes."

After about an hour or so of talking with Levi about the history of this town and the gardens they were in, Reece sat up and turned to face him. His lips were so desirable, and his soothing voice had her mind wishing to return to their rooms. Levi knowingly grinned, prompting Reece to refrain herself from kissing his lips in that moment. She wasn't sure, but being out in public like this with civilians walking by made her feel as though it would be improper.

Levi's eyebrow arched. "Mrs. Oxley? What, may I ask, is going on in that delightful mind of yours?"

She sighed. "Well, as beautiful as all this is, I think I'm ready to go back to our room now."

Levi stood and offered his hand to help her up. He brought his index finger to her chin, and to Reece's great delight, he brought his lips down to hers.

He withdrew from her tender kiss. "You need only to say the words."

"Let's get out of here," she said with a grin.

With that, he drew her arm back into his and led her to where the carriage awaited them. Once they were back at their rooms, Levi led her directly to their sleeping quarters and secured a strong, passionate kiss from her. Without hesitation, Reece began unraveling the intricate knot of his cravat and tossed it aside. She felt Levi chuckle, and then he stepped back, though he was still close enough for Reece to start unbuttoning his waistcoat.

He watched her deft fingers work. "Well, my lovely wife," he spoke in amusement and disbelief, "it appears that I may have unleashed a little tigress within you!"

She lifted her chin and successfully removed his waistcoat, draping it over the chair next to them. "I think you might have, and I'm about to show you how much I've missed being in your arms over these last few hours."

"Well, if that is the case, I am yours to do with as you please."

# Chapter 11

"Well, gentlemen, that's the game!" Harrison said as he cleared the entire billiard table on the first break once again.

"Harrison, could you at least give us a chance to play?" Tomas rejoined with laughter.

Harrison grinned. "I did try doing that, my friend, but if you cannot figure out how to sink a ball into a pocket when breaking, it will eventually be my turn," he said as he placed his stick on the stand, "and I believe you understand by now that I do not intend to lose."

"How do you manage to sink every ball in each pocket without one miss? It is inexplicable to me," Tomas returned.

Harrison folded his arms. "Inexplicable?" He nodded toward the table. "You have just borne witness to my doing so for the fifth time tonight. As I said, if you cannot clear the table while it is your turn," he grinned, "I will be happy to step in and show you how. You must give me some credit for allowing you an opportunity to play; I did let you two go first."

"Boring your opponents once again, I see, Harry," King Nathaniel said as he walked over to Harrison.

"Wrong term, Father," Harrison said with a laugh. "'Entertaining' or 'educating my opponents with my impressive skills' is more accurate."

King Nathaniel smirked. "Clearing the entire table after their one miss is indeed quite boring." He looked over at Tomas. "Am I not correct?"

Tomas nodded. "Your Majesty, I would never be so foolish to argue with your assumptions."

"Well then, I stand corrected. For fear of boring anyone else tonight," Harrison laughed as he gripped King Nathaniel's shoulder, "I believe I shall step aside and let the great King Nathaniel take my place for the evening." He grinned at his father mischievously. "Not only will your opponents have the opportunity to play the game, but they will also walk away from the table knowing the victory of beating an Oxley at a game of billiards."

The group of men laughed, and his father arched his eyebrow at him. "Do not forget who taught you to play, son. I may be old, but I can still run the table like none other."

Harrison chuckled. "This, I must see!"

For the two evenings since Levi and Reece's ceremony, Harrison chiefly spent his time in the company of his father and the other kings. If he wasn't among them, he was engaged in commanding the Guardians at the command center.

Most of the kings and their families were still taking up residence at the palace, and even though the noblemen were excellent company, Harrison was starting to grow weary of all the talk about running their kingdoms and how these particular men felt they could help Levi with the transition to being their new emperor. The only one who didn't seem to bother him was King Marcelle's son, Tomas. He was the young prince who had married Isabelle, King Hamilton's eldest daughter. Given the closeness of the Hamilton family and the Oxley families, Harrison couldn't be happier for Isabelle, as she and Tomas appeared quite taken with each other. It was nice to finally see Isabelle move on from when Levi ended their relationship, and she seemed to have found a man who was a perfect fit for the kind woman she was.

Even though Harrison had partnered with Tomas in order to have someone closer in age who he could agree with, tonight he had reached his limit of being in the company of this particular group. In need of fresh air, Harrison thought it best to seek his entertainment outdoors for the rest of the evening.

Searching for a proper excuse to make his exit, he watched as his father ran the table, dropping each ball into a pocket one after the other before any man had the opportunity to play against him. *Arrogant man can't help himself either*, Harrison thought with a silent laugh.

"Tell me, Harrison, how are you getting along commanding our Guardians since the most unfortunate loss of Samuel?" King Maxen asked, interrupting Harrison's thoughts.

King Maxen stood at Harrison's side, yet Harrison would not turn to acknowledge him. Instead, he folded his arms while watching his father clear the last of the table and grinned. *All too predictable, you underhanded old man!* Harrison thought in annoyance at King Maxen's question.

King Maxen was a very wise man. Disappointingly, however, he always seemed to underestimate Harrison's abilities in everything he had ever done. Out of all the kings in Pemdas, Harrison liked him the least. He respected King Maxen because he was wise beyond his years, but Harrison didn't appreciate being looked down upon in such a way either. As far as King Maxen was concerned, Samuel had also not been fit to be the Guardians' chief commander.

Harrison continued to stare at the table as he answered, "I will not mislead you in any way, Your Majesty; it has had its challenges. There are some Guardians who are making it very clear that I must earn their respect as their new commander."

Harrison glanced over at King Maxen, only to see him displaying a proud and knowing grin, but Harrison wasn't finished.

Harrison turned to face the man. "Even so, I expect nothing less from our warriors. Commanding the fiercest and bravest men in existence requires skill and dedication that is not easily acquired. I have no qualms with proving myself to the many of whom I fought alongside. Those who may be wary about my utmost concern for their safety and the protection of our realm need have no fear, and I will prove that with every decision I make. So with that said," he took a sip of his wine and stared directly at the man's somber expression, "yes, I have had my trials. But you must know by now how much I love an excellent challenge."

The man's lips quirked in frustration, but King Hamilton, who stood at King Maxen's side, laughed in return.

"That is one thing that has always delighted me about you, Harry, and I have no doubt that our warriors are in great hands with a man like you commanding them. Samuel has been missed greatly, as has our fallen emperor, and yet you and Levi are doing an excellent job of keeping Pemdas moving forward after losing men of such distinction."

"Indeed," said King Nathaniel as he handed his pool cue off to another young man in the room. He walked toward where Harrison stood facing King Maxen and the other kings now at the men's side. "Both men have risen to meet their respective challenges admirably," said Nathaniel. "As an uncle and father, I could not be more proud of Levi and Harrison in their new positions."

King Maxen cleared his throat. "That is certainly good to know. I must say, I was a little concerned when Levi selected his closest friend to hold such an honorable and exceedingly crucial position in Pemdas."

Harrison instantly became annoyed, and fortunately his father recognized it. "I am not surprised that a man like you would have as much to say, Maxen," King Nathaniel said. "However, you have not only insulted a nobleman and his father, a king, in your presence, but you have insulted your emperor as well."

"I meant no offense by it, Your Majesty." Maxen nodded toward King Nathaniel.

"I say let King Maxen have his opinions, and let the emperor and me prove him wrong," Harrison retorted.

King Hamilton laughed. "That is very bold of you, Harry."

Harrison cocked an eyebrow and stared directly into King Maxen's eyes. "Yes, King Hamilton, it is; however, it is not as bold as to insult the emperor in his own home, especially when he is not present to defend himself." Harrison stepped back as he saw King Maxen's cheeks flush red. Harrison eyed the men in his company. "Gentlemen, if you will excuse me." Without waiting for their reply, he turned to leave.

As he walked out, Tomas came up along his side. "May I inquire as to what that was about?"

Harrison sighed. "Simply another opinionated king questioning his young and supposedly naïve emperor's decisions."

Tomas shook his head. "They shall all get used to it. I believe everyone simply needs time to get past the death of Emperor Navarre. Perhaps that could be the reason for their constant concern."

"Believe me, I am not that disturbed by their opinions, as I have been listening to this nonsense since they arrived; but honestly, I have reached my limit this evening. My father and Hamilton can entertain the doubtful kings; I, on the other hand, will seek my diversions elsewhere tonight."

They walked up on a small group of young men. "Gentlemen," Harrison acknowledged them. The men turned abruptly to properly acknowledge Tomas and Harrison. "Are you all enjoying your stay at the palace?" Harrison asked as he walked into the sitting room to pour Tomas and himself a glass of wine.

"Yes, Your Grace, we are, thank you," one young man responded nervously, trying to find a way out of the conversation.

Harrison grinned and handed Tomas his wine while taking a sip of his own. "I am curious, are you gentlemen lost?"

One young man laughed. "Excuse us, Your Grace—"

Harrison shot him a knowing look. "You may call me Harrison," he said as he took another sip. "Now, before you say anything more, there is a lovely game of billiards being played in the parlor with most of the men. The Duke of Bryndal and I were just leaving, as I was growing tired of losing to all of those noblemen. I believe they could each learn a lesson from such young and able men as yourselves."

The young man stared at him blankly, seemingly searching for a response to get out of the proposition that would interrupt their intended plans for the night. "Sir, I do not believe we were invited to join them because of our ages."

"Well, how old are you?" Harrison asked, knowing very well the young man was trying to find a way out of his suggestive offer.

"We are between the ages of fifteen and seventeen."

"Oh, that is not too young. Now run along, and be sure to let the wise kings know that the Duke of Vinsmonth personally invited you to join them."

"Um, thank you, sir," the young man stammered before the group scurried off

Tomas stared at Harrison with uncertainty. "Why would you send them off to join the kings? Do you know who they are? I am having trouble keeping up with all of these new visitors."

"I know exactly who they are," Harrison responded dryly. "They are the grandsons of King Dresden and King Falun, two of the other kings who have chosen to vocalize their concerns about our *young* emperor. But the sly, young man who I was just speaking with? Well, I have watched him take notice of my cousin Elizabeth more than once. Those boys were gathered here in these hallways in hopes of finding a means of joining her and the other young women outside."

Tomas laughed. "So you sent them off to play billiards with the kings?"

Harrison and Tomas walked outside the palace. "Indeed, I did. Those boys are up to no good, not to mention that I know it will drive King Maxen insane to have a bunch of young, foolish kids in his company." He exhaled. "So I think it best they all should suffer the consequences for annoying me tonight—especially King Maxen!"

Tomas laughed as Harrison led them out through the palace gardens. The sounds of laughter from the ladies led Harrison to the location of where they were gathered.

"I need to check on Elizabeth anyway. She has been doing an excellent job of entertaining all of these young women, and I am sure she'd enjoy some help from her good cousin."

Tomas shook his head. "Harrison, my friend, I do not believe I have ever met anyone quite like you."

"And you never will again," Harrison said as they approached the clearing where tables and chairs were set up for outdoor entertainment.

Harrison stopped abruptly when he found himself face-to-face with Annalisa and Suzanna Sterlington, daughters of the unfortunate Magnus Sterlington. *Looks like the crazy train accidentally dropped off the stalking step-sisters,* he thought as his stomach twisted in knots. Suzanna's eyes bored into his, bringing back a memory of one of the biggest mistakes he had ever made in his entire life.

"Your Grace," Suzanna said with a curtsy. As she rose up, she extended her hand to Harrison, and he quickly folded his arms in response, rudely declining a proper greeting. Suzanna's countenance changed to that of fury in an instant. "What have I done to become so disagreeable in your eyes, Harrison?"

"This is not a conversation I wish to have here, nor anywhere else, at any time, ever," Harrison responded. *Will this desperate psychopath ever go away?* "I am confused as to why you would wish to be in my company at all. After all, I was one of the men to personally escort your father to his prison chambers once we learned of his corruption and scheming with Michael and Simone."

Suzanna's cheeks colored red under Harrison's icy glare, but she pressed the matter. "You must understand the shame and embarrassment our father has brought upon our household. To think that he was using my sister and me to gain more wealth and status by trying to marry us off to the most eligible noblemen was simply horrible. I am so desperately happy he is out of our lives."

Harrison rubbed his chin and grinned. "Ah! Well, allow me to be the first to congratulate you on your selflessness. However, I am unsure as to why you are here at the palace if your intentions are not to be with a man of wealth or status."

"Our aunt was invited, of course, and she extended her invitation to us. We are honored to be here to celebrate our emperor and new empress' union."

"Well, then forgive me for keeping you ladies. The servants have just brought out cakes and other treats for your comfort here at the palace. In case we do not meet again, I wish you both the best in finding a suitor who has no wealth or power so you can be truly happy, contrary to your father's wishes."

"Harrison," Suzanna called out. "You are the man that I desire."

Harrison glanced over at Tomas, who was visibly uncomfortable by the awkward conversation. Harrison quickly took Suzanna's arm and led her away from the group. "Allow me to make myself perfectly clear to you," he spoke in a low voice. "You need not make a fool of yourself in front of guests you do not know. You cannot imagine the extent to which I am *not* the man for you. I believe it is best if you move forward with your life and quit chasing dreams that will never come to fruition."

"You are an arrogant fool," she spat as she reached out and slapped his cheek.

"That, my lady, I have been told more than once. Take no offense from my words; there is no lady that I will allow myself to fall victim to."

A slap to his other cheek brought forth a burst of laughter from Harrison. "Forgive my brazen words, but that is the man I am. Now if you will kindly excuse me, I fear I have no cheeks left to slap, and I am in search of my cousin Elizabeth before this drama fuels my need to leave the palace indefinitely."

Harrison turned and nodded toward Tomas. "I believe your lovely wife also awaits you in the gardens."

Tomas nodded, and the men continued along the path that led to the sound of ladies in conversation. "If I may be so bold, Harrison…"

"There is no need to be polite, friend. That woman was a dreadful mistake I made long ago, and no matter how hard I try, she will not go away."

Tomas laughed once again at Harrison's effrontery as they approached the area that Elizabeth and most of the guests had retired to.

*Poor Lizzy,* Harrison thought as they approached the outdoor location. More young men and most of the young women had retired to this location. Of course, the young men seized this opportunity to be in the company of the beautiful young princesses. *I guess I cannot blame the boys. If I had a coin for every princess party I ambushed, I would be richer than the emperor,* he thought. Nevertheless, he was thankful he came out in search of Elizabeth.

"Is it just me, or did the crowd of guests enlarge after Levi and Reece left? I believed it to be only kings and their families who were invited to this celebration. Where have all of these people come from?" Harrison whispered in a low voice to Tomas.

Tomas chuckled. "How easily you seem to have forgotten the part where everyone who wasn't invited to the private ceremony was invited to Pasidian to celebrate the addition to the Royal Family over the ensuing days."

"Remind me to thank Levi and Reece for this upon their return." Harrison sighed. "Well, we should at least enjoy the sight of the beautiful women while they are all gathered together.

The loud and joyful group grew quiet when Harrison and Tomas came into view. Tomas walked directly to where Isabelle sat and joined her. While looking for a seat himself, Harrison took notice of a young man sitting next to Elizabeth. *Well, well, well...it looks like someone surely picked the wrong seat this evening,* Harrison thought, noting Elizabeth's discomfort and her friend Angeline's mild irritation with the young man who sat between them as though he belonged there.

Elizabeth noticed Harrison staring intently at the young man. She smiled in distinct relief. "Cousin!" she called out delightedly. "It is wonderful to have you join us. I do not believe that I have seen you since Levi and Reece departed."

Harrison grinned as all eyes in the group looked in his direction, yet he ignored the surrounding guests. He didn't care whether his current disposition caused any of them discomfort or not, as his sights were set only on King

Maxen's oldest grandson, the young man who was sitting between Elizabeth and Angeline Hamilton. The boy had earned a reputation upon his arrival at the palace of being rude and disrespectful to the palace servants, and that was something that did not sit well with Harrison, as the servants were always to be treated with the utmost dignity and respect at Pasidian. In Harrison's personal opinion, this incompetent boy was a little too close to his sweet cousin, and her unease was his primary concern.

"That is sadly correct, sweet one. Forgive me for disappearing on you. I believe my duties have kept me distracted of late," he answered.

He stared down at the young man who looked up at him in confusion, despite having a smug grin on his face.

"Commander, could I have someone get you a chair?" he asked in an offhand tone.

*Commander? Who does this kid think he is?* "There will be no need for that. You can simply get up and out of mine."

Elizabeth grinned. The young man swallowed hard and hesitantly stood. He smiled overconfidently at Harrison, and it only irritated Harrison more. The group that sat in a circle around them quietly watched the exchange.

The young man was presumably trying to keep his composure as he stared up into Harrison's unwavering eyes. "Forgive me, Commander. I—"

*Why does this boy keep referring to me as his commander?* "Tell me, have we been introduced?"

"Commander, I am King Maxen's oldest grandson, Luke Maxen. Yes, we have been introduced, do you not remember?"

Harrison gave the boy a challenging arch of an eyebrow. No one referred to Harrison as Commander unless they were a Guardian warrior or recruit into the Pemdai army.

This young man was neither, but he was trying to act as if he were.

*If I remembered, I would not have asked, genius,* Harrison thought as he cleared his throat. Instead of allowing the young man to taunt him, he exhaled and proceeded to play along. "Ah. It is not often my memory fails me, but apparently in this situation, it has." He turned and sat on the long bench between Elizabeth and Angeline where the young man previously sat. He looked up at the boy's annoyed expression and grinned. "Tell me something. You keep referring to me as though I am your commander. Since my memory is so poor tonight, I must have you refresh my recollection as to whether you are among the new Guardian recruits? Because I do not believe I have ever seen you in any of our trainings. And by the looks of you, you appear to be too young to be even considered as a recruit. What is your age, boy?"

The young man's face turned red, and Harrison felt Angeline giggle at his side. "I am fifteen, and I have every desire to join—"

*Fifteen? This kid needs to get lost!* Harrison refrained from laughing aloud. "Yes, young man, I am sure you do have every intention of becoming a Guardian one day. But for now, run along. On our way out here, His Grace and I passed a group of your friends in the palace corridors. They said they were heading down to the music room to practice the harp or some such instrument." He looked over at Tomas. "Wasn't that right, Your Grace?"

Tomas' lips pressed into a hard line. Fortunately, he kept a straight face, as Harrison could tell he was about to erupt into laughter at any moment.

"Uh, yes. I believe they made mention of a flute as well, Your Grace," Tomas responded.

Harrison's eyebrow's shot up, feigning excitement. "Yes! Indeed, they did," Harrison said as he looked up at the young man's angered expression. He stretched his long legs out in front of him and crossed them, dismissing the man with his gaze alone. The young man said nothing more and quickly turned to leave.

"Young Mr. Maxen," Harrison called out, stopping him.

Luke turned and glared down at Harrison. "Most refer to me as 'Your Grace,'" he sneered.

Harrison chuckled, "Oh! Well, please forgive my disrespect, *Your Grace*. I just wanted to say that I shall be sure to let the emperor know he personally owes you his gratitude for keeping such a watchful eye over his beloved sister in his absence." Harrison smiled wryly. "I am most positive he will be extremely interested to know about your concern for her welfare."

The young man said no more, yet spun on his heel and stormed out of the area. The group around them softly laughed as Harrison directed his attention to Elizabeth sitting to his left. "Do not tell me that boy has been following you everywhere. If so, I am deeply apologetic for allowing my other duties to distract me over these past few days."

"Cousin, I am simply glad you showed up when you did. Mr. Maxen has indeed been keeping close company with us, and I had not a clue as to how to get away from him."

"Lizzy, I do not believe we will have a problem with him anymore after tonight," Angeline interjected. "Oh, and if we do, I will not mention that you did not refer to him as *Your Grace* a moment ago," she smiled.

Harrison burst into laughter. "Indeed *not!* Has it been that bad?"

Angeline chuckled, yet said nothing. Harrison stared down at Angeline. "Angie?"

"Let us just say for now that Lizzy and I are extremely thankful you showed up tonight." She arched her eyebrow at him.

The expression on her face had Harrison's eyes now locked onto hers. They were a brilliant bronze color, and they seemed to dazzle against her flawless olive complexion. It was undeniable that she had grown up to be a profoundly beautiful woman, and he could only wonder how miserable it must have been for her and Elizabeth these last few days with all of the young men visiting the palace. He grinned. "Well, I will consider it my duty to make sure you both have peaceful evenings until these senseless men finally leave the palace." Both women laughed as Harrison brought his attention back to the rest of the group sitting around them.

The rest of the night passed easily while Harrison entertained the crowd of young couples in the gardens. It was a nice break from being in the company of the kings and listening to incessant talk of ruling kingdoms, politics, and the superficiality of things that, in Harrison's opinion, only fueled egos.

After breakfast the next morning, Harrison was in the command center with the Guardians who were reporting to him about the recent assignments they had returned from. After his unexpected run-in with the Sterlington ladies the night before, there was no place he'd rather be. Once he finished with his usual duties, Harrison set out to check on the new recruits going through training in the training center. A good workout with the men would ease his irritability with the palace's numerous guests. He walked the corridors with Gerald, the senior Guardian instructor who had requested his assistance in the training center.

"Give me a moment to change into my combat attire, and I will meet you there," Harrison informed Gerald.

"Very well, Commander."

As Harrison crossed the foyer, he spotted Elizabeth and Angeline walking toward him. They were caught up in humorous conversation and unaware of Harrison's approach.

"Ladies, it is easy to see that you are both having a much more enjoyable time than you were last evening." He stopped and grinned down at them. "Or do the wolves only come out at night?" he asked with a smile.

Elizabeth returned Harrison's humored expression. "If you must know, this is the first morning I believe we have not ducked into darkened alcoves to avoid the *wolves*," she said with a laugh. "Angie and I are both grateful for what you did last evening. It is obvious you frightened the young men off."

"I am pleased to hear that I was successful in that regard." He looked over at Angeline, who had a delightful grin on her face. "Tell me, where are you lovely ladies heading off to this afternoon?"

"We had planned to change and take a horseback ride," Angeline answered.

"Ah, that is an excellent idea! Well, I shall not keep you any longer." He nodded at both women. "Enjoy your afternoon."

Elizabeth and Angeline offered Harrison a smile of gratitude before they brushed past him. Strangely, Harrison couldn't resist the urge to turn back and take in the image of Angeline as she and Elizabeth walked through the halls. For the first time since he had known Angeline Hamilton, Harrison allowed himself to admire the beauty of the young woman. He turned back and shook his head while continuing to walk down to his rooms. His eyes no longer saw her as that young girl constantly trying to tag along with him, Levi, and her brother Julian. At nineteen, she appeared to be a picture of absolute beauty. How had he not noticed before? *Well, a man has every right to appreciate the fine beauty of a woman,* he told himself, excusing the idea that he could be attracted to his cousin's closest friend.

That evening, Harrison kept to his word and searched for Elizabeth and Angeline to ensure they weren't being bothered by the young men again. As he walked alone through the palace's grand hall, he encountered his aunt.

"Nephew, it is refreshing to see your face," Lady Allestaine said as she extended both hands to embrace him.

Harrison happily returned her embrace. "Aunt, you look as beautiful as ever."

She chuckled as he kissed her cheek and stepped back. "Thank you, Harrison. So how are you managing these days without Levi around? I know you, my child, and you are usually lost without him," she teased.

"Fortunately, commanding the Guardians has kept me busy, and most recently I have made it my duty to ensure that Lizzy and Angie can have some peace without these young men chasing them all around the palace."

Lady Allestaine laughed. "You should know their intentions very well, dear nephew. Elizabeth told me about last evening, and I am grateful that you took the time to help her and Angeline. But this evening you should not have to concern yourself, as Elizabeth seems to have fallen somewhat ill. She has opted to spend the evening in her rooms, and Angeline has volunteered to keep her company."

"Ill? That is strange."

Lady Allestaine smiled. "Do not worry over her. She is perfectly fine. I believe she has overexerted herself lately, and she could use the rest."

"I certainly understand. May I ask, how are *you* managing since Levi and Reece's departure? You must be exhausted as well with all of these guests. I cannot remember the last time that Pasidian had so many visitors at once."

Lady Allestaine laughed. "I am surprisingly well, and I do admit that it is nice to have the distraction. Do not worry over me; your mother seems to be making sure that I am not overdoing myself with all of the entertaining."

"That is good to know."

"Now," she smiled, "speaking of your mother, she is waiting for me in the sitting room with a few other women. You enjoy the rest of your evening, and I will see you tomorrow. You must join us all for breakfast."

Harrison grinned. "Excellent! Until then."

Harrison was up earlier than usual the next morning. An unexpected issue had come up with a few Guardians on assignment. Once again, he was forced to take his breakfast in the command center and unable to dine with the rest of the guests. After a few debriefings from the Guardians who had returned from Earth, he decided he would step out for a moment to check on Elizabeth's health.

"Vincent, I will leave you to handle reports for now. I shall return within the hour," Harrison said as he pulled his coat on.

"Very well, Commander. If anything should come up, I will have one of the men search you out," Vincent responded.

With that, Harrison turned and exited the command center.

Vincent was turning out to be a great help, and Harrison understood why Samuel had depended on him so much. As Harrison walked up to the first floor of the palace, a door to one of the rarely used sitting rooms was open slightly, and it jarred his interest. He opened it further, and when he did, he saw Angeline curled up on a chaise, reading a book in solitude.

"So this is what it has all come to?" he asked to announce his presence to the room.

Angeline turned and looked to the doorway where Harrison stood. He noticed the relief apparent in her expression when she saw it was only him invading her privacy. "Yes, I guess it is," she answered with a laugh.

Harrison took a seat across from her. Angeline sat in a proper position, closed her book, and offered Harrison her undivided attention. For a moment, Harrison was overcome by her beauty and struggled to remember why he stepped into the room. Fortunately, he kept his composure and was able to think rationally. "Is Lizzy still unwell?"

"Yes, I left her to rest. She is recovering easily, only suffering from minor weakness today. Doctor Fletcher paid her a visit this morning and diagnosed her with fatigue. He says she should remain in bed for the rest of the day."

Harrison sat back. "Poor thing. She never has been one for entertaining large crowds. I am not surprised she would fall ill as a result."

"I believe she is missing her father as well," Angeline said with concern in her voice.

Harrison grew troubled at the thought, not realizing that Elizabeth would obviously still be grieving the loss of Emperor Navarre. With Levi and Reece gone and Lady Allestaine constantly monopolized, there really was no one but Angeline for Elizabeth to turn to for solace.

"I have been so distracted lately that I fear I have entirely forgotten about my sweet cousin." He ran his hands through his hair. "I feel awful."

Angeline laughed, bringing Harrison's attention back to her. The smile she wore was brilliant, showing off a single dimple in her left cheek, engaging her eyes and enhancing the beauty of them. Once again, Harrison was spellbound by her. *Wow!* This was no longer the young Angie he forever teased as they grew up together; she was now a remarkable woman.

"Harry, you are being much too hard on yourself. You have no idea how delighted Lizzy and I were that you intervened on our behalf the other evening. I am confident she will feel better soon enough."

Her smooth voice and maturity added to her physical attractiveness. "She is fortunate to have a friend like you, Angie. I am quite confident that your spending the next few weeks with her will help her cope as well."

Their conversation was halted when Harrison heard voices out in the hallway. The sounds of young men had Angeline visibly tense. *Looks like it's time to rescue the damsel in distress*, Harrison thought as he stood up and extended his hand. "Come. Allow me to offer you a much better hiding place until Lizzy has recovered."

She took his hand and stood. "Really, Harrison, you should not concern yourself over me."

"I beg to differ. If those prowling hounds are to remain on a constant hunt for you ladies in the hallways, you will likely end up in Lizzy's condition." He offered his arm. "And we cannot have that," he said with a wink.

Angeline laughed and took his extended arm. "Thank you, but I believe you will exhaust yourself finding a place to avoid those young men; believe me, I have tried."

Harrison chuckled. "Trust me, I have an excellent place in mind, and hopefully it won't bore you. At the very least, it will give you a break."

They walked out of the room and nearly ran into the group of young men lurking outside. It was plain to see they were waiting for Harrison to leave Angeline alone. *This is absurd. I am sure I never had to try this hard when I was their age.* Angeline's hand gripped tightly to the bend of his arm.

"Gentlemen," he called out deeply. "Are we lost in the palace corridors again?"

Luke Maxen stared impudently at him. "As a matter of fact, Your Grace, we are not. We were only seeking out Princess Hamilton so as to inquire after the condition of Princess Oxley."

*At least he figured out my proper title.* "I must say, that is truly astounding for a man such as myself to hear."

"Your Grace?" Luke asked in confusion.

Harrison sighed. "I find it very odd that young noblemen have suddenly lost their manners when it comes to concerning themselves over a woman's well-being, especially if they know not what her ailment is. Tell me something, have you been personally provided with any information in regard to the princess?"

"Not formally, but we did overhear as we dined this morning that—"

"Ah!" Harrison interrupted him. "Young men finding their entertainment with gossip. This indeed is a problem, especially when it is in regard to Princess Elizabeth."

"You are mistaken, Your Grace," Luke snapped back brashly.

Harrison had enough. His glare alone had Luke swallowing hard in return. "Get outside," Harrison ordered him darkly. "If word should come from Lady Allestaine that she wishes to inform you of Princess Elizabeth's current state, only then will I tolerate your concern for her." Harrison's baleful expression did not falter against Luke Maxen's. "Now," Harrison continued, "if you will excuse Princess Hamilton and me, we have wasted enough time in your presence."

With that, they marched forward, forcing the group to divide and let them through.

"That boy needs to find his place, and quickly."

Angeline laughed. "Well, you were provoking him."

Harrison rolled his eyes. "Do you have any clue as to when they are all departing?"

"My mother informed me that their families are preparing to leave by the end of the week."

Harrison looked down at her in disbelief, and she laughed in response.

"Where are we going anyway?" she asked.

"Well, it may not be that exciting of a location, but those boys will come nowhere near it."

"The *command* center?" she asked quietly.

"Do not fear. There are isolated rooms with comfortable seating for you to enjoy your reading without distractions."

She gripped his arm tightly, forcing him to look down at her. She smiled with excitement. "No, you do not understand, I am thrilled. I have always had a profound interest in our warriors. To see them in person, to watch how the command center works…" She trailed off.

Harrison smiled down at her, amused. "Really? I have never known of a princess who would be intrigued by such things."

She arched her eyebrow up at him. "Have you forgotten who I am already, Harry? I was the little girl who as a child always wanted to play with you, Levi, and my brother. I was always upset when I was scolded for it and told it was not ladylike." She chuckled.

Harrison laughed. "I do remember now. You used to drive us insane."

"I have not changed much, and so you can understand why visiting the command center would delight me greatly."

*Oh, you have certainly changed. That is one thing I am rapidly being made aware of every time I look at you,* he thought as he continued their walk toward the command center.

That evening, Harrison sat in his office unable to remove the images of Angeline from his mind. Even though he was kept extremely busy with meetings and debriefings, he still managed to discreetly watch Angeline through the glass walls of his office. She remained mostly in the company of Vincent, watching him interact on the transparent screen with the men serving on Earth. It intrigued him to see such a lovely and proper woman finding all of it so fascinating. Never once would he have thought that a woman in Pemdas could be so interested in such things.

Harrison was baffled by this woman, to say the least. He was gradually forgetting the young girl he used to view her as. He saw her now as a very captivating and delightful woman who had unexpectedly captured his interest. She stayed for only a couple of hours before she felt she needed to go check on Elizabeth, and even when she gave him a friendly and grateful hug before she left, he found himself somewhat taken by it. Her delightful fragrance strangely assaulted his senses and heightened her appeal to him.

He inwardly laughed at himself for feeling such a way. He knew very well it was not right. Him being twenty-seven years of age, and her being his cousin's closest friend, he could not allow emotions to overrule his judgment by developing an attraction for her. But now, he began to wonder if that was already happening.

# Chapter 12

Harrison was returning from the Guardians' training unit when he nearly ran over Angeline walking through the servants' passageways. He had no doubt why she was discreetly using the private corridors through the palace, but he wondered why she was alone.

"Forgive me, Angie," Harrison said as he gripped both her arms to stop himself from running into her.

Angeline laughed in response. "No apologies are needed, Harry."

Harrison stood there, bewitched by her shiny bronze eyes, forgetting that he was still wearing his combat clothing, which was the reason he had chosen this private route to begin with. He blinked a few times and cleared his thoughts. "Are those young men still prowling around the palace?"

Angeline smiled. "Indeed."

"Tell me you aren't the only one that got away. Has Lizzy fallen prey to their foolishness?"

"Certainly not. Lady Allestaine invited her and me to join her on a trip into the city today. I opted out of the tempting invitation, as I knew it would be more pleasant for Elizabeth to spend this time alone with her mother."

"That is very generous of you. And it is a pity you are unable to roam freely throughout the palace for fear of being harassed," Harrison said. "Allow me to extend an invitation to join me for a horseback ride. Perhaps that will offer you a change of scenery."

"That sounds marvelous."

"Very well, then. If it is agreeable with you, I shall retrieve you from your chambers after I have changed into my proper attire and notified Javian to saddle our horses."

"I will see you then," she responded. With a quick curtsy, Angeline brushed past Harrison, leaving him to continue his journey to his private rooms.

Once changed, Harrison paid a short visit to the command center to inform Vincent that he would be leaving the palace for the afternoon. A servant was dispatched to instruct Javian to saddle the horses, and nothing was left but to retrieve Angeline and rescue her from the young men pestering her at the palace. He hopped up the steps to the second floor and strode quickly through the corridors toward Angeline's rooms.

Harrison was surprised to see Angeline answer her door instead of her maiden after he knocked briefly. "Angie?"

"Harrison?" she bantered with a laugh.

"Well, it is clear that you are ready to leave the palace without wasting any time." He offered his arm. "Shall we?"

As they walked toward where the horses awaited them, they encountered the group of young men at the stables. "They all leave tomorrow, correct?" he asked Angeline.

She laughed. "Yes, I believe so."

Saracen was the only Guardian horse amongst the other saddled horses awaiting their riders. Harrison sighed as he watched the young men trying to interact with his massive black stallion. *Touch the steed, and lose a hand,* Harrison thought as he sensed the irritation radiating from his horse.

"I see you have all taken my advice and decided to involve yourselves in more masculine ventures," Harrison called out upon his approach. The young men glanced back, yet said nothing in return. They walked away from Saracen, trying to ignore Harrison and Angeline's approach.

Harrison led Angeline over to the white horse that was saddled for her. The group of men stood a distance away, and Harrison felt their gazes on him and Angeline. *This should give them something to brood over while we're gone,* he thought in humor, knowing it would create gossip in the palace.

As he helped Angeline at the mounting block, Javian approached. "Master Harrison, may I have a word with you before you depart?"

Once Angeline was on her horse and settled, Harrison turned back to Javian. "What is it, Javian?"

"Sir, I understand you have been extremely busy, but I wanted you to know your mare is close to birthing her foal."

Harrison laughed and clapped Javian on his shoulder. "That is excellent news. Have you any idea when we might expect our new colt?"

Javian grinned. "I would say no later than tomorrow evening. Also, it appears that Emperor Levi may see his new foal soon as well. I am hoping his mare will wait for him and the empress to return. Her Royal Majesty seemed very excited that the mares would be giving birth soon."

"Why does that not surprise me?" Harrison turned to walk toward Saracen. "Just wait until Arrow sires one of the foals; she will probably let it live in the palace with all of us."

Javian chuckled, and then turned to leave Harrison to mount his horse. Once on Saracen, he guided him over to where the young men stared at him darkly. Without hesitation, Angeline brought her horse alongside of Saracen.

"Gentlemen, I am curious. Your horses are saddled, but you are not riding them? Are you waiting for riding lessons?"

Luke Maxen stepped forward arrogantly. "Forgive me if I am out of line, Your Grace, but it almost sounds as though you have a problem with all of us."

Harrison grinned. "That is positively absurd. I do not have a problem with *all* of you; my problem, *Your Grace*, is with only you. I do not like you or your attitude, nor do I appreciate the way you treat the servants in our home. Now that we have cleared that up, allow me to issue you a proper warning to stay away from my cousin, Princess Elizabeth."

"I do not take orders from you."

Harrison's eyes narrowed. "This is not your domain, little duke. You are in the Royal Family of Pemdas' home, and you should guard your words and your actions wisely.

If I should hear another word from anyone about any additional disrespect or impudence on your part, you will face the consequence of doing so." He pulled his foot out of its stirrup, smiled, and pressed the heel of his boot into Luke Maxen's chest. The unexpected gesture was not meant to inflict pain, but to make the boy stumble backward.

As Luke lost his balance and fell back into the soft mud behind him, Harrison nodded. "Let that be my final warning, you stubborn young fool," he finished as he pulled back on the reins, backing Saracen away from the group.

"Good day, then," Harrison said before he and Angeline rode swiftly away from the palace.

They raced along the banks of Pasidian River for nearly an hour before Harrison directed Saracen toward a large meadow surrounded by a grove of trees. They dismounted their horses and allowed them to wander off to graze freely in the meadow.

Harrison and Angeline spent the next hour or so in casual conversation, most of which consisted of Angeline updating Harrison on her years of growing up. She sat upright next to him as he reclined lazily on his side facing her, captivated by the many attractive and animated expressions that crossed her face. Being away from the formalities of the palace, she seemed to open up more, and it was refreshing to watch her as she told him stories about her adolescence. Her amusement was undeniably contagious, and Harrison had never felt as contented in any woman's company.

"I still cannot believe that our Harry is the commanding officer of all the Guardians," Angeline said as she plucked a flower from the tall grass.

"Is this a bad thing?" Harrison returned with a mischievous grin.

Angeline arched a knowing eyebrow at him. "Well..." She trailed off in a teasing voice

Harrison smirked. "Well? What?" he said with a laugh.

"Well...it is not a bad thing, if I should choose to forget the Harrison Oxley that I grew up with," she returned playfully.

"Indeed? Well, it is quite obvious that I am still the strapping man you grew up with. I believe that not only have my handsome features increased with age, but my profound knowledge and wisdom has as well," Harrison returned smugly.

Angeline tilted her head to the side, studying him. "You are certainly the most arrogant man I know!" she returned with a laugh. "But on a more serious note, I will say after the battle of Armedias and the burial of Emperor Navarre, I have noticed a significant change in you, my friend. I also know that guarding The Key on Earth and becoming the Commander of the Guardians have always been some of your greatest desires."

Harrison also plucked a vibrant yellow flower and handed it to her. "And you, Angeline Hamilton—what is your greatest desire? You are nearing the age where one might start fulfilling those wishes."

Angeline touched the flower to the tip of his nose. "I wish I could say that I was the perfect princess who had her entire life mapped out, but I must admit that I do not."

"The Princess of Sandari Kingdom has no idea what she wants out of life?" Harrison said dramatically. "This is, without a doubt, disturbing news, and one that some would believe to be shameful." He cocked an eyebrow, feigning reproach.

Angeline tucked a lock of curly auburn hair behind her ear and rolled her eyes. "Unfortunately, there will be rumors flying around that King Hamilton's daughter is wildly out of her mind. She has no desire to sit around her father's estate all day, join the ladies in the sitting rooms, or assume the proper role of a future queen."

"The Sandari Kingdom will likely fall due to this." Harrison's brow creased as he shook his head. "We must inform the emperor that there is no future for our favorite kingdom."

Angeline laughed. "Yes, we must!"

Angeline's eyes locked onto Harrison's, and though she went on, he heard nothing more. He was entranced by the very essence of this moment with Angeline. The wind whipped through the tall grass that surrounded them and enhanced the splendor of the woman sitting in front of him. Her personality was delightful; she was proper and graceful, and her excellent sense of humor and charming wit were unlike any he had ever encountered.

Eventually, the questions turned back to Harrison. Angeline was fascinated by his service on Earth and the privilege that he and Levi shared in protecting Reece. She strongly desired to hear more of what Earth was like, and he could see in her eyes that she longed to visit the planet one day.

"So television…" Angeline's brow creased in concentration. "I am trying to imagine what that must be like. You say there are humans who portray a life that is not theirs, and it is watched on a screen where the fictitious story appears to be real?"

"In a way, yes. Those humans you are referring to are known as actors." Harrison grinned. "It is very similar to attending a live event where our talented people portray individuals in books we have read on the theatrical stage.

Although, when those on Earth use their technology, the television can become quite entertaining."

"That is interesting," she answered. "Do many on Earth enjoy this?"

Harrison laughed. "Most have a great interest in the technology. It is their favorite pastime, and there are at least two or three televisions in an average household."

Angeline's lips twisted. "Do you think Reece misses the ability to watch television? We do not have anything like that in Pemdas."

Harrison coughed out a laugh. "While guarding Reece on Earth, we learned quickly that she wasn't engrossed with entertaining herself with television." He glanced past Angeline. "Which makes perfect sense as to why she never complained about missing that technology."

"How would she pass her time?" Angeline asked, intrigued.

Harrison sighed. "Let me just say that Levi and I grew extremely tired of coffee shops and learning about Earth's medical practices."

Angeline laughed. "Do you believe she misses her life on Earth?"

Harrison grew somber. "She lost everything when she lost her father. We watched her suppress the grief of his death. It took great strength for her to flee from her hometown and take up residence in a new place. In ignoring her grief, we watched her fight instead. She excelled brilliantly in college and medical school, but she wasn't entirely whole without her father in her life."

Angeline's expression changed to that of sorrow. "How awful to be all alone in such a big world," she answered.

Harrison nodded. "She managed well enough. Seeing her live her life firsthand for so many years, I can honestly say that I could not be happier that Levi was the one to give her something to live for again."

"Who would have ever believed a woman would catch Levi's interest in such a way."

"Indeed!" Harrison chuckled.

Angeline folded her arms. "I will admit, I have never seen Levi so undeniably happy until I first saw him with Reece at my family's ball."

Harrison smirked, plucked a stone from the ground, and tossed it out toward the trees. "Yes. He is quite the sappy romantic man these days."

Angeline nudged Harrison. "Harry! How dare you say that?"

Harrison's eyebrows shot up. "It is a fact! Believe me, when Levi thought he lost Reece for good, he was the most miserable man I have ever kept company with." Harrison shook his head. "I only knew of one way to fix his misery at the time, and that involved arranging romantic escapades for him and Reece to enjoy on Earth." He looked at Angeline and sighed. "My excellent plans to renew their love nearly had me strangling both of them during that visit."

"Something deep inside of me tells me that you probably deserved it," Angeline said as she tried to cover a laugh.

Harrison eyed her. "Once again, someone finds humor while I was tortured beyond belief!"

Angeline burst into laughter but managed to quickly compose herself. "In order to end our rude gossiping and you insulting your emperor and empress, allow me to change the subject. What is your—"

Every sense of casualness left him as he studied the charming woman in front of him. "You have definitely grown up to be a lovely young woman, Angeline," he said, cutting her off mid-sentence.

The interruption seemed to shock her, but he didn't care. He had no idea what it was she was saying at the time, as he was more taken with her at that moment than with her words.

Angeline's cheeks lightly colored, and she looked down. Harrison grinned uncertainly, knowing he had created an awkward moment. He thought he should probably change the subject. He stood up and extended his hand to her. "Come. Let me show you my and Levi's favorite tree to climb when we were boys."

Angeline quickly recovered and smiled. She took his hand and rose up. He walked them into the grove of trees, and they came to the largest one, which had a trunk over five feet wide. He looked up at the many large branches and remembered climbing and swinging joyfully amongst them.

"Wow!" Angeline said as she gazed up into the magnificent tree.

Harrison laughed. "This tree must be thousands of years old. I believe I may have broken nearly every bone in my body at some point in my childhood as a result of playing in this tree."

"You were always quite the daring young man. You always seemed to have acquired some form of an injury whenever you were around." She laughed. "Do you remember the time when you broke your ribs falling from the bridge at our house and our parents were so upset with you?"

Harrison shook his head. "I believe I was the only child in Pemdas who always received punishment instead of sympathy in return for his injuries."

Angeline leaned back against the tree and gazed up. "I remember telling you that I loved you, even if your parents did not." She looked at Harrison and laughed. "I was so little. It seemed to me that if your parents would not comfort you after such an accident, they most certainly did not love you."

Harrison stared intently into her eyes, utterly lost in them. Slowly he approached her, and her smile faded. His lips curved up on one side as his hand came slowly up to touch the softness of her face. He watched as she swallowed hard in response to his tender touch. "I remember you telling me that when you grew up, I would be the only man you would ever marry."

She inhaled deeply as the back of his fingers traced along the softness of her face. Even if he wanted to, he couldn't have resisted the temptation to touch her and feel the silkiness of her skin. Never once had a woman influenced him in such a way. He couldn't think sensibly as he stared down at her tempting lips; the overwhelming desire to place his own upon them was inexorable. He breathed deeply, struggling to maintain his discipline. If this was wrong, certainly Angeline would give him an indication.

She stood with her back pressed into the tree, helpless against Harrison's seductive touch. He looked into her eyes for reassurance. Her breathing picked up as her striking bronze eyes gazed longingly into his. She appeared as exhilarated by this moment as he was.

"I have never kissed a man before," she innocently admitted.

She softly laughed, embarrassed by the forthrightness of her confession. Her declaration didn't help Harrison's resolve, for now he was losing all sense of self-control. He knew very well that he should walk away, but she was intoxicating. His other hand came up and tenderly embraced the base of her neck. "We can easily change that," he said in a low voice.

Fully expecting her to reject his advances toward her, he remained entranced by the look she gave him. Angeline must have wanted him to do this. She only waited for him because she so innocently didn't know where to start. As both of his hands gently cradled her head, he fought against this next urge. *Harrison, don't!* he demanded of himself, but it was too late.

Then his lips were on hers, slowly and gently pressing against them. Her hands held onto each of his sides as his lips played against hers, wanting more from their kiss. Her breathing was fast as he left moist kisses along the lines of her alluring mouth. He slowly continued, feeling her lips move softly against his in return. He continued to lead her every move, while ardently waiting for her to accept the passionate kiss he was desperately wanting.

Harrison brought his cheek to hers. "Do not fear, Angie; it is only a kiss," he breathlessly whispered into her ear. Unexpectedly, Angeline wrapped her arms tightly around his waist, drawing him closer to her. Harrison smiled appreciatively before he pressed forward with the passionate kiss he was waiting to give her. She softly moaned with pleasure, spurring him on. At first, his hand slowly caressed her cheek, guiding her and leading her. Harrison was so caught up with her innocent, yet affectionate kiss that he had no control over anything anymore. All sensibility had left him, and he yearned for more.

His hands left her face, searching more of her perfect body. His lips left hers, wanting to taste more of her delicate skin. Wild with passion and desire, Harrison pursued more of this perfect woman for his own satisfaction. His mouth moved hungrily along her décolletage, and it still wasn't enough. So caught up was he with the passion of this daring moment, Harrison barely heard Angeline call out to him.

"Harrison—" she exhaled. "Please—" she softly moaned.

Unable to think of anything but the breathless sound of her pleas for him, he brought his lips to her throat while his sturdy hands tried to find the buttons on the back of her dress. At that moment, a sharp pain pierced through the top of his boot, nearly collapsing him where he stood. Unable to mentally overcome the pain, as he should have been so easily able to do, he found himself instead reaching to brace himself against the tree where Angeline had stood only a moment ago.

Before he could turn, Angeline had swept her foot around the back of his legs, bringing him hard to the ground. He stared up into her furious bronze eyes, amazed that she had not only brought him to the ground as a Guardian would, but that she had disarmed him, now holding his dagger in her hand.

She looked dangerously into his eyes. "Do you think me to be such an ignorant girl?" she asked, letting his dagger fall point first into the ground between his legs for him to retrieve.

"Angeline, you must forgive me, though I am unclear of what I did that may have insulted you!" He was trying to figure out how he went from gazing into her perfect eyes one moment to having the heel of her shoe sharply gouged into the top of his boot before she took him down to the ground in the next. He sprung quickly to his feet to face her.

Her lips were pressed into a fine line, her arms crossed, and her eyes were like flint. "Unclear?"

Harrison reached out. "Forgive me, but—" He ran a hand through his hair. "Angie, you must tell me, how did you learn to fight in such a way, never once—"

"Have you forgotten my eldest brother already? Julian taught me how to defend myself ever since he became a Guardian. But that is hardly the point at the moment," she snapped back. "I am not required to tell *you* anything."

*Julian,* Harrison thought with great remorse. "Angie, I beg of you to please forgive me. I am still deeply regretful for the loss of your brother in the battle of Armedias."

"I do not need *your* sympathy, Harry," she said as tears filled her eyes. "My brother met his death with great honor, as did all of our Guardian warriors." She placed both hands on her hips. "Our family is dealing with the grief of his loss very well, and now I am even more grateful that he taught me the ways of a Guardian warrior, so that I may defend myself against selfish men like you."

Harrison reached for her hand, but Angeline jerked away and took a step back. "Do not touch me."

"Believe me when I say I never had any intention of our outing ending in this manner." He rubbed his forehead and exhaled. "I don't know what came over me."

"But of course you did not, Mr. Oxley," she said with disgust. "Had I not stopped the beast of a man you were turning into, I believe your intentions would have been that I fall victim to your charms, as every other pitiful woman in this land has."

"Angie, please know that—"

"Who do you think you are, Harrison Oxley?" she interrupted him with a deliberate and icy tone. "More than that, who exactly do you think I am?"

Harrison sighed as remorse washed heavily over him while he stared down into Angeline's fiery gaze. *What was I thinking?*

"Angeline, I am so dreadfully sorry."

"Indeed, you are. You are a pathetic excuse for a man, and I am sorry that I believed myself to be different than every other woman you have so egotistically taken advantage of."

"Angeline."

"I should have known you were no better than the boys you have made it your mission to insult every time you see them. I do not care how handsome you are, Harry; I will not be so easily taken advantage of by a man's base desires. Ever."

He could say nothing. She was right, and his words of apology were meaningless. He stared at her, unable to speak.

"Take me back to the palace," she demanded.

Without another word, Harrison nodded to answer Angeline's demand of him. She was right in every possible way about him, and Harrison wondered if he would ever gain Angeline's forgiveness for what he had done.

# Chapter 13

The next morning, Harrison walked into the command center after a restless night. He sent for his breakfast to be taken in his office to avoid anyone for the time being. He sat numbly sat at his desk, trying to focus on the papers in front of him, but failed. His thoughts were consumed with the way Angeline smiled at him while they sat in the meadow together. He couldn't remove the memories of gazing at her radiant expressions as she spoke and her newfound openness and trust in him, which he in turn destroyed immediately after.

Harrison was glad for the distraction from the haunting images when a group of Guardians contacted Vincent from Armedias. He walked briskly out of his office and joined Vincent in front of the glass that displayed the holographic images of the men.

"Gentlemen, what have you discovered?" he asked.

"The lands are recovering well, and the new ruler is complying with all of Emperor Levi's requirements for their rebuilding. It appears that Armedias will soon be brought to a friendly peace with Pemdas once again."

"Is there any new information on the four priestesses whose bodies were never recovered?"

"None."

Harrison placed both hands on the table in front of him. *They couldn't have just vanished into thin air*, he thought in disbelief. "We shall find them and bring them to justice soon enough. I have men searching in all of the dimensions, and we will eventually uncover their whereabouts." He cleared his throat. "Gentlemen, other than that, you bring good news. I will have a group of Guardians deployed tomorrow to relieve your posts in Armedias. I believe a week's vacation is owed to you all."

"Thank you, sir."

"Until then, gentlemen."

As soon as he finished that conversation, another Guardian was standing by, having returned from Earth with a report of another impending abduction. It was like any usual morning in the command center, Harrison was kept extremely busy, and his mind was no longer left to wonder about the situation he was in with Angeline.

After all of the morning's reports from the Guardians, Harrison had a chance to go over his notes. As he sat at his desk sipping from a hot cup of tea in silence, he became concerned when two Guardians walked into his office after having returned from their assignments on Earth earlier than expected. As the men prepared to give their reports, Harrison glanced over at the entrance to the command center, only to see King Hamilton waiting patiently with Angeline at his side. *It was only a matter of time!* Harrison thought, wishing that his office was not enclosed with glass walls. He nodded toward King Hamilton, acknowledging their entrance.

He brought his attention back to the Guardians across from him. "Gentlemen, it appears that King Hamilton has arrived unexpectedly." He gripped the arms of his chair and stood. "Give me a moment to greet him and the princess, and I will return for your report. In the meantime, help yourselves to some tea."

"Very well, sir."

Harrison exited his office and crossed the command center to where King Hamilton and Angeline stood. "Your Majesty," he acknowledged the King. "Princess Angeline," he respectfully dipped his head toward Angeline, "this is a surprise, indeed. Is there something I can do for you?"

"As a matter of fact, there is. If it wouldn't be too much trouble, my darling daughter has requested a tour of the command center. She has always had a great interest in the Pemdai Guardians and begged me to gain your approval so she could experience firsthand what it is our brave men do."

Confused, Harrison glanced at Angeline, wondering why she would request such a thing, having been here already. She arched her eyebrow at him and grinned. Harrison smiled mildly in return and brought his attention back to King Hamilton.

"I would be delighted to give her a tour; however, I must take a report from my men before I will be able to do so.

Until then, I believe Vincent will be of excellent assistance."

King Hamilton clapped Harrison on his shoulder. "Go to work, Harry. We shall be out here with Vincent."

One more glance to Angeline to find her restraining herself from laughter, and Harrison turned with great relief to debrief his men. He walked into his office and took his seat.

"Gentlemen, forgive the interruption. I will make this quick, as you both appear to be exhausted. Tell me, were you able to successfully educate the Broisions on how to properly respect the humans on Earth?"

Both men laughed. "Yes, Commander, we were."

Harrison leaned onto his armrest. "So tell me, what made these creatures believe they could bring a human into the Broisiduate dimension? Were they able to make contact with anyone?"

"Sir, they did make contact with a man on Earth, a doctor. After our interrogations, they claim their intentions were to enhance his intelligence by giving him knowledge of their advanced medicine. They also claim they intended to return him to his family once his mind was improved so that he might spread this knowledge to others."

Harrison rolled his eyes. "What a surprise. Have these creatures no imagination anymore? It would seem as though they took a chapter from the universe's bestselling book, *101 Excuses to Tell the Pemdai about Why We Abducted a Human.*" Harrison exhaled. "Anyway, how were they dealt with, and did you have any contact with the human?"

"We did have contact with him, and we subsequently used our devices to erase his memory of the events. The doctor was quite traumatized when the Broisions chose to appear to him in natural form to persuade him to go with them. The man was overcome with fear at the sight of them."

"Who wouldn't be disgusted by their appearance? Vulgar beings." Harrison sighed in annoyance. "I will be in contact with their ruler today, and I shall remind him that if his people should choose to visit Earth again, they must shift into human form in order to do so. Go on."

"Once we were assured the doctor had no memory of his encounter, we escorted the creatures back to their dimension and returned to Pemdas from there."

Harrison nodded. "How long did the assignment take before the mission was completed?"

"Given that the Broisions were unaware that we were watching them, from the moment they selected the human until we returned them to their dimension took roughly eight hours."

"Excellent work, gentlemen." Harrison sat back in his chair. "Anything else I should be aware of on this particular assignment?"

"None, sir."

"Very well, then." Harrison stood. "I will see you tomorrow when you report for your new assignments. Other than that, enjoy your families on your short furlough in Pemdas," he said as he shook their hands before they made their exit.

Before he could walk out of his office, Angeline stepped in. Somewhat uncomfortable, Harrison looked around for King Hamilton.

"Vincent has my father quite entertained at the moment," she said with a warm smile.

Harrison guided Angeline to the settee situated along the wall and sat in a chair opposite her. "Would you care for some tea?"

She smiled. "I am fine, thank you. We finished breakfast not long ago, and I was rather concerned as to why I hadn't seen you at dinner last night or at breakfast this morning."

"I believe you are perfectly aware of why I would not burden you with my presence after what transpired between us yesterday." Harrison rested his elbows on his knees and clasped his hands together. "Angeline, I do not know how to begin to apologize to you for insulting you in the way I did. To approach you in such a manner without your consent is entirely unforgivable."

"Harrison, please do not apologize. I had to come here and see you because I feel you should know that you are not the only one at fault for yesterday's events."

"No—"

"Let me finish," she said in amusement. "I am partly to blame as well. I knew better, but I did nothing to stop it. I have always been attracted to you since I was a young girl, and I innocently believed that one day I would grow up and be the one to capture your heart. It was wrong, and I was foolish to believe in such fantasies." She laughed. "Harry, I am here because I do not want to lose our friendship over what happened between us. Your friendship is more important to me than any fantasy I had as a young girl."

Unexpectedly disappointed by her words, Harrison felt a knot form in his stomach. "Angeline, I do not see yesterday as a mistake." He shifted in his seat. "Of course, my approach and my behavior were regrettable and unacceptable, but I can assure you that before I insulted you, our time together was something I will never regret. Please allow me another opportunity to make this right with you."

Angeline stood, prompting Harrison to do so as well. She brought her hand to his cheek, and Harrison's flesh burned against her touch as he absently leaned into her delicate skin.

"I want nothing more than your friendship. If you must know, I wish to be with a man who will love and need me wholeheartedly. He will earn my love in a gentleman-like fashion, and not one based on selfish desires." Angeline tilted her head to the side. "You are not that man, Harry. You know yourself that you are not that man. So we must find a way to get past this awkwardness, because I will not lose you as my dear friend."

She was right, he wasn't that man. *Love?* He had vowed never to let himself fall victim to that emotion. In his opinion, love was a dangerous state, and one that would never hold him hostage.

Harrison took her hand and brought it to his lips. "You, Angeline Hamilton, are an amazing woman, and wise beyond your years. The man you seek will be a fortunate one indeed. You are correct; I could never live up to those standards." As he said the words, a strange feeling stabbed him in the chest. For a brief moment, he began second-guessing letting go of her like this. He quickly recovered, feeling selfish. "Angie, I can assure you there will be no awkwardness between you and me from this day forward."

"Thank you, Harry. I will always be grateful for your honesty and friendship." With a simple smile, she curtsied and left him alone in his office to contemplate whether or not he truly did carry feelings for her. Watching her leave with these words seemed all too wrong!

*What are you thinking? You know it is best to let her go,* he thought as he walked back toward his desk.

Before he could sit, Vincent walked into his office with a grave expression.

"Vincent? Is anything the matter?"

"Commander," Vincent started. "Something interesting has taken place. William and Travis have returned from their assignments only moments ago, and they encountered a strange being down at the gates. When they questioned the man, he said he wished to inform the Emperor of Pemdas of extremely important news."

Harrison crossed his arms. "Important news? Well, there are desirable ways for this man to get the emperor information, and showing up at our gates unannounced is certainly not one of them. Did Will and Travis return this individual to his dimension with the proper instructions on how to request a meeting with our emperor?"

"That is why this situation requires your immediate attention. When they went to do as much, the man simply vanished before their eyes. When they believed he may have transported himself back to the dimension he came from, the man spoke out. He was nowhere to be found, but the men continued to feel his presence among them."

Harrison's brow furrowed quizzically. "What? He has an ability to cloak himself?"

"It appears so, and he refuses to leave our gates until a meeting with Emperor Levi has been granted."

*Demanding creature, isn't he?* Harrison thought in annoyance. "If that is the case, I will handle this matter myself. Finish taking Will and Travis' reports on this matter, and I will go over them more thoroughly upon my return."

Vincent nodded. "Yes, Commander."

Harrison pulled on his greatcoat. "Position a troop of Guardians to stand at the gates until Javian has Saracen saddled and I am prepared to leave."

"Your Grace," King Hamilton called out as Harrison walked hastily out of his office. "You appear quite distressed; is there a problem?"

Angeline watched with concern as Harrison responded seriously, "No, Your Majesty. There is simply a matter that requires my personal attention."

He pulled his sheathed sword off the hook where it hung next to other armaments. As he strapped it around his waist, he continued, "Please, stay and enjoy the command center as long as you may like."

King Hamilton smiled grimly. "It appears that this situation calls for a little more than conversation."

Harrison grinned. "One can never be too prepared."

"Good man," King Hamilton rejoined. "We were just leaving anyway. I am very curious to hear what has summoned you toward this sort of action."

Harrison nodded. "I will be glad to report my findings upon my return. I will probably be seeking your and my father's advice, as this matter regards the emperor.

"We will await your return."

After Saracen was prepared, Harrison bolted toward the gates where this mysterious being was waiting. As he reached the gates, which were surrounded by the Guardians he had requested to stand watch, he dismounted Saracen and walked over to the men.

"Where is this creature?" Harrison asked.

"He has shown himself again and stands over by those trees."

As soon as Harrison saw the peculiar man, he set out in his direction.

"You are not the emperor, but you will do for now," the man said in a mysterious voice.

He had white hair, his skin was a healthy golden color, and his eyes were white in color.

"Who are you, where are you from, and what business do you have with the Pemdai Emperor?"

"Oh, sir, you will soon discover who I am and where I am from. But you must allow me to speak with the emperor first," the man responded with a strange accent.

"I will not adhere to any of your demands, and I do not make bargains. You will tell me who you are and what your business is, here and now, or I will have you removed from our borders." Harrison grinned. "And believe me, when we remove you, we will not be gentle."

The man smiled in return. "You would not want to do that."

Harrison turned to leave. "Gentlemen, remove the intruder."

"Would you care to know where the four priestesses are, Commander?" the man spoke out.

Harrison stopped and spun around. "I am in no mood for games. I will not be mocked or lied to."

"You can search all of the dimensions for the women you seek, but you will waste your time."

"In order for me to trust this information, I must see it as truth within your mind."

The man smiled. "I will gladly comply with that."

The man's confidence had Harrison concerned. "If you are not showing me truths, but rather forcing images into your mind that are fallacies, I will know."

The man nodded. "There is no reason for me to mislead you. Once I allow you inside of my mind, you will understand why I am here, and why I am required to speak to the emperor of your people."

Harrison sighed and proceeded to read into the man's thoughts. He saw a fortress where the priestesses resided. Suddenly, Harrison jerked back to stare intently at the man. "There is no possible way."

The man smiled again, and one of the Guardians approached out of worry for Harrison's response to the images he saw.

"Commander, is everything okay?"

Harrison looked at him in disbelief. "Emperor Navarre is alive and being held captive!"

# Chapter 14

The day had come when Levi was to bring Reece to the location that he had secretly planned for their honeymoon. Spending the evening with Reece in this posh city exceeded all of his expectations. Levi was up before the sun and enthusiastic about making preparations to make this journey.

Once the imperial guards were given their instructions, Levi wasted no time in preparing himself before Reece woke. After a rejuvenating shower, he promptly went through his routine of preparing himself for the day.

He chuckled when Reece surprisingly came up behind him, wrapping her arms around his waist tightly. She peeked around his side and watched as he drew the blade of his straight razor over the last of the stubble on his cheek.

"Good morning," he said as he studied the mirror for any remnants of facial hair that he might have missed.

"It is a wonderful morning," she answered in a sleepy voice. "I'm curious about something."

"Curious?"

"Yes," Reece answered, staring at him through the mirror. "I thought your butler would be the one who shaved your face."

Levi shook his head as he splashed water over it. Reece handed him the towel he had placed on the vanity before him.

After blotting his face dry, he turned. "And what makes you think that?"

"I just figured that Henry was pretty much like Jasmeen, insisting on doing everything for you." She laughed as he embraced her.

"Henry learned many years ago that I prefer doing some things on my own, shaving being one of them."

"That's right," Reece said, acting as though she had a revelation, "you're a Pemdai warrior."

Levi laughed and nuzzled her neck. "Indeed. And let us not forget I am also your husband and personal Guardian as well."

Reece lifted her chin and ran her hands down the center of his bare chest. "Well, if you are the bold warrior you claim to be, why aren't you shaving with your dagger?"

Levi stared into Reece's teasing eyes, and instead of responding he scooped her up into his arms as she squealed with delight. "You are full of questions this morning, are you not?"

He gently laid her back on their bed. "I'm just curious about my husband's morning routine." She ran her hands along his cheek. "Silky smooth."

Her eyes beamed, and Levi could no longer resist his wife. "Have you called for your maiden yet?" he asked with a kiss to her throat.

"Why, Emperor Oxley!" She softly laughed. "What are you planning now?"

Levi's voice was muffled against her chest. "To enlighten you on the newest addition to my morning routine," he said, loosening the silk tie of her robe. "If it pleases my lovely wife, that is."

Reece sighed and ran her hands up his back and through his dark, wavy hair. "I'm definitely interested in learning more about this particular part of your morning routine," she answered as he fulfilled his aching desire by bringing his lips down onto hers.

By nightfall, the imperial convoy arrived at the final destination Levi had planned for their honeymoon. Levi discreetly observed Reece's reaction as they stopped in front of the massive caverns. She stared upward, studying the appearance of the illuminating rock caves. Without looking at Levi, she unconsciously brought her hand to the stone dangling from the chain on her neck. "Where are we?" she whispered.

The door to the carriage opened, and Levi turned to help Reece from it. "The caverns of Lixlea," he told her as he brought her arm into his to ascend the glimmering stone stairs. With each step they took, the stones swirled into new, vibrant colors. "These caverns are Pemdas' most sought-after destination, and it is nearly impossible for reservations to be made."

"I'd love to call you a show off right now, but I simply can't get over the majestic beauty." She chuckled. "I never would have guessed we'd be staying in caves."

As they entered the large atrium, Levi led Reece through two stone doors that branched off to a small room. Before she could question why they were in what seemed to be a closest, the stone doors closed, leaving the imperial guards on the other side of them. She gripped Levi's arm when she felt the energy of the room pulling them up. The walls illuminated brightly as they were hoisted up to the private chambers they would be staying in.

Levi found it amusing, having visited before. He kissed her head. "Love, you act as though you have never ridden in an elevator before."

Reece nudged him. "That's not fair, and you know it. Ever since I entered this dimension, there have only been grand staircases. I've hardly been around anything of a technical nature."

The doors opened to the large, cavernous room that overlooked the Silean Sea. Large stone archways lined the walls of the room, each one leading to a private balcony. Levi led Reece to the largest open archway in their room. It led out to a balcony where a shimmering pool was situated to overlook the sea.

Levi wrapped his arms around Reece's waist and rested his chin on her shoulder. "The water is warmed by the energy of the caves."

Reece leaned back into him. "After our long trip here, taking a swim in a warm pool sounds very inviting. I know I've probably said this a hundred and eleven times since you've brought me to Pemdas, but this is the most beautiful place I have ever been."

"More like one hundred and twelve," he teased. "My family and I have vacationed here since Lizzy and I were children," Levi said as he led her across the room toward another balcony. "When you are up for it, I plan to take you on quite the adventure through these forests in the next day or so."

Reece released her hold on Levi's arm and walked onto the balcony that overlooked an enchanting forest. She stood quietly, listening to the critters beneath them sing in infinite harmonic melodies. "You've officially done it," she said as she turned to Levi, who was approaching her. "I really don't know what to say. This location, the splendor of this room," she walked into the room and glanced up, "the dark ceiling looks like stars are sprinkled all over it. The illumination of everything is fascinating."

Levi grabbed her by the waist and spun her around. "You, Reece Oxley, are fascinating."

"Biased, as usual," she said with a smile as she brought her lips to his for a quick kiss.

"Come. Allow Jasmeen to help you freshen up, and we shall dine under the vibrant stars of Pemdas together."

"Later, can we take a swim?"

Levi grinned at her daring expression. "Anything you wish."

After two days of exploring more of the unique caves in this remarkable region, Levi and Reece were anxious to see the forest. With the intent of a day spent racing along the seashore before venturing inland, Levi arranged for Areion and Arrow to be saddled and brought to a private exit at the back of the cavern they were staying in. Now Levi could also surprise Reece with the place where he had prepared for them to spend their night alone.

Levi stood with a group of servants, giving them all the information needed for them to set up the location where he and Reece would be later. He spared no detail in order to make this night unforgettable for Reece. Once he was assured that the servants would have everything set up for them before nightfall, he went to retrieve Reece.

"She is fully prepared," Jasmeen said as she approached Levi. "I hope you enjoy your evening, and I will have everything ready for her upon your return tomorrow."

Levi nodded toward the bag that Jasmeen held in her arms. "Are those all of the items she will need for the evening?"

"Yes. It has everything she will require to remain comfortable for the night."

Levi reached out for the bag. "Thank you. I will have Henry take this along with my items down to the servants who are preparing to depart."

Levi watched as Jasmeen's cheeks colored lightly, and he studied her perplexed expression with amusement. He continued, "You are free to enjoy the rest of today and tomorrow in any way you wish until we return."

"Emperor," Jasmeen started. "Please allow me to bring the luggage to Henry so that you waste no more time waiting to leave."

*It would appear my lovely wife is correct in her assumptions about this young maiden.* Levi subtly grinned and handed her Reece's luggage. "Very well, then."

Jasmeen snatched the bag and offered Levi a quick curtsy. "It is always my pleasure," she said as she brushed past Levi and exited the sitting area.

Levi walked through the two stone doors that led into their private chambers and found Reece sipping her tea, leaning against the balcony. As she gazed into the forest, Levi came up behind her. He brought his arms around her waist and brushed his lips against her cheek. "Do you approve of your new riding outfit?"

She turned in his arms. "I absolutely love it! Thank you *again* for surprising me with yet another amazing gift." She gave a quick tug to her riding coat. "Are you sure it won't shock all of the guests here to see their new empress wearing what they would refer to as a man's riding outfit?"

Levi pressed his lips against her forehead. "One day you will learn that I care nothing about the opinions of others." He stepped back and studied her brilliant eyes. "Although I was fairly confident it would concern you, so I made arrangements for an inconspicuous exit." He offered his arm. "Shall we enjoy our day outdoors together?"

Reece smiled. "I can't wait to explore the places my husband enjoyed so much as a child!"

***

They walked out to where Arrow and Areion were saddled and waiting for them. Reece marveled at Arrow's gorgeous saddle and blanket that Levi had made for her. She ran her hands along the polished black leather that had silver arrows garnishing it. Her initials were stamped into the leather on each side of the saddle. The saddle blanket was a velvet material, which was taupe in color and matched new her riding outfit perfectly. Arrow's bridle was also made of rich black leather. Silver medallions with Arrow's name carved into them sat on each side of his face, close to his temples. Reece couldn't get over Levi's creativity when it came to designing anything he felt would please her.

She gripped Arrow's halter and smiled. "Another gift?" she asked when she noticed Levi's proud expression.

"For Arrow, of course," he returned.

Reece stood on her toes and kissed Levi's cheek. "Of course."

Levi helped Reece onto her massive stallion, and Reece noticed his hesitation at Arrow's reaction. She inwardly laughed, and she knew his concern was wasted when Arrow showed no signs of refusing her mastery of him. Instead, it was quite the opposite; the horse gazed into Levi's eyes with a look of annoyance before bringing his attention to Areion, who was impatiently waiting for Levi to mount him.

"Still worried about Arrow?" Reece asked with a laugh.

Levi sighed. "Simply amazed, is all." He turned toward Areion and hoisted himself onto his powerful steed.

"How does a ride along the shore sound?" he asked as he guided Areion over to Reece.

"How about a race?"

Levi grinned. "Even better."

They guided their horses toward the shore, and without hesitation Reece called out loudly to Arrow and the horse joyfully responded.

After spending most of the morning exploring the shoreline and racing the Guardian horses, Reece brought Arrow to a halt and glanced at Levi. "You'd think Areion would get sick of losing races to Arrow by now, wouldn't you?"

She laughed when Areion looked directly at her and grunted. "My love, Areion and I enjoy allowing you and Arrow your victories."

"Yeah, right."

Levi arched an eyebrow at her. "You should know that I enjoy the sight of my wife riding ahead of me. In truth, Areion does dislike it, but he will eventually get used to it."

She narrowed her eyes at him. "What am I going to do with you, Levi Oxley?"

He laughed. "Absolutely anything you desire." Levi gripped the reins. "Have you worked up an appetite for lunch?"

"Now that you mention it, I am starving."

"Follow me," Levi said as he turned into the thick forest and started up a steep mountainside. *Steep hills? Where is he taking us?* Once at the top, Reece could see the entire sea, and it felt like they were truly at the highest point in all of Pemdas. A white, blanketed shelter was set up amongst a large group of trees, and it was complete with what appeared to be a mattress and pillows.

"Would you care to join your husband in slumbering under the stars tonight?" Levi asked as he dismounted Areion.

Reece hopped down from Arrow, walked over to Levi, and wrapped her arms around his neck. "Your thoughtfulness amazes me more and more every day."

"That is my hope." Levi brought her arm into his. "I have arranged for the servants to prepare a small lunch, and while we explore this place together, they will return with supper."

Once they finished their meal, they returned to their horses and led them toward the opposite side of the mountain. Reece swallowed hard. "Where are we going? I'm not sure I'm comfortable riding down that steep a mountainside."

Levi grinned. "Just lean back and brace against your stirrups."

"Levi—" Her voice cracked in fear.

"Relax, love. Arrow is bred to protect his master; therefore, he would not take one step down that mountainside if he had some notion it would bring harm to either of you."

Reece inhaled deeply. "Okay. This had better be worth it."

"There are beautiful waterfalls deep in the forest, and it is absolutely secluded. I truly believe you will find this ride enchanting."

Before they started down the mountainside, Levi halted Areion and looked over at Reece. "Give Arrow his head, and he will comfortably follow down behind Areion and me."

"What?" she asked nervously.

Levi grinned. "Loosen the reins, my love."

Levi started down the trail in front of her, and Arrow gracefully followed in step. She loosened the reins and used the stirrups to brace herself as she leaned back. It was incredibly steep, and she trusted Arrow with every step he made, yet she closed her eyes, unwilling to watch the descent. Reece could sense that they were nearing the bottom when she heard Levi laughing aloud. "Why, Mrs. Oxley, have your eyes been closed the entire ride down that hill?"

Her eyes opened to find Levi and Areion patiently waiting on a thick mound of vibrant green grass. The forest illuminated in a grand display of colors all around them.

She smiled at Levi. "You call that a hill? *That,* my love, was a cliff. And yes, Captain Adventurous, I did have my eyes closed the entire way." She grinned mischievously at him. "Now that I survived that, where are these magnificent waterfalls?"

Levi winked. "Right this way, My Lady."

Levi dismounted Areion and helped Reece off Arrow. "We hike in from here," he said as they began to walk deeper into the glowing forest.

Reece felt she should be used to this by now, but she wasn't. It was magical and enchanting to watch nature and the insects illuminate all around them. She gazed up into the massive trees, which were so tall that their tops disappeared into the skies above them. Then she noticed something. She stopped, forcing Levi to halt with her.

Glistening winged creatures sprung from the treetops, leaping from the branches that formed a canopy over the area. Like monkeys, these winged creatures danced through the trees in a playful manner. Reece watched as a multicolored glittering trail followed them with each leap.

"Those are zorflaks," Levi stated as he gazed up into the trees above them.

A rustle in the bushes brought Reece's attention to another mysterious creature in the forest. Before she could scream, Levi spun her behind him and speared his dagger through the head of a dragon-like serpent. Reece watched in horror as the creature's body shook as though it were electrocuted. A vivid blue color glowed so brightly that she squinted her eyes, unable to turn away. The dazzling light of this loathsome serpent displayed the size and length of its body, which extended so deep into the forest that Reece couldn't see if it ever ended. As the serpent's life slowly ebbed away, the bright color of its body started to dim.

"What was *that?*" Reece asked shakily, her heart pounding in her chest.

"A krewin," Levi said in a subdued voice. "It is an extremely hostile creature, only to be found in this forest."

"Why exactly are we hiking through this place again?"

Levi went to retrieve his dagger. "I certainly hoped we would not have come into such close proximity with one, as I take no satisfaction in killing creatures who are merely surviving in their natural habitat. But had I not, Pemdas would be in need of yet another emperor and empress." Levi grinned at Reece's narrowed eyes.

After wiping off and sheathing his dagger, Levi bent to kiss her. He chuckled when Reece turned her lips away from his. "As my personal Guardian on Earth, I'm fairly confident that you know I don't do well with spiders." She nodded toward the enormous serpent whose body was now turning into a pile of dust. "My heart can't handle the sight of a snake, so if this forest is filled with those things, count me out," she said with a reproachful glare.

"Mrs. Oxley," Levi returned her gaze with a humorous one, "have you lost faith in my protective abilities already?"

Reece sighed. "No more potentially life-ending surprises, okay?" she teased.

"You have my word."

They continued their hike through the forest, listening to a serene harmonics coming from the creatures leaping through the trees. Soon a clearing came into view, and the musical sounds of the forest were replaced with the roar of rushing water.

They approached a river flowing rapidly through carved rocks and walked up to it. The sky was a brilliant shade of blue above them, and the diamond-like sun sat directly over their heads. The higher they climbed, the more the river began to spill into pools of sparkling water. The cliffs that surrounded the pools of water glistened under the light of the brilliant sun, enhancing the majestic beauty of the water.

"Am I forgiven?" Levi asked.

"This is so remarkable."

"What is *remarkable*, love, is what awaits us behind that curtain of water." He smiled as he led her up to the waterfall. "Behind that waterfall is a large cave. I believe you will be astounded by the beauty of it. It is very deep and seems to go on forever, but the inside of the cave illuminates with patterns like ribbons of jewels glowing along its surface."

Levi started to lead Reece up to the waterfall when she stopped him. "Wait, I need a moment to take in all of this first." She stared into the numerous pools of water that surrounded them, and without warning the scenery changed.

Reece was suddenly in a dark forest packed with snow, leaning against a saddle and shivering under two Guardian cloaks. She watched as Levi was in conversation with Harrison and other Guardians dressed in their warrior regalia. She sat exhausted, irritable, and waiting for Levi to return to her. He was in discussion with Harrison and the other men, and Reece had no energy to think about what they could be discussing. As her heavy lids started to close, Levi approached her as the rest of the Guardians joined where she sat around the fire. Levi reached down to her, and she reflexively placed her hand in his and reluctantly stood up.

He pulled Reece off to the side and away from the group of Guardian warriors. "Come with me. I believe you shall be grateful for what I am about to show you."

He gently took her arm and led her away from the large campfire that illuminated the area. She was confused but followed alongside of Levi up a hill through deep snow. At the top of the hill was a steaming pool of water surrounded by trees and tall, icy glaciers. Steam rose off the water and filled the entire area. She was instantly overwhelmed with the desire to dive head first into the water to freshen up.

"Allow me to help you out of this," Levi said as he unfastened her cloak.

"Are you sure no one is going to walk up on me?"

Levi kissed her nose. "After all of your complaining, I am surprised that you are concerned over that. But to answer your question, no. They are down the mountain, keeping watch."

Her heart reacted at her favorite grin, and then another overwhelming desire came over her. She brought her hand up to his face. "Will you get in with me?"

Levi's eyebrow arched. "That was one of the main reasons I was thrilled when Harrison told me about this pool of water."

Once Reece was completely undressed, she stepped into the water. "Levi, there's nothing in here that will bite my toes or anything like that, is there?" she asked as she got an uneasy feeling.

She turned, and the sight of her husband half-dressed made her forget about everything else. Moments later, Levi grabbed a bag, walked over to the side of the snowy ledge, and set it down. Then he was in the water and she was in his arms. His mouth found hers in a powerful kiss that sent a surge of energy through her.

Reece's head snapped up, and she was back with Levi in front of the massive waterfall. She looked over at Levi, trying to clear her head. "That was strange."

"Indeed!" Levi answered. "Was it another vision?"

"Why would you think that?" she asked.

"I watched your entire expression change, and your eyes—" Levi studied her. "Your eyes went from their usual blue color to a brilliant green."

"What's happening to me?"

Levi shook his head. "I am unsure. I know I am being repetitive with these questions, but are you confident that these visions are not tormenting for you in any way?"

"No. They're just very unexpected and bizarre." She laughed. "I was wearing the uniform of a Guardian, and we were in a dark forest with deep snow covering the ground all around us."

"Again, we shall seek Queen Galleta's advice upon our return. I am extremely curious as to why these visions are occurring."

"You and me both," Reece said as she rubbed her forehead. She lifted her chin and smiled at Levi's concerned expression. "Until then, let's enjoy our honeymoon and check out this cave."

They walked along a narrow ledge and slipped behind the rapidly flowing waterfall. As they strolled through the darkened cave and the daylight started to disappear, Reece found herself in total enchantment once again. The noise of the thundering waterfall began to diminish in the distance, and the cave started to glisten with countless shimmering bands of color. Levi brought his arm around her as she slowed to take in the majesty.

"Once again, I'm dumbfounded. This place is astounding," Reece said as they walked deeper into the cave.

Levi kissed her on her head. "Is it not? I used to explore this cave when I was young. There are many different tunnels that lead to various places."

Levi turned down a tunnel that ended at a large body of water. Another waterfall poured out of a separation in the rocks and fell gently into the vivid aqua pool. The entire space was illuminated by the glowing from this basin.

"Care for a swim?" Levi asked in a teasing tone. "The water should be quite rejuvenating after our hike up to this location."

Reece crossed her arms and stared into the tempting water. "If we had swimsuits, I'd definitely take you up on that offer."

"What happened to my spirited wife? Has the sight of the menacing krewin lessened her adventurous personality already?"

She challenged his mischievous grin with a smirk. "Are you sure we are in total isolation?"

"Yes."

She pulled her coat off and shoved it into his chest. "Fine, let's get a little crazy."

Levi gripped her arm and laughed. "Here," he said, pulling a swimsuit out of a bag he'd brought, "this for you. I want you to fully enjoy yourself, and worrying that someone may see us is the last thing you need."

Reece grabbed the suit and smiled at him. "You are having way too much fun at my expense today."

"True." Levi smirked. Then he brought an arm around her waist, pulled her in close, and started to unfasten the buttons of her silky shirt. "However, the point is for *you* to be the one enjoying yourself today, not just me. Allow me to make it up to you."

Reece's heart fluttered as she recognized the expression Levi held for her. They swam for a while until they wound up in each other's arms as the waterfall poured down over them. Levi's blue eyes glittered as Reece locked her gaze onto them. She smoothed his wet hair back, and his lips were instantly at the base of her throat. His hands ran up her sides as he brought his lips to her shoulder. Reece stood on her toes in the shallow water and brought a kiss to his jaw as Levi proceeded to undo the strap of her swimsuit.

"I can't believe we're doing this," she whispered breathlessly.

Levi kissed the side of her neck. "I can," was all he said before Reece was lost in the passion that only her husband could ignite within her.

That evening, Reece lazily reclined against Levi's chest as they stared into the fire he had made by their shelter. She leaned her head back into his shoulder and gazed up at the millions of shimmering stars scattered throughout the brilliant sky. Levi used this opportunity to place kisses along her neck.

"Will you ever know precisely how much I love you, Mrs. Oxley?"

She smiled sweetly as she ran her hand up through his hair. "The question is, will *you* ever know how much I love you? Levi, my life has changed so much by having you in it. I don't deserve you." She twisted in his arms. "I think we should actually thank Movac for this."

Levi chuckled. "I never would have thought of it that way, but you are correct. If the Ciatron weren't aggressively pursuing you, I would still be standing in the shadows protecting you, all the while longing for you to take notice of me."

Reece turned and settled back into Levi's embrace. "And I would probably be stressed out about med school."

They laughed but were soon interrupted when Reece noticed the most adorable critter she'd ever seen approach their location. She sat up slowly, trying not to startle it. Whatever it was, it looked like a tiny bear with big, triangular ears. Its eyes were like yellow jewels, and they were overly large and round with long lashes. It was white with patches of brown and black on its fluffy coat of fur. It blinked slowly, and Reece giggled.

"What is it?" she questioned in a very soft voice.

As the fluffy creature came closer, it seemed frightened, but hopeful. "That's a young zorflak, the same as the creatures you saw in the forest canopy today. It appears to be orphaned."

Levi held out his hand, and the fluffy zorflak slowly crawled over to him, his tiny wings sticking out from his back. Reece watched in amusement as the animal sat there on his legs. It reached its hand out, and its tiny, chubby fingers touched Levi's long ones. It blinked again and made a small humming sound as it looked up into Levi's face. Reece was completely enamored by the little guy.

"Poor thing, he is orphaned," Levi said. "We will have to bring him back into the village tomorrow. Maybe they will know what to do with him."

Reece impulsively spun around in Levi's arms. "Can I care for him?"

Levi laughed. "Reece, these little guys feed on tenillians. I am certain you will not want him around the palace grounds. He shall be fine out here."

"Please? I won't let him eat any tenillians. Is that all they eat?"

Levi sighed. "I should tell you yes, because I know where this is going."

Turning, the little guy hopped over to Reece and jumped into her lap. She immediately cradled it in her arms and looked up at Levi, begging him with her stare. "Please?"

The zorflak seemed to be pleading with Levi also as he made another humming noise, mimicking Reece's plea to Levi.

"Do not look at me like that, Reece Oxley. Your eyes already have far too much control over me."

She continued to look into his eyes as she felt the zorflak snuggle into her embrace and latch his tiny hand onto hers. Levi glanced down, and then a tiny smile drew up the corner of his mouth.

"You do realize how much hassle you are going to receive from everyone at the palace for this, do you not? Especially from Harrison."

Gleefully, Reece kissed Levi. "Thank you!" she said with excitement.

Levi laughed in surrender and brought his fingers to scratch the baby zorflak's head. "Well, it looks like you are going to have to come up with a name for the little monster."

Reece giggled. "Oh, I will!"

# Chapter 15

The following morning, as daylight reached the land, a soft harmonic melody alerted Levi to the zorflak at Reece's side. Levi had been awake since before sunrise, and he relished the comfort of having Reece in his embrace. As the humming continued, Levi leaned over to see if Reece was still asleep. She was curled up on her side with the zorflak nestled in her arms. He laughed inwardly when he saw that it was singing its tune exclusively to Reece. It had its hand on her cheek while she lay there smiling at the song it was humming for her.

Levi kissed her shoulder. "It appears I may have competition already."

Reece laughed. "Isn't he the cutest little thing you've ever seen?"

"He may be adorable, but I fear I am already growing weary of him."

"Him?" she asked, staring into the zorflak's large eyes.

Levi sighed. "Yes, *him*," he answered, feigning annoyance. "You have rescued an orphaned male zorflak, and he and I already have an issue with each other."

Reece rolled onto her back and smiled up at Levi's amused expression. She laughed. "Really? What did he do to you?"

The zorflak hopped onto Reece's stomach, bringing her attention back to him. Levi shook his head, and Reece giggled.

"Well, to start with—"

As soon as Levi began to speak, the zorflak starting singing again, interrupting him. *Is he trying to get thrown off the mountain?* Levi sat there, baffled that the little baby zorflak was actually competing with him for Reece's attention. Levi went to speak again, but before a word came out the zorflak put his tiny paw to Reece's chin as it hummed an even louder melody.

"First of all—" Levi spoke out, yet the zorflak's humming continued to drown out his deep voice. He sighed while he narrowed his eyes at the critter.

Reece started laughing, and then sat up, gripping the little guy softly while placing him in her lap. "Listen, little buddy, you're about to get us both in trouble. You need to let Levi finish talking, or he's not going to let me keep you."

The zorflak gazed up at Levi, frowned, and then curled up into a ball in Reece's lap, using his long, pointed, furry ears to cover his eyes. Reece returned her humored look to where Levi reclined on his side.

"You were saying?" she politely asked him.

Levi sighed. "I think the little monster just proved my point. I would love to think he was sound asleep so that I could have you to myself; however, I believe he is merely waiting for me to finish so that he can begin serenading you again."

Reece got up and placed the zorflak back into the bed Levi had crafted for it the previous evening. The orphaned zorflak's wings began to illuminate in different colors as they slowly flapped back and forth, and Reece hoped the tiny critter was falling asleep. Once she believed it was completely out, she came back to where Levi patiently waited on their cushioned bed.

Reece placed a tender kiss to his lips. "There. He's asleep, and now you have me all to yourself."

Levi encircled his arms around Reece, drawing her down onto him. "You must know I tend to be selfish when it comes to sharing the love of my life."

"Selfish?" Reece traced the lines of his forehead. "I would have never imagined you could possess such a negative emotion," she teased.

"Unfortunately, when it comes to anything trying to steal my wife away, I most definitely am."

Reece brushed a finger over his chin. "Well, I'm here now, and I'm all yours."

Levi grinned. "Indeed." He brought his hands through her long golden hair and secured a passionate kiss. As Levi proceeded to indulge himself in his wife, the harmonious serenading began again. Levi instantly froze in place. "Unbelievable," he said while staring intently into Reece's eyes.

Reece burst into laughter as she saw the zorflak was now by Levi's head and singing to him.

Levi turned his head and gazed sternly at the zorflak. "If I allow you to come back with us – and believe me, it will only be because of the profound love I have for my wife – you will be caged, and you will sleep outdoors," he scolded.

When Levi looked back at Reece, she had both hands covering her mouth and her eyes closed tightly. It was obvious that Levi's irritation by the zorflak's intrusion was greatly amusing her. This was a fortunate thing for the animal, as Levi could not resist how charming Reece appeared at this moment.

When she opened her eyes, Levi grinned at her. "I will start building his cage today, if I must," he playfully groused.

Reece brought her hand up to his cheek. "I'm sure you will. Maybe we should head back to the caverns, and I'll see if Jasmeen will take him for the rest of our vacation. This way, we can have our time alone without any interruptions." She laughed. "I'd hate to see the poor fellow be thrown in prison by the Emperor of Pemdas already," she mocked.

"Splendid idea, love. He obviously has no idea who I am," Levi teased as he smiled smugly at the zorflak.

"You know what they say about wild animals, they just have no respect for aristocracy anymore!" Reece laughed aloud as she kissed Levi's cheek.

After a quick breakfast, Levi and Reece left the outdoor retreat to journey back to the caverns where Jasmeen and the rest of the servants awaited them. Upon their return, they dismounted their horses as the imperial guards retrieved them. After handing their horses off to the groomsmen, Levi dismissed the guards and escorted Reece up the stairs and into the back entrance. There were no patrons in the large foyer when they entered it, and they discreetly headed toward their private chambers.

As they crossed the secluded foyer, Levi stopped dead in his tracks, abruptly halting Reece at his side. *Harrison?* he internally questioned when he noticed his cousin reposed on an oversized chair. He had his arm propped up on the arm of the chair, and his head was resting on it with his eyes closed. Distress was apparent on his face, and Levi couldn't help but wonder what had gone wrong.

"Harrison?" Levi called out in disbelief.

Harrison's eyes jerked open, and he nearly sprung from the chair to greet Levi and Reece.

"Levi, Reece—" his words were cut short when he glanced down at Reece's arm. "Reece? However did you manage to capture an infant zorflak?"

She smiled. "He's going to be our new pet. Isn't he adorable?"

Harrison faintly smiled and shook his head. "Only you, Reece," he said in bewilderment.

Levi frowned at his cousin's terse response. Fear washed over him, knowing something must be wrong with his mother or sister. There was no way Harrison would show up unexpectedly, or behave in this manner, for any other reason.

"Harrison, you look as though you haven't slept in a month. What has happened?" Levi demanded.

Harrison ran his fingers through his hair, forcing Levi's heart rate to increase.

"Tell me at once! Are my mother and sister okay?" Levi asked in a raised, somewhat panicked voice.

Harrison inhaled deeply. "Forgive me; everyone is perfectly well."

Reece stood in silence, studying Harrison's odd behavior as well.

Harrison's lips twisted. "I have news for you," he paused and exhaled, "however, during my journey here, I have pondered the many ways I could deliver it properly to you. I believe the best way is to have you see everything through my mind."

"If that is your wish," Levi answered calmly, yet confused.

"If you do not mind, Reece?" Harrison asked in a grave tone as he extended his arm out to her. Once Reece was at Harrison's side, he nodded to Levi, prompting him to read his thoughts.

As Harrison's mind opened up, Levi saw the events at the gates from Harrison's eyes and memories. When the image of his father alive came into sight, Levi called out, "Father?" as if waiting for Navarre to look over and answer him.

If it weren't for the wall next to him, Levi was sure he would have collapsed to the ground in complete shock, disbelief, relief, anguish, and bemusement. He stood there for a moment, holding onto the wall with one arm, trying to gather himself. He listened as Harrison quietly informed Reece of what had been revealed to Levi. Navarre was alive. Words couldn't describe what he was feeling at this moment. Levi sensed the room growing silent, waiting for him to recover. He knew he should turn back to Harrison and Reece, but he couldn't. Emotions ripped through him violently as he held on to the image of his father, alive and still wearing the Guardian uniform he last saw him in.

"There is no possible way," he muttered to himself.

Levi turned, bringing his back against the wall for added support. Against all self-control, he felt a tear stream down his cheek. He brushed the emotions away, bowed his head, and covered his eyes, trying to force himself into a stronger mindset. He needed to speak with Harrison, but he couldn't utter a word if he tried. He closed his eyes and took a few calming breaths, forcing himself into the only mental state in which he knew could control such emotions. Once he did, the Pemdai warrior within him was awoken. A warm calm came over him, soothing every distressed nerve in his body. His thoughts were clear, and he looked up to find tears streaming down Reece's cheeks as Harrison held a protective arm around her.

Levi stepped away from the wall and stood tall, his body rigid and commanding. "Who is this man, and where is he now?" Levi wanted to know.

"He refers to himself as Mordegrin. He is currently under heavy guard in the prison unit of the command center."

"Very good. Has Lady Allestaine been informed about any of this?"

"No. Only my father, King Hamilton, and a select few Guardians know that the emperor is alive. We believed that you should be the one to inform your mother of this news." Harrison cleared his throat. "This stranger will give us no further information until he speaks with you."

Levi gazed intently at Reece, using her presence to calm himself further. Her endearing smile in turn helped to silence the warrior within him.

He exhaled as his features softened. "Forgive my temperament."

Reece's eyes widened, and she shook her head. "There is nothing to forgive," she answered compassionately. "Levi, you must speak with this being at once."

Harrison remained unusually quiet as he and Reece waited for Levi's response.

Levi closed his eyes, struggling to figure a way to handle this. He was grateful for Reece's response, and he completely agreed with her. The urge to retrieve Areion and ride in haste back to Pasidian was nagging at him, but he could not abandon his new bride in such a manner.

"Levi?" Reece softly implored as she slowly approached him.

He extended his arm to accept her embrace. She leaned into him and looked up into his eyes. "You should leave with Harrison immediately and question this being yourself. You need to find out where your father is and find out what this individual's intentions are."

He sighed. "I cannot desert you like this so far from home."

"Levi," she responded in a gentle voice, "I will be fine. I have the imperial guards with me, and Jasmeen will be a great companion on our journey back to the palace. Please," she begged, "go with Harrison."

Levi sighed as he gazed into her tear-filled, yet hopeful eyes, and he brought his hand to her cheek. "Very well. I will go with Harrison, but my only request is that you leave today as well. I will make arrangements for the guards to take you on a more private route to Pasidian. There is a small inn along the way for you to stay at. You will not be bothered by having to entertain the citizens without me in that town."

Reece smiled. "I will leave today, and please don't worry about me."

Levi stared into her brilliant eyes. "Are you certain?"

"I have absolutely no doubt that you must handle this matter immediately."

Harrison approached where they stood. "I had four other warriors ride with me. I will have them stay and assist with the escort of the imperial convoy."

Levi looked over at Harrison. "Very well, then."

Within the hour, Levi and Harrison were riding away from the caverns as fast as their stallions could carry them.

By the time they had departed, the attendants had already begun to leave with the luggage.

Having not stopped once, and with Areion and Saracen's great speed, Levi and Harrison reached the palace as nightfall covered the land. Levi chose to enter the command center through a secluded entrance, so as not to be noticed by any visitors at the palace. He marched through the halls of the command center and down toward the cell where the being waited for him. The guards positioned at the door stepped aside to allow him in, but when he entered the cell, he found no one there.

He abruptly turned to Harrison. "Has he escaped?"

Harrison wore a severe expression as he stared into the corner of the room. "No. This entity has the ability to cloak himself."

"Show yourself, creature," Levi spoke out.

At that moment, a blurred image of a being came into view in the corner of the room. Levi watched the image of the being become a solid figure with great disbelief.

"Emperor Oxley, it is a great honor to finally meet you," the being said as he gave Levi an exaggerated bow.

"I am told you have extremely important information for me?" Levi did not trust this being at all. Something was not right about him, yet Levi couldn't pinpoint it. "Please tell me who you are, and where are you from?"

"I am Mordegrin, from Oltenia."

"Oltenia? What dimension is that realm situated in?"

The being grinned. "Forgive me, Emperor, but it is an entire dimension, not a realm within a dimension."

Levi gazed darkly at the being. "Do you think I am a fool? There is no such dimension in all of Earth. You have shown us that my father is alive; and if that is true, then tell me which dimension is he being held in?"

"Your father is in another dimension, to be sure, but not one of Earth's. He has been transported into another galaxy."

"That is impossible," Levi returned.

The being walked toward Levi with an odd limp. "It is possible," he said in his strange accent, "or you and I would not be having this conversation."

Levi stared at the being in disbelief. "Intergalactic travel does not exist." He exhaled. "Even if it did, how is my father alive and well? We buried his body close to a month ago, and I watched him die in my own arms."

"You watched him *dying* in your arms. Your father is alive, Emperor Oxley, and he waits for you to rescue him."

"IMPOSSIBLE!" Levi roared.

Never before had any being ever entered or exited this universe. Levi was growing exceedingly agitated in this entity's presence, but he needed to calm himself so he could get more information; and most of all, to learn if this was a lie or if this stranger was speaking the truth.

"Emperor Oxley, I can appreciate your struggle to accept this information—"

"Tomorrow—" he loudly interrupted the being. "I will have a group of my men with me, and you *will* take us into the dimension where he is being held captive. We will retrieve him and bring him home. I shall thank you for your help at that time."

"That is impossible, sir."

"Truly, these are lies that you speak, then."

"If you do not trust that I speak truth, then you will never have your father back, and my coming here to help him will have been for nothing."

"Help him?"

"Yes. You see, you are not the only ones who have been victims of the Olteniaus' evil doings."

"Olteniaus?"

"Ah, yes. They misled your kind into believing that they were priestesses of some sort. They are not. They are from another galaxy, and their dark ways are purely malevolent. They have taken over our entire galaxy and cursed nearly every dimension and world within it. This is where your father is being held captive."

Levi stared intently at the being. "I will consider the possibility of entering other galaxies for now, against all reason. With that much said, you must tell me how we are expected to travel into your world to retrieve my father. Is there a particular vessel that can transport me and my men?"

The individual sighed, seemingly relieved that Levi was starting to cooperate with him. "There is but one way that you and your men would be able to achieve such travel. A portal must be opened."

"Is this portal not already open? How were you able to enter our galaxy otherwise? How were the priestesses able to bring my father into their galaxy?"

"It is a strange power that the Olteniaus have in their possession. It is what they used, and what I used, to travel in such a way. However, it will not work for anyone but those who are Olteniaus. The only reason your father was able to successfully pass through with their power was that he nearly had no life left within him when they transported him to my galaxy."

Mordegrin was being vague with his answers and causing Levi to grow even more confused and frustrated. There were too many questions in Levi's mind already, so he had to prioritize what was most important, and that was getting his father back.

"You say a portal must be opened. Do you have any way of accomplishing this for us?"

"I cannot open the portal for you."

Levi huffed with exasperation. "Then tell me—as my patience is nearly all but lost—who or what can open this portal through which we must travel?"

"Oh, Emperor, there is but one being who can achieve such an arduous feat. It is the one whose powers are unique unto them alone, the one whose powers cannot be replicated. The one who is the descendant of Paul Xylander, and she is known as the—"

"My wife?" Levi snapped back aggressively. "She cannot do such things; she is a human. It would be wise to stop speaking to me in riddles, and tell me now how we open the portal."

"Ah! But that is where you are mistaken. Did you truly believe The Key was of a purely human descent?"

Before Levi could think, he pinned the being up against the wall. He held him up off the ground, restraining him with one arm, his hand gripping the being's throat tightly. "You come into my world and show me my father is alive, then you speak absurdities about intergalactic travel and great evil powers." His grip around the creature's neck tightened. "And now you wish to make insinuations that The Key, my wife, is not fully human?" Levi's voice boomed in the cell. "Clearly, anyone who carries an interest in her is not to be trusted."

The man's eyes slowly closed, and he became invisible. Levi removed his strong grip on the being and heard him drop to the ground. He turned around and brought both hands up through his hair, gripping his head tightly. He looked over at Harrison's blank expression.

Levi turned hastily to find the being was visible again, sitting on the ground holding his throat. He gazed up at Levi with fear in his eyes.

Levi needed to step away and gather his senses so that he could have an open mind to all of this information. Recovering his father could only be achieved by involving Reece? Unacceptable.

Levi stared intently down at the man. "I will send for you when I am ready to discuss this in more detail. As of now, I must have time to contemplate everything you have made me aware of."

The being closed his eyes and nodded his head in response. "Thank you, Emperor Oxley."

Levi turned and walked out of the room without saying anything more, and Harrison walked silently at his side. "What are your thoughts?" Levi asked while they walked through the command center.

"I believe I am at a complete loss for words at the moment."

"Thankfully, I am not the only one who feels that way."

Levi stopped before exiting the command center. "I am not ready to inform my mother of my father's potential condition just yet. As desperately as I want her to know, I must have more facts and information. I will not give her hope until I am assured there is a possibility that he is indeed alive and that we can recover him."

"That is understandable."

"Search out your father and King Hamilton. I need to meet with all of you in my study immediately. Until I am ready to speak with my mother, I do not wish for anyone to know I am here. Also, when I am ready to speak with that being again, I want Queen Galleta present."

Harrison nodded. "I will retrieve my father and King Hamilton, and I will meet you in your study momentarily."

With that, Levi went directly to his office. When he walked in, he stopped and stared in astonishment at the large-scale picture that was hung over his fireplace. It was a portrait of Reece sitting on Areion in a brilliant crimson gown. He walked over to it, letting the beauty of her image settle his nerves. She was breathtaking. Her smile slowed his racing heart and made him feel almost as if she were there in the room with him. *This was your gift for me?* His heart twisted in pain, knowing she probably had planned to have him receive this gift differently. Under the present circumstances, he was not only unable to receive the gift properly, but he also had to abandon her on their honeymoon.

He studied her smile and the way her entire expression was alight with joy. As he fought with the impossibilities of knowing his father was alive and being held captive in another galaxy by means of intergalactic travel, he began to think about Reece's reaction to the realization that there was life outside of Earth. Her reality was turned upside down in an instant, and though it was a difficult transition, her open-mindedness is what brought her through it.

He smiled at her portrait. *If you can accept the unimaginable, then I must have an open mind with it as well.*

Levi walked over and poured himself a glass of wine. He sat on the sofa that was positioned to face the portrait and let Reece's image ease all of his tension despite the new situation he faced.

# Chapter 16

Harrison walked hurriedly through the corridors and found the nearest servant. "Send a rider to Insworth Castle immediately. Have them notify Queen Galleta that her counsel is required at Pasidian at once."

The servant bowed. "Yes, Your Grace."

"Also, might you inform me of King Nathaniel and King Hamilton's whereabouts?"

"Your Grace, the kings are in the east sitting room."

"Thank you," Harrison said as he swiftly brushed past the man.

Harrison, still having difficulty comprehending the last twenty-four hours, couldn't imagine what Levi was going through. The way Levi handled himself during his first interview with the stranger did not surprise Harrison at all. Even though the being was trying to be cooperative, Harrison could sense that he was with withholding more information than he was revealing. Even so, the information they were given was unfathomable. Emperor Navarre was being held captive in another galaxy, Reece was not entirely human, and she was also the only way to achieve the impossible? *Intergalactic travel,* Harrison thought with disbelief. *I can only imagine the expression on my father and Hamilton's faces when they hear about this.*

He walked into the sitting room where Angeline and Elizabeth entertained Lady Allestaine, his parents, and the Hamiltons with melodies from the piano and violin. He discreetly walked over to where his father sat, so as not to cause a scene. He bent over and whispered Levi's request into his father's ear. King Nathaniel nodded in understanding. Both King Hamilton and Nathaniel exchanged knowing glances and stood to exit the room.

King Nathaniel addressed the women in the room when their standing silenced the music from Elizabeth and Angeline. "Ladies, please excuse Hamilton and me, as there is a matter we wish to discuss with Harrison."

Harrison managed a grin when his mother looked back at him in concern. Fortunately, his father made their exit quick.

"How is Levi handling the news, son?" his father asked as they walked through the corridors.

"As well as is to be expected." Harrison stopped and faced both kings. "There is more to this being Mordegrin's story; and I tell you this because Levi is not the only one struggling to fathom such unimaginable news."

"Go on," Nathaniel said.

"Levi has summoned Queen Galleta before he speaks with this being again, as the most serious news involves Reece. The stranger has informed us that Emperor Navarre is in another galaxy, and our only way of retrieving him is for Reece to open a portal, as there is no other way of travelling into this galaxy."

King Nathaniel and Hamilton exchanged glances. "If such travel is possible, how does this stranger suppose a human is capable of accomplishing such things?" King Hamilton asked.

Harrison inhaled. "He has informed us that, unbeknownst to us, Reece is not entirely human."

"What?" both men exclaimed in unison.

"As you both can imagine, Levi is troubled by this information most of all."

"I would imagine so." Nathaniel resumed walking, prompting Harrison and King Hamilton to follow. "When will Galleta be here? We need more information from this stranger known as Mordegrin."

"She should arrive within the hour, if not sooner."

They walked into Levi's office and found him staring up at the portrait of Reece. Harrison's heart sank when he saw Levi, wondering how his cousin was coping with the information.

"*That* was definitely an interesting experience for Javian and me," Harrison said, announcing the men's entrance to the room.

Levi stood from his sofa and turned. "Experience?"

"Indeed," Harrison said, nodding toward the portrait. "She was extremely tenacious in her quest to ensure that this portrait was made, despite our warnings. We could not dissuade her, as she insisted on having this portrait made upon Areion's back." Harrison grinned. "I stand amazed that Areion allowed it."

"Quite the determined spirit you have for a wife, my boy," King Hamilton said as he poured glasses of wine for the men in the room.

Levi chuckled, and relief washed over Harrison, seeing that Levi's expression and demeanor had elevated from before. He seemed to be in a better frame of mind, and Harrison was hopeful they could decide upon a plan of action.

"She certainly has a distinctive way of charming any creature that crosses her path," Levi said as he walked toward his desk.

Harrison, Nathaniel, and Hamilton took their seats across the desk from Levi. "Could that be another reason we will soon have a zorflak living amongst us at the palace?" Harrison asked as he took a much needed sip of his wine.

Nathaniel laughed. "A zorflak? Do not tell me—"

Harrison grinned as Levi's features seemed to lighten even more now.

"Yes, Uncle, I believe I am utterly at my wife's service."

King Hamilton laughed aloud. "It has been my personal experience that if you remain humbly at your wife's service, you shall have an excellent marriage all of your days."

Harrison smiled. "My cousin's predicament is precisely why I shall remain unmarried for the rest of my life. There is no way—"

"Son, your words sound confident," Nathaniel cut his son off, "but when the time comes, a woman will enter your life without notice, and she will hold your heart hostage whether you desire it or not."

For a moment, Harrison's mind shifted toward Angeline. He grew more calloused against her each time he thought of her, as he was set in his ways and determined not to be transfixed by any woman in such a way. Harrison rolled his eyes as the men in the room laughed together.

"When the day comes, I shall commend that young woman, for she will have achieved the impossible," Hamilton said before adding, "she will have also given us all a great delight in teasing Harrison mercilessly."

The banter in the room seemed to relieve the tension weighing in the atmosphere even further. Harrison was grateful for the shift, despite his own discomfort with the topic of conversation. *If only you knew, Ham,* he thought as he raised his glass to his lips and took a large gulp of wine.

"Uncle and King Hamilton, first of all, I am grateful for your attending this meeting. I desperately desire your wise counsel in regard to the events that have unfolded."

"Yes, Harrison has told us of the new information." King Nathaniel leaned on his armrest. "So it appears that the impossible may be possible after all? I must say, it is always delightful to learn that there is more going on out there than we thought, would you not agree?"

Levi exhaled. "I suppose you are correct. I seem to lack your optimism at the present time, as it is difficult for me to unite the many facets of this overwhelming predicament."

"I understand. In this situation, I believe you should wait until Galleta uses her strong mental abilities to prove whether or not any of this is true. We should listen to what the being has to say; however, I suggest that we do not place much merit upon his words until Galleta confirms that they are truths."

Harrison leaned forward. "I cannot understand why someone from another galaxy would make it his business to help our emperor."

"If this individual speaks the truth, there is no doubt in my mind that this being shall desire something from us in return," King Hamilton added.

Levi sat back in his chair. "Of course there is something he wants from us. His world is under a curse cast by those we believed to be Lucas' priestesses in Armedias. This being says they are not priestesses at all, but dark creatures known as Olteniaus. It seems very likely that he seeks our warriors' help in destroying them and bringing peace to his land."

"We will find out what his intentions are once he has been questioned further," King Nathaniel interjected. "And of course, only if Galleta assures us Emperor Navarre is truly alive."

"Did Harrison inform you of what Mordegrin has revealed about Reece's lineage?" Levi asked.

Nathaniel sat up. "Indeed, he has. How are you handling that news?"

"If it is true, my principal concern in this matter is for Reece. I do not wish to frighten her with such unexpected news about who she may or may not be." Levi looked back at her picture. "However, if past events are any indication, she seems to adjust well to life-changing, inconceivable news." He brought his gaze back to Harrison and the two kings in front of him. "If Galleta sees this as truth in Mordegrin's mind, I must find a way to inform Reece without bringing her fear. At the current moment, it is my greatest urge to keep this from her."

"Understandable. Do you plan on making your mother aware of your father's current situation?" Nathaniel asked.

Levi's lips tightened. "That is another concern I am burdened with at this time, and another reason I need more facts. I do not know if we will be able to recover him.

Mordegrin said the only way in which we could do so is by opening a portal to that galaxy."

"Very well," King Hamilton stated. "Force this being to open the portal, and we will retrieve our emperor.

Levi rubbed his forehead. "That is the problem. According to Mordegrin, since Reece is The Key, she is the only one with the ability to open the portal. I need to find out if there are dangers, and until I can determine all of the factors involved, I remain uncertain as to whether I will give my mother the hope of rescuing him."

Harrison looked at his father's expression. He was deep in thought, staring directly at Levi.

"Levi, this is a lot for you to consider and to decide upon. Of course, we must gather more facts in order to determine what must be done, and if it can be done at all. Reece may not even be able to do what the being suggests, but we will not have any clue about that until we learn more.

"All that aside, you know the woman your mother is; she is strong and unwavering. In my humble opinion, I think it best she know that her husband is alive and there is a possibility to save him, even if it might not work. She is as brave and resolute as the rest of us, and she will understand your dilemma as well. She was a great counsel to your father in difficult times, and I know she will be of great counsel to you. She would never consider putting Reece's life in jeopardy to bring her husband home; however, she can offer wise advice to us all when given the opportunity."

Levi sighed.

Harrison cleared his throat. "Levi, he is correct. Your mother will most likely handle all of this news better than we did. She knows your father best, and you should trust her wisdom. It would be an injustice to keep such knowledge from her."

Levi's eyes bore into Harrison's as he remained deep in thought. After a long moment, he nodded. "You are both correct. I will make her aware of this once I have questioned the queen and Mordegrin."

A servant made entry into Levi's office to announce the arrival of Queen Galleta.

"Please, show her in."

The three men stood to acknowledge her properly, and when she found her seat, Levi began to question her.

"Your Eminence, my deepest apologies for any inconvenience I may have caused you. Thank you for arriving much sooner than I expected."

"It is my pleasure, Emperor Levi. Now, please tell me what has transpired to cause such an urgent request, Your Royal Majesty."

Levi cleared his throat. "Have you any knowledge that Paul Xylander was not entirely human?"

Harrison watched as Galleta's brow furrowed. "None at all. But you must understand, Emperor, I was not in contact with any on Earth before the battle that took place with the Ancient Guardians. I only understood Paul Xylander to be an incredibly intelligent and talented human."

Levi exhaled. "So this is news to you as well, then."

"If I may, what has caused you to make such a presumption?"

"A stranger has shown up unexpectedly at our gates. He brings with him peculiar information, and I am struggling to understand it. He has shown Harrison that the four priestesses we have been searching for are in another galaxy with Emperor Navarre, who is alive and presumably well."

Harrison watched as Galleta's expression changed to that of absolute shock. Never before had he seen the queen with such an expression.

She looked at Harrison. "Are you sure he was showing you truths, and not forcing suggestive thoughts or images into your mind?"

"I felt as though I were in this room with my uncle, and that if I spoke, he would answer. There was nothing created about it; this being has been in the room with the emperor."

Levi spoke, "I will have the being brought here. We wish for you to use your abilities to reach his mind and see if all he has shown us is truth." Levi continued to focus on Queen Galleta. "Until then, he has made us aware that the priestesses from Armedias were not what they appeared to be. This individual says they are also from another galaxy, the same one he is from. They have dark powers, and they are referred to as Olteniaus. They carry a great power that has given them the ability of intergalactic travel."

"This is astounding to hear. I have heard of the possibility of such travel but never knew anyone had found a way of doing so. In order to achieve this, one must possess a great power."

"So it is feasible that one could travel to other galaxies?" King Nathaniel asked.

"Your Majesty, anything is possible if you carry an ability to do so. In all my years, I have never heard of an entity capable of successfully traveling in such a manner. More than that, no object has ever been created to travel out of our galaxy, and that is why it would seem impossible to all of us to travel into other galaxies. I cannot imagine anyone surviving it."

Harrison looked quickly at Levi to find him staring intently at the queen. He said nothing.

"Queen Galleta," Harrison spoke up, "this stranger says Reece is the only one who can help us travel to his galaxy. He said she is not purely of human descent and that somehow she has the capability to open a gateway by which we could pass through to retrieve Navarre."

Queen Galleta cocked her head to the side. "Did he tell you what bloodline she is from? What other blood runs in her veins to give a human such talents?"

Levi stood. "No. I will send for the being. It seems all we are doing is talking in circles and getting nowhere. I will not sit here and try to analyze this anymore." He looked at Galleta. "Once he enters, I need you to observe his mind and find out if all of this is true."

Harrison stood. "Allow me to retrieve him."

"Very well."

Harrison walked out of Levi's office and marched to the command center. His thoughts were engrossed by this situation, and he nearly charged directly into Angeline and Elizabeth as they were walking toward him in the corridor.

He prevented himself from falling by gently gripping one of Angeline's shoulders, and by Elizabeth grabbing his belt.

"Cousin, are you okay?" Elizabeth asked.

"This would be the second time your cousin has nearly run me over in the corridors," Angeline added with a laugh.

For a moment, Harrison's senses were filled with the soft fragrance of Angeline's perfume, bringing him back to the day of their kiss once again. He straightened up, and his eyes locked onto Angeline's. He breathed deeply, trying to gather himself.

"Forgive me, ladies; it would seem that my mind is elsewhere at the moment." He looked at Elizabeth. "Angeline is correct. I believe this is the second time I have nearly injured her while racing carelessly through the palace. Forgive me if I startled you both."

"We are perfectly fine," Angeline said. "But it appears that you are quite distressed this evening."

He glanced at Angeline but did not return her friendly smile. Instead he ignored her, bringing his attention to Elizabeth as he managed a smile. "I am well, thank you," he stepped past them, "please forgive my rudeness, as there is an urgent matter I must attend to with a few of my men."

Elizabeth nodded, and Harrison did not fail to notice that his ignoring Angeline caused the captivating woman's smile to fade.

"Very well, cousin. If we do not see you this evening, I hope all remains well."

"Do not fear. It is always well, sweet one," he said reassuringly before hastily continuing on his path.

Once Harrison had Mordegrin restrained in cuffs, he led Mordegrin through the private corridors of the palace. He had two Guardians ahead of them, making sure that no one would encounter them. After his surprising run-in with the women, he opted to use the servants' passageways for his return to Levi's office.

"It would be wise not to test the emperor's patience this time," Harrison advised Mordegrin before they entered Levi's office through a side door.

Once within, Harrison directed Mordegrin to an empty chair in front of Levi's desk. "Mordegrin, allow me to make myself perfectly clear before I question you and your motives for being here. When I ask you a question, I expect to receive thorough and concise answers in response," Levi said.

"Emperor Oxley, I will humbly respect your wishes. I will answer you as best as I know how. You must understand that I am using different languages and word meanings to communicate with you, so it is difficult at times," Mordegrin responded.

Harrison watched Levi's eyes narrow as he studied the stranger. The kings remained in their seats, and the queen was now positioned behind Levi as Levi began to question him.

"First of all, I do not trust you, nor do I believe any of your words." He glanced back at Queen Galleta and nodded. "Queen Galleta will know if what you speak is truth or deceit. I warn you that if all you have relayed to us are lies, you will promptly be escorted out of Pemdas. Are you confident that you wish to stand by your word and vow that everything you have spoken to us already is in truth?"

"I vow that the information I have given you, and will give you, is all in truth."

"Very well, then. Tell me, why have you come here to deliver this news to us? What do we have that you need?" Levi asked.

"Emperor, your people are fearless and fierce warriors. I have come here because after I sought counsel with Emperor Navarre, he told me about the powerful Guardian warriors and their many battles."

"My father would never freely discuss such things with strangers."

"But he did, or I would have never attempted to seek out you and your people."

"Tell me, then, why he did speak with you?"

"You see, once I told him why he was captured and brought into our galaxy, he became interested in what our world was like before he was brought there. Our world was once as your planet Earth, with many dimensions and human-like beings inhabiting it. Our planet had dimensional travel as well, but then a dark power invaded and managed to imprison all of the inhabitants and beings from all dimensions. All dimensions were destroyed, and our world—" The being stopped and looked down.

Harrison looked over at Levi, who listened to Mordegrin unflinchingly. "Your world? Go on, what became of it?" Levi asked.

The figure looked up at Levi. "Our world became cursed with doom and filled with many different beings, beings who were imprisoned and brought there to live. The wicked Olteniaus use these individuals to harvest their energy in order to gain so much power that no being in our world could overcome it. We are enslaved in a desolate land, and we are at their mercy."

"Tell me why I should trust this is not a trap for me and my men," Levi returned. "How am I to know that these dark creatures aren't using you to deceive us and destroy our galaxy and world?"

Unexpectedly, Mordegrin softly laughed. "Forgive me," he said as he smiled sympathetically at Levi, "your father told me that if you were to question my motives, that I should tell you the name of your first Guardian horse and the reason you named him. Should that not prove that I have spoken with your father, and that he trusts my motives in seeking your help?"

Levi strummed his fingers on his desk. "I am expected to believe that my father gave you details about my first stallion as a means for conveying his trust in you?"

Mordegrin smiled. "The name of your first Guardian stallion was Bucephalus. He was named after a ruler's horse on Earth—Alexander the Great. That man appealed to you in many ways by how he was a bold and fearless warrior. Your first horse resembled his in temperament so much so that you believed that would be the perfect name for him."

Levi remained expressionless and nodded. "That is true, and it is something known only to me and my father," he answered. "It would seem as though you have had detailed conversation with him, which sets my mind slightly more at ease." Levi leaned forward. "I need to know everything you know about why my father was brought into your galaxy and imprisoned there."

"The Olteniaus have not only sought out to imprison and control everything in our galaxy and the dimensions existing within it, but they are seeking out other galaxies as well. Their next plan is to do the same with this galaxy and Earth. They captured your father in the belief that he was you."

"If these beings are so great with their powers, how could they mistake me for my father? And why would they need me in order to achieve any of this to begin with?"

"Because the Olteniaus female who you enslaved in your kingdom communicated telepathically with the rest that you had unlocked the map to the stone," Mordegrin answered. "They want the stone's powers."

Levi's eyes closed as he exhaled.

"They know that I have knowledge as to where the stone is located?" Levi asked. "This is unbelievable."

"It remains an undisclosed subject in our world, and will remain that way," King Nathaniel interjected as he gazed knowingly into Mordegrin's eyes.

Mordegrin nodded. "That is understandable. I confidently vow that I have no means to tell any being that the emperor knows the location to the stone. To be the one who carries such a valuable piece of information must—"

"Moving on," Levi interrupted Mordegrin. "You mentioned earlier that intergalactic travel is only possible for us by opening a portal. Before I inquire how this is to be accomplished, I would like to know why you and the Olteniaus are able to do it without a portal. Are there others who have achieved this?"

"Only the Olteniaus. They are entities with superior and overwhelming dark powers. I, too, am an Olteniaus, and the last of our kind." Mordegrin cleared his throat as he glanced at everyone in the room. He finished by locking gazes with Levi's questioning expression. "I do not possess dark powers, this I assure all of you."

Levi brought a tightened fist to his chin, "Very well. But if you are an Olteniaus, then why have you not used your powers to stop them?"

"I am no match for the dark powers they possess. It would kill me if I attempted to overpower them."

"But you have the same power of intergalactic travel, how do you manage that?" Levi questioned.

"We are able to travel to other galaxies with minimal power. We enable ourselves to sleep deeply in our world and transport the image of ourselves into whichever galaxy we wish to be in."

Levi shifted in his seat. "Then how is it we are speaking to you now?" He leaned forward across his desk. "How was I able to nearly crush your throat earlier? I felt your flesh with my own hands."

"You did. But it is not the flesh you believe it to be. This form which you see, which you have touched with your own hands, was created with my power. It is fashioned from the particles of your world and changed into molecules, and therein I am able to speak and exist in your world while remaining in mine."

"That is absurd!" Harrison blurted out.

Mordegrin smiled. "You may call it whatever you wish, but it is a fact. That is why you believed that Armedias had priestesses and you continued to search for their whereabouts until I informed you that they are no longer here."

"I destroyed the one we held captive. Are you telling me she never died? That she is alive in your galaxy?" Levi asked.

"She is in our galaxy, but she is unable to awaken due to her death while in this galaxy. It was so swift that she did not have a chance to remove her energy from the form she occupied while imprisoned."

Harrison looked at Queen Galleta, as she seemed transfixed on Mordegrin. His father and King Hamilton both wore the same bemused expressions while they remained silent. Levi was quite the opposite, and his expression grew dark.

Levi continued to stare. "How many of your kind are there? How were you not able to form your entity inside of Pemdas, but instead remained at our gates beyond our protective barriers?"

"Pemdas is a very puzzling dimension, and my energy cannot penetrate the protection that surrounds it. I tried, but my energy was deflected and drained by the void. It is astounding; did someone create it for you? How are your horses capable of transporting our created beings into your dimension when we cannot transport ourselves?"

Levi grinned, and Mordegrin was silenced. "Do you believe I am foolish enough to give you those answers? I am the one asking the questions. Now tell me, how many of your kind are out there?"

"The entities you know as the priestesses and I are the only ones left of our kind. There *is* one other who carries our gene; however, it is muted down with human blood in—"

"My wife," Levi returned gravely.

"Why, yes. Her ancestor was the child of an Olteniaus female and human male."

Levi's eyes closed, and he deeply inhaled. Harrison knew that the questions swirling around in his head were most likely nothing compared to the questions in Levi's.

Levi looked back at Queen Galleta. "I am curious as to your response to this. Does this being speak truth about Reece?"

Queen Galleta nodded. "There is nothing deceitful in his words."

Levi nodded acknowledgement. "You knew Paul Xylander. Had you any clue as to who his parents were?" he asked the queen.

She looked at Mordegrin as she spoke. "Paul never knew his parents, Emperor Levi. I believe now we may have the answer as to why."

Mordegrin nodded. "The Olteniaus female's form was unable to survive the birth of a human child. When the human male lost this woman, he took his own life shortly thereafter."

"What were the reasons for such a relationship? Why would an Olteniaus female desire such things when her true form was not on Earth to begin with?"

"The Olteniaus never believed such a thing could happen. But once it did, it was too late. The child grew swiftly in her womb and drained her energy, thereby evaporating her form on Earth and her life on our world."

Levi tapped his fingers on his desk; the expression on his face was unreadable. King Nathaniel addressed Mordegrin, "So this is why you say the emperor's wife has the ability to open a portal, because she has Olteniaus genes within her?"

"Paul Xylander created a powerful stone, did he not?" Mordegrin asked in an unnerving tone as he stared strangely at Galleta.

"He did," Levi said, bringing Mordegrin's attention back to him. "What does that have to do with the question I have asked you?"

Mordegrin grinned. "Emperor, that stone is the only way that the descendant of Paul Xylander can unlock the hidden talents buried deep within her mind and create the portal."

Harrison watched Levi's jaw muscles twitch as he clenched his hand into a fist. "How does the stone have the power to do such a thing? How would you know what it can do?" Levi asked.

"Paul Xylander created that stone with purpose. I know of it because I followed the child as he grew. I watched how Earth came under the threat of being altered, and how it almost saw the same fate as my world. I saw how he used the power he gained from his mother while in her womb to create that stone from the particles of Earth. He gave that stone his powers, and that is why Earth remains protected to this day. I lost track of Paul and the stone soon after he used it to destroy Atlantis."

"If Paul could use his Olteniaus powers to create a stone that can open portals to another galaxy, why can you not do the same?" Levi asked.

Mordegrin cleared his throat. "Because I am not in my true form on Earth, I have no power to use to create such an object."

Unexpectedly, Levi leaned forward with a lethal expression. "Fine. Tell me why my wife is the only one who can do this? Why can I not use the stone to open the portal?"

"She is the only one the stone will respond to. It was designed to answer only to the ancestral line of Paul Xylander. However, she must begin the process of unlocking her Olteniaus powers first."

Levi abruptly stood. "Enough!" He placed both hands firmly on his desk and leaned forward, staring severely at Mordegrin. "My wife will not be required to start the process of anything! My wife will NOT be the one to open the portal," he spoke deeply. "If the stone is what is required to open a portal, we will find a way to do so, but I will not require my wife to change the person she is and has always been!" He looked over at Harrison. "Remove him from the palace. I want him imprisoned at the holding unit at Casititor. I do not want this being and his bizarre powers anywhere near Reece when she returns." He looked back at Mordegrin. "Although you state you come in peace, the last time we had one of your kind brought into our world, my wife suffered greatly. I will not allow any being of your kind to be around her."

*We are definitely not going through THAT again,* Harrison thought. He didn't fully trust that Mordegrin wouldn't try to get into Reece's head like the Olteniaus female they had imprisoned did.

As Harrison stood, Levi spoke out, "There are still many questions I have for you, but for now I have heard enough." Levi crossed his arms and gazed darkly at Mordegrin. "In the time before we meet again, you *will* find a solution for me and my men to open that portal. My wife is not the answer."

"Sir, there is no possible way—"

Levi grinned without mirth. "I have been saying that to myself with every word you have spoken to me since I first met with you. You will find a way. If I were you, I would start by using the great powers that you so boldly made us aware of."

Harrison gripped Mordegrin's arm and firmly jerked him to his feet.

Levi gazed somberly at him. "Get this creature out of my palace."

Harrison turned, leading Mordegrin out of Levi's office and once again through the servant's corridors. He remained silent as he walked Mordegrin down to the command center.

Once the Guardians positioned a holding carriage for Mordegrin to be escorted in, the men were off and journeying to the prison unit of Casititor. During the ride, Harrison didn't question Levi's concern for having this being near the palace. After everything they had been through since bringing Reece into Pemdas, no one could be trusted. Once Mordegrin was handed over to the guards who would stand watch at his cell, Harrison gave the final orders and left the prison. He dismissed himself from the two Guardians who were with him and instructed them to inform Levi that he would be in late, as he felt the need to check on the person who was responsible for the other beings learning about who The Key really was. That was Simone.

Thoughts of Angeline crept into his consciousness, but he immediately dismissed them. *Why would I think of that woman at a time like this?* he thought uncertainly. Harrison could not bear the thought of having anything distract him in such a way. He could already sense these emotions weakening him, and he refused to allow them to continue. His irritation with the beautiful Angeline was now turning into animosity for her. He no longer cared whether they carried a friendship past what had happened that day in the meadow or not; they were never close before. She was Elizabeth's friend, and that was exactly who she would remain.

After traveling for a great while to the rock island where Pemdas' evilest of prisoners were held, they finally reached their destination. Harrison leapt out of the wooden boat and onto the wet stone surface of the damp dock. The place exuded depression, darkness, and abandonment, and even a man like Harrison felt desolate as he marched up the jagged rock steps to where the prison units were. Without the natural power source that fueled Pemdas, only auburn candles with dripping wax lit the dark pathways he walked through. He met with the lead guard who guided him down toward the cell where Simone was being held captive. Harrison was tall for the average Pemdai, but this man towered over him. Totally withdrawn from society in Pemdas, the guards who protected these units were beastlike men, and in Harrison's opinion they were born for this duty.

Wailing and moaning filled the halls and grew louder as the prisoners heard the rattling of the guard's key.

"In here," the man said gruffly.

The door to Simone's chamber opened, and Harrison held a lantern into the room to search out her location. He spotted her in a corner, legs curled up and rocking back and forth. She was muttering hateful words that Harrison could barely make out. Harrison walked toward her, finally catching her attention.

"Get out of my home," she snarled.

Harrison studied her worn face. Her eyes were sunken with dark circles, and her usual shiny, pitch black hair was now matted and almost entirely gray. She looked like the beast that resided within her.

"My, my, Simone," Harrison said in a low voice, "it seems as though your appearance has come to match your personality."

"Why are you here?" she spat out. "To mock me? Did you bring your little pet, Reece Bryant, along so she can finally see what she has done to me?"

Harrison held up the lantern and studied the small stone room they were in. It was damp, with no blankets, no bed, and no place for light to peek through. "Might you be referring to the new Empress of Pemdas, Reece Oxley?"

"Vile," she spat out. "This entire realm is vile. The only decent place is this island, and I am proud to take residence here. Now, allow her in so that she may look upon me in this state."

Harrison chuckled. "Do you really think the Empress of Pemdas would be allowed anywhere near this forsaken island?"

"Still playing the damsel in distress, is she? Enjoying everyone pampering and protecting her?"

"Quite the opposite, actually. She is well and adapts to her new position in this world with confidence." He grinned sardonically at her. "There are none who disapprove of her as their empress."

"Why are you here?" Simone growled wickedly.

"Perhaps my morbid curiosity has finally gotten the better of me. You know, I would have chosen death for you. It was obvious that was Levi's desire as well." He tilted his head to the side. "Unfortunately for you, Reece made the choice. I suppose she knew that there are some fates far worse than death. Seeing you suffering in this manner after all you have done to our world has led me to believe that she made a wise decision. Death would have been too kind for such a malevolent woman."

Simone laughed wildly. "I beg for death every day! They keep me nourished enough to survive this torment."

Harrison nodded. "Then all is as it should be." Harrison turned to leave. "Before I leave, I do have one question; do you ever regret the day that you let your hatred consume you, or that it led to the death of many brave warriors, including your own father?"

Simone's lips pulled up into an evil rictus. "No," was all she said before laughing maniacally.

Harrison left her chambers, unable to understand how such hatred could be borne by anyone. Because of everything she had done, they had now to face the impossible. Her callousness toward everything, even the death of her own father, proved to Harrison that Simone was receiving the proper punishment for the darkness that dwelled within her.

# Chapter 17

As the carriage ascended the mountainside toward the palace, Reece looked out the window in anticipation of seeing Levi again. She was concerned about how he was coping with the unexpected news about his father. It broke her heart to watch him nearly collapse in front of her and Harrison when he heard the news. She wished she could have been more of a support for him, but after Levi decided to ride back with Harrison, there was no time to have a private conversation. She knew the best support she could offer was to send him away to get the answers he needed.

They traveled over the bridge that brought them into the courtyard of the palace, and her heart reacted to the sight of the tall, handsome man standing nobly on the palace steps. He stood properly in his ivory and black striped waist coat, crisp white shirt, and black trousers. His handsome face appeared worn with exhaustion and stress, but once the carriage stopped and he walked down the steps, his easy smile erased all evidence of anguish in his expression.

The door opened, and his hand was immediately there to receive hers. She stepped out, and he brought her into a tight embrace. "It is such a pleasure to see you and have you safe in my arms again. I have so desperately missed you," he said.

She wrapped her arms tightly around him and peered up into his sapphire blue eyes. "I've missed you just as much."

As Jasmeen was preparing to step out of the carriage, Levi extended his hand to help her. "Jasmeen, I am indebted to you for keeping Reece comfortable in my absence."

"Emperor Levi, it is my pleasure and honor," she said, and then turned toward Reece. "Would you like me to care for Mozart this evening?"

Levi shook his head and reached for the zorflak asleep in Jasmeen's arms. "We shall take him." He smiled as he softly laughed.

"Very well, then. I will see you before dinner, Reece." Jasmeen curtseyed before she turned and walked up into the palace.

Reece smiled as Levi looked over at her. "Mozart? That is an interesting name you have come up with."

Reece studied Levi's eyes, and although they were lit with amusement, she saw beyond that and could see the stress Levi was burdened with. She refrained from asking any questions about Navarre at this time. She knew she would get the full story soon enough, and she decided to keep this moment, however brief, as lighthearted as possible.

"Yes, I named him Mozart," she answered him with a smile, "because his humming reminds me of an orchestra. He's such a funny little guy; he has different humming sounds that tell me his needs and emotions. If he's hungry, his hum sounds like a violin. When he's happy, it sounds like a flute. The funniest one is when he's sad and he hums like a cello. So I just started calling him my little Mozart. He's quite the musician!" she laughed.

Levi brought his hand to Reece's cheek. "It is refreshing to have you with me again, my love. You have no idea how much I have longed to have you in my presence."

Mozart's ears opened, uncovering his eyes, and his little arms stretched while his illuminating wings fluttered. He looked up at Levi and stared.

Levi grinned. "Welcome to your new home, Mozart," he said. "I believe you will enjoy meeting the rest of your new family, but for now," he held his arm out to Reece while gazing adoringly at her, "I have something to show my charming wife."

Reece took his arm, and he led them down toward the stable yard. As they walked through the well-lit stalls, Reece looked up at Levi. "Don't tell me!" Reece exclaimed with excitement.

"Yes. Our mare has foaled, just this morning," he said while turning down another long row within the large building.

Reece clenched his arm. "What did she have? A boy? A girl?"

Levi chuckled. "You shall see."

He walked toward the large open area, and inside were two baby colts suckling on their mother.

"Twins?" She stared up at Levi in disbelief.

He nodded, and Mozart started humming a flute melody. "Go have a look at them," Levi said with a brilliant smile. "I believe you will need to find more names now."

Reece laughed as she walked through the gate and up to the mare. "Hello there, momma! Look at what you made." The mare nudged her, and the two young colts both brought their attention to Reece. As she held out her hand, the colts came over to her and rubbed their noses along it.

"Astonishing," Levi said from the other side of stable.

"What is it that has you so astonished?" Reece laughed while the two baby colts returned to feed from the mare.

Levi nodded toward the foals. "The fact that two baby Guardian colts stopped eating in order to make your acquaintance, and that they actually showed any interest in you at all. It reminds me of the morning I encountered Arrow taking an interest in you when he should have had no desire to approach you naturally."

Levi brought his attention back to Reece, and his piercing blue eyes studied her closely. Reece was somewhat puzzled by the way he was watching her. It was obvious there was more to this encounter than he was telling her. It was almost as if he knew something about how this could happen and why it amazed him so greatly.

"Levi?" she questioned seriously.

His entire demeanor changed, and he smiled warmly at her. "You are quite amazing, that is all. Now, you must decide upon a male and a female name. Do you have any ideas?"

"I'll come up with something," she said. "I'm sure whatever I figure out, you will probably laugh at them, like you did with Mozart."

Reece gasped as her surroundings abruptly changed and she found she was still in the carriage on her journey back to the palace.

"Is everything okay, Reece?" Jasmeen asked as she glanced out of the carriage window in the direction Reece had been staring.

*Must have been another vision,* she thought, trying to maintain a normal expression. She reached for Mozart, sitting in Jasmeen's lap. "Just daydreaming, I guess," she managed.

"You have been staring out into the countryside for quite some time," Jasmeen worried with a nervous laugh. "I am sure you are anxious to be back at the palace."

"True." Reece ran her fingers through Mozart's soft fur. "Any idea as to how much longer this trip is going to take?"

"We are only moments away."

No sooner than Jasmeen had mentioned it, the palace came into view. As the carriage traveled over the bridge that led them into the palace's courtyard, Reece glanced out the window to find Levi standing nobly at the top of the steps waiting for them.

Reece blinked her eyes, more than once. *This is exactly like the vision I just had!* she thought as she took in the image of Levi standing there in his ivory and black striped waist coat, crisp white shirt, and trousers. Once the carriage came to a stop and the door opened, she went through every motion in disbelief, not once changing a thing about her responses to Levi as he brought her into the same tight embrace he had done in her vision, while saying every word to her exactly the same.

She watched in astonishment as everything played out in the same fashion as her vision. Levi took Mozart from Jasmeen and laughed at the name she came up with for him. Reece wanted to tell Levi what was happening, but she decided to see how long this bizarre déjà vu would last. Levi led her down to the stables to see the twin colts. As eerie as it was, she continued to play along.

Reece didn't know what to think. It was not just déjà vu; everything happened exactly as it had in her vision, down to the last word. She walked out of the large corral that held the mare and two baby colts, took Levi's arm, and answered him after he told her she had to come up with their names.

"I'll come up with something," she said, "I'm sure whatever I figure out, you will probably laugh at them, like you did with Mozart."

Levi chuckled. "My love, you must know that I delight in the names you decide upon. Do you realize the moment you told me of Arrow's name, I wanted to take you in my arms right then and there? That was when I knew you must have feelings for me, and it gave me the courage to profess my own to you."

She laughed as she took her husband's offered arm. "Is that so? I remember you having difficulty trying to get the words out."

Levi leaned into her, giving a quick kiss to the top of her head. "You are correct about that. I believe the fear of your rejection was overwhelming at that moment. However, your expressions had their own way of confusing my thoughts and words at that time as well."

Reece gripped his arm. "I love you so much." She stopped and looked up at him before they entered into the palace. "How are you doing? I've been very worried about you since you left with Harrison yesterday. We didn't have much time to talk about this news, and I can't imagine what you must be thinking right now."

Levi gently removed Reece's hand from the crook of his arm and turned to face her. Mozart leaned out toward Reece, prompting her to retrieve him from Levi. Once she cradled him in her arms, the zorflak softly hummed in repose.

Levi gazed at Reece and Mozart with a pleasant smile. "I am dealing with all of this to the best of my ability." He looked at Reece in consternation. "I had Queen Galleta probe into this being's mind, and she has confirmed that my father is indeed alive—" He stopped, exhaled, and looked past Reece.

"What is it, Levi? Did he tell you where your father is?"

He looked back at Reece and cocked his head to the side. "You may never believe this, as I continue with my struggle to understand it all for myself."

Reece brought her hand up to his cheek and arched her eyebrow at him. "After everything I've learned and witnessed since coming to Pemdas, I'm sure I can believe anything at this point."

"I have learned that my father is not in any of Earth's dimensions. Apparently, he has been transported into another galaxy." His smile died as he intently studied her expression.

Reece laughed out loud, and Levi stared at her as if she'd lost her mind. "Now we have *more* life out there? Your father is in another galaxy?

"You have no trouble believing this is possible?" Levi questioned.

"Why should I? It wasn't too long ago that you and Harrison abruptly made me aware that aliens really existed and that there were other worlds and dimensions outside of Earth. So why should I have trouble believing that there are other galaxies with life existing in them also?"

Levi released the breath he had been holding and smiled at Reece. He bent to kiss her and rose back up. "It is not only that there are galaxies beyond ours that exist, but there has never been a being that has successfully traveled through different galaxies."

Reece smiled. "This may be surprising to you, but until I watched that car almost crash into that mountain the day you brought me into Pemdas, I would have never believed that anyone or anything could travel through dimensions." She looked up at him, astonished that news like this would surprise him. "After everything you have showed me, I'm surprised this news comes as a shock to you."

Levi ran his thumb along her jawline. "Until this being appeared, no one dreamed such travel was viable."

"So this isn't something you believed could ever be accomplished?" Reece wondered in confusion.

"Never," he answered with a laugh. "This means of travel has never been attempted, nor does it exist. Reece, when my father was taken into this other galaxy, it was accomplished in a most unimaginable way." He looked past her again. "But the being who delivered this news to us has done it." He gazed back at Reece. "He has been with my father and had conversations with him."

"That is what has me confused." Reece shook her head. "I am trying to wrap my mind around the fact that your father is alive. We saw him dead. We attended his funeral."

"I know. But the fact remains that my father is very much alive. Queen Galleta has volunteered to speak with this stranger tomorrow, as I have very little patience with him and his bizarre way of communicating with me. She will gain more information from him for us all."

Reece nodded. "Do your mother and sister know yet?"

Levi cleared his throat. "I have told my mother, yes."

"How is she coping? I can't even imagine."

"I have always believed my mother to be an admirably strong woman." He exhaled and shook his head. "She wept in utter disbelief and has been restored with hope knowing that her husband lives. Truth be told, I think she is handling this better than I, as she was the one to console me in the end."

Reece smiled. "I don't know what to say. Her strength of will is an inspiration, to say the least. I am very relieved that she has taken the news well. So have you and the men decided when you will go and rescue your father?"

Levi shook his head. "No. Entering this galaxy is not as simple as you would imagine. We are working on a plan, but as of now we have no way of entering the galaxy."

Something wasn't right about the way Levi was informing her about all of this, and she could sense it. "If this man can do it, then why can't the Guardians?"

Levi's eyes grew dark as they bore through hers. His somber gaze sent a shiver coursing through her.

"What is it?" she asked softly.

Anguish came over Levi's face, and he glanced away from her.

"Levi," she reached for his face, bringing his attention back to her, "what aren't you telling me?"

He caressed her cheek with his hand. "Come, it has been a long journey home for you, and you should freshen up some." He reached over to Mozart, who remained surprisingly quiet during their discussion. Levi scratched Mozart's head. "I am confident that Lizzy and Angie would be delighted to meet Mozart."

Reece narrowed her eyes at him. "Don't avoid my question. There is more to all of this, isn't there?"

Levi ran his hands through his hair. "Yes."

"Then tell me, Levi. I'm your wife."

Levi shook his head. "Please allow me more time. I must have more information."

Reece sighed. "Does it bother you that much to tell me?"

Levi's expression was grave. "It bothers me greatly not to. Please understand that I have no intention of keeping anything from you; however, in this situation, I feel as though I must for now. I beg of you to forgive me, and most of all to trust me."

"Whatever you are the most comfortable with." Reece was confused, but the pleading expression on his face helped her concede to his request. "You mentioned Lizzy and her friend would want to meet Mozart?" She smiled.

Relief was apparent in Levi's features when he returned Reece's smile. "They would be absolutely delighted to hold a zorflak in their arms."

He offered his arm. "Allow me to escort you and Mozart to them."

As Reece took his arm, she thought back to the vision she had that came to pass. With Levi being so overwhelmed by current events, she thought it best to wait until he was more relaxed before she would tell him that she thought these visions were actually premonitions. She needed to know why they were happening to her, but for now she would wait until a more opportune time.

That evening after dining, Reece and Levi strolled together in the palace gardens. The dinner guests had retired to the sitting room, but Levi and Reece opted for a few peaceful moments alone before rejoining the group.

"Your mother really does seem to be handling everything very well," Reece said as they wandered past the glowing foliage.

"Indeed, and surprisingly enough, Elizabeth is also. Even though she worries over my father's current condition, I see she is finding great support in my mother's and her friend Angeline's confidence." He paused and brought her into a loving embrace, tenderly kissing the top of her head. "Lady Allestaine will also cope better having you around the palace again."

Reece rested her head against his sturdy chest, absorbing his rich fragrance. "All of this has to be so much for you to deal with. I want you to know I will be there for you in any way I can."

She could easily discern that what was bothering him earlier was still on his mind. The way he was treating her led her to believe it all had something to do with her. Every time he even glanced at her, his eyes had shown nothing but sympathy and concern for her. His gaze seemed somewhat possessive, yet protective.

"I know you will, and you have no idea how much you have already been there for me." He withdrew from her and used his index finger to bring her eyes up to meet his. "Oh, I almost forgot to tell you about the most lovely, breathtaking portrait of an exquisite woman hanging above the fireplace in my office."

Reece grinned. "Really?" She arched her eyebrow at him. "Well, I'm not sure if I approve of this picture," she teased. "Please enlighten me, what does this lovely woman look like? Should I be worried?"

"She is the most fascinating woman I have ever laid eyes upon." Levi softly chuckled. Then he became serious as his eyes locked onto Reece's. "Her brilliant blue eyes pierce my soul, soothing every nerve in my body." His thumb traced along her bottom lip. "Her smile eases my spirit in a way I could never explain." He ran his hand up her arm. "Her flawless body will forever take my breath away." He brought his lips to her forehead while bringing her into a tight embrace. "I will always be grateful for that portrait of your exquisite beauty."

Levi stepped back and studied Reece's face, forcing Reece's heart to beat faster. She reached up, placed both hands on his cheeks, and brought his lips down onto hers. After a few small kisses, she withdrew from his embrace.

Levi's eyes opened, and he displayed her favorite grin. "I'm glad you liked the gift," she said.

"You will never know how much that portrait means to me. I walked into my office the night I returned, so upset by the news I had been given, and I was feeling utterly lost. As I stared up at the portrait of you, all of my anger and tension faded. I felt as though you were with me." He smiled. "It probably sounds strange to hear, but I do want you to know I will treasure it always, and I am thankful beyond words for it."

"You are very welcome. Elizabeth did a wonderful job with the detail; I think she might have enhanced it in a few areas." She laughed.

"There were no enhancements necessary, beloved. Even as I gaze into your eyes at this moment, I am soothed by them." His demeanor became concerned again. "Reece Oxley, I want you to know I will forever love and protect you with my own life."

*Why is he talking like this?* Before she could answer him, he offered his arm. "Let us go back into the house. I am sure Mozart is missing you by now."

Reece chuckled. "Oh, he seemed pretty taken with Angeline and Lizzy earlier. I have probably lost my little pet already."

"Well, I did extend the invitation for Lizzy to care for him for the night."

"Did she accept?"

"Before I could even get the words out of my mouth."

"Then let's try to make this visit short. I've missed you for too long already," she said with a sultry look in her eye.

Levi's eyebrows shot up. "We can bypass spending time with Lizzy and Angeline, if that is the case."

Reece laughed. "As enticing as that sounds, we would be teased mercilessly for our little disappearing act if we did."

Levi offered his arm. "Very true. Let us grace them with a few moments of our time."

As they walked into the sitting room, Reece laughed aloud. Angeline was playing her violin while Mozart hummed along, harmonizing as he sat in Elizabeth's lap. All eyes in the room were on them, and it seemed everyone was humored by the zorflak's performance.

Levi and Reece sat on the sofa near the fireplace, and it was not long before Elizabeth and Angeline walked over to join them in conversation. As soon as they approached the sofa adjacent to Levi and Reece, Mozart's wings began to flutter and he reached for Reece. Elizabeth laughed and handed him over to her.

"Reece, I can hardly believe that we really have a zorflak as a pet. Mozart is so delightful," Elizabeth said while sitting on the couch next to Angeline.

"He's the funniest little critter, I will tell you that," Reece said while Mozart curled up into a ball, ears covering his eyes, as he positioned himself to peacefully sleep in her lap. Reece smiled at Elizabeth and Angeline. "How did the celebration go after Levi and I left the palace? It seems like all the visitors have finally left."

Angeline laughed. "I must say, I am grateful they are gone." She looked at Levi. "King Maxen's grandson's joined him for the celebration."

Levi immediately looked to Elizabeth. "Did Luke give you any trouble?"

Elizabeth smiled. "Harrison did an excellent job of keeping him and the rest of the young men at a safe distance from us."

Levi laughed. "He of all people would know what those young men were up to at such an event. I am glad he was attentive to that in my absence."

Reece looked at Levi in confusion. "Where is Harrison anyway? Why wasn't he at dinner tonight?"

Levi brought his arm up around Reece and reclined back into the couch some. "He and a group of men traveled to Casititor tonight. I demanded he leave the palace for a while and unwind his nerves. He has not stopped since he learned of my father."

Reece laughed. "I have to admit, I've never seen him so distressed as the day he arrived at the caverns."

"He left for our destination as soon as it was confirmed my father was alive." Levi shook his head and looked back at Reece. "He had ridden the entire night through, without any rest. Apparently, he was only at the caverns for a few moments before you and I returned to find him there. As you know, it was an hour later that he and I rode back to the palace. The poor man has not rested for at least two days now."

"It does make sense now why he nearly ran right into Angeline the other night," Elizabeth sympathized.

Angeline chuckled. "It was strange; as he walked toward us, he was looking directly at both of us. We smiled at him, but his expression never changed. The next thing I knew, Harrison nearly collided with me."

As they all laughed, they were interrupted as Harrison walked into the room. Levi sat up as Harrison walked over to where they sat. "Harrison? What brings you back to the palace so quickly? I was sure you would remain out the entire night."

Reece's eyes widened when she noticed Harrison look directly at Angeline with an interesting expression on his face. Reece's eyes remained on Angeline's reaction to the subtle glance. Angeline's cheeks colored lightly, and strangely, Reece could feel the beautiful woman's excitement that he had walked into the room. Reece looked around to see if anyone else noticed what she had. Somehow, she was the only one who seemed to be aware that these two must have feelings for each other. *If I'm not having premonitions, I'm getting weird vibes from everyone. What is going on with me?* Reece thought in confusion.

Harrison took a seat next to Reece and sank into the couch. "I believe I have had enough entertainment for one day. Besides, it would have been rude of me not to welcome the lovely Mrs. Oxley back home."

Reece laughed, but it was Levi who spoke up. "When have you ever grown tired of being entertained? Especially when you are out with the men, and no doubt amongst all of the women who so enjoy your company?"

Reece watched as Levi gave Harrison a knowing grin.

Harrison took a sip of wine. "My good cousin, I was having an excellent time, and then Suzanna Sterlington decided to join in the festivities."

Reece laughed when she remembered the story about the woman's bizarre obsession with Harrison.

"But that is not the pressing issue here." He looked over at the zorflak. "Tell me, Reece, are we going to have two young colts roaming the palace as well?"

Reece laughed. "Why would you say that?"

Harrison reached over to pet Mozart. "Well, your husband has already admitted the reason we now have a zorflak with us is because he is helpless against any of his wife's wishes."

"You give Levi such a hard time, dear cousin; however, your time will come soon enough. Some woman will come along, and you will be just as eager to appease her wishes of you," Elizabeth teased.

"I look forward to *that* day, more than any of you will ever know," Levi added in humor.

Reece watched as Harrison didn't seem to find the comment as funny. Instead, he glanced at Angeline intently before looking at Levi, and then his smile returned. "Keep looking forward to it, my friend. I do not ever anticipate that day's arrival."

Reece remained quiet, discreetly studying Angeline and Harrison's glances for each other.

She was surprised when Angeline laughed in disbelief at Harrison's comment. She gave him a challenging grin. "And so you plan to live the rest of your life as a single man, all due to your fear of women?"

The group laughed, but Harrison was noticeably not amused. In Reece's opinion, it was not like him. He gazed intensely at Angeline.

"I never said I was frightened of women; I simply choose not to fall victim to their many charms," Harrison answered.

While everyone laughed, Reece felt the tension building between Harrison and Angeline. Angeline's lips tightened, but she quickly recovered and returned Harrison's smug grin directed solely at her. *No*, Reece thought, *Harrison and Angeline?* She wanted to laugh aloud but refrained.

Levi sighed. "I believe it is best we change the subject. Harrison's arrogant opinions regarding love and women will eventually drive us all insane."

Harrison laughed and seemed to revert back to his good-humored self again. "A brilliant idea."

As they had planned, Reece and Levi kept their visit in the sitting room short. Levi properly excused them from their company, and when they arrived at their new living area, Reece sought to question the odd exchange she noticed between Harrison and Angeline. "Did you notice how Harrison and Angeline acted toward each other tonight?"

Levi's brow furrowed. "Nothing more than simple friends, as they always have been."

Reece stopped Levi before entering their private rooms. "No, there was a *lot* more than friendship in their exchange."

Levi laughed. "Not this again. First it is Jasmeen and Henry, now Harrison and Angeline?"

Her lips twisted. "You really didn't notice how he was treating her? How she reacted when he walked into the room?"

"First of all, my eyes were not on Angeline as my cousin entered the room; they were on my lovely wife. Not to mention that I am having great difficulty with this conversation, given that I would rather be indulging myself further in your beauty."

Any thoughts of Angeline and Harrison immediately faded as the expression Levi now held for her had her aching to be in his arms again.

Levi laughed, and then gathered her into his embrace. "Now, Mrs. Oxley, allow me to welcome you to your new home in the palace."

They walked in, and Reece was in awe of the room. It was nearly the size of the large estate Levi had purchased for them. A grand staircase was the first thing to greet them, with furniture and other rooms surrounding the foyer they were in.

"This room seems to be the same size as the house you bought us," Reece said as they reached the third floor.

Levi chuckled as they walked down the hall, "My love, our living quarters in the palace are actually larger than our home."

"What?" she asked in disbelief. "I thought your family only had their private living quarters on the third floor?"

"Well, yes. You can access our new living quarters from the third floor, but also from the main level as well."

"That's interesting. I probably should have known, given the size of the palace."

"I am grateful you were unaware of it, as now I can happily surprise you with our new living area."

"So this is why you had me freshen up in the rooms I've always stayed in." She laughed. "You always have something planned in that mind of yours. Now, please enlighten me as to where exactly we are?"

Levi kissed her forehead. "Well, our private quarters are in the west area of the palace. There are only two living quarters set up in such a way, the others being my mother and father's rooms at the opposite of end of the palace. These rooms are designed to give us our seclusion and peace away from the rest of the palace. You even have your own private courtyard on the first floor."

"Oh? I've always dreamed of having my very own private courtyard," she teased.

Levi laughed. "Now that you have a pet zorflak, it will be a lovely place for him to pass the time when you are engaged in other activities."

They walked into a large room that held an enormous bed. The fireplace was lit, and the room was complete with two chairs and a long chaise situated in front of it.

"Do you approve of the bed chambers?"

She couldn't remove her eyes from the luxurious bed that awaited them. "I love it," she absently answered.

Levi brought his arms around her waist. "Would you care for some tea?"

Reece gently removed his hold on her and sauntered over to their grand bed. She turned and gracefully lounged across it, staring as Levi stood paralyzed watching her.

She ran her hands over the silky smooth fabric of their luxurious comforter. "No tea for me. This bed is too inviting." She arched an eyebrow at him. "Care to join me?"

Levi was at her side in a moment, his lips covering hers as his hands aggressively searched for the buttons of her dress. Reece ran her hands through Levi's hair, so thrilled to be here and in his arms again.

Later that night in bed, Reece lay awake and was concerned more than ever about Levi. His sturdy body was molded tightly around hers, arms protectively wrapped around her, while his chin rested atop of her head. He hadn't let go of her since he drifted off to sleep, and the tension in his strong arms made her wonder why he was being so sheltering of her.

As much as she enjoyed having him hold her in this manner, her mind couldn't rest easy. She knew something wasn't right with him. She lay there, gently running her fingers along his arm. She had to get him to talk to her, and she resolved to do it the next morning. He was bearing a burden, and she knew it had to do with her.

# Chapter 18

Levi sat on the sofa in his office, sipping tea and staring into the roaring flames in his fireplace. To say he was conflicted by recent events would be the biggest understatement of his life. He sat in solitude, his mind consumed by thoughts of his wife.

On this particular morning, he remained in bed with Reece until she woke, even though he had already been conscious for hours. He didn't move a muscle; instead, he held her tight and brought his face into the softness of her hair, absorbing her intoxicating fragrance. He could not accept that Reece was the only answer to recovering his father. Descendant of Paul Xylander or not, his wife should not have to be subjected to these sorts of things. It was the Guardians' duty to protect her journeys, not the other way around.

As if trying to figure out a way to keep her out of that danger wasn't enough, Levi was burdened with the task of telling her that she wasn't entirely human. *How many times can I turn this innocent woman's life upside down?* he worried as he held her tighter. He wasn't sure what the most distressing information might be, the fact that she descended from an alien bloodline, or that it was the same bloodline that tortured her for months, nearly driving her insane.

When Reece awoke, she twisted in his arms and gazed adoringly into Levi's eyes. He wished they could stay in that moment forever. Instead, everything was about to change, and Levi knew it. When Reece told Levi of her premonition before arriving at the palace, he tried not to show his shock. Her omens seemed to validate Mordegrin's statements, and it took a great deal of restraint for him not to tell Reece that her true lineage was most likely the reason for the emergence of this ability.

Now, as he sat in his office and watched the flames consume the wood, he felt more and more conflicted about telling Reece who she really was. *If her visions are truly premonitions, would it not frighten her to have no knowledge of why or when these events were to take place?* He looked up at her portrait, letting the beauty of it calm his frazzled nerves.

The door to his office opened, and a servant admitted his mother, Harrison, King Nathaniel, and Queen Galleta.

It was after noon, and Galleta had returned with information from her interview with Mordegrin.

Levi stood and turned to greet them. Lady Allestaine was the first to approach him. "Levi, darling, how are you feeling?" she asked as she placed a quick kiss to his cheek.

"I believe I will feel much better once I know how to retrieve my father. It is my hope that Galleta will have that answer for us now," he offered with a faint smile.

Everyone took seats around Levi's desk. "Queen Galleta, please tell me we have better answers from Mordegrin today? Did he figure a way to accede to my demand that Reece not be a party to opening the portal?"

"Emperor—" Galleta started with an expression that was not comforting.

"Yes?" Levi prompted.

She sighed. "I have had quite an interesting conversation with Mordegrin. First of all, he is correct; a portal must be opened to retrieve your father. It is beyond Mordegrin—or me, for that matter—to fully understand how your father was successfully transported in the manner that he was. However, the Olteniaus females were able to collectively form a powerful barrier around his nearly lifeless body to achieve that task."

"Why did they take him?" Levi asked.

"They believed he was you. The Olteniaus females recreated themselves in our galaxy in search of the stone. They chose Armedias because that land had the weakest-minded ruler. They had been here for quite some time, seeking out who The Key was in order to take the information from her mind and locate the stone. It wasn't until Reece was presented to the Council of Worlds that they learned exactly who The Key was. After Reece was brought back to Pemdas for protection, they knew they had to find a way to draw her out. Once they collectively learned that you knew where the stone's location was, they derived a plan to draw Reece out of Pemdas in order for Armedias to provoke a war with our men. This war was their only means of bringing you near death in order to take you into their galaxy. They mentally persuaded Lucas to take issue with the Pemdai, and of course Simone and Michael were more than happy to accommodate their plans."

"Why would these beings have any desire to locate the stone?" Levi wondered. "And how was that female we held captive not able to see the location in my mind? She obviously saw that I knew where the stone was."

"The map must be extracted from your mind in order to see its location. The Olteniaus need you to be in their galaxy and among their true forms in order to accomplish this. It is the only way they can physically extract the information from your mind. They cannot do it with their created forms, as their mental powers are not strong enough to reach past the barriers that protect the map within your mind. Again, this is why they provoked war in order to bring you near death and transport you into their galaxy. Their plans failed when they learned it was your father and not you they had transported into their presence."

"It still makes no sense as to why they have taken an interest in our galaxy and the stone that protects it," Levi stated.

"They do so for the same reasons that the Ciatron have a great desire to take possession of the stone. According to Mordegrin, the Olteniaus females' motivations are much stronger. They have taken over an entire galaxy with their powers. They have imprisoned the inhabitants of the galaxy they are currently in. They use life forms to obtain power, and the powers they currently have will be multiplied greatly if they can use the powers within all of Earth and within all the dimensions of the planet," the queen explained.

"Does this creature Mordegrin have any clue as to how they plan to do this? How will the stone help them if they cannot make use of it?" Levi asked. "It seems clear that if we choose to open a portal, they will be *physically* destroyed if they try entering through it."

"Emperor, if they obtain the map to the stone, they will create their presence on Earth once again and go to the location. Once at the stone's location, they will mentally draw from the power it has to open a portal into our galaxy. When this takes place, they will physically enter our galaxy and take the energy of the life forms in all of the realms of Earth. After they accomplish this, they will personally take the stone into their possession and use it to open gateways to other galaxies."

Levi rubbed his chin, trying to control his rage. "These entities appear to pose a very grave danger. Who would ever have known a threat of this nature could exist?" He stared at the walls and past the people sitting in front of him. "However, if these beings are as intelligent as Mordegrin portrays them to be, how is it that they mistook my father for me?"

"It was a mistake on Michael Visor's part. Michael must have believed your father to be you on the battlefield. It was not until Emperor Navarre was successfully transported and recovered in the Arsediean galaxy that they realized Michael had delivered to them the wrong man."

"Michael knew about these entities being in another galaxy?" Levi asked in disbelief.

"No, he only made an agreement with them. The Olteniaus females mentally impressed upon him a vision that he would rule over Armedias and Pemdas. In order to achieve this, he was instructed to give you a fatal wound; however, it was to be a particular wound that you would not die instantly from. They gave Michael no further information after that. We do know from Mordegrin that they needed your father nearly dead so they could use the energy of the vortex and their own power at the exact moment the horse passed through to replace your father with an exact replica of the individual on the horse."

Levi gazed at everyone in front of him. "Has Mordegrin given you any information on how we will retrieve my father and end this new threat to our world? These beings must be obliterated!" Levi leaned over his desk. "Even if we open this portal and enter it, do we have any clue as to how we destroy these dark beings?"

The expression on the queen's face gave Levi the answer he dreaded. *Reece,* he thought as he stood abruptly and turned his back to everyone in the room.

"Emperor," the queen softly spoke, "Reece is the answer to all of those questions. Reece is the only being that can destroy them, as they can only be—"

"Enough," Levi nearly spat in frustration with what Queen Galleta declared.

"Son," Lady Allestaine gently cautioned.

Levi held up a hand, as if to stop anyone's approach. "No," he ordered.

He walked over to the windows behind his desk and shoved both hands into his pockets as he stared at the gardens below. Levi could hear his heart pounding in his chest. *Why?* He looked up toward the sapphire skies, watching the birds fly peacefully across. *Why is Reece the only answer?* His mind recalled the night before Harrison arrived with all of this outlandish information. Reece was in his arms, looking up at him and telling him that if it weren't for the Ciatron, they would not be there together and married on that night.

He placed a hand on his hip, and his other covered his mouth. He closed his eyes and softly chuckled. *Well, if it weren't for the Ciatron, my love, I believe your love for me would not be coming at a price for you now.* His father awaited him and the Guardians' rescue, yet he had a sick feeling within him that this would involve a dangerous act for Reece. Even if opening the portal was no risk to her life, she would have to travel amongst them into an entirely new galaxy, risk the dangers of the absolute unknown that awaited them—and now she was the only one who could destroy the Olteniaus? She was the only one that could protect their galaxy? *How am I to place such a burden solely on my wife?*

His thoughts were interrupted when he felt his mother's hands around his waist. He reflexively brought his arm around her shoulder while he studied the serenity of the gardens outside his window in great turmoil. If he were to say no to Reece helping them into this galaxy, he would be choosing his wife over his own father. He knew he wouldn't be able to face his mother again once she understood that he had chosen to protect the only woman he could ever love and ignore the hope of Lady Allestaine's husband's return.

"Darling," she said, "I know the torment you are suffering. I know you are struggling with one of the hardest decisions you will most likely ever make in your entire life. No one deserves such a dilemma."

"Mother—"

"Let me finish, son," she kindly interrupted. "The last thing your father or I would ever request of you is to feel as though you had to choose between him and Reece. I know that is what you are struggling with as you stand here. I speak on behalf of myself and your father when I say that you should not forget your father gave his life so that you could recover Reece and keep her safe."

Levi's chest heaved as he struggled to fight back tears.

"Levi, have you no clue as to how strong the woman you married is? I know you do not wish to frighten her by her lineage, but I am certain that Reece would get a good laugh out of it."

Levi nodded, realizing his mother was most likely correct about that. "If I told her, she would feel obligated to help us. In doing so, I place an enormous, very dangerous burden on her, which is not hers to bear."

"I ask of you to recall the day that Samuel informed us that Reece was free to return to Earth, and we were all misled to believe the Ciatron had lost interest in Reece being The Key."

"How does that have anything to do with this?"

"After you and Harrison left to retrieve Reece's clone, Simone threatened Reece's life if she were to tell any of us what she and Michael had done. Reece could have kept Simone's secret for fear of her own life, except she chose not to. She immediately informed your father in the hope that it was not too late to stop you and Harrison from being placed in danger upon your return to Earth. Reece told your father, knowing it could have led to her death. She is very courageous and wise, Levi."

"I know, Mother."

"Then you must trust her. She has shown her bravery time and again. You feel as though you must choose for her, and in doing so, you are not allowing her to make her own decisions. You are smothering her with worry in not telling her about her true ancestry and what is really happening. Let her be your wife, your equal. You and she must determine together if she should be a part of the plan to recover your father or not."

Levi stared down at his mother. "And if she says she will?"

"I am confident that she will be trained properly and protected well by our fierce warriors."

Levi sighed, bent over, and softly kissed his mother on the top of her head. "I will do my best to bring him back to you. I simply must have more time to make a decision, and I must be assured Reece will be safe if she chooses to help us recover Navarre."

"I agree completely. Now, let us hear more answers from Galleta, and then you and Reece should spend the evening in the home you bought for her. You can explain all of this to her then."

After he gathered himself, Levi turned to sit again. "Forgive me; I needed a moment to think," he said.

"It is understandable," the queen affirmed.

Harrison and King Nathaniel's expressions were both sympathetic and grave, all in the same. His mother returned to her chair, sat straight up, and waited for Levi to continue questioning the queen.

"So tell me, why can this man not achieve what I demanded him to do? What are his excuses? Why is Reece the only answer?" Levi asked directly.

"Without being in his natural form on Earth, he does not carry the ability to open a portal. He also advises that no one is to alter the stone. The stone was not created to respond to anyone except a being with Olteniaus blood within them."

Levi's lips tightened. "You are telling me that it won't even respond safely to a Guardian warrior? What was Xylander thinking when he took this power from us?"

"He definitely has proven his point, that he trusted no being with such great power other than his own kind—not even after the alliance he made with the Guardians in the ancient times."

"If only he had known that *his own kind* could lead to the absolute destruction of our entire galaxy." Levi exhaled and looked over at Harrison.

Harrison had closed his eyes and pinched the bridge of his nose, obviously enduring the same absolute frustration Levi was experiencing. He looked over at Levi with an icy stare. "I am glad we are learning all of this now," he said dryly.

"It appears there is no other way out of this." Levi shook his head in discouragement. "Well, what are Mordegrin's suggestions, then? How does Reece accomplish this? What is she required to do?" he inquired sternly.

"You must take Reece to the location of the stone. When you have reached it, it will illuminate and respond to her presence. She need only touch it, and a surge of energy will transfer into her. Slowly, her Olteniaus genes will begin to awaken and take over." The queen folded her hands in her lap. "Mordegrin also said that she carries the ability to use some of these talents now, though she may not have control over them. If they manifested themselves, they would be involuntary. The stone will help her gain control over these abilities."

Levi's breathing halted, and he turned to look up at her portrait. *That is what was happening on our wedding night when her thoughts and emotions projected into my mind. And now the visions? The premonitions?*

He exhaled deeply. "I believe she is already experiencing these abilities. But why now? Why so suddenly?"

"When did she notice anything different?" Queen Galleta asked.

"After our wedding, she was able to project her thoughts and emotions into my mind. More recently, she told me of a vision she had, and shortly thereafter this vision came to pass. Are these the special talents she carries?"

"Yes," answered the queen, "and she may have even more abilities. Until she visits the stone, we will never know how strong these abilities are. Do not forget that she is mostly human; the stone is what will change all of that for her. Her mind will have the capability to use all of its mental powers. Along with that, she also has the means to alter other minds and manipulate them. But Mordegrin does not believe these powers will work in their entirety because of her human descent. I might tend to believe there is some possibility, however, since somehow she has influenced your mind, as you stated."

"She never manipulated it. I only felt her emotions and saw her thoughts at random moments."

"Then that may be how that particular talent will work with her," the queen answered. "All of her senses will be heightened. She will be able to judge people and become extremely intuitive, as if she were reading their minds. The premonitions she appears to be having could have something to do with her senses already becoming attuned to that."

"How will all of this help her to open the portal?" Nathaniel asked.

"With the power of the stone, she will know. She must have the stone with her as well," the queen answered.

"Remove the stone from Earth and break all of the treaties with the other worlds?" Harrison challenged with a laugh.

"They need not find out about it," Queen Galleta answered with a subtle grin. "No one knows its location except for you, Levi; and Earth will not be altered any time soon. Do not forget how long it took the Ciatron to create their domain on Earth in an attempt to alter it."

*She is right. Earth will not be in danger.* "The stone is not in an easily accessed location, Queen Galleta. It will be an extremely dangerous venture to bring her to its location. Is Mordegrin certain Reece will know how to remove it without altering Earth?"

"She will know," the queen answered.

Levi sat back in his chair and stared intently at the queen. "Is there any way you can help her with these talents before we visit the stone? I will feel more confident bringing her to this location if she is able to defend herself mentally as we are able to. Her abilities must be more heightened than they are currently. She will not survive the journey to the stone in her present state."

"As long as her powers are awakened, I will help her to heighten them to the best of her ability without the stone's force."

Levi stood. "Very well. I will discuss all of this with Reece tonight. For now, I have no more questions until she gives me her answer about whether or not she is willing to do this at all."

Harrison walked over to Levi and clapped him on the shoulder. "Levi, you will not be dealing with this alone. You have all of us. We will help you and work to help Reece as well. I know you fear of telling her this news, but Reece has proven her resilience. You know that she will be accepting of this and stand at your side to help you through the difficult decisions that must be made. Allow her the right to know more about who she is, and give her the freedom to decide of her own will."

"You are correct. I believe in the end she will prove I was the one who overreacted." Levi crossed his arms. "Once I find Reece, I will bring her to our estate for the evening. Tomorrow, we will reconvene our meetings with Reece's answers."

"Until then," Harrison replied, and with that everyone left the room.

Levi immediately sought out Reece's whereabouts. A servant informed him that she was at the stables with Elizabeth and Angeline. As he walked down toward the large buildings, he saw Reece riding Arrow out in the fields. He went over to the split-rail fence and stepped a foot on the bottom rail while resting his elbows over the top. He leaned over, clasped his hands together, and watched Reece nonchalantly riding the high-spirited Guardian horse.

The horse responded joyfully to her every command, and anyone watching would believe she had been raised to ride horses. Levi studied her, and Arrow's response to her. A large tree was on its side, and Levi tensed as Reece directed Arrow in its direction in order to jump it. He remained silent, watching and knowing that if Arrow believed she could be injured with the jump, he would change the course she had him on. Arrow was more than loyal to Reece; he was extremely protective of her. The horse gathered himself and gracefully cleared the obstacle.

Levi shook his head as Reece screamed in delight. She patted Arrow on his shoulder, and then turned him back to jump the fallen tree again. Indeed, there was something captivating about her. Arrow sensed it, and he was drawn to her the moment he first encountered her. The Guardian horse knew of her importance long before anyone else did. He knew she had abilities, and Levi understood now why the horse was enthralled with her.

Areion came out of the forest and trotted over to where Levi stood watching Reece. The moment Reece noticed Areion, she smiled brightly at Levi. She called out and raced Arrow toward Levi's location. Levi pushed off the fence as Reece approached. Just as Arrow stopped, she swung a leg over the saddle and prepared to leap from the horse and over the fence.

Before he could discourage the action, Reece's feet were on the top rail, and then she was in his arms. She giggled as Levi securely embraced her. He gently put her feet on the ground, and she gazed up into his eyes. "Did you see that? Did you see what Arrow did?" she asked in excitement.

Levi said nothing; instead, he brought one hand to cradle her neck and the other encircled her waist to pull her in closer to him. He was rewarded with a passionate kiss. He forgot about all of his surroundings and let this kiss consume him. Too quickly, he felt Reece trying to push him away.

"Levi," she mumbled, her lips still captured by his.

He finally let her go and smiled. She stared up at him with bewildered eyes. "My loving husband, what has gotten into you? Angie and your sister are just over there!" She laughed in shock.

"Then they can look in another direction." He smiled as he cajoled her in to resume their fervent kiss.

After a few more moments of indulging in her tasteful kiss, he slowly withdrew. "My love, Jasmeen is preparing your things. We are returning to our estate for the evening. Does that agree with you?"

She stared at him quizzically. "You're acting odd, what's going on?" she asked with a nervous laugh. "Do you have good news about your father?"

"I will inform you of everything over a quiet dinner tonight. For now, I will have Javian saddle Areion, and you and I will have an enjoyable ride together to our home before we retire for the evening."

"That sounds wonderful, but are you sure you want to leave with everything that is going on?" she asked.

"At the current time, yes," he grinned and went on, "and of course Lady Allestaine insisted."

"Then we'll go and have some time alone. Let me make sure Elizabeth is okay with taking Mozart, then." She smiled up at him.

"I am surprised you would even need to ask," he laughed.

# Chapter 19

Javian brought Areion to the mounting block saddled and ready for Levi. Before their departure, Levi had returned to the palace to make preparations with the staff to have their estate prepared for them when they arrived that evening.

While waiting for Levi to return, Reece walked over to Elizabeth and Angeline, with Arrow following closely behind her. "It looks like Levi has made unexpected plans for us and we will be spending the night at our home. Will you two mind keeping Mozart company for another evening?" Reece asked with a sympathetic grin on her face.

"Without a doubt, of course!" Elizabeth said with excitement.

Arrow stepped forward and brought his nose down to investigate Mozart, bringing the critter's attention to the massive stallion and away from Reece. Arrow sniffed and grunted before stepping back behind Reece, no longer interested in the zorflak.

Reece laughed as Angeline stood up and approached Arrow. "I cannot believe that a Guardian horse has taken to one who is not a Guardian warrior," she said in disillusionment. "It is so intriguing to me."

Reece turned to find Arrow standing tall and imposing as he studied Angeline. After a quick nod, Angeline smiled and reached out slowly to pet him.

"Maybe it's because Arrow and I became friends when he was a colt." She smiled at Angeline's expression.

"Has Levi not told you, even as colts, these horses do not take to just anyone?" Angeline answered.

"He has, but Levi seems to have a way of over exaggerating certain information when it comes to things taking an interest in me," Reece answered with a laugh.

"I believe she won that horse's heart with all of her bribes and snacks," Harrison said in amusement as he walked briskly toward the stables. "Isn't that right, Arrow?"

Arrow grunted as Harrison playfully nudged the horse in response. He called for Javian to saddle Saracen before walking back to where Reece stood with Angeline.

"Harrison, are you coming with us?"

"No. I have a matter of business that awaits me in Casititor."

"Is everything okay? I'm surprised that Levi insists that we leave the palace for the night."

Harrison glanced at Angeline, and Reece didn't miss it. *What is going on with those two?* She could feel the tension between them. She forced herself to turn and pet Arrow, when she noticed Angeline staring up at Harrison, seemingly questioning his demeanor. Even with her back turned to the couple, she could feel Harrison's irritation with Angeline. *For crying out loud, why is this happening to me, and why do I even care?* she thought in frustration. Fortunately, Levi approached and the energy surrounding the group changed.

She turned back and focused solely on her husband, letting the emotions radiating from Angeline and Harrison leave her.

"Harrison. Angie," Levi acknowledged them on his approach.

"I will handle the matter you requested," Harrison told Levi, "and I will see you tomorrow."

"Thank you. If anything should come up, send for me," Levi returned.

"Relax, my friend, enjoy the evening with your lovely wife," Harrison said and quickly walked toward the stables.

"Are you ready to depart?" Levi asked Reece.

Reece looked at Angeline and Elizabeth, who now approached with Mozart. "Thank you again, ladies." She leaned over and gave Mozart a small kiss to his head. "Be good, little guy. I will see you tomorrow," she said while Mozart hummed his melancholy cello tone.

"Angie and Lizzy, I believe you both may have to take him to the music room," Levi said in amusement. "It appears as though you may have a cello accompaniment to go along with your piano and violin music while Reece is away."

"Mozart, you will be fine," Reece instructed the zorflak as the girls laughed.

"Both of you have a wonderful time, and don't worry about Mozart," Elizabeth said.

Reece laughed and turned to allow Levi to help her onto Arrow's back. Soon after, Levi was on Areion and the two young women stood back with Mozart and waved them off.

Once they were through the forest that sat behind the palace, Levi turned in a direction she had never gone before, where a narrow bridge arched over a rapidly flowing body of water. Levi halted Areion before crossing over it. As Reece came up alongside of Levi and Areion, he looked over at her with a mischievous grin.

"It appears to me that you and Arrow enjoy a little excitement as you ride?" He arched his eyebrow at her.

Reece's lips quirked in humor, and she lifted her chin. "We do," she said proudly.

Levi nodded as he smiled at her. He gripped his reins tightly, and his eyes seemed to sparkle in excitement. At that moment, Areion began stamping his feet impatiently. Arrow, sensing the powerful energy emitting off Areion, began stamping his feet as well. Reece felt the adrenaline rush through her body.

"Care to see what Arrow is really capable of?" he asked with a tiny smile.

Reece narrowed her eyes at him. "What exactly do you have planned?"

Levi glanced over at Arrow, who was mimicking his impatient sire. "You shall see."

Levi loosened the reins, and Areion lunged forward powerfully. Reece did the same, and soon both horses were racing over the bridge and through the dark forest at a faster speed than Reece had ever ridden Arrow before. It was incredible. The power in the horse, the crisp air whipping through her hair, and most of all, the high speed they were traveling. Both horses' hooves mightily dug into the ground as they exited the dark forest and traveled through an open meadow with tall grass.

Large estates lined the horizon in front of them, and a road to their left had several carriages traveling on it. Reece wondered if they were heading into a city as Levi guided Areion toward the road. Once ahead of the travelers, Levi turned Areion to race on the road covered in black sand. Reece was behind them, filled with excitement as Arrow followed in step with every move Areion made in front of them.

They traveled the road for a few moments before Levi changed course, leading Areion off the road and toward a hillside. Aggressively, the horses dominated the grassy hillside and traveled along a stone fence line. Reece saw a large structure in the distance and farm life feeding off the pastures surrounding them. As they passed this, the structures and fences were replaced with trees and large boulders. As they traveled swiftly across another grassy meadow, a wide river with trees surrounding it came into view. As soon as Reece questioned where the bridge was, Levi glanced back and grinned. Then Areion gathered himself, and in one graceful movement he leaped into the air, clearing the wide river effortlessly. *I can't believe he's letting us do this,* Reece thought as Arrow lunged forward and nimbly sent them through the air, leaping over the large river.

Levi glanced back as soon as Areion reached the other side, yet he never stopped his horse. Once Arrow efficiently landed on the other side, he found another speed as they continued to follow Areion and Levi.

"Good job, boy!" Reece shouted as Arrow continued at this new, aggressive speed.

They came up over another hill before Levi finally halted Areion. Arrow slowed, and as Reece came up alongside of Levi, he reached over with one arm, wrapped it around her, and leaned over for a quick kiss.

He sat back up in his saddle. "I am very impressed, Mrs. Oxley," he said with amusement.

"Why, thank you, Mr. Oxley," she answered with a laugh. "To be honest, I'm pretty impressed myself. I can't believe we jumped that river."

Levi laughed and brought his attention to the tall mountains lining the horizon, which appeared to be about a mile away.

"When we approach the peaks of those mountains—"

"Peaks? What?!" Reece said in astonishment.

Levi grinned. "Yes. We are headed toward that mountain range, and once we reach the top, give Arrow full control. He will follow Areion's exact speed and step." He pulled back on the reins again. "You want to see what he is capable of, do you not?"

With that, he winked at her, and they were once again racing through the meadows. It wasn't long before they reached the bottom of the enormous mountainside. Reece gripped the saddle horn and stepped her feet hard into the stirrups as Areion and Arrow lunged themselves up the rocky mountainside. The ridge they were climbing was narrow, and the ground below seemed to drop quickly beneath them. The higher they climbed, the smaller everything below them became. Reece knew she should have been frightened, but she wasn't. Maybe it was her trust in Arrow, as he showed no hesitation with the arduous climb.

Levi glanced back every now and then but continued to lead Areion up the hill without slowing down. As they neared the top of the mountain range, Reece could feel the energy in Arrow building up. Areion lunged onto the top, and Arrow followed. Reece did exactly as Levi instructed her and loosened Arrow's reins, fully giving him his head. The horses found a new speed, a speed that Reece only encountered on Areion when he leaped over the Pemdas protective barriers.

*No, he isn't,* she thought before the gray mist came into view. The stallions simultaneously leaped into the air, bringing Levi and Reece together over the gray mist.

Once they were both across, Levi turned Areion hard to the right and they followed along the gray mist divide. He turned into an area where a forest surround a large opening and halted Areion. Before he could say anything, she dismounted Arrow and walked over to where he sat on Areion.

Once he took notice of her off the horse, he dismounted himself.

She placed both hands on her hips and gazed up into his vibrant eyes. "Jumping barriers all of a sudden? What was that about?"

Levi's expression was radiant as he wound his arms around her waist, lifting her off the ground. She smiled down at his expression and brought her lips to his for a quick kiss.

She ran her hands through his hair. "Answer me. Why would you trust me to jump the barriers when I have never attempted a thing like that in my life?"

"You tell me," he answered her.

He placed her on the ground, and she continued to stare into his searching eyes. He had a reason for this. He was trying to prove something to himself. But why? Levi's eyes studied hers, waiting.

"Tell you what, that you are acting really strange? What's going on? You've been acting different with me ever since I got back to the palace."

He inhaled deeply and brought his hand to her cheek. His eyes never left hers. "I love you so much." He cleared his throat, and then shook his head and looked past her.

He seemed tormented, and she knew there was something he was withholding from her.

"Yeah, I know. That doesn't change the fact that I feel like you are keeping something from me, I know you are."

"You are correct in that assumption." He tilted his head to the side, intently gazing into her eyes. "Do you wonder why you are correct in that assumption? Why you were correct about your assumptions of Henry and Jasmeen?" His eyes then glistened with humor. "And most likely correct in your assumptions of Harrison and Angie?"

She fidgeted with her fingers on one hand as she listened to what he said. "I noticed this afternoon, with Harrison and Angie again, they were acting strange toward each other. It's like I could tell how they were feeling toward each other. I tried to ignore it, but their emotions were so thick, I couldn't. It is really starting to annoy me, because I've certainly never bothered putting myself into other people's business. But it was as if my mind wouldn't let me stop thinking about it."

She looked at Levi, whose expression was stern. She ran her fingers along his face. "Right now, you seem angry, but you're not. You're worried, and you are afraid to tell me something. You're afraid that I won't take this information well."

He nodded and took her hand. "Do you remember when we brought you into Pemdas and I explained to you that you needed to keep your mind open to everything I was about to tell you?"

"Yes," she returned hesitantly.

He stopped, and his tortured eyes gazed into hers. "This creat—" He stopped himself. "The man that has given us the news of my father has also given us news about Paul Xylander's ancestry as well." He studied her expression, and then went on. "Paul Xylander's mother was not a human from Earth. She was known as an Olteniaus, a being from the galaxy that my father is currently in." He inhaled deeply. "Apparently, she gave her love to Paul Xylander's father, and Paul was born on Earth as a result of their affections."

She raised her eyebrows, and then laughed aloud.

"Reece?" He questioned.

"Seriously?" she said as she continued to laugh. "I'm part-alien now?"

Levi let out a sigh of disbelief and relief all in the same. "Sweetheart, you are not part-alien. You are the descendant of a man who was half-Olteniaus and half-human. You only carry some qualities of this supernatural gene. You *are* a human, Reece."

She shook her head and laughed at his concerned expression. "This is what you were so worried about? Levi, I accepted the impossible when your father told me I was Paul's descendant and that I was *The Key*," she said reassuringly. "I kind of felt like I wasn't your average human being when I found out that I have a mystical map to a magical stone imbedded in my DNA." She brought her hand to his cheek. "You worry too much."

Levi said nothing as he searched into her eyes.

"It's fine. When we have children, they will be super-alien Pemdai humans!" she teased.

Levi's lips twisted, and she stared in concern again. "That's not all, is it?"

"Will you please allow me more time before—"

She abruptly cut him off, "Don't do this. You are trying to shelter me from something, and all you are doing is making me scared. Please, trust me and tell me. I won't freak out, I promise."

Levi sighed. "You are correct. You must know that I have not taken any of this lightly. It has taken the support of many others to help me accept this news."

She gazed promisingly into his eyes. "Okay," she said reassuringly.

He led her to a mound of grass and guided her to sit next to him. He held her hand and allowed his thumb to softly caress the back of it.

"Reece, in order to recover my father, we must travel into another galaxy. It is not possible for us to do so at this time, as it would seem as though a portal must be opened in order for us to achieve this way of travel."

"I'm the one who has to open it, aren't I?" she answered him.

He exhaled, and she saw the pain return to his eyes as he stared off into the distance. "Reece, I have tried to come up with any other possible solution to this dilemma, and I fear that I was unsuccessful. Queen Galleta has confirmed that the only one who has the ability to accomplish this task is you."

He looked at her with sorrow deeply set into his eyes.

She gently caressed his cheek. "Please, don't worry. I mean, I have no idea how opening portals works, that's not really something I learned in medical school," she laughed, "But if this man and Queen Galleta say I can do it, then I'm sure I'll figure it out. Why are you so upset about this?"

He exhaled. "Because you will have to travel with us to retrieve my father and destroy the beings that took him. I cannot fathom putting you in such a dangerous situation. We know nothing of this other world, how to battle its inhabitants, how much danger we will encounter, and most of all how to go up against the evil power these beings possess. I cannot risk your life in such a manner, but if I do not consider the option, Earth will be in grave danger and my father will be forced to live out—"

"Levi!" Reece interrupted him firmly. "There is no question in my mind about what needs to be done. If I am the only way we can bring your father home and protect Earth, then you guys better figure out a way to keep me safe as we go through this other dimension."

"Reece—"

"No! You aren't talking me out of this." She arched her eyebrow at his sympathetic expression. "I'll go with or without you, how about that?" she taunted. She then ran her hand through his hair, his expression unwavering. "I know that you've had a couple of days to think about this and consider all the possibilities. I also know that if you thought I couldn't do this or it wouldn't work, you would have never told me. You should know me well enough to know that I will do whatever is required of me to keep everyone I love safe, and I think that you shouldn't be afraid of putting me in danger when there are so many other factors involved that come with serious consequences if nothing is done."

He looked at her and seemed slightly relieved.

"Why does this man believe the Earth girl is supposed to be able to achieve the unimaginable?"

He shook his head. "You question none of this?"

She laughed. "Why should I? I believe I accepted the impossibilities of many things somewhere in-between you taking me from Earth and me having to wear corset dresses."

Levi faintly laughed. "This is different."

"How is it any different? You're the one who told me when I first got to Pemdas that it would help if I had an open mind before I learned everything about myself and how the universe works."

"This is different because we are specifically putting your life in danger in order to recover my father."

"What better reason to have my life put in danger?" She ran her hands along his arm. "Wasn't my life specifically put in danger when we had to face the council on Earth so we could retrieve the Guardian warriors? I have no doubt that you, Harrison, and the Guardians will figure out a strategy in order to safely get your father, destroy these beings, and keep me safe as well."

He brought his hand to caress her cheek. "My love, I have no words to describe how much I love you and your ability to be steadfast when I am lacking confidence."

She grinned. "I feel the same about you. Now, will you tell me everything that is going on?"

He brought his lips to hers, laying her back into the soft grass. She indulged in the kiss for a moment before she gently removed his lips from hers. "Trying to avoid the question?"

He softly chuckled. "I will explain everything in further detail over dinner tonight. The hardest part, I believe, is finally out of the way."

She shifted her head to the side. "Why did we jump over the protective barrier anyway?"

Levi's hands gently caressed her cheeks. "I thought you would like to see what your horse was capable of."

She laughed. "What if I fell off?"

Levi chuckled. "Beloved, do you think we would have taken this particular ride if I were afraid you would fall into oblivion?"

"How would you know if I would or wouldn't?"

He gave her a kiss on her nose. "Arrow would not have followed us as he did. He feels your energy and your strength. If for any reason you felt hesitant, he would not have jumped over the river or carried you up the mountain ridge, and he definitely would not have crossed you over the barrier."

"He can sense all of that?"

Levi kissed her chin. "Just as you are sensing other's emotions; however, his senses are highly attuned to yours, which is why he was taken with you as a young colt. He has always sensed your uniqueness and has left all of us in awe as to why he is undeniably at your service. Now we know why."

"So it would appear that I'm a Guardian warrior now?" she teased.

Levi laughed, and then stood and reached for her hand. "Indeed, you are. Now, let us see some more of your astounding abilities."

They crossed back over the Pemdai barriers and rode through more aggressive terrain, leading them to the mountaintops where Levi first brought Reece when he showed her their estate by horseback. Reece remembered the ledge they traveled upon, and fear washed over her. As Levi went to guide Areion over the ledge, Arrow whinnied loudly when Reece forced him to stop. Levi turned back with a smug grin.

"Are we no longer a brave warrior, my wife?"

Reece narrowed her eyes at him. *The horse won't go if he knows I can't handle this.* Reece lifted her chin. "Still here," she lied. "I'm just enjoying the scenery before we make our descent down 'death's mountainside.'"

Levi laughed aloud and motioned for her to lead. "I believe I shall follow you."

"You really are trying to challenge me, aren't you?"

Levi shrugged. "I believe I would like to enjoy the scenery as well."

"Fine, we'll take the lead."

They began their descent, and Reece's stomach was in knots with the thought that the horses could possibly lose their step and send them all thousands of feet below to their death. Finally, they were at the bottom and riding over the vibrant pink moss trail. The moment the trail opened, Levi raced Areion past Arrow and led the way along the aquamarine river that led to the back of their estate. As the estate came into view, Levi turned into the forest of lavender trees, and Reece followed.

Once in the forest, Levi dismounted Areion and pulled Reece from Arrow, bringing her softly to the ground beneath him.

Reece laughed in delight as Levi kissed her chin. "That was phenomenal."

Levi brought his lips under her neck. "You are absolutely phenomenal."

He proceeded to place kisses on her, and then Reece brought his eyes back to meet hers. "There is no way," she answered, knowing his expression very well.

Levi laughed. "Oh, really?" he said, bringing his lips to hers. "No way? I believe you explained to me how I need to have an open mind. I believe you should regard your own sound advice."

She kissed his humorous lips. "What am I going to do with you? What if someone walks up on us?"

"You worry too much."

"Trying to use my words against me? And yes, in *this* case, I do."

Levi continued to kiss along her shoulders, and she gazed up into the glistening trees above them, letting every kiss Levi gave her relax her and fuel her desire for more.

Soon, she was wholly at his mercy and not concerned about anything but being with him in this moment.

Later that evening, they had a quiet dinner on the balcony of their manor. Levi explained all the details to Reece about everything they had learned from their meetings with Mordegrin and Queen Galleta.

Reece took a sip of her wine. "With all that you have made me aware of, I still can't figure out why these abilities I have sprung up on me out of the blue."

"That is confusing to me as well. That is why I have had Mordegrin removed from Pasidian and detained in a different city. Being that he carries the Olteniaus gene within him, he could possibly be playing a part in awakening these abilities within you."

"Why wouldn't the priestess—" she stopped and corrected herself, "the Olteniaus woman that was here, why wouldn't she have started the process of awakening these talents that I have?"

Levi glanced past her.

"Levi," Reece spoke deeply, "you're doing it again, keeping something from me."

"I believe they feared you." Levi's gaze bore through her. "These Olteniaus beings seek to destroy Earth and all dimensions that exist within it, as they have done to the galaxy they currently reside in."

"Go on."

"With the powers the stone will give you, Mordegrin has informed us that *you* are the only one who can permanently destroy them. Knowing this, I believe the last thing they would desire is to awaken the Olteniaus powers within you."

Reece forced herself to maintain a confident expression and refrained herself from gulping the entire glass of wine sitting in front of her. Levi's eyes never left hers, and she knew he was waiting for her to back out of this.

She smiled. "This should be interesting."

"I can hear your heart racing from here," Levi answered. "You are fearful of this, and I perfectly understand. This burden should not fall on you. The Guardians and I have been born and raised to protect Earth; we have been sworn to protect you." He ran a hand through his hair. "And here we sit with everything changed. You are the only one who can help us protect Earth from its greatest threat, and the only one who can help recover my father."

Reece smiled and reached for his hand. "Maybe this is why Paul and the Guardians made this treaty. It is possible that Paul knew that one of his descendants would most likely have to help the Guardians protect Earth, just as he did when they all battled the Ciatron. Think about it, he not only created that stone to protect Earth, but didn't he use it to destroy Atlantis?"

Levi tilted his head to the side. "It does make perfect sense. I simply struggle with the knowledge that this fate has befallen my wife."

"You're going to have to get over that. Like you said, I have to go to the stone and get these powers from it. I'm pretty confident that if Paul could destroy an entire civilization on Earth with it that I can take out a couple of bad guys."

"Four," Levi corrected her. "Four dark and evil beings from another galaxy that we know nothing about."

"When do we go to the stone? How soon do we leave for this world?" Reece asked, knowing that if she gave Levi any more time to contemplate everything they were up against, he would let his doubts finalize a decision she didn't agree with.

"You are confident you wish to be a part of this?"

"When do we go get the stone?" she demanded.

"Galleta has informed me that since your abilities have been awakened within you, she would like to work with you in order to expand and hone them. She has a natural ability of working with mental talents and supernatural abilities. The stone is located in an area that a normal, above-average human being could never obtain. We cannot go to its location until I am assured that you can control your new abilities and use them to get there."

"Can you tell me where it is?"

"With Mordegrin in our world and my uncertainty of his abilities, I do not trust speaking the location aloud or opening the map up within my mind. I fear he may have stronger abilities than he is leading us to believe. I do not trust him, and I cannot risk him seeing the location in my mind."

"Do you think he can read your mind?"

"I am unsure, but as I said earlier, I believe he is the reason your abilities have been awoken inside of you. There is no other reason it would start happening to you when he arrived here."

"True."

"Promise me this now, if any strange things begin to happen to you such as they did when those dark beings were here before, you will let me know immediately. I will find a way to remove that man from Pemdas and imprison him elsewhere if I feel he is attacking or controlling you in any way."

"I'm definitely not going through any of that again. I will let you know if I experience any weird things."

Levi stood and walked over to where she sat. "Care to join me for a walk in our gardens?"

Reece stood and took his outstretched arm. "That sounds marvelous."

They spent the rest of the evening walking leisurely through their vividly glowing garden, changing the subject entirely from what awaited them the next day.

"Levi?" Reece asked as she took in the beauty of their home.

"Yes, love."

"Let's call our home, Oxley Manor."

Levi stopped and looked down at her. "That sounds nice. Why do you choose to give it a name when we will be living in the palace, though? As much as I love to visit here, we should not get too attached."

Reece laughed. "I don't know about you, but once your father is back at the palace, I'm not living there anymore. I have plans to move into our new home."

Levi's eyes brightened. "My love, we do have a profound challenge that awaits us, but I believe I must start accepting our success as well. You are correct. We will return my father safely to Pemdas, you and I will happily live in Oxley Manor for as long as possible." With that, he scooped her up into his arms and walked swiftly back into their large home.

# Chapter 20

It had been two weeks since Levi informed Reece about everything that must be done to recover his father and to protect Earth. It was obvious to Harrison that Levi remained skeptical of her involvement, but Harrison was relieved when Levi shared that he would not let his wariness of the situation influence her decision negatively.

At Levi's command, Harrison was instructed to visit Casititor every day and learn more about this galaxy, the dangers they would be facing, and about how Reece was to destroy these beings. Harrison was relieved to see Levi more relaxed in his protectiveness of Reece, and he was thrilled to know that he would be the one training her once Galleta had finished heightening Reece's abilities.

From what Harrison was learning, the Arsediean galaxy was similar to theirs. It had planets, which were the same shapes and sizes of those surrounding Earth, except each one of these planets had the capability of sustaining living beings. The galaxy had a sun and a moon, oxygen, plant life, animals, and they all seemed extraordinarily similar to Earth. It seemed as though the Olteniaus females had control over all of these planets, and it was the reason they achieved their advanced abilities and supernatural powers.

The greatest problem for their entering this galaxy was that it was under a very dark and oppressive curse. When Mordegrin mentally showed Harrison the current state of this galaxy, it was dark and mostly uncivilized. He saw small villages with huts and barbaric beings in battle with each other. This world was in constant warfare because as people died and oppression flourished, the Olteniaus females gleaned from that to keep their energy levels strong. To say the very least, it was bizarre, horrific, and unimaginable all at the same time to Harrison, yet he was anxious to undertake the new challenges that awaited them.

He looked forward to entering this world to conquer these entities and return this planet back to its previous state. Developing the strategy of doing so seemed rather simple. They couldn't bring their cars into this world due to the primitive way of life that was there now. Even though there was a time that different parts of this world used vehicles, that would have been many years before they were overtaken and cursed. If there were vehicles then, Harrison knew there would be no traces of them now. Anything of a technical nature would simply have deteriorated and turned to dust.

It seemed more prudent in Harrison's mind to bring their war horses than their vehicles anyway. Because the horses' instincts were so intuitive, they were essential when the Guardians went into potentially dangerous situations, especially when battle was most likely to ensue.

Once back at Pasidian Palace, Harrison guided Saracen over to the stables before he dismounted and turned the horse over to Javian. It was late afternoon, and he'd been gathering information from Mordegrin nearly all day. Knowing that Levi had already returned to the palace, he was eager to meet with him in order to form a battle plan with the new information he had been given.

"Good afternoon, Harry," Angeline called out.

*Just when my thoughts were finally no longer consumed by you, Angeline,* Harrison thought as he forced a smile on his face. The thought of her beautiful bronze eyes haunted him by day and had begun to invade his sleep. Now, once again, they bore into his, igniting every nerve in his body. Her lips were inviting, her olive-toned skin was tempting, and her daring neckline was not helping him to overcome any feelings of attraction for her. It was highly irritating trying to fight these emotions, but he would not fall for Angeline Hamilton, if it was the last thing he did. His frustration of being in her presence started to grow by the second.

"Good afternoon, Angeline." He wanted to so desperately give her a short nod and walk past her, but he was battling the desire to stay and continue absorbing the beauty of this woman. She softly laughed, and she was exquisite.

"Am I not *Angie* to you anymore?" she pleasantly responded.

Harrison sighed. Over the past few weeks, he tried his hardest to maintain the friendly relationship he and Angeline had before he destroyed her opinion of him by the overwhelming kiss that he still could not remove from his mind. He tried to maintain his friendship with her, but he couldn't. In some strange way, she was so appealing to him, and being in her presence made him want more. *Why you?* he thought in annoyance. *How do I overcome this vixen's hold over me?*

"Harrison?" Angeline softly asked. "Is everything okay?"

He furrowed his brow in question. "Everything is fine. Forgive me; there is a lot on my mind these days."

"Is everything going well with the plans to recover Emperor Navarre?"

"As well as can be expected." He looked past her.

"Harry, please forgive me if I am out of line here, but things seem to have changed with you—with us." Her eyes displayed her remorse. "Did you not vow that things would remain the same? Are you angry with me for some reason?"

Harrison cleared his throat. "Angeline, a lot has taken place since the mistake we made by engaging in a kiss. You must understand that I have been so busy attending to Guardian affairs that I must have completely forgotten the promise I made you, as I seem to have forgotten anything had taken place between the two of us at all until this conversation."

It wasn't true, and he knew it, but right now he did not have the courage to tell her why he had changed toward her. He watched as she swallowed hard in response to his lie

"Really?" she said as her expression became severe. She arched her eyebrow at him and folded her arms. "Well, I suppose I know now why it is no secret that most of the young women in my father's kingdom despise you. I am only sorry that I have fallen victim to you as well."

"Victim?" he said in disbelief. "Ms. Hamilton, it was a kiss, nothing more. I would have imagined you would have forgotten such a minute thing."

"What?" she spoke out angrily.

Harrison knew the expression on her face very well, as it was the same look he had received time and again before he was slapped by all of the other women. Maybe that's what he needed, Angeline to slap some sense back into him so he could think straight again.

Her expression quickly changed, and she smiled at him. Her hand came up to his face, but not to slap it. Her eyes roamed over his features, and Harrison was paralyzed by her tender touch. He hadn't remembered what he had just said, thought, or done, and now he had no idea why he was so fortunate this moment was happening to him.

"I pity you," she said in concern. "You are a good man, Harrison Oxley. Yet you are so prideful and arrogant that you will never see that. You will never find love, and you will probably never desire it." Tears filled her eyes. "I will never forget that kiss, our kiss. Not only was it a dreamlike experience for me, but it also saved me the heartache of ever making the mistake of falling in love with you." She withdrew her hand. "Fortunately, I still admire you, Harry. I delight in your company, and for that reason I will forgive the harsh words you have spoken to me." She gave him a small curtsy. "Good day, sir."

Harrison stared intently at Angeline as she gathered her long yellow dress and briskly strode back up to the palace, not looking back at him once. *You're the biggest idiot in the universe!* he thought. He shook his head with regret that he would say something so callous and so contrary to his truth.

He walked into Levi's office and found his cousin staring intently at the paperwork on his desk.

"So when does the lovely wife return to Pasidian?" he said as he sat in an empty chair across from Levi.

Levi glanced up and grinned. "She should be arriving within the hour." He stood. "Cousin, you look like you have just returned from battle." He laughed. "Join me on the sofa; it looks like we could both use a drink."

Harrison gladly accepted the offer and sat on the sofa, waiting for Levi to bring him his glass. After Levi handed Harrison his glass, he took a seat next to him and relaxed into the sofa.

"I must say, you are doing better than I expected since your new bride has been away from you for over a week." Harrison looked over at Levi and grinned.

"Indeed, I have. I believe it is the business I have been handling and our strategizing about how we will travel into this other world that has kept my mind otherwise engaged. I fear if Reece were here, she would be extremely neglected by me as of late anyway."

"Have you heard if she is making any more progress with the queen?"

Levi nodded. "Queen Galleta seems to be extremely impressed with how she is coming along. We will know the final results when she returns."

"Can I ask you something completely off the subject?" Harrison asked without thinking.

"Of course you can. What is on your mind?"

"Well, I do not really know how to approach this," Harrison thought aloud.

"Approach what?"

He looked over at Levi and sighed. "If you do not mind my intruding on your personal affairs, I was wondering about something. When you first kissed Reece—" He stopped himself. *This is definitely not the conversation to be having with Levi, or with any man for that matter.* He thought as he exhaled.

Levi softly chuckled. "Go on."

"I do not know why I am asking this." He looked over at Levi again, only to find his eyes alit in humor. *I can only imagine how long he has been waiting for this day to come.* "When you first kissed Reece, did it upset her at all? I mean, did you kiss her in such a way that it would insult her?"

Levi laughed aloud but abruptly stopped himself and cleared his throat. "Harrison, I am not concerned over the fact that you are inquiring about mine and Reece's first kiss, what I *am* concerned about are your reasons for asking about it."

"Forget it."

"No, you will tell me. Who has finally gotten through to that stubborn heart of yours? I would like to know who this woman is that has finally made you feel guilty about your heartless advances toward women in general."

"I know you find this humorous, Levi, as well as you should, but I will not mention any names. Will you just answer my question?"

"Fine. When I first kissed Reece, it did not upset her; however, I did not dare to do such a thing until after I confessed that I had feelings for her and she told me her feelings were mutual."

Harrison sat back on the sofa and took a sip of his drink. "I must say, I envy the gentleman in you."

Levi laughed again. "Since when does the *great* Harrison Oxley care that I am a noble gentleman? I am sure you have been possessed, my friend, because I have no idea who the man is that is speaking to me now."

Harrison leaned forward, resting both elbows on his knees and gazing intently into the fireplace. "You are probably correct. I am possessed, bewitched, or something of that nature."

"Who is she?" Levi asked in amusement.

Harrison shook his head. "It does not matter. Let us talk about something else."

Levi sat up some. "Very well, then. What else have you learned from Mordegrin about this other world?"

"It appears that our journey will take us through some very harsh terrain. The horses will be challenged, as it will be nearly a five-day journey to the fortress where the emperor and these dark beings are."

"Do we need to have Javian and the Guardian horse trainers start conditioning the horses for such travel?"

Harrison grinned. "I believe we shall all need to be conditioning ourselves for this journey."

"Is there an alternate, less rigorous route that we could take instead?"

"From the map that Mordegrin has shown me in his mind, it appears this is the safest way of travel to avoid confrontation with any other dark forces."

Just then, the door opened to the room. "Emperor Levi, the empress' carriage is entering the village below."

Levi stood. "Allow me a moment to greet Reece, and then I will return."

"Take your time," Harrison said as he stood. "I believe I will take my lunch in the command center for now."

"Very well, then. Maybe a nice lunch will help you clear your thoughts?" Levi finished with a laugh.

Harrison sighed. "My thoughts are perfectly fine," he said as he followed Levi out of his office.

Fortunately, Vincent had much to report to Harrison once he reached the command center. Vincent had been doing an excellent job standing in for Harrison while he was occupied with Levi and Mordegrin.

After finishing his business in the command center, Harrison noted the time had not passed as quickly as he imagined. He felt it best to return to his chambers and freshen up.

After a brief shower and a quick change of clothes, Harrison sat on his sofa and gazed out of his windows which over looked the palace's front lawns. With nothing to distract him, he finally felt some peace.

Just as he thought he would be able to enjoy this newfound peace, a knock on his door interrupted it. He had already excused his butler for the evening, so he pulled himself reluctantly up from the couch and went to open his door.

"Harrison," Angeline said with a warm smile. "May I enter?"

Harrison absently stepped back and motioned for her to enter his rooms. "Is there something I can do for you, Angeline?" He watched her saunter past him, and he could not peel his eyes away from her tempting physique.

He walked down to where she stood pouring herself a glass of wine and refilling his. *That's a bit out of the ordinary,* he thought as she grinned and handed him his chalice. "Angeline, you must know, it is highly improper for you to be in my rooms without company."

Angeline giggled as she sipped her wine, never taking her eyes off his. "When has anything improper ever disturbed you, Harry?"

*Is this really happening?* he thought as he took a sip of his wine. "Angeline—"

"Please stop referring to me as Angeline." She walked over to him and ran her fingers along his face. "When can I be Angie to you again?"

Harrison saw the sultry expression in her eyes, the desire they held for him, and he was finding it highly irresistible to refuse her at this moment.

"As you wish, Angie."

She brought her hands to his knotted cravat and easily removed it. Harrison inhaled deeply and caught her hand. "Angie, no."

She arched a brow at him. "I know that you have feelings for me." She started to remove his waistcoat and proceeded to unbutton his shirt. He stood paralyzed, watching Angeline fulfill what he'd been longing for.

"Do not make me beg for you, Harrison," she said as she stepped back and uncovered one of her shoulders. "I know you want this as much as I do."

All sensibility had left him. He walked toward her and took her slender frame into his arms. His lips were on her shoulder, tasting the sweetness of her fragrance that consumed him every time he was around her. Her silky soft skin was highly irresistible, and her pleas for him made this moment highly intoxicating.

He stepped back, and her eyes reopened. "I cannot do this." He sighed. "Not with *you*, Angie."

She stepped toward him and removed his undershirt, caressing his sides and leaving him breathless. "Yes, Harrison, you can. I want you to."

Her lips found his in a crushing kiss, and he could not help but to return her advances. "I love you," he said absently as he cradled in her arms. "After this night, you *will* know that I am not that man that other women speak of."

She ran her hands through his hair as he walked briskly into his bed chambers. "It doesn't matter to me, I want you either way."

Harrison laid her gently on the bed and brought his eyes to meet hers. "If we do this, I vow to make an honest woman of you."

Angeline didn't respond with words. She pressed her hands firmly down his back and brought her lips to his throat.

Five hard knocks to his door startled Harrison awake. *Not again!* He flung the throw pillow he had been resting on across the sofa and abruptly stood. *This woman will be the death of me.* "I *love* you?" he grumbled. "Love? Give me a break." *Yes, I am bewitched by Angeline Hamilton. These dreams must stop.*

Two more knocks on his door, and he walked briskly to it. He opened his door with force to find Levi standing there, staring at him in shock. "Taking a nap? What has gotten into you?"

*Nothing you are going to find out anytime soon,* Harrison thought as he ignored his cousin's question. Instead, he turned and walked down to pour a drink. He gulped it down like water and turned back to find Levi watching him with a questioning expression.

He refilled his glass to another large drink and narrowed his eyes at Levi. "What?"

Levi nodded toward the empty glass. "It appears that something has you quite distressed? Care to tell me about it?"

Harrison straightened his waistcoat. "There has just been quite a lot to deal with these days." He clapped Levi on his shoulder. "I am amazed at how well you are coping."

Levi studied his cousin and grinned. "Fortunately, my wife is an excellent support."

"Quit prying. My current disposition has not been brought about by a woman."

Levi's lips tightened. "I wasn't implying that a woman would be the cause of your distress."

"There is no other reason you would have that ridiculous grin on your face." Harrison sighed and stretched his arm toward the exit of his room. "Let us go. I am confident you have searched me out for dinner, and I am in no mood to continue this conversation."

"I have had the servants send our dinner to the command center. King Hamilton and your father will be joining us as well. We would like to go over the details of the map Mordegrin showed you, and go into further detail about what you learned from him today."

*Thank goodness. The last person I need to see right now is Princess Bronze Eyes,* he thought. He grinned at Levi and thought, *Sounds like an excellent idea to me.*

Once the men finished their meals, Harrison called for the lights to dim in the command center, and he brought up the holographic image of the destination they were to journey to. Harrison pointed toward the far left of the map, where the atmosphere was red and lingered over rugged, snow-capped mountains.

"The machine has enhanced the map I saw in Mordegrin's mind; however, I believe you can easily see the ruggedness of this terrain where the portal must be opened. It is essential that we travel through these icy, treacherous mountains when we enter this galaxy." He turned back to the men.

Levi studied the map for a moment. "You are positive there are no other locations from which we can enter this domain?"

"We need to be as discreet as possible once the portal has been opened. So discreet, in fact, that we must not stop for anything for at least a few hours in order to take us away from the portal as swiftly as possible. We cannot allow anyone in this galaxy to know the location of the opening into Earth's galaxy."

"How many Guardians do you believe we will need to assist on this journey?" Nathaniel asked.

"We will have close to three thousand men with us; however, we will not all travel through at the same time. My thoughts are that close to one hundred men will travel with Levi, Reece, and myself. The other men that come through the portal behind us will come through one hundred at a time. I will go over the details with them about where we will all join together after they enter." Harrison pointed at the map again. "They will be out in these areas traveling alongside us."

"We all are very aware that King Nathaniel must remain as reigning emperor while Levi is away," King Hamilton spoke up. "Now the question is, which group of men shall I lead into this galaxy?"

"Your Majesty," Levi responded, "you should not burden yourself with this. The Guardians are expertly trained to handle this without risking the life of one of our greatest Pemdai kings."

King Hamilton twisted in his seat and grinned at Levi, "With all due respect, Emperor Levi, your father and I were not only the best of friends, but also great warriors in our day as well. I *will* join our men on this mission and help to lead them."

Levi sat back, crossed his arms, and grinned, "I believe you and my wife are the only two who have challenged my concern over their well-being on this mission."

The group laughed in unison.

"Very well, King Hamilton shall lead an army of warriors in; which one do you believe it best for him to lead?" Levi asked Harrison.

Harrison stared at the king, wishing he would change his mind.

"Harry?" King Hamilton spoke out.

"I believe the fourth group in should suffice," Harrison answered.

King Hamilton sat back in his chair. "That will do."

"Emperor Levi, when are you going to send for all of the kings and personally inform them of this news?" Nathaniel asked.

"I have notified them all about the news that Emperor Navarre is alive; however, until we have made all of our preparations, I will not have them at the palace for meetings at this time."

"Is there a particular reason for that?" King Hamilton asked.

Levi took a sip of wine. "I do not desire to hear their doubts, nor their opinions."

King Hamilton laughed aloud, and Harrison's attention was brought back to him while the men remained in conversation. *Why must he insist on joining us?* Harrison thought in concern. His thoughts returned to Angeline and how she would manage another death in her family if her father did not survive this mission. With concern for Angeline, his thoughts became consumed with her again. He couldn't remove the images and feelings he had for her in the most recent dream he had and how he wished with all he was that it was reality.

"Would you not agree, Harrison?" Levi asked in amusement.

*Oh great! Now I am tuning everyone out while I obsess over her?* Harrison shook his head, inwardly begging himself to concentrate on the men staring at him with humored expressions.

"Forgive me, agree with what?" He cleared his throat.

Levi's features lightened. "No apologies needed. I can see a lot is going on in your mind. I was only speaking in jest about the fact that King Hamilton will most certainly end up begging you to lead the second troop in on this journey instead of the fourth."

Harrison faintly smiled. "Indeed." He glanced over at King Hamilton. "I mean no disrespect, Your Majesty, but your family has already grieved the honorable death of Julian, and it is my wish to keep you as safe as possible. Journeying into this galaxy with the fourth regiment of troops assures me of your safety.

Hamilton laughed aloud. "Boy, I do not know what has come over you, but I will do as requested by our commander."

Harrison had completely given himself away, and he knew it. Levi knew exactly who the young woman was that he was obsessing over, and he only hoped that his generous cousin would not question him about her.

After their meeting, Levi and Harrison joined the young women in the sitting room. Being in Angeline's presence again had Harrison reeling with frustration. He inwardly wished he would have joined his father and King Hamilton in the parlor with their wives and his aunt.

Angeline sat next to Reece as Mozart hummed to her. Everyone was in excellent spirits, and Harrison tried with all of his power to join in. Unfortunately, his usual good humor was replaced with sharp, sarcastic, and snippy remarks to the entire group, and especially toward Angeline.

"We should have all known there was something special about you, Reece. Not only because you are from Earth, but with the way the animals admire you as they do." Angeline laughed as she touched Mozart's nose. "I must say, all of it is all so astounding."

"Astounding, is it?" Harrison snapped.

Angeline's bright expression faded when she looked over at Harrison. She had been doing very well with all of his harsh remarks toward her; however, it appeared she was reaching her limit with Harrison's attitude.

Her eyebrow shot up sharply. "That is exactly what I said."

"Well then, it appears that everyone except for you has gotten over their amazement by Reece's ability to be the animal whisperer of Pemdas."

The comment he made was not only rude toward Angeline, but degrading toward Reece as well. In truth, he agreed with Angeline, and he was probably more astounded by Reece's abilities than she was. Fortunately, when he went to apologize to Reece for his rude remark, he found her and Levi stifling a laugh. *Great, they both know. Why is this happening to me?* He had to leave the room. What he really needed was some fresh air in order to get his mind straight again.

"Well, maybe it is no longer amazing to you, Harry, and that is most likely due to your arrogant attitude about everything." Angeline smiled wryly at him. "I, on the other hand, will always find it amazing."

"You are absurd," Harrison said with utter disgust in his tone. "Arrogant? You have yet to encounter me utilizing my *arrogance* to its full advantage."

Angeline shot him a knowing, fiery gaze. "I believe you are very much mistaken in that regard."

Harrison couldn't ignore the reactions of those who just witnessed him make an absolute fool of himself. Levi was using his fist to conceal a smile while he fixed his eyes on the table before him. Reece and Elizabeth remained silent, seemingly in shock while Angeline continued to gaze up at him severely. He studied Angeline's expression, knowing she was waiting for his response. For the first time in his life he had no response to someone challenging him. Instead, his eyes became spellbound by hers, and he was helpless against her beauty once again.

"Harrison, what has gotten into you?" Elizabeth asked uncertainly.

Levi coughed, most likely preventing himself from bursting into laughter, and Harrison didn't fail to notice Reece place a hand over Levi's in understanding. He glared over at their amused expressions. *Looks like I just elected myself as the source of their pillow talk tonight,* he thought in anger.

He abruptly stood. "Forgive me, but I believe I have grown weary of trying to keep company with anyone today," he said, looking directly at Angeline. "I will leave you all to enjoy your evening, as I am finding myself rather annoyed by having to sit in this room any longer."

He forced his eyes from Angeline's and briskly left the room. He approached the front doors of the palace and strode out to the front gardens, desperately seeking fresh air and a change of environment. He wasn't far from the steps when Angeline called out to him.

*Will this never end?*

"Harrison Oxley!" Angeline sternly called out to him again.

He turned to find Angeline's expression fierce. "What?" he retorted. "Am I not *Harry* to you anymore?" he said, mocking her words from earlier.

Her eyes narrowed. "After what has transpired between the two of us in that sitting room, and the scene you caused, I am afraid not." She approached him and crossed her arms. "First you embarrass me in front of everyone, and then you mock my desire for friendship with you?

What is wrong with you? Why do you despise me so greatly?"

Harrison firmly ran both hands through his hair. He had to think straight. He tilted his head to the side, entrapped by her again. *Just say it, you idiot!* He couldn't bear hurting her anymore.

"Angeline, I do not despise you in the least," he said softly.

"Then why are you treating me like this? It makes absolutely no sense to me."

"I know. And what you have done to me makes no sense to me either." He softly laughed.

"What I have done to you?" she asked in disbelief. "Please, enlighten me. All I have asked of you is for your friendship."

"Angie, please understand that what I am about to tell you goes against everything that I am. To feel this way about any woman—it is unlike me. I fear I have been quite angry with myself for feeling these emotions. I never wanted this. I never believed I would ever desire a woman's love so much, but apparently I do; and believe me when I say that I have gone through great efforts to fight the feelings that I have been having about you. I do not know how to deal with any of this, even now."

He stepped closer to her and brought his hand to her face, letting the softness of her skin soothe him. Her expression never changed, she only stood there staring intently at him. *What was she thinking?* "Angeline, I must have you know that against all of my power, I believe I may have somehow fallen in love with you."

Angeline stepped back out of Harrison's reach. "In *love* with me?" she returned, shaking her head incredulously. "Wow. I must say that after such a flattering declaration of love, I suppose I should be thrilled?"

"As I said, this is all so difficult for me to accept. If it came out wrong, I am sorry. You must believe me; I truly believe I am in love—"

"Harrison, stop," she interrupted him in a dismissive tone. "Allow me to educate you on something. In order to love someone, you must enjoy being in their company. You would smile at them instead of glaring at them all of the time. You would not tell that person that you loved them against everything that was in your power. And you most certainly would not cast the blame on them for the feelings you wish you never had. You are pathetic." She turned to leave.

He gently reached for her arm, halting her. "Angie, please do not leave me like this. This is all coming out wrong."

"It is making perfect sense to me." She jerked her arm free from his gentle grip. "You are a narcissistic, selfish man, and I hold absolutely no attraction toward a man such as you. My father informed me that he wishes to remain at the palace, and I had planned to do the same. However, after tonight, I believe I would have better company at my family's estate. It would seem that both of us could use some time away from each other. Perhaps when we meet again, you will revert back to your normal self."

"You are correct, Princess Hamilton." He stared intently into her eyes. "Time away from you is exactly what I need. Forgive me for wasting your time this evening. I do hope you have a safe journey home."

She shook her head. "You are unbelievable."

With that, she turned and marched into the palace. Harrison watched her leave him in shock. As he stood there trying to breathe, it had felt as though a knife had been stuck into his cold heart. He numbly walked down the path, unable to comprehend what he had done. He came up on an isolated stone bench, sat down, and dropped his face into his hands.

"You are a complete wreck," Reece said in laughter.

He never lifted his head to acknowledge her, yet he felt her sit next to him while bringing her arm around his back.

"Reece, please, leave me be. What are you doing out here anyway?"

"Well, after your display in the sitting room this evening, Levi was on his way out to find you; however, given his current lack of sympathy for your situation, I felt it would be best if I gave you some support instead."

He sat up and stared at her in disillusionment. "Reece, none of this is what you or Levi might think it to be."

"It's no secret now that something is going on between you and Angie."

Harrison sighed. "I am in no mood to talk about it."

"I know. That's why I convinced Levi to let me come out and talk to you alone."

"Levi has indeed waited for the day when a woman would have some kind of a power over me like this."

He felt Reece softly laugh again. "I see nothing wrong with that. Angeline is beautiful, talented, and has an excellent personality. To be honest, I believe you both suit each other very well. Why would you be so upset about being attracted to her?"

"I do not know. I cannot even think in her presence. Since the day I kissed—" He stopped himself. "Never mind. Please, I merely need some time alone and to get my thoughts straight. There are bigger issues for me to be dealing with right now that have nothing to do with women."

Reece stood up. "Good luck with that," she said with a laugh.

"What?" he said, looking up at her.

"It's completely obvious that you've fallen in love with her. If you actually admitted that to yourself, I think you could tell her about your true feelings a lot more easily." She smiled. "I've seen the way she looks at you; I think she would probably be overjoyed to know you feel this way about her."

He softly laughed. "I did tell her."

Reece stared at him expectantly. "And?"

"And now I am the last person in Pemdas she ever desires to be in the company of."

Reece's expression lightened with humor. "What did you say to her?"

"I told her that I did love her, and it was against everything that was within me—"

"Harrison! Are you out of your mind?"

"I really believe that I am."

"Well, you have successfully ruined that declaration of love."

"Do not remind me."

"You need to accept it, get over yourself, and stop being such a jackass."

Harrison looked up at Reece, and for the first time since he returned to the palace he smiled. "Aren't you just the helpful therapist?"

"You want a helpful therapist?" she started. "Let Angeline calm down for the evening, and while she is doing so, I believe you should take some lessons from Levi in the 'declarations of love' department." She laughed. "I can tell you that as a female, she will eventually get over this, but it will not happen unless you apologize to her first."

Harrison stood. "I will try to find a way to apologize."

For the rest of the evening, Harrison returned to his duties at the command center, knowing it would be an excellent distraction. Who knew what the days ahead of him would bring, but struggling with the fact that the one woman he loved vowed to never return his feelings seemed to be troubling him more than anything.

After a restless night, Harrison found himself tormented knowing that he may never see Angeline again. Even if he did, she would always despise him for the way he treated her. He had to make it right with her somehow. Reece was correct, he had to apologize, and hopefully she would offer him another chance and remain at the palace.

Just as the sun was rising, Harrison gathered information from the servants that Angeline was prepared to leave before breakfast. He sought her out, only to find Elizabeth returning from the front lawns of the palace.

"Has Angie left already?" he asked in concern.

Elizabeth stared up at him. "Yes. Cousin, what did you say to her? She will not confide in me about it, but I cannot understand why she would change her plans so abruptly and leave first thing. Forgive me for being so bold, but I believe it was your irrational behavior toward her last night."

Harrison sighed. "You are correct, Lizzy. I must apologize to her at once. How long ago did she leave?"

Elizabeth smiled up at him in relief. "Only a few moments ago."

Harrison impulsively brought Elizabeth into an embrace. "I will make things right again, sweet one. I am sorry I insulted your dearest friend."

With that, he jogged down toward the stables. He called for Saracen and walked into the tack room, grabbing his horse's reigns.

"Master Harrison, I can have him saddled for—"

"There is no time for that, but thank you," Harrison interrupted Javian.

He spun around and walked out to the stable yard. Saracen was not in sight, and he urgently called out to him again. After a few moments, he heard Saracen's hooves echoing in the distance before he appeared from over the mountainside, racing aggressively toward Harrison.

Harrison abruptly hopped the fence, and as soon as Saracen approached him, Harrison pulled the reins up onto his head. Once buckled and secured, Harrison quickly hoisted himself up onto his stallion's back and led him at full charge over the fence and off toward the location where Angeline's carriage would be.

The carriage was out in the countryside when he finally approached the convoy. King Hamilton's guards abruptly halted their travel when they saw Harrison rapidly approaching them.

"Your Grace, is there news of which we should be made aware?" the guard on the lead horse questioned, most likely wondering if Harrison was informing them of a dangerous situation ahead.

"Have no fear; I do not bring you urgent news of any sort. However, I must speak with Princess Angeline for a moment."

The man nodded, and Harrison was off Saracen before the footman could open the carriage door. Harrison dismissed him, and when he opened her door he found her staring at him in utter amazement.

"Harrison, what are you doing?"

"I must speak with you. Please allow me a few moments of your time," he asked.

She smiled. "Harrison, it is fine. Please—"

"It is far from being fine. Now, if you will join me on a short walk?"

"Very well."

She placed her hand into his and allowed him to help her from the carriage. The guards and the coach pulled further off the road, allowing others to pass while they waited. Harrison drew Angeline's arm up into his and led her out and away from the carriage and guards.

"Angeline, I desperately owe you an apology for my uncouth behavior over these past few weeks. I really do not know where to begin."

Angeline smiled sympathetically. "Are we going to have *this* conversation again?"

Harrison stopped and turned to face her. "When I told you that I had forgotten our kiss, it was indeed a lie."

He cheeks colored lightly, and she diverted her eyes from him.

"Angie, please look at me," he softly pled. "I have not been able to concentrate on anything while in your presence since that day. I understand my manners have been entirely rude and harsh toward you as a result of that. I could not understand why I would obsess over such a thing. I did not know why I was unable to concentrate in your presence, and it was highly frustrating for me. Instead of accepting the truth of what was happening to me, I fought it greatly."

"Harrison, you really do not have to do this."

"Yes, I do. Angie, everything I spoke to you last evening was in truth. Falling in love was never something I wanted, with you or with anyone. Unfortunately, my pride stood in the way of telling you what I understand now."

She looked at him with trepidation. "And what is that?" she said with irritation hinting in her voice.

"Angeline, I am deeply in love with you. You are an astonishing young woman, and you have captured my heart. I would give anything to feel my lips on yours again, to hold you in my arms, to take peaceful walks alone with you. To hear you say that you love me in return." He tilted his head to the side. "However, I have brutally destroyed any good opinion you may have ever held for me, and I believe that love is probably the last emotion you could ever feel toward me now."

"Harrison," she smiled, "you will always have a special place in my heart; however, I truly do not believe—"

He took her hand. "Give me another chance, I beg of you. I can be that man whom you desire to love one day, allow me to prove this to you. Angie, I can be him. I have never desired a woman's presence in all my life, such as I desire yours."

Tears filled her eyes. "Harrison, please."

"For the next few weeks, I will be extremely distracted by my duties at the palace working to recover the emperor, and I believe I will not have the time to prove it to you. But I will, Angeline. For now, will you at least accept my apology for my detestable behavior toward you?"

"I do forgive you, Harrison." She smiled guardedly.

"Will you consider returning to the palace?"

Angeline looked past him. "I believe it is best if I do not."

He brought her hand to his mouth and gently kissed it. "There is no woman I have ever loved but you, Angeline Hamilton. Please do not leave."

She studied his eyes for a moment. "I really must be going. Please reassure Lizzy that everything is fine with me. She seemed quite distraught by my abrupt change of plans."

"I will," he answered, knowing he could beg her no longer. He had lost the only woman he ever imagined he could love, all due to his arrogance and pride.

"If I do not see you again before you all leave to rescue Emperor Navarre, I do hope you all remain safe." Her eyes pleaded with him. "And please, if you truly love me as you have said, then you will do this one thing for me."

"Anything."

"Ensure that my father is safe on this journey." Her eyes filled with tears. "I cannot bear to lose another whom I love so greatly."

"You have my word." He offered his arm. "Allow me to escort you back to your carriage."

His heart felt broken, and he began to feel a strange emptiness form inside of him. If she couldn't trust his love for her, then he must accept it. He only wanted her to find happiness, whether or not he was the man she sought it from.

# Chapter 21

Reece woke to Levi gently brushing his fingertips along her arm. She turned over and lazily wrapped herself around him, snuggling further into his warm body.

She softly kissed his chest. "I'm surprised you're still in bed."

"That is because this is the first time in over a week that I have had the luxury of waking up with my beautiful wife by my side," Levi smiled, "and I believe this will be the last morning we will have like this until my father has been recovered. I desire as much time with you as I can get."

"It's good to be home."

"It is good to have you home again, love." He sat up some. "We have not discussed many details about the lessons you had with Queen Galleta. I will send for her today, as I am curious about her opinion regarding your developments."

Reece propped her head up against her hand. "Are you wondering if I passed my tests?" she teased. "What if I didn't?"

Levi grinned. "Then I will have words with you, Mrs. Oxley, for leaving me for such an extended period of time, and for no reason."

He studied her eyes for a moment. "Your eyes—"

"What about them?" she asked skeptically.

He ran his hand along her cheek. "I noticed yesterday when you first arrived home that they appeared to be more vibrant than usual, but it would appear now as though they are changing in color somewhat."

Reece chuckled. "Yes, I noticed that too. Do you see the bright yellow flakes in them?"

He nodded with an intrigued expression on his face. "They seem to be turning green in color, as they did when you had your vision. They are very beautiful, indeed, like jewels. I wonder why that is?"

"Well, it kind of scared me in the beginning, so I asked Galleta. She told me that my eyes would continue to do this the more my abilities emerge and my mind opens. It's strange because ever since I started to unlock these powers within my mind, I not only think more clearly, but colors and details of my surroundings are very vivid to me; it's as if everything is so much brighter to me now. And then my ability to learn and retain things is extraordinary. Can you believe that I read a Pemdai medical book and understood everything without even trying to learn it? And now all of that information is saved in my mind, like I memorized the book just by reading it."

"So you were successful then?"

"We did a series of meditations, and it was like all of a sudden something clicked in my mind. I could control that weird intuition I was having difficulty with. It's like I can turn it off or on," she laughed, "which is really good because I was beginning to feel like a busybody intruding on everyone's private feelings."

"Well, it did come in helpful with Harrison and Angeline."

"I wasn't reading their emotions last night."

Levi's eyebrow arched. "No? Well, I would have thought Harrison was out of his mind yesterday had you not told me beforehand that something was happening with him and Angie."

"Poor guy. You have to feel sorry for him a little bit?"

"Not in the slightest," he countered. "Believe me, this is good for him. You have no idea what that guy has put me through with his concept of women in all our years together."

"Levi, he really does love her. He is just having a particularly difficult time conveying it to her. I hope he doesn't ruin this for himself, though; I think Angeline is perfect for him."

"Harrison will be fine, and I do hope Angie does challenge him in his pursuit. Harrison could use some lessons on how to treat a lady."

"And if he screws it all up?"

Levi raised his arms up and clasped his hands behind his head. "Then hopefully he will have learned something from his egotistical mistakes."

"Oh, don't be so heartless," Reece teased as she ran her hand along his side and he jerked slightly in response.

Her eyes widened. "Are you ticklish?"

Levi frowned. "Of course not—Reece!—Don't!"

Reece giggled in delight as she found her husband's weak spot. He jerked again and laughed as she tickled each of his sides. She didn't get to marvel in torturing him for long before he was on top of her, pinning her hands above her head.

"Now that you have uncovered the only secret I have intentionally withheld from you, I do hope you will not take advantage of this new revelation."

Reece grinned. "Promise me that you will be supportive of Harrison if he comes to you again for advice."

"Giving me orders now, are we?" He kissed her chin. "What else did the queen help you learn about your hidden talents besides your new assertiveness toward your husband?"

"I will show you another thing I learned, but you have to promise to help Harrison if he asks."

Levi's head tilted to the side. "Another lesson you learned?"

She bit her bottom lip while smiling at him and nodded. "You will appreciate it."

His eyes narrowed. "It is not in my nature to succumb to bribery; however, I believe it would be wise to do so in this case."

"Very wise."

Levi exhaled. "Very well, then. If Harrison seeks my counsel, I shall try my best to be helpful."

"That's the generous man I fell in love with." She gave him a quick kiss. "Now, let's make the best of our last peaceful morning together. Relax while I show exactly what

327

my mind is capable of when it comes to passionately loving my husband."

Reece sat in her vanity room in her bathrobe, waiting for Jasmeen to finish pulling her hair back into an intricate braid.

"Jasmeen, you don't have to be so creative; I'm just going down to the Guardian training unit."

"You look dashing, Mrs. Oxley," a deep voice called out from behind. "Jasmeen, Henry notified me that if you are ready to take your breakfast, he will gladly escort you."

Jasmeen's cheeks flushed as she gave Levi a curtsy. "Allow me to finish with—"

Reece grinned. "I'm fine, Jasmeen. Go have breakfast with Henry."

After Jasmeen left the room, Levi approached Reece, kissed her softly on her head, and placed a large box in her lap. "For you, my love; it is a gift from Harrison."

Reece glanced up at Levi in amazement. "Harrison is giving me gifts now? Are you already teaching him to practice for Angeline?" she teased.

Levi shook his head. "Just open it."

She did, and she found a black training outfit neatly folded inside. "Well, it looks like someone's excited to work out in the training center today."

Levi chuckled. "More than excited, actually. After learning of your progress with Queen Galleta, Harrison is looking forward to testing your new limits."

Reece stood up. "Do I change into it now? We haven't had breakfast yet."

"We shall take our breakfast in my office this morning after our meeting with Harrison and Queen Galleta. I want to go over more of what you learned with the queen before you attend the Guardian training. Harrison needs to know more so he can take the proper approach in training you as well."

After Reece was dressed, Levi escorted her down to his office. A few moments after they arrived, a servant admitted Queen Galleta and Harrison to the room. Once everyone was seated in their chairs around Levi's desk, Levi addressed them.

"Thank you for joining us, Queen Galleta. It appears as though Reece has done very well with your help, and I am greatly appreciative for your assistance with that," he said.

Galleta smiled at Reece. "Emperor, she has exceeded all of my expectations, and I believe she will be ready much sooner than we had expected."

"I am fully aware that we are in an extremely urgent situation. Under any other circumstances, we would have commenced the recovery of my father the moment we found out where he was. With each passing day, my concern for him and his current condition grows stronger. It is my greatest desire to charge through the portal this instant in order to retrieve him and bring him home; unfortunately, this is a situation that we must be overly prepared for, or we will not only put his life in grave danger, but our lives, and the lives of every being on Pemdas, Earth, and all of the dimensions that are interconnected." Levi shifted in his seat, glanced at Reece, and then brought a somber expression to both Harrison and Galleta. "I also will not risk Reece's life any more than I already am by her involvement with this. I will not rush anything; therefore, I must be certain that you are confident in your assumptions of her preparedness."

"That is understandable, Your Royal Majesty; nevertheless, I believe you will find Reece's success as remarkable as I have," Galleta returned.

"I do hope you are correct. If all goes well, and I am confident with Reece's condition, then I believe we can make our plans to retrieve the stone by the week's end. Now, how exactly do her talents work? How will they protect her?"

"She has not reached her full potential with her abilities, as only the stone's power will give that to her; but she is able to control the new abilities that were happening to her without warning."

Reece looked at Galleta. "What will change with me when we go to the stone?"

"The moment you make contact with the stone, its powers will ignite the Olteniaus genes you carry within you. At that moment, you will have full control over your mind without having to concentrate so greatly, as you are doing now. Everything will come naturally to you. And with your mind functioning in such a way, you will know then exactly how to open the portal."

"How will she respond to the Guardian training with what she is able to do now?" Harrison asked.

"All she will need to do is to watch the Guardians' combat training sessions for an hour or so; after that, it will be imprinted into her mind, and she will know exactly how to fight as they do."

Levi looked at Harrison. "Of course, Reece must gain strength before she is trained in such a way."

Harrison rolled his eyes. "Levi, I am not going to have anyone trying to kill her just yet."

"The one thing that does intrigue me, Emperor, is what you mentioned about Reece being able to project her thoughts and emotions into your mind," Galleta said.

Reece's eyes widened as she stared at Levi, hoping he didn't tell her what they were doing during the only times this particular ability had manifested itself. Levi looked at

Reece and grinned. *Levi, please tell me you didn't tell her the situations we were in when it happened?* she asked him telepathically, knowing now how to do so at will.

Levi slightly shook his head in a negative response to Reece's question, and she sighed in relief.

Levi cleared his throat. "Yes? What about this ability of hers intrigues you?" he asked.

"Well, it appears that she is only able to do this with your mind." She tilted her head to the side. "I am unsure why that is."

Levi looked at Reece. "That is intriguing. And it appears she can use this particular talent at her own will now as well," he said as he glanced in Reece's direction.

"Yes. I believe this ability is very powerful."

"I do wonder why my mind is the only one she is able to do this with."

"It must be the way your minds are connected, and it must have started sometime after you took the information about the stone from her mind," Galleta responded.

"Is Reece able to read anyone's mind if given the opportunity?" Harrison asked.

"No. In that regard, her talents are reversed. Instead of reading one's mind, she can persuade it."

Levi leaned forward. "Persuade a mind?" His eyes widened some. "As the Ciatron are able to do?"

"Yes."

Harrison looked somberly at Reece. "That is what that priestess woman was doing to Reece when she was here." He shook his head. "Wow. That was a terrible situation for you, Reece." He sat back and grinned. "But maybe when we meet up with them personally, you can pay back the favor."

Reece crossed her arms. "Don't think I hadn't thought about that when I first found out that I could do this."

"When Reece goes with us to where these Olteniaus females are, will they have an effect on her like that again? Is her mind capable of being protected?" Levi continued.

"Reece is susceptible to mental persuasion, yes," Galleta answered as she looked at Reece. "But you will continue to use the techniques you learned in order to protect your mind from it, correct?"

"I will."

Galleta nodded. "As long as Reece maintains this focus while in that world, she should be able to block them."

Levi's lips twisted.

"Levi," Reece said firmly, "I will be fine. Don't let that worry you. We are going there together, no matter what."

He inhaled deeply. "Very well." He looked at Galleta. "The premonitions that Reece was experiencing in her dreams, they have apparently stopped happening to her. Why would that be?"

"They have ceased as a result of the control she is gaining over her mind and the expansion of her talents. There is no explanation for it, but she does have excellent intuition over certain things."

"Such as?" Levi asked.

"It would seem to depend upon the circumstance; however, if placed in a situation that makes her uneasy, or if she senses danger, do not hesitate to act upon her feelings, whatever they may be."

"Is there anything more we should know before she begins her trainings?" Levi asked.

"Not at this time," Galleta answered. "For now, we will all continue to work with her and help her to strengthen her abilities."

Levi stood. "Queen, this information has been very helpful for me." He walked around his desk and approached Galleta. "If it is no trouble for you, my mother wishes to speak with you. I believe she awaits you in the parlor."

Galleta nodded. "Very well."

After Galleta left, breakfast was brought into Levi's office. Harrison used that time to inform Reece of the combat training she would be undergoing. Levi was hesitant with all of it, but he knew he had to trust that Reece could do this.

After they had finished, Harrison walked Reece down to the training facility. "For now, we will test your endurance. Has the queen worked with you on mentally forcing your body to go through exhaustive situations so that you can use your mind to overpower your body's exhaustion?" Harrison asked.

"Yes. I am still having some difficulty with that. It's hard to stay focused at times, so it doesn't work for me well all of the time." She gripped Harrison's arm. "But we won't tell Levi that, will we?"

"He understands that you aren't going to master all of this in one week. He only wants to be sure you can use these abilities to shield yourself from any fatigue or distress you may experience when we venture to the stone."

Reece exhaled. "And apparently once I get a hold of that thing, all of these abilities will work better."

"Queen Galleta believes so," he answered her. "Now, the combat training will not begin for another couple of hours or so. I want to use this time in-between to help you discover more of the endurance abilities you possess."

At that moment, Reece mentally focused on letting her body know it had the energy, strength, and power to do anything Harrison required of her.

"Up for a run?" he asked.

"Sounds great, but don't you think we should stretch a little first?"

"Do you think your muscles need that?" he challenged her with his expression.

"Right," Reece thought, mentally focusing on the fact there was no need to warm her muscles up.

She focused on the fact that they were already warmed up, and almost immediately she felt her legs muscles loosen up and beg for her to run.

"Well, let's go," she said.

Harrison grinned, and then took off running through the field that led down and around the forest behind the palace. They ran rapidly, and Reece's mind maintained excellent focus on keeping her heart rate and breathing steady. It was almost like magic. How was it possible to push her body in such a way, yet have no fatigue or exhaustion? She should be gasping for air, her heart rate soaring, and her legs begging for rest.

As soon as she started questioning the way her mind was controlling her body's current state, she felt her leg muscles start to burn, and she started breathing heavily. She tried refocusing, but it wasn't working. She managed to keep up with Harrison, desperately trying to refocus her mind and hoping he wouldn't notice she slipped up.

After about a half a mile of this exhaustive run, she had to stop. She brought her hands to her knees while gasping for air and trying to catch her breath.

"I am impressed that you made it a half-mile in this state."

She stood and began walking, slowing her heart and catching her breath. "I told you, I haven't quite mastered this 'mind over matter' ability I have."

"The more you practice it, the easier it will become. What do you suppose made your mind tell your body to find limits?"

"I was just marveling at how incredible it was being able to run so swiftly and for so long, yet my body felt great. I wasn't tired, and it was like I wasn't even running. After that, I began to feel the exhaustion of running with you."

"It really is incredible. I can only imagine what it is like for you, as a human, to never have experienced anything like this before, and then all of a sudden you have abilities like us."

She chuckled. "Must be nice to be born with such a talent. You know something?" She stopped. "In Greece, Levi was free diving and holding his breath for close to twenty or thirty minutes at a time. How was he able to do that? Will I be able to do that?"

Harrison nodded. "It is another way our minds can control our bodies."

"How do you do that, though?"

"It is quite simple. We simply tell our body it does not require oxygen, and therefore our bodies will not ask for it."

"And I will be able to do that?"

"That is uncertain; however, I believe that with some work, you can discover whether or not you have the ability to do such a thing."

"Looks like I am really a super-human then!" She laughed incredulously.

"That would be one way to put it." He looked down at her and smiled. "Well, do you think you can refocus, or are we going to have to walk twenty miles back to the palace?"

"You mean twenty-four and a half miles, right?"

He grinned. "It appears your intelligence has improved as well."

Reece began to focus again, and her exhaustion left her. "Let's race," she said, and then both were swiftly running back toward the palace.

Once they were at the training unit, Harrison instructed Reece to stand at the back of the room with him to observe the men in their combat training. She watched every move they made, absorbing everything. Not long after, she was confident that she could fight as a Guardian would. They moved swiftly with their fighting techniques, but somehow she felt she could move faster if given the opportunity. It wasn't much longer before Harrison had her out with the men and going through a series of moves. Reece did very well up until the point where she lost her concentration, her exhaustion would set in, and she would lose her footing.

Once they were done running drills, Harrison escorted her to the palace. "You did very well today. Maybe we will work on hand-to-hand combat tomorrow. I may be held up in meetings, but I will have my lead instructor work with you if I am unable to do so myself," he told her.

"Okay," she sighed, "I hate the fact that I lose my focus. I have to work on that."

Harrison chuckled. "You will master that soon enough."

After they walked into the palace, Harrison turned to her. "If you wish to go and freshen up, I will notify Levi that we have returned and about your progress."

After Reece had freshened up, she spent the rest of the afternoon in the company of Lady Allestaine. They had a quiet lunch on the balcony before retiring to the gardens. Reece laughed as Mozart hopped through the grass, chasing a variety of insects. "He's such a funny little thing."

Allestaine smiled brightly. "I would have never imagined we would have a zorflak as a pet, my dear, but he is very entertaining to watch and listen to."

Reece smiled before she looked to Allestaine with concern. "Levi is somewhat confident that we may be able to travel to the stone before the week is over."

Allestaine smiled. "That is what he mentioned to me earlier." She grew more serious. "I want nothing more than to have my husband home with me again, but you must know that I am concerned for your well-being. Please do not rush yourself in your trainings. We must have you safe before Levi can decide when he will bring you to the stone."

Reece nodded. "I understand, but I feel stronger with my abilities every day."

Allestaine took her hand. "Your bravery is astounding, Reece. I am honored to know such a strong woman, and even more proud to call you my daughter. Navarre and I have always been grateful that our son found love with a woman like you."

Reece embraced her. "We are going to bring him back to you. I promise."

When she withdrew, Allestaine's eyes were filled with tears. "I know, darling."

"If you don't mind my asking, how have you been faring since hearing the news?" Reece asked.

Allestaine sniffed. "Forgive me." She brushed a tear from her cheek. "It appears my emotions had gotten the best of me for a moment."

Reece smiled sympathetically. "It's perfectly understandable. I, for one, would be in constant tears if I were in your position."

"I am doing well. I am greatly concerned for Navarre; however, I am also concerned for you, Levi, and all of our warriors. I am hopeful this will be a successful mission, but I worry about lives being lost in the process. I know this will not be the first time you have put your life in the hands of our warriors, but the journey you must take with them distresses me greatly. Hearing your confidence that my husband will return home to me safely restores my confidence as well. I cannot express how much I miss him, and I am so grateful to know that he still lives."

"Well, whether this is my newfound intuition talking or not, I feel extremely confident about this mission. I know we will be successful in recovering him. I feel as sure about it as if it has already happened."

Allestaine smiled warmly. "Thank you, Reece."

They spent the rest of the afternoon strolling through the gardens, Mozart entertaining them along the way, until a servant notified Reece that Levi would not be attending dinner that evening. Harrison, King Nathaniel, King Hamilton, and Levi would be taking their dinner in the command center, still meeting and strategizing how the Guardians would battle enemies in the new galaxy.

That evening as everyone was preparing to retire to their rooms, Reece was feeling too restless to fall asleep. She took a couple of books from the palace library and headed back to her and Levi's private living quarters. She changed into her long silk nightgown and robe and headed downstairs to their sitting room.

She curled up on their sofa, completely engrossed in books about Pemdas' history. Once she quickly absorbed all of the information from them, she closed the last book and let her mind relax. She settled into the sofa and allowed the flames in the fireplace before her soothe her further. It was the last thing she remembered doing before she woke the next morning in her bed. It was obvious that Levi must have returned to their rooms, but she was uncertain if he had stayed with her or if he had slept at all.

"Jasmeen?" she called out while getting out of bed.

"Right this way," Jasmeen answered.

Reece walked into her vanity room and found Jasmeen laying out the items for the day.

"Levi brought more training clothes for your combat lessons with Harrison today," she said while turning to leave the room. "Let me pour your tea."

Reece followed her out. "So Levi did come back last night?"

"He did, but it was only to bring your training attire. He returned to the command center shortly thereafter."

"He hasn't slept at all?" she said in astonishment.

"Not that I am aware."

Reece sipped her tea, somewhat concerned about Levi. She knew that he was working relentlessly to ensure that when Reece was ready to retrieve the stone, they would all be ready to recover Navarre.

Once she was prepared to train with the Guardians that day, she headed to the training unit. Having seen no sign of Levi and Harrison, she prepared to join the other Guardians alone.

When she walked into the room, she was greeted by a warrior she had not met before. "Empress, the commander has been detained in meetings with the emperor at this time, and he has given me specific instructions on what he wants you doing in this training today."

She nodded, somewhat intimidated by this man. "Please, call me Reece; and forgive me, but have we met before? I don't think I remember your name."

The man grinned. "Please forgive my rudeness. My name is Brandon, and it is a pleasure to finally meet you, Reece."

"It's nice to meet you as well. So what will I be working on today?"

Over the next few hours, Reece followed the training instructions very well. She worked mainly with Brandon as he showed her new styles of fighting and ways of defending herself. She got through the entire training, this time without losing focus. It was an excellent idea to have someone she didn't know working with her, as the entire time she never once marveled at her new abilities; instead, she remained intently focused on his movements and countering them.

"I am very impressed by your fighting skills, Reece. The commander and emperor will enjoy hearing of your progress."

"Thanks. I was definitely able to focus better today."

Brandon nodded. "For now, we are finished with drills. Unless Commander Oxley requests for you to return, you are free to enjoy the rest of your day."

When she left the training center, she was surprised to find that it appeared to be late afternoon. She stopped and gazed up at the palace. She was hungry, but she decided to test her abilities further. She focused on removing the need for food from her mind, and her body immediately reacted. She felt nourished and pleasantly full, as if she had just eaten. She was no longer in the mood to return to the palace, but instead decided that a horseback ride with Arrow sounded more enjoyable.

After Javian finished saddling Arrow, he walked him to where she waited, watching the colts out in the field with their mothers.

"Thank you, Javian," she said as she approached the mounting block.

Once she was on Arrow, she looked down at Javian. "I think I'm going to take a longer ride than usual today. If Levi asks about my whereabouts, please let him know that I rode along the Pasidian River with Arrow."

Javian nodded. "I will. Enjoy your ride, Empress Reece," he said and turned to leave.

Reece pushed Arrow as hard and as fast as the day she and Levi rode together. She followed along the river for quite some time, and then halted Arrow completely when she approached an enormous lake. Trees lined the entire shoreline, and she decided to ride along it. Once reaching the north side of the lake, she heard the sound of a large waterfall deep within the forest in front of her. She followed the sound, guiding Arrow in that direction. After some time, the trees opened up to reveal an enormous waterfall spilling into another large lake.

*I heard this waterfall from that far away?* she thought as she noticed yet another change in her.

She dismounted Arrow and allowed him to wander off to drink from the vivid blue water. She walked over to the shade of a large tree and sat down, listening to every sound. In the distance, she heard small steps being made. *They must be rabbits*, she thought as she listened to the way they made their movements. After that, she tuned those sounds out and searched for more. One by one, Reece listened intently to all the animals that surrounded her in the forest.

It wasn't long before she heard the sound of a large animal. *Areion,* she thought as her heart began to race. It was easy to identify him by the steadiness and power in his gallop. Her mind recalled the distinctive stride Areion made while being held back and yet wanting to ride faster. His gallop slowed to a trot, he was closer. Reece felt the excitement rushing through her, knowing she would soon open her eyes and be face-to-face with her husband again. She maintained her focus and never once opened her eyes or turned to see if he had made it to her location yet. Areion was at a walking pace now, and Reece immediately sensed Levi's emotions. Instead of blocking them, she gladly let them consume her.

He was extremely exhausted and desperately missed her. His exhaustion faded, and his heart leapt when he spotted her. He halted Areion, yet continued to gaze at Reece, absorbing the sight of the woman he loved. She felt his distress for her, and his overwhelming desire to protect her from everything they were about to go through. She began to feel as though she were intruding on his emotions and immediately blocked them from her thoughts.

She listened to him as he dismounted Areion and slowly walked over to her. As he approached her side, she could hear his heart rate increase. He knelt down in front of her, and she opened her eyes to take in the sight of the man she loved.

Levi's eyes widened some, and he reached for her face. "Sweetheart, your eyes have enhanced in their new color once again."

She reached her arms around his neck, bringing her face up to meet his. Powerfully, he answered her urgent kiss, and she gently encouraged him to lie back. He did, and his hands soothingly massaged along her sides and up her back. The fragrance of him consumed her senses, and she believed she could stay like this forever. Levi gently cupped her face with both of his hands, slowly ending their ardent kiss.

"I've missed you," she told him. "How did you find me all the way out here?"

"I followed Arrow's fresh tracks through the forest. What brings my beautiful wife out to this part of the land?" His eyes became serious. "You must tell me, are you concerned over all you have been dealing with? I do apologize for my absence as of late, but—"

She smiled and sat up, allowing him to as well. "I'm not worried over anything; but from the look on your face, it's seems more like you're the one who is worried and hasn't slept in a week."

He pulled her onto his lap, kissed her cheek, and stared out at the water. "Indeed, I am; worried, that is."

"Are you having difficulty with your planning?"

"No. But the plans we have to make when we enter this new world have me concerned for your safety when we journey through it."

"Like what?"

He shook his head. "The people of this land are barbaric, and the creatures are unlike any we have encountered before. It seems to be a very dark place, one that I do not desire you to have to travel to; however, I know you must be with us."

"I'm extremely confident we will recover your father." She brought his eyes to meet hers. "Remember when Galleta said you should listen to my intuition?"

His eyes lightened in humor somewhat. "Exactly how confident are you, my amazingly talented wife?"

She leaned in to kiss his lips. "As confident as I am right now, knowing that when I place my lips on yours, you will gladly return this kiss." She did, and Levi tenderly gripped the back of her neck, deepening their kiss further.

He kissed her nose and stared proudly into her eyes. "Brandon informed Harrison and me of your excellent training today; he was very impressed."

"I was able to keep my focus much better today than I have been; I think that's why I didn't slip up this time."

"Harrison is looking forward to testing your new skills tomorrow as well."

"There's another thing that I can do now," she said in excitement.

Levi arched his eyebrow at her. "Is there?"

"Yes, it's my hearing, it is enhanced now, too. I heard this waterfall from the entrance to the forest. Then I listened for a while to little critters playing around in the forest, and then when you were heading this way, I heard

Areion. I could easily distinguish that it was him by his gallop."

Levi brought his hand to her face. "That is quite astounding. Do these new abilities frighten you in any way when they happen spontaneously?"

Reece shrugged and shook her head. "Not really, it's actually kind of exciting. Should I be worried?"

"No. I am simply curious because your mind is beginning to function similarly to the manner in which our Pemdai minds do. Obviously, I was born with these abilities, so it is curious for me to imagine what it would be like to live life without them and then to have them manifest themselves so suddenly."

"That's what Harrison said yesterday. So I have to ask, what pulled you away from your meetings? Did you finally start missing me?" she teased.

Levi's eyes darkened somewhat. "I always miss you when we are apart; unfortunately, that is not why I excused myself from our meetings. After speaking with Brandon about how well you did in your training, I decided you might be ready for the next test of your abilities."

"What are you going to test me on?"

"Reece, one of my greatest concerns about taking you to the location of the stone is that we must travel underwater for quite some time to reach its location. The underwater terrain will not allow us to use diving gear or oxygen tanks."

Reece swallowed hard, and for the first time she became worried. "I have to learn how to hold my breath like you did in Greece?"

Levi's expression changed, and she could feel his angst. "I will be at your side the entire time. I will not push you beyond your limits. We will do this as slowly as possible until your mind can fully take over and you can control your ability to force your body not to require oxygen for long periods of time."

Reece exhaled and brought her forehead to his. *What will happen if I can't do this?* she thought as her apprehension skyrocketed. She closed her eyes in defeat, knowing she had accidentally impressed this thought of her fear into Levi's mind.

# Chapter 22

eece?" Levi said with concern in his voice.

He gently caressed her cheek, encouraging her to pull her forehead from his and bring her eyes back to his. She stared into his brilliant blue eyes, searching for strength.

"Sorry about that. All of this gets a little overwhelming for me sometimes."

He nodded and gently kissed her lips. "I know it is, love, whether you tell me so or not." His eyes were set with purpose. "It is persistently overwhelming for me as well. I have battled with this since I first learned you were to be involved, as I have told you before. It is my greatest desire to have you remain safely at the palace, waiting for us to return with my father." He shook his head. "However, in order to bring him home and ensure the safety of Earth and her dimensions, it cannot be that way."

Reece forced away her natural human fear and focused on regaining her courage. She did not want Levi to start worrying over her again or start second-guessing her helping their cause. Whatever had to be done, she would do it. She had the genes within her to help her, and she would maintain a great focus on the new abilities that resided within her.

"I know." She smiled. "Well, the way I see it, the longer we sit here talking about what I need to do, the longer it's going to take for me to learn it." She sighed. "So when do we start the underwater challenge?"

Levi faintly smiled and looked out at the sparkling water in front of them. "We can start now, if you are ready. I informed Harrison that I would spend the rest of the day out of meetings helping you with this."

"Did you bring some swimsuits for us?" She laughed.

"Do we really need any?" He kissed her nose. "Of course I did." He laughed.

Once changed into their swimming attire, they got into the water. Levi took advantage of the moment and brought Reece into his arms, starting this new training with a heartfelt kiss. As he did, Reece's mind began to unwind and calm down. She seemed to absorb the strength and power that always seemed to radiate from him.

She gazed intently into his eyes, relaxed and ready to proceed. "How do we start?"

"It is as simple as what you did with Harrison on your run the other day, and when you worked with Brandon in the training unit. Clear your mind of any fear. Simply stop breathing, and convey to yourself that you do not require oxygen. Your body shall acquiescence, so long as you believe that you do not need the oxygen."

She closed her eyes, trying to figure out how to tell her body it wouldn't need oxygen underwater. Breathing was such a natural thing. She never felt as though she had to tell herself to breathe, so telling herself not to do so now was difficult.

"Are you ready to try?"

She nodded.

"Open your eyes, love."

She did.

"Reece, do not fear. If you cannot do this yet, we will keep working on it until you are able to."

"Call me crazy, but trying to turn off an involuntary bodily process seems a little bit unnerving," she said uneasily. "Not to mention the fact that I've had a fear of drowning since I had a close call at the beach when I was little." She sighed. "So nice of that memory to return to me at this point in time." She thought for a moment. "The man who saved my life, he came from nowhere and reached me before the lifeguard did. Was he my—?"

Before she could finish, Levi grinned and nodded. "Your Guardian? Yes."

"Wow, you guys weren't messing around, were you?" She shook her head in disbelief. "All right, here we go. Let's hope I can do this."

"Remove fear from your mind." Levi ran a hand over her hair. "Allow your mind to relax. Let us start first by going under water. Hold your breath, and see if you can mentally overcome your need for oxygen."

She inhaled deeply. "Okay."

Levi nodded. "Whenever you are ready."

With that, she held her breath and went under water. She closed her eyes and tried to focus on not wanting to breathe, but it seemed the more she focused on that, the more she wanted to. She began to panic mildly, and her body would not comply with her mental command. She desperately needed air.

*If I couldn't do this, Levi wouldn't be attempting to try this with me. I don't need to breathe. I don't need air.*

It was too much. She erupted out of the water, gasping for air. Levi was there with her, smiling with encouragement.

"I'm so sorry."

"Do not apologize. When you are ready, we shall try again."

She bit her bottom lip in concentration. Maybe it would help this time if she opened her eyes and focused on Levi. "Go under with me," she requested.

"As you wish."

They went under the water together, but her plan didn't work. She could not do this at all. She came up from underneath the water breathless, her lungs screaming for oxygen.

"I really don't think I can do this," she said in remorse. "I think you guys may be wrong about me. If I can't do this, how are we to go to the stone?"

Levi kissed her softly. "I believe the reason this is not working is because you doubt yourself. You have the ability, and you are already demonstrating that you can control your body with the power of your mind. You simply have to believe you can master this particular skill, and it will happen."

She shook her head. "Easy for you to say, Mr. *I was born with these talents!*"

"Ah! A new pet name for me?" Levi teased.

349

"I'm glad you're finding this all humorous."

Levi smiled at her sweetly as he tucked her wet hair behind her ear. "Reece, close your eyes. Allow your mind to drift off and relax. Focus on something that will take you out of this moment."

She exhaled, somewhat frustrated. "Levi, I can't do—"

He pulled her in close to him and brought his lips to her neck. He softly began placing tender kisses along her skin, and Reece closed her eyes with satisfaction. She let her head relax back into the palm of his sturdy hand. Her mind calmed as Levi continued placing kisses along her jawline. Her heart rate slowed, as well as her breathing.

His lips were at her ear. "Hold your breath," he whispered.

She did. They remained above the water, and Levi continued to kiss her. She thought about the desire to breathe and no longer fought the need for air. At that moment, the sensation of wanting to inhale or exhale vanished. She was doing it. *It was that simple?* she thought. After five minutes of not breathing, Levi slowly brought them under the water again. He released her from his embrace, allowing her to do it on her own.

She kept her eyes closed and continued to focus on remaining calm. Being under the water was somewhat of a change, but as long as she remained calm, her mind did an excellent job of persuading her body to not seek oxygen. In her mind, she knew that exactly ten minutes had passed, and she still had no desire for air. She opened her eyes and saw Levi's brilliant ones staring back at her.

She couldn't resist the urge and impulsively brought her lips to his. The next thing she knew, her heart was racing and she needed to breathe. *Nice job, Reece!* she thought while pulling away from him and popping her head up out of the water.

She smoothed her hair back with both her hands. "Ugh! I was doing a good job, too!"

"You did an excellent job," he said with excitement.

She sighed. "Let's do it again."

"Will you require my assistance in order to help you concentrate again?" he said with a mischievous grin.

"As wonderful as that was, no, I don't think so."

She wanted to do this on her own. Her mind grew calm, her heartbeat followed, and she halted her breath. Slowly, she went beneath the surface of the water. She gracefully pushed off the soft sandy surface beneath her and began swimming through the water. She let the beauty of the unique fish swimming throughout this body of water calm her. So entranced by the beauty of swimming through the waters, she had no idea how long she swam beneath the surface.

The water became increasingly less visible the deeper she swam. She watched as Levi gracefully dove down toward the darkness below them. Feeling much braver, she followed him. She thought of nothing more than how enjoyable this was. To swim with Levi in this way, and to have the same talents that he possessed, was indescribable.

*How deep is this lake?* It became extremely dark, and the only light was far above them at the surface. *Oh no!* Reece thought as she felt panic begin to set in. What if she needed to breathe? How long could she go without oxygen? The thought made her body wretch by the need to breathe. She began swimming upwards, hoping she would make it to the surface while she fought the urge to inhale water into her lungs. She wasn't close enough, and she knew there was no way she would make it. Then without warning, she was in Levi's powerful embrace. He covered her mouth with his and breathed into her mouth, filling her burning lungs. She was weak and lightheaded with relief.

She clinched her eyes shut as Levi swam them both to the surface. Once at the top, he held her in his arms, swimming them to the shoreline. Reece was barely able to stand once they were in shallow enough waters.

Levi kissed her forehead as she looked at him in pity. "Sorry about that," she managed.

"I am exceedingly proud of your efforts today," he said with his usual striking grin. "I was not sure that you would make this much progress in such a short amount of time."

His words were encouraging, and Reece felt proud of herself. She could do this, she was doing this; she had no other option but to believe in herself fully from this point forward. She embraced Levi tightly, excited that they would be journeying to the stone soon.

At the palace, Levi helped Reece off her saddle. He drew her arm up into his as he led her up to the gardens of Pasidian. Excited by her accomplishments from earlier, she couldn't remove the idea from her mind that they would be headed back to Earth to get the stone soon.

"Levi?"

"Yes?"

"Do you think I did well enough today that we'll be able to leave for the stone soon?"

Levi brought his other hand up and covered hers that rested in the bend of his arm. "It is still unclear to me at this point. You did very well; however, I am unsure as to how you will react in the dark water of the ocean right now."

She recalled her panicking in the deepest part of the lake. *That's why he dove down. He was testing how I would react to that.*

"Is it really that bad?" She sighed. "That deep?"

He halted their walk. "The stone is located amongst isolated islands. These peculiar islands have numerous rugged caves everywhere. There are very narrow passageways, and in order to get to the location of the stone, we must dive deep below the ocean surface and swim through those underwater caves."

Reece's eyes widened as she imagined the reality of the task at hand. "There's no access to this place from the surface?"

He shook his head. "Unfortunately, there is not. The images that the map has displayed within my mind show this as the only route." He gazed past her. "It is strange, the way that I view this location and see the map, it's as if I am seeing the memory of Paul Xylander making this journey himself." He looked down at Reece.

"That is strange, but believable, I suppose. I wonder if that's what the map really is, a memory of Paul's that passed down genetically."

"It would make sense, yes. However, I also have coordinates and graph images, as a map would have."

Reece grinned. "Where is this stone anyway? I've never thought to ask you about it before, but since we're so close to going there, can you say?"

Levi grinned. "As desperately as I want to tell you, I cannot. While Mordegrin is in Pemdas, I do not feel it is safe to say. I am unsure as to how powerful his abilities might be. I almost told Harrison the stone's location, but I had a strange feeling that Mordegrin may somehow be able to listen in on our conversations."

"Well, we've learned never to be too careful in the presence of anyone who takes an interest in the stone, haven't we?"

"I don't trust that man." He touched her cheek. "It is why I have him far from the palace. I cannot trust his intentions around you. He gives me a bizarre feeling whenever I am close to him."

"With all that has been happening with me, is there any way that you will start to consider a time frame for us to get the stone?"

"After witnessing your swift progression with your abilities," Levi inhaled, "I believe I can. If you continue to improve at this rate, we may journey to the stone before the week is over."

She sensed his uncertainty. "I'm not really close to being ready, am I?"

"You will be, in time." He sighed. "I will not allow you to take such a journey if there is a possibility you might panic and put yourself in grave danger."

"I'll keep practicing."

He drew her arm back up into his, resuming their walk. "I know you will."

Reece remained quiet, walking alongside of him. She needed to find a way to prove to him that she could be ready faster. She was the hold up; she could see it in his eyes. She could tell he desperately wanted to get all of this done and over with. She figured that if she was more successful today, there would have been a better chance of leaving for Earth either the next day or day after that. *How do I find a way to improve faster?* she thought.

"Levi, Reece!" Harrison said enthusiastically as he approached them.

"On your way to the training center, I presume?" Levi returned.

"Yes, the Guardians we have chosen to journey into this new galaxy are slowly starting to arrive at the palace. Most of them will be here within the hour, and the rest by tomorrow morning. I plan to start their training as soon as possible."

Levi nodded. "That is excellent news."

"How did you do today, Reece?"

"I didn't do as well as I would've liked. Would you mind if I joined you and the Guardians as they train tonight?"

"I am certain you have not eaten anything today. Would you prefer to freshen up after swimming in the lake?" Levi answered.

"If you keep trying to pamper me, I'll never be ready." She smiled confidently at him. "I'm fine." She looked back at Harrison. "Well? Are you up for a little hand-to-hand combat with me?"

Harrison grinned. "Why, I thought you would never ask!"

Levi gazed sternly at Harrison. "Go easy on her, Harrison. She is doing very well, however—"

"Levi," Reece firmly interrupted him. "Please, have a little more faith in me. I need more challenges if I'm going get better at this."

"She will be fine, Levi," Harrison said, then he looked at Reece. "And you are correct, you must indeed be challenged." His smile broadened. "And I shall be delighted to be the one offering the challenge to you." He winked, and then looked back at Levi. "My father and King Hamilton are still going over some of the details we discussed after you left the meeting this afternoon."

"Very well. I will search them out so they can inform me of any new information." He looked at Reece. "If I am able, I will dismiss the meeting early in order to spend the evening with you."

She smiled. "Sounds great!"

With that, Harrison dramatically raised his arm. "Shall we then, my lady?"

Reece laughed and gladly took it. "Hopefully after tonight, you won't be referring to me like that."

Levi softly laughed as he left Harrison to walk Reece toward the training center.

"I believe tonight is the night we prove you and Levi both wrong, what do you say? Then I shall refer to you as a brave Pemdai warrior instead."

Reece gazed up at him in confusion. "What do you mean by that?"

"Well, neither one of you believe that you are ready, or my cousin would not have that look on his face."

"I know, I was thinking about that, too. I panicked in the water, and I think that's what's concerning him."

"Reece, there is no better way to gain your confidence other than to go at this head on. We shall start with the combat skills." He stopped before walking in. "If we can do this, and really prove it to Levi and mainly *yourself*, I guarantee your outlook and reservations about your abilities will change."

"Gonna beat it out of me, eh?" she teased.

Harrison opened the door and smiled mischievously at her. "Absolutely."

At first it was only Harrison and Reece in the training room, and then close to an hour later, others began filtering in and started performing their drills when the instructors gathered in the room. Harrison kept Reece off to the side, working on his own combat drills with her. They went through a lot of the same fighting moves that Brandon had done with her earlier that day, and Reece was becoming bored with all of it.

"So when are you going to show me how you really fight?" she said with a laugh.

Harrison raised his eyebrows at her. "That's the spirit." He squared up to her. "You ready?"

She prepared herself for the attack. "Whenever you are."

Harrison swiftly advanced on her, planting a foot and throwing a straight arm punch directly at her, which she easily deflected. Harrison quickly countered, pulling her into a powerful embrace. She should have felt the pressure of the tight embrace, but she didn't. She felt nothing but power, and she knew what her next step was. With Harrison standing behind her and the wall before her, she used it to climb it swiftly with her feet, flipping herself up and over his head and freeing herself from his grips. Before he could turn around to face her, she squatted down and swung her leg around his ankles in an attempt to bring him to the ground.

She was almost successful, but Harrison quickly regained his balance. She was on her feet at that time and was ready for his next move. Every move Harrison came at her with, she countered perfectly. She wasn't as strong as he was, but her mind kept her ahead of his every move and out of harm's way. They went aggressively like this for close to two hours, never stopping to take a break. She wasn't breathing heavily, and her heart wasn't racing, she was simply fighting him. No matter what he did, she was just as fast, if not faster, than he was. He tried more than once to pin her, but her mind easily calculated a way out of the position he held her in.

As she went to counter with a jab, he caught her fist and laughed in delight. "Now, that is what we want!"

She gave him a smug grin. "You quitting so soon, Commander?"

He shook his head. "As much as I desire to continue our match, I must send for Levi. He needs to witness this for himself."

She cocked her head to the side. "I did it, didn't I?"

"Reece, you were brilliant. I believe you can guard on Earth now if you like. Your speed is phenomenal, and the style in which you fight was even a challenge for me at times." He grinned. "That is why Levi must witness this for himself. You aren't thinking about anything as you fight me, are you?"

"No. It's like my body has full control. If I start to think about how I am doing it, I'll screw up."

"Go hydrate yourself. I shall be back in a moment."

While sipping on her water, she watched the other Guardians as they went through their drills together, learning more moves in the process. They fought with their long swords, and it was mesmerizing for her to learn this new skill by simply observing them.

"Reece, remember what we have been working on. You can do this again. Levi will be here at any moment. I want him to see this," Harrison said as he walked back into the room.

*Wait! What?* This was very familiar to her. *Wow!* She had done this before. The men fighting in the room around her, Harrison approaching her—but when?

"Harrison, we've done this before. Haven't we?" she asked in disillusionment.

Harrison laughed. "Very funny." He looked past her. "Ah, he has arrived. Wait here," he said in enthusiasm.

She turned and saw Levi dressed in slacks, shirt, and waistcoat, opposite of Harrison and the others in the training unit. Levi's expression was somber as Harrison approached him in conversation. He glanced briefly at his cousin before he directed this very grave expression toward Reece. He nodded, stood back, and crossed his arms. In that moment, Harrison turned back toward Reece. His expression was radiant with excitement. Then she remembered; everything about this was identical to the vision she had on their honeymoon. *Another premonition coming to fruition!*

Harrison squared up into position. "Now, we will start slow. When you feel your body taking over, just go with it like you did before."

In that moment, Harrison jabbed out at her, and without thinking she deflected the punch. His grin widened. Before she knew it, she was fighting Harrison again, defending herself against the strong man's every move. Her mind knew what he was going to do before he did it, and as quickly as he moved, she countered back even faster. Harrison was trying to challenge her more than before.

When they finished, Levi walked out to where they stood. He grinned at Reece. "Truly amazing—"

"Exactly. See, she is ready. She will be fine," Harrison said confidently.

Levi smiled at Harrison. "She will be fine in combat should harm come her way. I can definitely see that." He looked back at Reece. "Tomorrow we shall practice your swimming again."

"Tonight!" she interrupted him. "If you can't go, then I will have someone else go with me."

Harrison laughed, and Levi stared at her in astonishment. "You need to take a break."

She shook her head. "No! I can do this. I want to do this."

Levi eyes were lit with pride. "There is a large pool in the eastern courtyard of the palace, we will practice there."

She shook her head. "I have a better idea. Give me five minutes, and tell Javian to saddle Areion for us."

With that, she jogged past Levi and Harrison out the door. She made it up to the palace swiftly and into her and Levi's living quarters. "Jasmeen, can you have Henry get Levi's swimming shorts? I need my swimsuit as well."

Jasmeen laughed. "Your swimming attire is at the front of your closet in the short cabinets. It appears you are in a hurry, so I will notify Henry immediately."

Once Reece retrieved their swimming attire, she walked quickly through the palace halls and out to where Levi and Harrison were waiting at the stables for Areion to be saddled.

"I'm not interrupting your meetings, am I?" she said to Levi.

Levi grinned. "The meetings can wait. I believe this is more important."

Javian approached with Areion, and Harrison clapped Levi on his shoulder. "Let me know if we will be leaving tonight or first thing tomorrow to retrieve the stone."

With a wink to Reece, he turned and walked back toward the training units.

Once they were on Areion, Levi asked, "Where exactly is it that we are going?"

"Find the closest, darkest lake. I don't care."

She felt Levi laugh, and then they were off. Not long after, they approached a large lake. They dismounted and prepared themselves to swim. Reece's mind was desperately ready for this, and unlike earlier, she was not afraid. Without waiting for Levi, she jogged out into the water and dove below its surface. Without the desire to take a breath, she swam in the dark water, watching the fish cast flickering, illuminating rainbow trails all around her. When she felt she was deep enough and she saw Levi at her side, she dove deeper. There was no need to inhale or exhale, she'd hardly breathed at all while fighting Harrison. Everything was coming to her now, and this was more enjoyable than anything.

She swam like this for close to forty minutes before she thought it was best to return to the surface to see what

Levi's thoughts were about her progress. Once at the surface, Levi pulled her swiftly into an embrace, and she squealed with delight.

"See, I did it!" She giggled.

Levi stared at her in astonishment. "I do not understand how quickly you were able accomplish this."

"You don't have to."

He laughed and kissed her lips.

"Now, when do you think we'll be able to go to the stone? Was that my final test?"

Levi nodded seriously. "Are you feeling that confident?"

"Levi, we could swim all night, and I wouldn't care." She laughed. "I haven't had anything to eat at all today, yet I won't allow my mind to think I am hungry. I'm doing all of this so much easier now."

"If," he kissed her softly, "you return to the palace and eat something, I will notify Harrison that we will leave for the stone shortly after you have finished your meal." He stared into her eyes. "Unless you would like to rest for the evening? In that case, we can leave first thing tomorrow morning."

"Tonight?" she said with determination and excitement. "You have been more desperate to go to the stone than you were letting on."

"I would never pressure you."

"Then we leave tonight."

He kissed her again. "Yes."

Reece could not be more relieved that this was all finally starting to move forward. It would not be long before they could all journey into this new galaxy and recover Emperor Navarre.

# Chapter 23

Once Reece finished her meal, she changed into her training attire, as Levi advised her to do. She walked down toward his office, where he was notifying King Nathaniel, King Hamilton, and Lady Allestaine of their plans to retrieve the stone that evening.

When Reece walked in the room, she was taken aback by the expressions on everyone's faces in the room. *What's wrong now?* she thought. Levi immediately stood from behind his desk and approached her.

"Is something the matter?" she quietly asked him.

Levi exhaled. "Forgive me, Reece. I believe I was so concerned over you being able to swim to the location that I failed to go over another major issue that you will encounter if you are not properly prepared."

She looked at everyone's somber expressions, and then back to Levi's. "What is that?" she said, slightly annoyed.

"We need to work on training your mind so that your body will not react to harsh climates," he said.

"Well, how do we do that?" she answered, still determined.

Harrison walked over to them. "I believe if Reece can easily go without breathing for forty minutes and nearly defeat me in a skilled match, she will be able to overcome her body's natural responses to harsh climates."

Reece nodded. "I'll do whatever it takes. Harrison's right, I feel like I've got this whole mind-over-matter thing down."

Levi's lips twisted as he studied her intently. "Very well; however, when we are on Earth—before we attempt our journey to the stone—I want to be positive you can handle the conditions we shall face."

Reece sighed in relief. "Let's just go and get this done."

At that moment, the tension in the room seemed to fade away. After everyone said their farewells, Reece, Levi, and Harrison were on horseback, riding toward the Pemdai barriers. This was the longest journey toward a vortex to Earth that Reece had travelled to yet, and she wondered where exactly their entry point would be. They had been traveling on the horses at a rapid speed for close to an hour before they began to ascend a steep mountain range.

Snow was present on the mountain range, and the temperature dropped drastically. As they crested the mountaintop, the barriers greeted them. They swiftly crossed over the gray mist and rode down toward the gates. When they arrived, they left the horses in the care of the stablemen who attended to these particular stables.

They walked toward a large, snow covered stone wall to retrieve the Pemdai car, and soon after Levi sped rapidly down the snow-covered road.

"Austria?" Harrison questioned as they came through the vortex into Earth.

Levi grinned. "It is where we will retrieve the Helicopter. I believe it is best to fly to the island instead of traveling by boat out of Norwegian harbors. I want this mission to go as quickly as possible."

Harrison shook his head. "Cough up the location, big guy. Where is the stone?"

"It is located deep within the caves of an isolated, barren island that rests between the Norwegian and Barents Sea," he answered. He glanced at Reece in the review mirror. "You can understand, now, my concern over Reece swimming in these waters."

Harrison looked back at her and grinned. "Nah, she will be fine. If anything, the icy condition of the waters will slow her mind even further, helping her to not panic or overthink." He laughed.

"True," she answered Harrison. "But I think I like Levi's idea of practicing a bit before I go diving head first into a sub-zero freezing ocean."

She looked out her window, trying to see where they were traveling to. They were travelling through the countryside somewhere, but she couldn't place anything. The sky was completely black, leaving the lights from their car as the only source of illumination.

"What time is it here, anyway?" Reece asked.

"The time is currently 5:47 a.m., Moscow Standard Time," the car answered her.

Reece's eyes widened, and she laughed. "What else does this car know?" She leaned forward and stared at the blue, transparent screen in the center of the dash, which currently displayed the time on it. "How cold is it outside?" she asked.

"Weather conditions for your current location are 19 degrees Fahrenheit; winds are at 8 miles per hour from the north," the car responded while displaying the temperature on the screen.

"That is so cool." She shifted into the middle of the back seat, gripped each side of Harrison and Levi's seat rests, and spoke again. "What time is sunrise?" she asked enthusiastically.

"Sunrise is at 6:53 a.m., Moscow Standard Time, rising in the direction of ninety-five degrees to the east of this current location."

"Seriously, Reece?" Harrison said as he looked over to Levi and laughed. "Only your wife would be more interested in playing with car features than on focusing on how she is going to be diving into freezing waters within two hours' time."

Levi glanced at Reece in the mirror and laughed. Before she could respond, they pulled into a private airport. Levi directed the car through the gate and over to an enormous aircraft hangar that stood alone, away from the other large buildings. As soon as the car pulled up to the large overhead door, it immediately opened. Reece was surprised by what awaited them inside.

Two large private jets and three sleek black helicopters were neatly arranged, ready to be used at any given moment. Once they were out of their car, a gentleman approached them. "We have your helicopter ready, Your Royal Majesty."

Levi nodded and led Reece and Harrison out of the shelter and over to where a huge helicopter sat alone on a helipad.

"How did they know to have that ready?" Reece asked.

Harrison became serious. "The secret to that is something that the Pemdai rarely share, but I will confide in you since you are facing a very dire situation. We actually call ahead and notify the Guardian standing post at the airport that we need our helicopter ready. You mustn't tell a soul!" he said as he wrapped his arm around Reece and laughed.

"You should be a comedian," she said dryly as she elbowed him in the ribs.

"You set yourself up for that one, smarty," he teased.

As they approached the helicopter, Harrison and Levi took their seats in the cockpit, leaving Reece to enjoy the comfort of the plush leather accommodations in the rear of the aircraft.

Levi quickly put on his headset and began flipping switches on the roof and the control panel around him. Reece watched his every move while she prepared herself for takeoff. The engines started, and the blades began rotating soon after. Without wasting any time, the men had the helicopter up in the air and were flying over the dark land beneath them.

Reece calculated everything Levi was doing, learning how to fly the machine in the process thanks to her new abilities. It was too dark to see the terrain they were flying over, but after about twenty minutes the sky began to display a ribbon pattern of purple and pink hues off in the distance. Shadows of rigid mountains lined the shorelines below with very rugged and snowy terrain.

As Levi directed the helicopter toward the sea, a bright golden strip lined the horizon as the sun began to rise. The view at this vantage point was utterly breathtaking. It wasn't much longer before an island came into view and large peaks poked up through a dense fog that covered most of the land.

"Is this the place?" Reece asked Levi.

He nodded as he directed the helicopter past the large, rigid cliffs over to a flat surface. Once safely on the ground, Levi shut the engines down. *How did Paul manage to make it out here?* she thought.

As they exited the helicopter, Reece could feel the bitterly cold wind stinging the flesh beneath her clothing. Instinctively, she wrapped her arms tightly around herself in order to stay warm.

"This would be an excellent time to test your body's ability to acclimate to harsh conditions," Levi said.

Reece nodded in understanding. "It is as easy as everything else you have done so far, is it not?" he said in encouragement.

Reece closed her eyes and instructed her mind to believe it was not cold. As she did so, she stopped shivering, and it was as if her body became numb to the temperature.

"That is such a trip," she said.

Harrison laughed. "Quit thinking about how unimaginable this is, or you will start shivering again, and you will never be able to dive into that water."

"As soon as Reece is ready," Levi interjected, "we must hike down these cliffs. It will take us close to a half an hour before we are at the water's edge."

Harrison and Reece nodded, and they set out, traveling through the icy, rugged cliffs of the lonely island.

"Does anyone live here?" Reece asked as they continued their descent.

"No human could inhabit this island, the climate and terrain is far too treacherous. It has a shelf of ice that never melts on its northern side," Levi answered as he continued walking toward the daring edge of the cliffs.

Reece avoided looking down to the ocean below as they reached the edge and began walking along a thin, icy ledge. Fortunately, the boots Levi had given her never lost traction. A slight crack in the face of the mountain before them opened into an enormous cave. Harrison and Levi barely fit through the narrow opening, but Reece was able to easily maneuver her way through it. Once she was through, Levi reached back and took her hand.

It was pitch black, and she couldn't see anything. "Where are the flashlights?"

"Harrison and I do not require illumination in order to see through the darkness," Levi answered. "Do not fear, Harrison is directly behind you watching your every step in case you slip for any reason."

"Well, can I do that, too?" Reece asked in amazement. "See in the dark?"

She forced her mind to try to accept that it wasn't dark, yet her vision never changed.

"If you are able to see in the dark as we are able to, these new talents of yours would really start to annoy me," Harrison said with humor.

"Why's that?" she answered while blindly making her way through the cave.

"Careful, Reece," Levi said, halting their walk. "You will need to step up," he advised her.

She reached out and grabbed Levi's waist, feeling him step up about two feet. She followed him, and then they continued walking on the flat surface again.

"The reason I would have a problem with it," Harrison said, "is because it took Levi and I nearly twelve years to master that ability for ourselves."

"Oh," she answered as she saw sliver of daylight peeking through the rocks in front of them.

"We are almost through this cave," Levi instructed.

The exit of this cave was larger than the entrance, and it led out to another long, narrow ridge that they had to follow down the side of the rugged, icy mountainside. As they drew closer, Reece stared in amazement at the large waves that were violently crashing against the rocky surface of the island.

"We have to swim in that?" she said in disbelief.

"No," Levi answered. "However, we are almost to the entrance where we must travel through the water."

Harrison gripped her shoulder with excitement. "You ready to do this?"

She laughed nervously. "There's no turning back now."

Levi gracefully jumped off the ledge onto a flat surface close to five feet below. He turned and reached up to help Reece land safely to where he stood. They walked down through the large boulders that lined the ocean, bringing them to the water's edge. They stood on the cliff, and Reece watched the waves as they crashed into the rocks surrounding them. Levi turned to his left, where a large pool of water rippled softly against the mountain.

"Where do we go now?" Reece asked, seeing no other way of passage.

Levi stared into the pool of water, and Reece felt some anxiety. Instantly, she became cold again, and she felt her legs weaken. *Don't do this, Reece. Not now.* The wind seemed to die down some now that they were in this hidden cove. Before Reece could pull herself together, Harrison lunged himself over the edge of the cliff they were on, diving straight into the water like an arrow.

Reece laughed apprehensively. *Show off!* When Harrison came up, he turned to face where she and Levi stood. He shook the water from his hair and smiled widely at her.

"Water's great!" he shouted. "Are you getting in?"

There was humor in Levi's expression as he looked at Reece, but quite a bit of concern as well. "Do you want to start off slowly?"

"Just dive in, Reece. You know you can do this," Harrison said as he waded in the water below.

Levi stared intently at her. "Reece, you are shivering again." He approached her and brought her into a warm embrace. He kissed the top of her head. "My love, you must stay focused. Your fear is overruling your thoughts. You can do this."

The cold air was causing her entire body to ache. "I know. Give me a second to get my thoughts straight again," she said through her chattering teeth. "Why couldn't Paul have hidden this stone in some cave in Tahiti?" she said as she rested her head against Levi's warm, sturdy chest, seeking not only warmth, but refuge in him also.

"I would love to assist you in helping calm your mind as I did yesterday; however, I believe we would make Harrison a little uncomfortable," he said with some humor in his voice.

Reece faintly laughed as she stepped back, bringing her eyes to stare into his. She reached her hand up to his face, encouraging him to lean over and kiss her. His warm lips burned like fire against her now icy ones.

He abruptly withdrew, and he gazed sorrowfully into her eyes. "I am so sorry, we should have waited."

In some way, the sorrow in his eyes gave her the strength to endure this. Her fears subsided, and she gained control over her mind again. Her body slowly warmed, and the achiness she was experiencing from the cold weather faded. Levi's brow furrowed as she grinned and stepped back.

"Are you okay?" Levi questioned.

She looked at the icy cold water below, knowing there was nothing to be alarmed by. Harrison's concerned expression was replaced with an understanding grin and a subtle nod.

She looked back at Levi and smiled at his concerned expression. "See ya in the water," she said as she lunged herself over the side of the cliff and dove into the water below.

As she plunged herself underwater, she felt nothing but the sensation of her body swimming gracefully through the water. She swam for a few minutes beneath the surface, testing her ability to hold her breath. Everything seemed to be working just as it should be. Relieved, she swam up to the surface of the water. Levi was in, and he and Harrison swam over to her.

"You had me worried there for a minute, Reece," Harrison said with a laugh.

Levi's eyes were alit with excitement. "Well done, love," he said proudly. "Now, let us go get this stone."

With that, Reece witnessed Harrison and Levi do something she hadn't seen Levi do before he went beneath the water's surface, and that was inhaling deeply before going under. She thought for a second before she realized that they were most likely taking in as much air as they could in case she panicked and couldn't breathe again while under the water. *Smart idea!* she thought; however, she felt confident.

She followed them both, swimming deeply down into the ocean. Soon after, Harrison slowed and followed behind her. They dove deeply down for close to twenty feet, following the rugged mountain beneath the ocean's surface. Levi swam over to a narrow opening, turned sideways, and forced his way through, disappearing right in front of Harrison and Reece. Harrison motioned for her to go through next. The opening was extremely narrow, and even Reece had to find a way to maneuver her way through it. *How did you find this place, Paul?* she thought as she finally managed to slip through the narrow opening. It was dark now, and Reece couldn't even see her hand in front of her face. Suddenly, she felt Levi pull her into his grips.

She felt Levi's hand come up and brush her face. *Must be checking on whether or not I'm about to lose it right now.* A moment later, he wrapped his arm around her waist, keeping her right at his side while swimming her through the black water. They swam this way for a few moments before Reece felt Levi place his hand on top of her head, directing her through a small tunnel. Reece reached out and felt the jagged rocks that surrounded her. She gripped the surface beneath her, bringing her stomach to it as well. She used this as a guide to bring herself through the passageway.

Suddenly, the water became lighter, and she could see shadows of the tunnel she was in. As she continued to swim forward, the water became much brighter, and she turned to see if Levi and Harrison had entered the tunnel. Levi was the first to squeeze through the small tunnel, and he pointed up toward their new direction. Reece nodded and proceeded to swim upward toward the surface.

When she was finally above the water, she marveled at the surroundings. She inhaled the fresh air deeply as she gazed in awe at the multi-colored water crystals that hung all around. They shimmered off the sun's rays that peeked through the cracks of the rock walls surrounding them.

"Wow." She looked at Levi. "Are we almost there?"

Levi grinned. "Yes."

Harrison came up alongside of them. "Excellent job, Reece. I am profoundly impressed by your focus."

They followed Levi up and out of the water. There were many different passageways; however, Levi led them toward the one that was directly in front of them. As they walked, Reece noticed the dampness in the air, and her wet clothes clung tightly to her body. The moment she noticed her discomfort, her mind became distracted and unfocused.

She was bitterly cold, and the only warmth she felt was Levi's sturdy hand gripping tightly to hers. The air was extremely damp, and her soaking wet clothes were icy cold. She became so cold at one point that she felt every bone in her body ache. Every muscle in her fragile body started to tense.

Levi squeezed her hand, and she looked up at him. He smiled, while his eyes glowed vividly. "Focus on what you learned, love."

As he said it, Reece's body became warm, and all pain she was experiencing disappeared in that instant. Her mind was easily able to conquer these feelings now, and she was grateful for it.

"Levi?" she said, somewhat amused.

"Yes."

"I had this vision our wedding night." She laughed. "Another crazy premonition."

Levi looked down at her. "Well, were we successful in retrieving the stone?"

"I don't know. The vision ended before that."

Harrison laughed. "So much for premonitions!"

They entered a large cavernous area, and Levi directed them to another passageway. They turned to the side, having to walk sideways to pass through it. Once through, another small room awaited them.

Suddenly, Reece felt an energy force pulling her. She was drawn to a smooth surface, and the rock instantly began to illuminate in a gorgeous aquamarine color.

"We're here," she said softly.

"Yes," Levi responded.

She reached out to the illuminating rock wall. She was amazed when her hand passed through the wall instead of stopping at the surface. *A mirage?* she thought, trying to understand how her hand went through the hard surface. Suddenly, she felt a hard pull of energy, guiding her fingertips to a rugged, yet polished object. As soon as she touched it, a surge of power jolted through her entire body. At that moment, she felt every nerve in her body ignite, and her mental strength heightened immensely.

She gently pulled the stone out from its place inside the rock wall. She turned slowly and faced Levi and Harrison. She never glanced up at them; instead, she flipped her hand over and opened it. She stared into the vibrant color of the emerald-like stone. Her mind gained more power, and she felt more strength within it than ever before. She looked around the room, watching rays from the stone reflect off the stone walls surrounding them like beams from a laser.

The air felt light, and it took less energy than usual to fill her lungs with oxygen. Her body was abundantly filled with energy, and her mind felt free of everything.

She looked over at Levi and Harrison as they watched her in awe. She turned and put the stone back in the exact position that she had found it.

She turned back to the two astonished men standing before her. Harrison grinned. "Reece, your complexion—I mean—" He stammered with his words.

"Your complexion is absolutely flawless, like I have never seen it before," Levi said with the same amazement as Harrison.

Reece held up her hand to examine it. They were right; her skin tone was glowing with a flawless, silky texture. It was almost as if someone airbrushed a creamy skin color onto her. She reached for her hair, only to find that it was not only dry, but it was a shimmering, golden blonde.

"Unreal," she said in disbelief.

"Reece, why did you put the stone back? We need it in order to open the portal, do we not?" Levi questioned.

Reece grinned coyly at the men. "No, we don't."

Levi's brow furrowed, and Harrison looked at her disbelievingly.

"Why do you say that?" Levi asked. "Mordegrin said that—"

"He was wrong, Levi." She arched her eyebrow at them both. "The stone can stay safely on Earth. I have the ability to open the portal without it now."

Levi cocked his head to the side, and Harrison laughed aloud incredulously.

Reece smiled mischievously at Levi. "And now it's time for me to ask you—do *you* trust *me?*"

# Chapter 24

After their return from the stone's location, they wasted no time getting back to the outside barriers of Pemdas.

Harrison sat atop Saracen, waiting for Levi and Reece to join him where he waited. Once on their stallions, Levi guided Areion over to Harrison, with Reece following closely behind.

"We will cross the barriers into Pemdas from another location," Levi instructed. "My wariness of Mordegrin continues to trouble me. He may well have an ability to see the barrier that we chose to cross out of Pemdas from. If we reenter Pemdas from a different location, perhaps it will make him question where we have travelled."

"Do you really think he could know that from so far away?" Reece said.

Harrison looked over at Reece. "This guy has some pretty strange abilities. It is certainly better to be safe than sorry where he is concerned. I do not trust him for one moment."

Levi nodded, and they began racing along the outside barriers of Pemdas. When they arrived at the palace, they met briefly with King Nathaniel, King Hamilton, and Lady Allestaine. Levi informed them they would be venturing to this new galaxy within the week. Levi requested King Nathaniel to summon all the kings of Pemdas to the palace in order to meet with them and explain in person about the plan to recover Emperor Navarre.

"I would like to meet and speak with Mordegrin as soon as possible," Reece said with a determined expression on her face during their meeting.

"Reece, I understand your request; however, Harrison can relay any questions or information you wish to give Mordegrin without you risking—" Levi said, somewhat troubled by the request.

"I will be fine," she confidently intoned.

Harrison studied Levi and inwardly laughed at how Reece's personality seemed to have changed since she gained her powers from the stone. *Here we go!* Harrison thought as the room fell quiet and Reece and Levi both stared sternly at each other. To Harrison's surprise, Levi's features softened, and he subtly grinned at Reece. *Ah, the beauty of marriage; the wife remains victorious every time,* Harrison thought in amusement as he watched his cousin become persuaded to do something against his own strong will for the first time.

"Well?" Harrison spoke up. "Is Reece going to visit Mordegrin with me or not?"

Levi's lips quirked up in humor when he looked back at Harrison. "I will send for Mordegrin this afternoon. Reece can speak with him then."

After the meeting was dismissed, Harrison, Levi, and Reece went their separate ways to freshen up, change into their usual attire, and join everyone in the breakfast room. As Harrison walked through the corridors on his way to breakfast, he encountered King Hamilton on his way to the dining hall.

Hamilton brought his arm up and around Harrison. "It delights me greatly that we are closer to retrieving Navarre. It all seems more and more promising."

"Are you prepared to leave with us, Your Majesty?" Harrison returned.

"I am more than ready. My wife shall be arriving at Pasidian tomorrow." He laughed. "My beautiful bride still desires to spend every last minute with her husband before he journeys to other worlds, dimensions, and now, galaxies."

Harrison laughed. "I believe she is only making her way here to scold you for doing such a thing."

"Indeed!" He clapped Harrison's shoulder. "However, I am prepared for it. That is what keeps the love alive, you know? A strong and feisty woman is needed to keep such a hard-headed man in his place."

"Do you know if Angie shall be accompanying her to the palace?"

King Hamilton stopped and eyed Harrison suspiciously.

Harrison cleared his throat. "She placed quite the burden on me before she left, informing me that I am to ensure your safety on this journey."

Harrison exhaled in relief when King Hamilton chortled, "That is my daughter for you. Angie is strong-willed in her own way. Her mother and I agree that she possesses the greatest qualities of both of us." He resumed their walk. "I do, however, pity the man who tries to advance her in any way."

Harrison looked toward the windows and rolled his eyes. "Yes, indeed."

That afternoon, Harrison returned to the palace with the convoy that escorted Mordegrin from Casititor. He gripped the man's arm, led him through a private door into the command center, and walked him down to a small, windowless holding chamber.

"When the emperor is ready, he will send for you. Until then, enjoy the delightful view," Harrison dryly said before leaving.

"I shall delight in meeting the empress," Mordegrin said strangely.

Harrison stopped in his tracks, spun around, and stared darkly at the man. "It would be wise to remain silent in the presence of the empress unless she asks you to speak." Harrison grinned. "Do not assume that you have that privilege to speak a word to her unless she requests you to. I am surprised that the emperor has allowed your meeting at all, so you would be wise not to test him, or I fear his reactions toward you this time will not be as gentle as they were when you first met with him."

Mordegrin waved his hand flippantly. "I understand your warning, Commander; and I thank you for making me aware of how I should conduct myself in this meeting."

Harrison turned and left. Mordegrin was annoying for sure, but somehow Harrison found a way to deal with him. Levi, on the other hand, could tolerate nothing of the man and hadn't seen him since the day he requested Mordegrin to be sent away from the palace. *This meeting should be an interesting one,* Harrison thought. He could only imagine Mordegrin's condemnation if he chose to play his strange word games with Reece in Levi's presence.

Harrison returned to his office and began going through the notes that the Guardian instructors had left for him. All but about seventy Guardians that were selected for the mission were at the palace, aggressively training for the journey they would embark on. The men were progressing in their training well, and Harrison became anxious to go into this world and handle matters with these Olteniaus females.

"Commander?" Vincent said.

Harrison looked up from his notes. "Yes? Is the emperor ready for us?" he asked.

Vincent nodded. "Yes."

Harrison stood up and gazed at Vincent. "This should be interesting."

Vincent chuckled. "Of that, I have no doubt. I wish you well."

Harrison sighed. "Thanks."

Harrison escorted Mordegrin into Levi's office. Levi, who was standing in front of his large corner windows, immediately turned at the sound of their arrival. Just as Harrison expected, Levi's expression was severe as he instructed Mordegrin to sit across from him.

"The empress will be arriving at any moment. Before she does, I would like to warn you—"

"Your Royal Majesty," the man smoothly cut him off.

Harrison sighed and stared at Levi's darkened expression.

"I have not asked you to speak!" Levi growled through his teeth.

Mordegrin dropped his head in a dramatic and humble nod.

"When—and only when—the empress wishes for you to speak, will you have the privilege of saying anything to her." Levi's lips tightened, and he stared deeply into Mordegrin's eyes, "If I sense the slightest discomfort or upset from her. she will be removed from this room immediately," a wicked grin played in the corner of Levi's mouth, "and then I will personally destroy your presence in my world without any hesitation. Do you understand me?"

"Your Royal Majesty, you have made yourself perfectly clear to me." Mordegrin exhaled. "I do not know what I have done to cause such mistrust and animosity from you. I have only come to you in peace, offering you a chance to recover your father and seeking your help in saving my world."

Levi's eyes narrowed, and his jaw was set tight. "I owe you no explanation for my opinion of you."

"If I may, I have been very compliant with all of your requests of me, why—"

"Indeed, you have," Levi interrupted him, "however, I am not unwise. I do not trust your motives, even now."

The servant opened Levi's door and admitted Reece into the room. Her eyes sparkled like green jewels since the moment she made contact with the stone. Her irises were the color of a brilliant emerald gemstone, very close to the color of the stone that illuminated within her hand when she held it in the caves.

Levi rose and walked toward her when she entered. He guided her to sit in a chair at his side. Harrison watched intently as she locked eyes and gazed somberly at Mordegrin from the moment she entered the room. Levi took his seat and brought his attention to Reece, who was seated at his side.

"Empress, as you requested, Mordegrin is here to answer any questions you may have," Levi formally spoke.

Reece tilted her head to the side as she stared at Mordegrin knowingly. "Why did you tell us that I needed the stone in order to open a portal?" she asked firmly.

Harrison sat back, very interested in what Reece's questions for Mordegrin would be.

"Empress, forgive me, but why do you feel you do not need it?" Mordegrin said with a look of suspicion, almost anger, on his face.

"Before I answer your questions, I would appreciate your answering mine," she responded coolly.

*This sounds familiar,* Harrison thought. *This idiot better not play games with her, or we will not be getting anywhere with information once again.*

"Ah! My manners have failed me, it would seem," Mordegrin said as he glanced at Levi and back to Reece. "You require the powers that are within that stone in order to create a gateway into our galaxy."

"I have the powers already, and I have the knowledge about how this can be done within my mind as well."

Mordegrin's lips tightened, and his eyes squinted, seemingly frustrated with Reece. In all of the times Harrison had encountered the man, he never had seen him appear upset. Harrison tensed, prepared to take action at any moment should he get out of line with Reece.

Mordegrin exhaled. "You do realize you will be bending time in a way, slowing it down, and altering your galaxy's physics when you create this portal; do you not?"

"I know exactly what I'll be doing, and I do not need the stone's power to do it, but I think you already knew that." Her gaze darkened. "Why do you want the stone?"

Mordegrin's expression grew fierce and daunting. "If you do not use the stone, all of the talents you have been enjoying these last few weeks or so will return to you void. Once you have expended all of the energy you carry within you to perform this task," he looked to Levi, "you could very well lose your life. Without the stone doing most of the work to open the portal, you are risking your very own life force, Empress." He sneered as he shifted his gaze back to Reece.

*What are you doing, Reece? What are you thinking?* Harrison looked at Levi uncertainly. Levi remained solemn and unaffected as he looked subtly to Reece, who was smiling in response to Mordegrin's insinuation.

"Why do you want the stone?" she asked again.

Mordegrin looked at Levi. "Emperor, she is overestimating her powers. She may meet her demise after the portal is opened. You must convince her to return to Earth and use the stone for assistance at once, lest you lose your wife in the pursuit of your father."

Levi grinned. "The empress overestimates nothing. It is you who underestimates her and my admonition to you about testing her before she entered this room." Levi leaned forward. "Why should I believe you fear for her life?"

"I fear for her life as much as anyone else in a situation such as this would," he answered steadily.

Harrison remained quiet as he watched the exchange intensify.

Reece laughed in what seemed to be annoyance. "Why are you avoiding my question?" she asked in a tone of disbelief. "Why do you want the stone?" she demanded in a deeper voice than usual.

Harrison leaned forward, knowing Reece was on to something. *Why didn't she mention any of this to us earlier?*

"I have not avoided your question." He smiled. "I have no interest in the stone—it serves no purpose for me. I am only concerned that you will harm yourself without using its powers to open the portal. You only have a certain amount of that stone's powers within your being; they will eventually drain from you." He cocked his head to the side. "This newfound confidence you have—the confidence that gives you the impudence to speak to me as you are—it will leave you. You are only human," he finished with a smug grin.

Harrison and Levi's fists both seemed to clench at the same time. The men stood when Reece got up suddenly and walked over to Mordegrin.

"Empress," Levi called out to Reece in a deep voice.

Reece ignored him and brought herself eye-to-eye with the man. Mordegrin's smile died. "You are a foolish child," he said forebodingly.

Before Levi and Harrison could respond, Reece spoke up. "When we come into your world for Emperor Navarre, we will come for you as well. I do hope you will be ready for the justice we will give you." With that, she gazed sternly at the man. "Your services are no longer required in Pemdas."

Mordegrin's eyes widened as he instantly gripped the arms of his chair. "You are incapable of such a thing!" he screeched.

Levi and Harrison stood in confusion about Reece and Mordegrin's exchange.

She arched her eyebrow at Mordegrin, and as she did, Mordegrin became invisible. Reece inhaled deeply and closed her eyes.

"You may come for me; however, you will not find me," Mordegrin's voice called out.

Reece's brow creased as she tightened her lips. At that moment, a large amount of water filled the chair Mordegrin was previously sitting in, and the water spilled down onto the floor around it. All that was left of the man were the cuffs that restrained him.

"What happened?" Harrison said, completely taken by surprise by what had transpired.

"Reece," Levi looked at her earnestly, "what did you do to him? How did you do such a thing?"

Reece's eyes reopened, and she shrugged her shoulders dismissively. "I simply mentally persuaded him to leave our world."

"Why?" Harrison asked.

"Levi's been right about him all along. He has been listening in on everything; I sensed it from him the moment I walked into the room," Reece answered.

Levi ran his fingers through his hair. "I knew it."

"At first, I only wanted to question him about why he would think I needed the stone. I thought that was strange." She looked up at Levi. "But when I walked into the room, I felt his dishonesty radiating from him."

"So is my father not alive, then?" Levi asked Reece in confusion.

Reece brought her hands around his waist. "Your father is alive. Mordegrin was the one that had him taken. He wants the stone, Levi. His plan all along was to have us bring the stone into his galaxy so he could have physical access to it."

"Is my father's life in danger now that we do not have the stone?"

Reece stepped back and shook her head, eyeing both Levi and Harrison. "He has no desire to harm Emperor Navarre. I don't know why, but right now he needs your father alive."

Harrison looked at Reece in confusion. "What would cause you to believe this?"

Reece's lips twisted. "The emotions I was sensing from him. He needs Emperor Navarre alive as much as he needs us to bring him the stone." She looked at Levi. "I don't know why, I just know that's the way he feels."

Levi brought a hand to his chin in concentration. "It is a relief to have the knowledge that my father will remain safe." He sighed and brought an arm around Reece. "So you are positively sure that you will not be harmed in any way while opening the portal without the stone?"

Reece nodded. "I will not be harmed; he was lying. It took a lot of energy for me to persuade his strong mind to leave, and I still can feel the stone's power within me." She stepped away from Levi and looked at Harrison. "We need to prepare everyone as quickly as we can. It is time to bring Emperor Navarre home and destroy Mordegrin and the Olteniaus beings."

Harrison walked over to Reece and draped an arm around her shoulders. "Get over here, you crazy thing," he said enthusiastically. "This shall be a remarkable journey, and I am certainly grateful that the Guardians have you on our side."

Levi studied the wet chair and floor. "Interesting that he used the element of water to manifest himself in our likeness."

"Yes." Reece smiled mischievously at both men. "It's the same way I will open the portal, too, and the reason why I don't need the stone."

"How so?" Harrison asked.

"The energy produced from a waterfall will easily work as a conduit for me to alter the physics of this universe in the way that I have to. I will harness its energy and use that to open the gateway into the new galaxy."

Harrison stepped back and shook his head and looked to Levi. "You deal with your wife; I am going to go make sure our warriors are ready for this mission."

Levi laughed, and relief was apparent in all of his features. "Find out when they and the horses can be ready. Have the silversmiths sent up; we will need them to prepare our weapons. I will advise your father that he shall be personally holding the meetings with the kings when they have all arrived." He smiled at Reece proudly. "It appears we may have my father back at the palace before they all arrive."

Harrison offered Reece a lively grin. "At this point, I might wager on it." He turned and marched swiftly out of Levi's office.

After three days of aggressively training and planning their departure to retrieve Emperor Navarre, the morning had finally come to enter Arsediean Galaxy. The kings and their families had already arrived at the palace, waiting to meet with King Nathaniel and learn more about the plan to rescue Emperor Navarre. Harrison was grateful for the distraction, due to the chaos in the palace at the time. When he was not distracted, he made it a point to see if Angeline had returned. When her mother, Queen Isa, arrived without her, he accepted that there was no reason to hope that she would return his feelings, even after his apology. It was obvious that she had taken great issue with him insulting her, seeing that she would not even show up to see her own father off before this mission.

Harrison focused on removing his regret from his mind. He had nearly a thousand men that he had to lead into this new galaxy to seek vengeance on Mordegrin and the four Olteniaus females, and he couldn't afford to be preoccupied by his mistakes. With the sun rising, Harrison's anticipation for this mission was elevated, and the warrior within him was craving the battle that awaited them.

He walked through the palace corridors, which were crowded with visitors. He had finished bidding private farewells to his family, Lady Allestaine, and Elizabeth, and he had only one more person to see before he left the palace. Once at the command center, he walked over to Vincent and extended his hand. "Vincent, the Guardians are yours to command until our return."

Vincent reached out and shook Harrison's offered hand. "Be safe, Commander. We will keep Earth and the other dimensions well protected while you are away."

Harrison grinned. "I have no doubt about that." He turned to leave. "Until then, my friend."

Once outside of the palace, Harrison looked around at the vast lawns of Pasidian, which were covered with thousands of Guardian warriors as far as the eye could see. They sat patiently on their horses, prepared and waiting to take this unimaginable journey. Harrison could sense their fierceness and readiness to avenge their emperor and return him to his home. In addition to the warriors, an enormous crowd of people had already gathered in the fields beyond the horse stables. The atmosphere was euphoric, and Harrison let the incredible energy consume and fuel him for the journey that awaited them.

He approached the stables where Saracen stood in his armor next to Areion and Arrow. Once on his stallion, he directed him to where the Pemdai warriors sat poised on their horses in perfect formation. Watching these brave men patiently waiting to march their horses into this new galaxy without reservation was a sight to behold. A surge of pride flooded through Harrison as he was reminded about how fortunate he was to command such a fierce and extraordinary group of men.

Harrison gallantly trotted Saracen through the lines of these brave men, greeting each one as he rode past the rows of horses. Once at the end of the line, he turned his steed back up the hill toward the palace, which was no longer in sight. The men were ready, and so was he. It was time to search out Reece and Levi in order to begin this journey.

Once at the top of the hill, he guided Saracen over to the men who would lead each combat unit through the portal at their designated times. After being assured the men were prepared for the mission, he spun Saracen around, and he spotted Levi and Reece in the fields with Arrow and Areion. The crowds that lined all around the palace had tripled in size since he first walked out the doors. As he approached Levi and Reece, he laughed at Levi, who was distressed about Arrow's halter while Reece sat on the stallion's back.

He brought Saracen to a halt and watched in humor as Levi grumbled over Arrow's tack. Levi was standing next to Arrow's head, while Areion stood a few feet behind him. "I told Javian he needed to create another notch for this halter," Levi muttered while pulling the dagger out of his sheath.

As Levi proceeded to puncture the halter and create another notch, Reece sighed. "Levi, it's fine. It's already tight enough around his head, don't you think?" Reece argued, and then shook her head while looking over at Harrison. "We don't need Arrow choking out while I am going through this portal."

"Excellent point, Reece," Harrison responded. "What exactly are you trying to do, Levi, strangle poor Arrow so we lose Reece somewhere in the portal?"

Levi exhaled while buckling the halter with the new notch he made. "I am not taking any chances after learning what Reece will most likely experience while opening the gateway. I am simply ensuring their safety," he said, sheathing his dagger and checking the straps of the saddle.

Harrison grinned at Reece's annoyed expression, "I must say, Reece, you definitely complement the Pemdai warrior attire very well."

She rolled her eyes. "Yeah, I bet. I didn't realize how heavy these clothes would be." She laughed as she shifted in her saddle.

"Use your mental powers, and get over it." He smirked. He looked at Levi. "The men are prepared to leave; I will see you both at the front of the line when you are ready."

Harrison turned Saracen back to where the men awaited him and halted his horse when a familiar voice called his name.

"Commander?" she called out louder this time.

*Angie?* Harrison spun his stallion around, and his heart instantly reacted at the sight of the beautiful woman standing in the crowd of people. She stepped out from the large crowd and proceeded to walk out to him. He swiftly dismounted Saracen and walked toward her hastily.

"Angeline, this is certainly a surprise," he said as he approached her. He stared into her shimmering bronze eyes, realizing that he forgot how mesmerizing they were. "I did not believe I would see you before we departed. I have spoken with your father, and I am assured he will be safe on this journey."

"That is not why I am here," she responded.

Without warning, and to Harrison's great pleasure, she reached up and tenderly caressed his cheek. It was obvious that the large crowd likely witnessed their exchange; however, Angeline didn't let it affect her, and Harrison certainly did not care if all of Pemdas stood witness to this.

Angeline tilted her head to the side, studying him. She smiled, and it halted Harrison's breath. "I could not let our brave commander leave and lead our warriors into another galaxy without a goodbye kiss from the woman he declares that he so desperately loves, now could I?"

"Angie?" he said, disillusioned by this moment.

Her eyes bore into his. "Harrison, I love you. With everything that I am, I do. I always have. I simply needed some time to be sure that you could truly return my feelings. I needed to know that your declarations were, in fact, true and authentic. Upon reflecting over my own stubbornness, it was easy to see that I was not just any other woman in your eyes."

Harrison was paralyzed. He was entranced by her eyes, her thick, curly, auburn hair, and the fact that this moment was truly happening. He had no idea what to do next. Fortunately, Angeline took the lead and brought her other hand up to his other cheek. He swallowed hard as he felt her soft finger tips glide softly along the lines of his face, resting on each side of the base of his neck. She leaned up and gently brought his lips down onto hers. Harrison softly sighed, feeling the softness of her perfect lips against his again. Her fingers ran through his hair, encouraging him and letting him know she wanted more than this tender kiss.

Fortunately, he wasn't too lost in this moment to know that they had most likely created an audience that was more than likely already conjuring up words of gossip. Without reservation, Harrison embraced her tightly and spun her around, his back now facing the crowd and shielding his and Angeline's passionate kiss. She pressed her body tightly into his, allowing him to hide their zealous kiss further. It was obvious that everyone knew what was happening at the moment, but Harrison did an excellent job of concealing it from them, protecting Angeline from their display of affection.

It took everything in his power to remove his lips from hers. Angeline stepped back, and her dazed, glassy eyes stared lovingly up into his. "I love you, Angeline Hamilton," he whispered.

She brought her hands to his face and kissed his lips softly again. She wrapped her arms tightly around his waist and embraced him. "Be safe, Harry. I will eagerly await your return."

Harrison leaned over and brought his lips to her neck, tasting of her delicate skin with a moist kiss, all while absorbing her sweet fragrance. He felt her body slightly shiver in response. "I will return to you," he said determinedly. He rose up and caressed her cheek once more. "And when I do, I want nothing more than to hold you in my arms and prove exactly how strong for you my love truly is."

Her cheeks colored red, and she gazed up at him shyly. "I will desperately be looking forward to that."

Harrison smiled and brought his hands up and around the back of his neck. He unknotted the braided leather band and removed it from his neck. "I carved this arrow as a young boy; I refer to this as my lucky charm." He softly laughed as he brought the black leather strap with a carved wooden arrow dangling from it to her wrist. As he wrapped it around a few times and fastened it, he watched Angeline softly caress the smooth arrow.

"This is beautiful." She glanced up at him. "But do you not think this is the type of mission that you should keep this particular charm for?"

"You, Angeline, are my charm." He leaned over and kissed her forehead. "Wear it, and use it to keep me close to you while I am away." He exhaled. "Now, I believe it is time that I must face your father about this moment we have shared."

"Yes, you do." She raised her eyebrows hopefully. "I am sure he will understand."

"After all of the arrogant opinions that I have shared about women in his presence," Harrison chuckled, "I am confident this will come at a price for me." He brought her delicate hand into his gloved one and tenderly kissed it. "However, to have your love is worth any price that I might ever have to pay."

Her eyes locked onto his seriously. "Please, be safe."

Harrison bent to kiss her once more, letting his lips linger for a moment before he rose up and turned to mount Saracen. He avoided all eye contact with anyone; instead, he gazed down at Angeline as tears began to fill her eyes. "I will return to you soon." He gave her a reassuring smile and a wink before he turned and hastily rode Saracen up to the front of the Guardian line.

# Chapter 25

After Levi finished inspecting everything on Arrow, he turned to where Areion and Navarre's horse awaited him. Reece looked over to where Angeline and Elizabeth stood next to Allestaine. Angeline gently caressed the necklace Harrison had wound around her wrist while she gazed somberly into the direction he rode off in. Elizabeth held Mozart, and from where Reece sat on Arrow, she could hear him humming in a low cello tone as he stared longingly at her. Reece shook her head, knowing poor Elizabeth would be listening to a depressed Mozart serenade her while she was gone. Reece continued to sit patiently on Arrow as she waited for Levi to say his farewells.

Levi walked over to where the three women stood together as Areion and Navarre's horse followed closely behind. He embraced his mother. "If all goes according to plan, we will return with father and have these beings destroyed within the week," he said.

Allestaine nodded. "I wish all of you great safety and courage." She reached out to pet Navarre's horse on his nose. "I look forward to seeing your master upon your back again, Haestron."

The horse nuzzled Allestaine in response, and Reece saw the tears began to form in Allestaine's eyes.

Levi turned to Elizabeth and embraced her. "Good luck with this little guy," he said while rubbing Mozart on his head. Mozart fluttered his wings in response. Levi glanced back at Reece with an amused expression before he turned to greet Angeline. He reached for her hand, and she gracefully placed it in his. He bent over and kissed the air over it. He rose up and looked down into her concerned, yet hopeful eyes. "Do not fear for him, Angeline. I always make a great, personal effort to ensure his safety on our missions; I will do especially so during this one."

Reece watched as tears pooled in Angeline's eyes once again. She gave Levi a small curtsy. "Thank you, Emperor Levi. But my wish is that all of you are safe on this journey to recover our brave emperor," she returned humbly.

After a nod of acceptance, Levi turned and hoisted himself up onto Areion's tall back. Reece gave a reassuring smile to the three ladies who looked at her with concern as Levi directed the horses out through the army of Guardian warriors. As Reece turned to follow his lead, the crowd began cheering loudly from behind them. When she was at the front of the line, Reece looked back once more toward the palace, in awe of the crowds of people watching them leave.

Levi trotted Areion to where Harrison sat in conversation with King Hamilton. "Gentlemen." Both men halted their conversation and looked at Levi. "Let us go and retrieve our emperor," he instructed. With Levi's command, they were off, riding swiftly north through the forest, out and away from Pasidian Palace.

They rode toward the only barriers in Pemdas that had powerful waterfalls and rivers running along their outer boundaries. Reece was relieved when she was informed that these waterfalls existed, because if they did not, she would have been forced to open the portal from within the lands of Pemdas. She knew very well that if she had to open a portal inside of the protective barriers, it would leave Pemdas more vulnerable than ever before. If anyone from this other galaxy were to find this portal and travel through it, it could place the protective realm in great danger.

Even now, she wouldn't explain to Levi the true reasons as to why she needed to use the waterfall as an energy force. She couldn't risk the idea of him demanding that she use the stone for her absolute protection. She knew Mordegrin wanted the stone, and bringing it with her would leave it at a great risk for Mordegrin to take it from them.

Mordegrin was correct: the stone would have conserved the power she held within her; however, she knew she would not be harmed. The water would supply enough power to aid her, and it would work excellently as a conduit. Regardless, she knew this process would possibly drain most of the powers she received from the stone. Luckily, combining those powers with the energy of the water would ensure she would be able to accomplish the task without losing her life in the process.

Her biggest worry was that losing her new abilities as they were entering this new, uncharted galaxy would leave her vulnerable, and she would have to fight to use her talents again. She knew she had the strength within her to use the training techniques Galleta taught her if she did, in fact, lose the stone's powers while opening the portal.

The horses lunged over the barriers, and they rode alongside the gray, misty void for close to an hour until a rapidly flowing river came into sight. They followed the river through the trees until a large waterfall appeared before them.

*This is it,* she thought. Before she could go any further, Levi was off Areion and walking over to her. Reece dismounted Arrow as he approached. Levi took her hand and led her away from the army of men, all slowly approaching this location from behind them. Arrow, Areion, and Navarre's horse followed them. Once they were somewhat alone, Levi brought Reece into a tight embrace. He held her like this for a few moments before stepping back and staring into her eyes.

"Reece," he said in a deep voice, "you know that I love you beyond measure, and so much more than my own life. To have you do this outside of my presence and protection distresses me greatly." His eyes penetrated into hers.

She nodded. "I will be okay." She caressed his cheek. "I will be the only one who will feel like going through the portal is taking forever while I'm opening this gateway. Once I'm successfully through it, for you it will only seem like I've been gone for a brief moment. As soon as you see the water begin to ripple after I have entered it, that is when the portal will be fully opened. For you and the men, going through the portal will be as instantaneous as it is when you travel to other dimensions." She smiled. "Although I'm not sure if there will be any blinding flashes of light," she teased.

Levi's lips quirked up in humor. "Are you positive that you can endure this alone?"

"It doesn't matter. I told you already that I have to do it by myself in order for it to work. If I don't do this, we will never get your father back. I'll be okay." She stood on her toes and gave him a quick kiss. She stared intently into his unwavering eyes. "You have to trust me."

Levi's jaws clenched, and Reece could sense his trepidation. "Levi, please stop. Don't do this, not now."

He let out a breath, and his eyes remained locked onto hers. Suddenly, she was secured in his arms, and his lips were on hers, kissing her ardently. She immersed herself in his fierce and dominating kiss, letting his powerful embrace and everything about this strong exchange of emotions fuel her confidence. Her hands gripped the well-defined muscles of his sturdy back.

She reluctantly slowed their kiss and tried to withdraw from Levi. She softly moaned, and then gently placed her hands on each side of his face, encouraging him to withdraw from her.

"Levi," she mumbled to him through their kiss.

He responded by finally allowing their lips to separate. He brought his strong hands up to rest on each side of her neck. His thumbs tenderly caressed back and forth along her jawline, while resting his forehead against hers.

"I do not know if I can bear for you to do this," he said in a weak voice.

"Don't fall apart on all of us now," she returned with a soft laugh.

"We will be right behind you." He lifted his forehead from hers, letting his lips brush over her nose and her forehead.

His grief-stricken eyes looked into hers. She had told him too much about what she knew she would experience going through the portal. She was grateful when his eyes closed and he softly exhaled. She knew it was time for him to turn his emotions off and embrace his Guardian warrior mentality.

He removed her from his embrace and stepped back. When his eyes reopened, they were set with determination and unyielding purpose. She no longer felt the anguish emitting from him; he had seemingly become a completely different man. His sapphire eyes were fierce, and Levi appeared to be a man ready for war.

She smiled in relief, but the warrior standing tall and commanding before her did not return her smile. Instead, he nodded. "It is time to open the portal," he said firmly.

Reece inhaled and followed him as he returned to Arrow. "Let us retrieve the emperor," was all he said as he helped her onto Arrow.

Once on the horse, Harrison walked Saracen over to where Reece waited as Levi secured a leather belt around Reece's waist, strapping her to the saddle.

"Reece," he grinned, "are you ready to do this?"

"Go where no Pemdai has gone before?" Reece's lips quirked up in response. "Yes, and I'm sure you're more than ready to get this all over with."

Harrison's grin brightened. "Beyond ready to put an end to all of this."

Once Levi finished securing Reece to the horse, he walked to the front of Arrow, gripping the horse's harness with both hands. Arrow grunted and nosed Levi in the chest in response. Arrow's massive hooves began rising up one by one. He ran his hand down the center of Arrow's face, and Reece watched as Levi's expression softened.

"Everything okay between you two, Levi?" Reece asked.

Levi's eyes were much brighter as he gazed up at her. He brought his hand to her leg, softly squeezing it. "Arrow is prepared to take care of you as I would." He reached for her hand. "Be safe, my love."

Harrison brought Saracen closer to Reece, leaned over, and brought an arm around her shoulder. "Time to work your magic," he teased. As he pulled back, he nodded toward the waterfall. "Do not forget, we must ride for at least two hours without stopping once we enter this new world."

"Arrow and I will keep moving once we are through the portal. I just hope you all can keep up with us."

Harrison smirked. "Oh, we will."

Levi walked to his horse, and in a swift, powerful motion he brought himself up onto Areion's back. He nodded at Reece. "Whenever you are ready."

Reece guided Arrow slowly into the swiftly moving river at the base of the waterfall. She stared into the waterfall and inhaled deeply, absorbing strength from the energy emanating from it and being pulled by gravity into the river below. Overcome with great power, she persuaded time to halt. As she did, the waterfall froze in that instant. She closed her eyes, and with every ounce of power she possessed within her mind, she created the passage for her and Arrow to enter into the waterfall. She guided Arrow toward the frozen water. It softly rippled, which confirmed she had created the opening correctly. She had to go through it to fully open the portal for the other Guardians to enter in from behind her. Once directly in front of the entrance, the waterfall vanished, leaving nothing but a dark opening for her to complete the process of opening the portal to the other galaxy.

*Now, time to alter physics and reality.* Reece knew this would be the most frightening part for her, but she had to continue to mentally alter time in order to open the portal. Arrow stepped through the dark entrance, and as he did everything changed.

Defying Earth's natural physics fought Reece's mental strength with brutality. She maintained superior focus as she no longer felt Arrow beneath her or his presence at all. A brief moment of utter loneliness gripped her entire being before it was replaced by a wave of heat surging through her body. *A fever?* No. A fever was mild compared to the scorching heat her body currently experiencing. She felt her mental strength swiftly draining from her.

Her body was scorching. She felt as though she were on fire, sitting in the middle of hot flames, being burned alive. With what was left of her mental strength, she suffered through these feelings of excruciating anguish. Instead of panicking, she forced her mind to escape the pain. It diminished somewhat, and she was able to concentrate on getting through this first part of the journey.

It felt like days had passed while she experienced this pain. Finally, the horrific experience was coming to an end, and the consuming fire ceased. The torture of the fire was replaced with the torment of becoming freezing cold, and she could not take in air. At this point, she wished she had the stone's power to help her, but she inwardly knew this was a small price to pay. If Mordegrin had the stone in his possession, the result would be far worse from what she was experiencing without it now.

It seemed to be an eternity of experiencing the feelings of suffocation before she finally gained power to take in oxygen again. She inhaled deeply, and for the first time of not suffering while opening this portal, she questioned Arrow's whereabouts. She couldn't feel him beneath her. All she could sense now was that she no longer carried the power of the stone within her. *How much longer? What was I thinking? I may not survive this.* Fear consumed her weakened mind. She was freezing cold, and she began to turn numb. Loneliness devoured her, and panic ripped through her. The darkness of this void became heavier, and her feelings of abandonment increased. *I can't do this. Where am I?* She wanted to scream for help, and she tried. When she opened her mouth, no sound came out. She tried to breathe to calm herself and regain power over her mind again, yet she didn't know how to anymore.

The air was thick, and everything was black. *I couldn't do it. Am I dead?* she thought, feeling that she was lost somewhere in this gateway, never to be recovered. The silence, darkness, and emptiness took her last bit of hope away.

After what seemed to be an endless amount of time being lost in the barren, black nothingness, she heard something. It was the faint sounds of a horse's hoofs clicking on a hard surface. Suddenly, it sounded as though broken glass were raining down all around her. High-pitched noises came and went from all around the darkness.

To her utmost relief, she felt Arrow beneath her, confidently walking through this dark place. She reached out in absolute gratefulness and roughly patted him on his strong neck. Her vision returned, and she could see Arrow's head in front of her, briskly nodding up and down as he aggressively walked straight ahead.

"We did it, Arrow!" she shouted hoarsely. "We did it, boy!"

Arrow whinnied in response, and soon after a large, bright opening appeared. Arrow picked up his pace and with a steady gallop swiftly brought them out of the dark place they were in. When they exited the portal that Reece had successfully opened, they stepped out into a deep snow drift. Arrow didn't waver, but he galloped at full speed through it. Reece inhaled joyfully of the brisk air. She was cold, but she felt alive. A thunderous roar from behind prompted her to look back. As she did, she saw Levi on Areion, leading hundreds of Guardian warriors through the portal.

As he approached alongside while Arrow raced violently through the snow, Levi grinned widely at her. He directed Areion in front of her and took the lead racing the horses through this harsh, snowy terrain. Once Levi was in front of her, the horses maintained an aggressive speed. Reece started to feel the result of exhausting all her mental power by opening the portal without the stone. She was freezing cold and wondered if she could endure these brutal temperatures for the next two hours. *If I could withstand opening the portal, I can endure this. I have to.*

The portal was opened, and the Guardians were well on their way to recover Navarre and defeat their new enemies.

# Chapter 26

The horses rode aggressively through this unforgiving environment, digging and scraping their hooves through the icy surface. The treacherous conditions were starting to have an effect on the powerful and relentless animals, but they continued to press on.

After a little more than an hour into this oppressive world, Levi could feel Areion wavering as he started up yet another icy ledge. Without hesitation, his powerful steed ignored his own exhaustion and lunged aggressively up the narrow ledge. Levi looked back more than once to check on Reece's condition. When they entered this world, he noticed a change in her demeanor. He desperately hoped Mordegrin was not correct about the possibility of her losing her abilities, because if there was ever a time when she would need them most, it was now.

When he first noticed her reaction to the weather conditions, he wanted to stop the horses to check on her; however, they had no option but to get as far away from the portal as possible after they made their entry. His fears subsided when he brought Areion alongside Arrow. Reece's entire appearance had changed, and she appeared to be using her mental powers to overcome the icy cold temperatures. She smiled reassuringly at him, and he returned Areion to the lead.

Over the last hour, he noticed moments where she began to shiver, but as they climbed the mountain ridge they were currently ascending, she seemed fine. Strangely enough, Levi was starting to feel the agitation of being in this environment, making him question why his mental strength couldn't overcome it. His usual confidence was beginning to be replaced with doubts about whether they would ever make it out of this harsh environment or not.

If there was a sun to be shown in the skies of this world, it was blocked out by the dark green clouds that blanketed the atmosphere all around them. Levi pondered how life could be sustained in such a place, and how they were able to take in oxygen here. Mountains and glaciers filled the entire area they were in, and the air was so extremely light that it was almost nonexistent. Breathing was no easy task, and he could tell that the horses were struggling with doing so also.

Once they crested the steep mountain, more snow and icy glaciers appeared before them, and they seemed to go on forever. Being in this land felt completely oppressive, and Levi felt his mood rapidly shift into extreme irritation. *"Harrison!"* he thought angrily.

*"What, Levi?"* Harrison answered him in the same mental tone of frustration.

*"How much farther must we travel until we are out of this desolate, dreadful area? Areion is tiring, and Arrow appears to be as equally fatigued."*

*"Just press on. You know very well we must travel at least another hour."*

Levi looked back at Reece to find that she was shivering again. *This is ludicrous!* Levi thought to himself. *Why is she doing this now?* His unreasonable anger began to consume his reason and logic. He shook his head violently, trying to remove his toxic mood. He gained some reprieve from the irrational mood swing and forced himself into his warrior mindset.

As the horses descended the face of another mountainside, he looked back to see Reece still brutally shivering. *"Commander?"* he mentally called out to Harrison in a calmer tone.

*"Yes, Emperor?"* Harrison answered telepathically in much the same mild-tempered manner as Levi.

It was relieving to know that Harrison was able to achieve his warrior mindset when Levi did. It meant the Guardian warriors had all done the same in order to protect themselves from the strange feeling that swiftly came upon them.

*"Reece doesn't possess the ability to shift into a warrior mindset; she appears to be in distress. Once we get off this ledge, you will need to take the lead for me, Harrison,"* Levi said as he glanced back at Reece. *"Reece is struggling to stay warm. I am going to bring her onto Areion with me. Have Garret take your place guarding the back of our line."*

Arrow whinnied loudly and uncontrollably, but there was nothing Levi could do at the moment. They were on a treacherous ledge, making their way down toward a flat surface. Once they reached level ground, Levi slowed Areion and paced him next to Arrow. He looked over to find that Reece's lips were blue, and her face was deathly pale as she was slipping out of consciousness. *"Harrison, move quickly! I need your help unfastening her restraints this instant!"*

Harrison rushed Saracen along the other side of Arrow, and he reached over and unbuckled the straps that harnessed her to the horse. Once Reece was freed, Levi gripped her waist and brought her onto Areion with him.

Levi tightly held her close to his warm body. He pressed her icy cheek against his and drew her head into his neck and chest to warm her freezing face. He brought her hood over her head and his cloak around her to shield her further from the bitter cold. He felt her weak breath softly against his neck as he held her closer.

*"How is she?"* Harrison asked him telepathically.

*"She is extremely weak, and she is suffering from hypothermia."*

*"Why do you believe she is having this reaction? Surely with the stone's powers, she would have excellent use of her mental powers."*

*"Something must have happened to her while opening the portal. I will not know until we can finally stop these horses somewhere and check on her."*

*"Finally!"* Harrison said telepathically. *"There are signs of vegetation off in the distance. We can make a shelter for her there."*

Levi scarcely opened the cloak that he used to surround Reece and trap the warmth from his body for her. Her eyes remained closed, but her lips were returning to a soft pink. She was still pale, but Levi noticed some color returning to her cheeks. He closed the cloak back over her and embraced her tighter.

Nearly forty minutes later, they had completely descended the punishing mountain terrain, and trees came into their view. They traveled through deep, powdery snow toward a dense forest. Tall mounds of snow surrounded them like boulders as Harrison guided them to an area where they could stop the horses and check on Reece.

Once halted, Harrison was off Saracen and walking quickly through the deep snow to Areion. He reached up and took Reece down into his arms.

"Oh, Reece," Harrison said sorrowfully, "what did you do to yourself?"

He turned back to where Levi approached and handed Reece over to him. "She is still unconscious. We need to create a fire immediately to warm her," Levi commanded Harrison.

After Harrison nodded and walked back to the Guardian warriors, Levi watched the interaction between Harrison and the men dismounting their horses as they looked to Levi with some confusion. From where he waited, he could hear every word exchanged.

"Commander," Garrett questioned him, "is there a reason we are stopping?"

"Reece is suffering from hypothermia. We must warm her as quickly as possible," Harrison said while walking past him. Then he stopped to face him. "Have five men retrieve wood from these trees. The rest of the men need to section off and protect the location we are currently resting in."

"Yes, Commander."

Levi held Reece close to him as he listened to Harrison give orders. "Harrison," he called, forcing Harrison to turn back to him. "Send scouts to check on our men who came through the portal behind us. If we must stop, I would like to be sure everyone is through and that no one from this world saw us entering at that location."

Harrison nodded and briskly strode out toward the rest of the warriors.

Not long after, a blazing fire was warming the area around them. Levi sat in quiet conversation with the five Guardians that remained with them and Harrison. Reece's heart rate was beating at a steady rhythm again, and her color had returned. She was in and out of consciousness as the fire warmed her. When she woke, she was too weak to keep her eyes open. Levi injected a serum into her veins in order to help her recover quickly, and he was grateful that he brought it for fear of something like this happening.

"Harrison, in my saddle bag I have some bread and a container of water; will you retrieve it for me?" Levi asked him as he felt Reece begin to stir again.

He looked down, and she gazed into his eyes. Her eyes were no longer the emerald color they had turned while having the power of the stone within her, but they had returned to the color she had when her abilities were first starting to awaken.

"How are you feeling?" he softly asked.

She rubbed her forehead. "What happened to me?"

He kissed her cheek. "I believe that is a question we all have for you, Mrs. Oxley."

Harrison approached and knelt down in front of where Levi sat cradling Reece protectively in his arms. "You look much better than you did before, Reece. Death is not a very becoming look on you," he said with a laugh. He offered her a slice of bread as he held Levi's water container.

Reece hastily took the bread and began eating it as if she hadn't eaten for weeks. Harrison and Levi both looked at each other in concern.

"Slow down there, kid," Harrison said humorously. "We do not need you choking and forcing us to save your life from that as well." He handed her the water and stood. "I will go get some more bread for her."

Levi watched her intently. Mordegrin was correct about her losing her power without the stone, but Levi was unsure why Reece didn't think that would be an issue. Now she was more vulnerable than ever before, and in the most treacherous place, no less. He wanted to ask her so many questions, but he knew it was best to let her rest, hydrate, and nourish her body.

She took another sip of water and gazed up to Levi shyly. "Are you upset with me?" she asked with hesitation in her voice.

Levi's brow furrowed in response. "Of course I am not. I am deeply concerned for your well-being."

Harrison returned with more bread, and then walked over to where he previously sat in conversation with the other men, giving Reece and Levi some privacy.

Reece nibbled on the bread and looked out at the fire. "I had to do it that way, Levi."

"Do what?"

She turned to face him and brought her hand to his cheek. "Please don't be upset with me." She sighed. "I knew from the moment I held the stone in my hand that if I didn't use it to open the portal, I would most likely be drained of the power it gave me."

"Reece," he said firmly, "why did you not advise me of that?"

She looked at him pleadingly. "I couldn't. I know you would have made me use the stone just to be safe."

He nodded. "You are correct. But I would have listened to your reasoning if you would have discussed this with me."

Her expression grew somber. "Mordegrin wants the stone," she said gravely. "I would not risk bringing it with us. You have to know that if I was worried that opening the portal without the stone would kill me, then I would have used it. I knew that using the energy from the waterfall would serve to protect me without having the stone with me. The worst case scenario was that I would lose the ability to do all of the super-human stuff that I'd learned, and I felt that it was a small sacrifice in order to keep Mordegrin from having access to the stone."

Levi sighed and brought his hand to her cheek. "So you sacrificed all of your newfound talents in order to keep the stone hidden on Earth?"

She took a bite of her bread and swallowed. "It was never a question in my mind."

"I should be upset with you for not telling me this beforehand." He grinned at her pitiful expression now. "The bread you are eating, I only packed because I considered that even if you had the ability to overcome hunger, something could change and you would require nourishment."

She softly sighed. "I'm sorry I didn't tell you, or prepare you, for this."

"If you would have at least prepared me, you would have much finer foods to nourish your body with while we are here."

Her lips twisted. "I'll be fine."

Levi looked over at Harrison. "Did any of you encounter any wildlife or things of that nature while you were out gathering wood for the fire? You said that the wildlife is safe to eat here, as it is on Earth."

Harrison looked directly at Reece. "Still hungry?"

Levi felt Reece chuckle. "I'm fine," she said.

Harrison and the other men stood. "We shall see what we can find; hopefully, Reece won't be too picky. Even though it is safe to consume, I am unsure about what the wildlife in this world will taste like."

Levi nodded. "Thank you, gentlemen."

When men disappeared into the forest, Levi pulled Reece closer to give her a kiss. With more energy, she turned to face him, and he gently pressed his lips against hers.

"Was it as difficult as you believed it would be when you opened the portal?" He watched a flash of pain cross her expression before she quickly recovered.

Reece softly sighed, and then brought her attention to the fire again. "The worst part was at the end."

Levi gently took the tie out of her hair and slowly began unraveling her messy braid. "Would you tell me about it?"

As Reece spoke about the events that she had gone through while opening the portal, he wondered how she could survive such an ordeal. It was much worse than he imagined it would be for her.

"I can still use my abilities somewhat," she said, looking back at him. "I just don't have control over whether they stay or go."

"What do you mean by that?"

"Well, when I came through the portal, I felt everything at first. It was bitterly cold, and I started to ache. The icy cold winds burned in my lungs, making it painful to breathe." She sat up and stared into the flames of their fire. "I thought I was in trouble then, but suddenly I had control over my mind again, so I acclimated my body to that atmosphere as quickly as I could." She diverted her eyes. "It seemed like as soon as I regained mental control, it was stripped away again suddenly. The power to control my mind came and went like that the entire ride. I tried my best to get through it when I started freezing again. The last thing I remember was becoming so tired that I couldn't fight the cold anymore." She turned back to him and smiled. "The next thing I knew, I was waking up in your arms in front of this fire."

Levi kissed her tenderly on her head. "We will do everything in our power to get you through this. For now, please relax. Hopefully, your abilities will start to come back to you again in a consistent manner."

Levi needed time to think. They were stopped in broad daylight, waiting for Reece to recover. Would she be able to withstand the rest of this journey? With the proper amount of warmth, rest, and nutrition, he had to believe that she would be fine.

Harrison and the men had returned with a large fowl. To Levi's surprise, Reece devoured the meat. Once she was completely satiated, she seemed to gain control over her mind again.

They returned to the horses, and Reece felt confident enough to ride Arrow alone. Levi and Harrison gave her their cloaks to stay warm in case she lost the ability to control her mind in the cold climate again. It was obvious that in order to maintain her abilities, Reece would need rest and nourishment, and that was how they planned the rest of their journey. They would stop for her in the evenings so that she could rest, and they would hunt the land in order to keep her properly nourished. Levi knew that traveling in such a way would set them back in their timing to retrieve his father, but there was no other option. His greatest fear with Reece not having full access to her mental powers was how they were to defeat Mordegrin and the Olteniaus females. Reece was in no condition to mentally battle anything, as she could hardly protect herself.

They would have to find another way to defeat their greatest threat, and being the fierce warriors they were, they would.

# Chapter 27

For two entire days, they traveled through deep, snowy terrain. The trees were abundant, keeping the Guardians well hidden as they traveled through this world. They hadn't encountered any civilians or beings in this new world, and that was exactly what Levi and Harrison had hoped by entering where they did.

All was going well, except for Reece; it was obvious in her features that she was growing weary of this journey. Even so, she never vocalized it. She was grateful when her mental abilities would absently start working again, because it felt as if they gave her a second wind. When the talents waned, she was miserable. Unfortunately, they weren't present at this moment.

It was morning, and they had left their camp close to an hour before. Without her abilities to cope, she was agonizingly hungry again. She forced herself to remain quiet over the issue, knowing she was already an inconvenience to the warriors on this trip. To her relief, none of the men made her feel guilty about slowing their mission down. Instead, they agreed that Reece did the honorable thing by leaving the stone hidden on Earth so that Mordegrin would not have access to it.

After three nights of sleeping outside under trees in this unforgiving environment, Reece was becoming agitated and extremely impatient. The only thing that kept her warm at night when she slept was being wrapped tightly in Levi's arms. He held her close to his warm body, but the thin blanket covering the icy ground beneath them did very little to protect her from the cold, even while she slept close to a warm fire. She didn't know how much longer she could suffer through this. Starving, exhausted, and highly irritable, she pressed on with the line of men.

Arrow galloped gracefully behind Areion. Under normal circumstances, Reece would have found the ride comfortable, but her stiff body was reaching its limits. The trail widened some, and Levi slowed Areion to pace alongside of Reece and Arrow.

"How are you feeling?" Levi asked as he looked over at her sympathetically.

"Like I should have taken the stone with me," she answered with a sigh. "I'll admit it, I'm completely miserable."

"Are you hungry again?"

*I'm ravenous!* she thought, but she wouldn't tell him. She wondered what going through that portal did to her, not only mentally, but physically as well. It seemed as though it was taking forever to restore her body's energy. She only felt good when she ate, and when she did she could access her abilities somewhat better. But even when she did eat, it wasn't enough. She was still hungry afterward. She was starting to be concerned about whether or not her body was gaining any nourishment from the food in this world. The men ate what she did, and they seemed to be satiated by their meals perfectly well. But they weren't human, and she was.

"Honestly, I just ate a little over an hour ago, and I'm hungry again? This is so maddening," she grumbled while absently rubbing her hand over the back of her neck. "I think I'm just sick of feeling filthy. I'm not sleeping well, *obviously*, and I'm…" She cut herself off. *Quit complaining, Reece. This isn't about you,* she thought in frustration.

"…and you are adorable," Levi finished her sentence. "Even when you are irritable," he finished with a compassionate smile.

Levi pulled out some berries in a satchel from his saddle bag and handed them to her. "Until we stop again, eat these. Drink the water I gave you also, it will help to control the need for food until we rest again."

Reece took the satchel and popped a crimson berry in her mouth. "I'm surprised anyone even found fruit in this desolate place."

"You can thank Garret later. He was equally surprised when he came upon a living plant life."

"Please tell me they're not poisonous." She laughed. "I'm pretty sure you all are probably contemplating putting the whining *Empress* out of her misery so you can all get this over with!"

Levi laughed. "Well, Garret is not dead yet, so I am sure they are perfectly fine, my love."

Reece looked over at Levi's amused expression after swallowing another berry. "I swore to myself I would not ask this question, but how much longer?"

"Harrison and I were just going over that. He believes the fortress is close to three or four days out, and that is if we continue our journey in the same way we have been over the last few of days."

*And then we have to go all the way back!* she thought as her mood swiftly changed from irritation to rage. She really didn't know if she could bear this any longer: riding all day long, enduring the same treacherous terrain day in and day out, eating bland meat that wasn't filling. She reached for her water container and started gulping it down in order to help cease her hunger and irritability.

"Reece?" Levi called her name in concern.

She shook her head, knowing if she opened her mouth all the wrong words would come out. Then, and not a moment too soon, she got her second wind again. It washed over her like a wave, and she sighed in relief. It seemed as though the moment she would reach her breaking point, that would happen. Despite her exasperation that she did not have full access to her abilities, she was grateful when they came to her, no matter how unexpectedly.

She looked over to see Levi's eyes dancing in amusement. "It is nice to see my lovely wife's vibrant eyes once again," Levi said with a chuckle. "Feeling better?"

Everything was brighter, lighter, and more peaceful now. The temperatures were comfortable again, and her sore muscles felt rejuvenated. She looked at Levi in utter relief. "You have no idea. I'm slowly realizing how much I hate my human genetics right now."

Levi's brow crinkled in humor, and he laughed aloud. "You never cease to fascinate me."

She laughed. "Fascinating is one of the many, many adjectives to describe me these days."

Levi shook his head, and the trail began to narrow again. He directed Areion up ahead of them and resumed leading the line of men through the dense forest.

Finally, nightfall was coming upon this forsaken land, and Reece was greatly relieved. Her abilities had come and gone throughout the day, and having them return when they did was the only reason she made it this far. It was nice to see that the scenery had changed somewhat. They were still in a forest; however, large rocks and cliffs surrounded them now. The men that traveled with them went through their normal routine of sectioning off an area to protect their location. A group of men would set out to gain information from the other troops riding out in the distance around them, and close to ten men remained with them to gather items to start fires, hunt for food, and scout for danger in their new location.

When they were stopped, Reece fell into Levi's arms when he reached up to help her off Arrow. She leaned into his warm embrace and closed her tired eyes, wishing she never had to open them again. Levi massaged her back with his strong hands, and it felt incredible. She leaned her chin up, and her heavy head collapsed back. She opened her droopy lids and pursed her lips in defeat as she stared up into his brilliant blue eyes.

"Levi, I think it's time that the Guardians remove the weak link. I'm done! Just put me out of my misery, bury me here, and move on."

Levi brought the palm of his hand to cradle her head. He cocked his head to the side, while his humorous eyes roamed over her face. "Unfortunately, the Guardians do not operate in such a way." His eyebrow arched. "And you are not the weak link, love, you are actually turning out to become quite the entertainment for all of us."

She sighed. "Figures."

That evening, after they finished yet another bland meal, Reece sat on her blanket and leaned back against Areion's saddle. She stared into the flames of the fire with Levi and Harrison's cloaks serving as blankets to warm her. She sat exhausted, irritable, and waiting for Levi to return to her. He was in discussion with Harrison and the other men, and Reece had no energy to think about what they could be discussing. As her heavy lids started to close, Levi approached her as the rest of the Guardians joined where she sat around the fire. Levi reached down to her, and she reflexively placed her hand in his and reluctantly stood up.

He pulled Reece off to the side and away from the group of Guardian warriors. "Come with me. I believe you shall be grateful for what I am about to show you."

He gently took her arm and led her away from the large campfire that illuminated the area. She was confused, but she followed alongside of Levi up a hill through deep snow. At the top of the hill was a steaming pool of water surrounded by trees and tall, icy glaciers. Steam rose off the water and filled the entire area. She was instantly overwhelmed with the desire to dive head first into the water to freshen up.

"Allow me to help you out of this," Levi said as he unfastened her cloak.

She looked down and realized she and Levi had done this before. This was the vision she had when they hiked to the waterfall on their honeymoon. She was about to say something to Levi when she realized that Levi was undressing her and the men were not far away.

"Are you sure no one is going to walk up on me?"

Levi kissed her nose. "After all of your complaining, I am surprised that you are concerned over that. But to answer your question, no; they are down the mountain, keeping watch."

Her heart reacted at her favorite grin, and then another overwhelming desire came over her. She brought her hand up to his face. "Will you get in with me?"

"That was one of the main reasons I was pleased when Harrison told me about this pool of water," he responded playfully.

Once Reece was completely undressed, she stepped into the water. "I really hope there isn't anything in here that will bite my toes," she said as she got an uneasy feeling.

She turned, and the sight of her husband half-dressed made her forget about everything else. Moments later, Levi grabbed a bag, walked over to the side of the snowy ledge, and set it down. Then he was in the water and she was in his arms. His mouth found hers in a powerful kiss that sent a surge of energy through her body.

He slowly withdrew, dunked his head, and came back up smiling. "I brought the bag Jasmeen packed for us."

"Bag?"

He laughed. "Yes. Do you not remember us laughing that she packed soaps, makeup, and a brush for our journey?"

Reece chuckled. "Why am I not surprised?"

He brought her in close to him, and his lips pressed against her chest. "Let us worry about washing our hair later." He kissed along her jawline as his strong hands massaged along her back.

Reece let her head relax back into the water as Levi gently guided her beneath the water's surface. The rejuvenation of simply getting her hair wet was incredible. All of a sudden, the temperature of the water was no longer warm; it was absolutely perfect. Her energy levels returned, and she brought her head back up out of the water. Levi's lips found hers in that moment, yet she pulled away.

She smiled brightly at him as his brow lifted, wrinkling his forehead in amazement. "My love?" he said as he watched her with a yearning look on his face. "It would appear as though you are feeling quite well again."

She bit down softly on her bottom lip. "Perfect timing, don't you think?"

Levi brought her into a powerful embrace, and her heart began hammering against her chest. "Indeed," he kissed her shoulder, "it is impeccable timing."

Reece's abilities stayed with her, and she felt magnificent. She reached for the soaps and happily began lathering the muscles of her husband's strong back. She was behind him with her legs locked leisurely around his waist. Levi remained perfectly still as she hooked her arms under his and gently massaged along the lines of his solid chest. The depth of the water went up to his shoulders as he stood there relaxing, staring into the distance. She kissed along his shoulder, now his neck. Levi languidly turned his head to the side, and her lips ran along the velvety stubble on his face.

She softly laughed. "I think I like this look on you," she said as she ran her cheek against the texture now present on his face.

It was very becoming on him, as the dark stubble highlighted his strong jaw and high cheekbones, giving further definition to them.

Levi softly chuckled. "You mean to tell me that you find an unkempt man attractive?"

He turned some and managed to bring his arm around her, pulling her in front of him. She snaked her arms around his neck, still hugging his hips with her legs. She gazed at his handsome face. "Well, if that's what you want to call it, then yes, I guess I do." She kissed him and laughed.

He brought his hand up around her neck. "Then I believe I will ignore the shaving supplies that Jasmine requested from Henry for now."

Reece softly nibbled his bottom lip. "That's an excellent idea." She studied his face. "Although, we'll need to keep it short and neatly trimmed."

Levi laughed. "I will be certain to tend to my newly grown facial hair for you on this journey."

That evening, Reece was surprised that her abilities hadn't left. She leaned lazily against Levi, and they sat in conversation with Harrison around their fire. Harrison's thoughts were obviously elsewhere that evening, and his eyes seemed to glisten as they reflected the light of the fire while he stared absently into the flames.

"Penny for your thoughts, Harrison?" Reece teased.

Harrison chuckled and looked over at her. "I should believe there is no penny required. I will unashamedly admit that my thoughts are with a lovely woman who awaits my return to Pemdas."

"You certainly got lucky with Angeline, my friend," Levi teased.

Harrison leisurely leaned back against the tall tree he sat in front of. "Truer words have never been spoken."

Reece smiled. "Has King Hamilton said anything to you?" Reece softly laughed. "You and Angeline created quite an audience before we left. Don't get me wrong, it was highly entertaining to watch that Sterlington broad—what's her name?" She looked up at Levi.

Levi chuckled. "Suzanna."

Harrison rolled his eyes. "I do hope Angie will not have to deal with that woman in my absence."

Reece laughed. "By the look on Suzanna's face, I don't think she's going to be talking for at least another week, much less giving Angie any trouble."

"In my opinion, Suzanna would do best to not go seeking trouble with Angie," Levi said with a laugh. "Any woman who has the ability to tame the wild heart of my cousin is not a woman I would consider entering into a quarrel with."

"I have been on the receiving end of Angeline's unyielding confrontations, and I will tell you, the woman has certainly taught me my lessons, and most profoundly so," Harrison responded.

"If you should ask me," Levi grinned, "I believe she should have let you suffer a while longer. She let you off too easy."

Reece softly elbowed Levi, while Harrison nodded and returned his gaze to the fireplace. "Indeed. However, I am most grateful she did not."

Without warning, and much to her disappointment, Reece's hunger returned forcefully, and her exhaustion was immense. She shivered violently as her body was slapped with the freezing temperature. She curled into Levi, and he embraced her tightly as she softly moaned in discomfort.

"This is like having the flu, aches and pains just coming and going as they please," she said through her chattering teeth.

Levi held her tighter and brought the cloaks up and around her. He kissed her softly on her head, and then brought her hood up and over it. "My love, I do wish there was a way that I could be of better help. Is there anything I can get for you?" He kissed her forehead. "I do know you get extremely hungry when you lose control over your abilities in this manner."

"I'm too tired to eat."

It was the last thing she said before the sun rose the next morning.

Much to her dismay, and right on schedule, they were back on their horses, galloping through the dense forest. They traveled through a narrow ravine for close to four hours before Levi suddenly halted in front of her, forcing everyone in the line to halt as well. Thundering hooves from behind gave way as Harrison charged up to where Levi was stopped, looking cautiously to the right of him into the trees.

Levi looked back at Reece. "Pull your hood over your head," he commanded her. His eyes were fierce, and his expression was gravely severe.

Harrison scanned the area around them, and Reece looked around as well. She didn't say anything, as it seemed both men were listening intently to their surroundings. Levi called out to Arrow, and the stallion walked up in-between Saracen and Areion.

"Levi?" she whispered.

"Quiet," he responded.

The next moment, Levi and Harrison removed the shields that were strapped at their horses' sides. Instantly, a loud sound from behind her alerted her that all of the Guardians traveling with them had done the same. An eerie whistling announced arrows flying directly overhead. Harrison and Levi swiftly brought their shields together, sheltering both of them and Reece.

Her heart soared with anxiety, and then a thunderous echo was pronounced off in the distance to their right side.

"Arrow—GO! NOW!" Levi shouted.

Before Reece could say anything, the horse raced rapidly up the mountainside to their left. She tried to halt him, scared and not thinking. Her eyes filled with tears, and she was terrified beyond belief. *Trust Arrow,* she commanded herself, knowing Levi would not have ordered the horse away had he not been sure Arrow would take her to a safe location.

She heard shouting in the distance from behind her, and she worried what the men were facing in this ambush. *How can this be happening? I can't lose any of them here.* Could Arrow lead her to the other Guardians that were out there somewhere if the worst were to occur?

Arrow ran swiftly and powerfully in this direction, completely off course for quite some time. They were on flat land now, still in a forest with snow all around them. Strangely, the trees of this forest were much wider in their circumference. Without warning, Arrow stopped. Everything was absolutely silent. Reece stayed quiet, watching Arrow's ears flick back and forth as he listened to something. Reece was frozen with fear, having no idea what she should do or where she should go. Arrow slowly walked forward toward a tall, snowy cliff. She gripped the saddle horn, feeling the surge of energy gathering in his muscles. Arrow whinnied loudly before he drew himself up to stand on his hind legs. His front legs crashed down onto the ground, and he whinnied loudly again.

"Arrow?" she called out.

Arrow started pacing violently, and when Reece tried to guide him away from the face of this mountain, he jerked his head in response. She watched in amazement as an opening appeared in the face of the mountain.

*What is this?* Arrow walked forward through it instantly. She turned back, and the opening dissolved into bright green ivory foliage behind her. She gazed in awe at the place they had entered into. Her surroundings had completely changed. There was no snow present anywhere, and large, massive trees filled the entire area. This forest appeared magical—no, enchanting. Reece remained silent as Arrow slowly walked ahead and deeper into it before he halted.

A woman with ebony hair, wearing a cream colored sackcloth robe tied with a blonde braided rope at her waist, approached them. She stared intently at Arrow, never once looking at Reece. The woman approached the stallion, yet he did not budge. He stood quietly and patiently as the woman brought her hand to his face. Arrow grunted, and then the woman's eyes grew fierce.

She shouted ferociously in a strange language, and in that moment a large mob of men with huge, feathered wings erupted out of the other side of these woods past Reece. They moved so swiftly that Reece could hardly tell what they were. She turned back and saw them disappear out of the ivy-like covered entrance she and Arrow entered from.

Reece hesitantly turned back around, wondering what was happening. The woman's skin was a beautiful dark caramel color, and she smiled warmly at Reece while motioning for her to dismount the horse. Reece gripped Arrow's saddle horn tightly, and his weight shifted beneath her. He grunted deeply and threw his head up in response to Reece's actions.

"You trust her, Arrow?" she asked her horse.

Arrow aggressively nodded his head up and down.

Reece slowly swung her leg over Arrow's back, hopping to the ground from there. No sooner had she dismounted did Arrow turn and rapidly flee the area. Reece panicked mildly, but the woman took her hand and walked her to a huge, wide tree. As soon as they approached it, a large arched door appeared in its trunk. It opened, and they slowly walked through it. This led them into a village that was secluded in a magical forest of trees.

Reece remained quiet as exhaustion washed over her again. *What is going on?* she thought. The woman stopped and turned to face her. People in matching sackcloth clothing slowly came into view, watching Reece and this woman.

Reece swallowed hard as the woman held her hand to Reece's cheek. Her hand was coarse and felt like sandpaper against Reece's flesh. She spoke in her foreign language again, and three young children with dark black hair approached. They held a wooden bowl with a white paste in it and handed it up to the woman. Reece's heart began racing, watching as an enormous crowd surrounded her.

The woman gave Reece a heartfelt smile as she dipped her thumb in the paste. She brought it to Reece's forehead, and before Reece had a chance to jerk back, the woman smeared it across her skin. Suddenly, Reece felt rejuvenated, like she did when she would gain control over her abilities. The woman took Reece's hands into her own and stared intently into Reece's eyes while she closed hers. When they reopened, the woman chuckled softly and shook her head. She turned and mumbled something.

The woman's eyes widened, and she motioned to her own mouth, as if to ask Reece if she was hungry. Reece was starving, but she shook her head negatively in response. The woman brought her hand to Reece's forehead and closed her eyes. They stood like this for close to a solid minute before the woman stepped back. She smiled pleasantly at Reece and reached for her hand.

"You are famished, sweet child," the woman said in an interesting accent.

Reece shook her head in shock. "You speak—I mean, you can talk to me?"

"Yes, child. I can communicate with you properly now."

"I'm not hungry," Reece said timidly.

The woman raised her eyebrows at her. "But you are, dear." She stepped forward and softly placed her hand on Reece's abdomen. "The young babe that grows within your womb—"

Reece jerked backward and rubbed her hands protectively over her abdomen. "Wait! What? How could you possibly know that?" She looked at the woman in astonishment.

"I can hear a rapid heartbeat beating within your womb very strongly," she said with a smile. "It is why you are greatly famished and exhausted. Your body desperately requires nourishment and is not receiving enough. Now," she took Reece's hand, "come with me," she said politely.

Reece eye's filled with tears while she softly rubbed over her stomach. *I'm pregnant?* It all made perfect sense now. The feelings of starvation she had been experiencing, her irrational mood swings, her exhaustion. *Levi! Where is Levi?* "Wait, my men need help, they were being attacked by something when—"

"Our warriors will bring your men here safely," she interrupted Reece in a calm tone. "Do not fear. They will rescue them from their attackers."

Reece sighed in relief. "Thank you," she responded as they entered a large, candlelit room.

She glanced down at her stomach. *I'm going to have a baby!* she thought with elation, wondering how she would tell Levi. *If I tell him now, he's going to be even more worried about me on this mission.* She resolved that it would be best to tell him when the mission was over and they were safely home in Pemdas.

# Chapter 28

After Arrow fled with Reece, the Guardians remained under attack as arrows constantly flew in their direction. Suddenly, the arrows ceased and all grew quiet. Levi peeked around his shield and noticed a black, swirling mist rolling in the sky above their heads.

*What is this?* Levi thought as the mist thickened. Out of nowhere, dark masses of what appeared to be creatures fell out of the sky. Before Levi and his men could react, they were surrounded by barbaric beasts that stood twice the size of a Guardian. Levi, Harrison, and the rest of the Guardians drew their swords simultaneously.

Levi locked eyes with the largest creature's deep red ones. Saliva dripped from the numerous fangs that were exposed on its long snout. "We mean you no harm!" Levi spoke out, hoping the scaly beast would let them pass without trouble.

Levi tightened Areion's reins when the creature shifted into the form of a fully armored man that towered over them. A loud roar boomed, and Levi watched as blades grew from the man's shoulders and hands. As he transformed, more and more of these creatures fell from the sky and did the same, surrounding the Guardians in every direction.

Instantly, Levi dismounted Areion, needing his horse's assistance to fight at his side. Areion lunged into the beast, giving Levi the advantage of protecting himself from another creature that was approaching at his side. Levi spun around and thrust his sword into his enemy's side, with absolutely no result. *Nothing!* Levi thought in disbelief that the blow had not affected the beast in any way.

Before Levi could charge the barbarian again, Areion aggressively threw his hooves into it, bringing the creature to the ground. Levi spun around swiftly when he felt a stinging sensation on his back. He turned to find the knives on one of a barbarian's hands swiping aggressively at him. Before Levi could think, Areion trampled the man and trounced him into the ground before he could make another move at Levi.

Levi turned and stood face-to-face with yet another barbarian. He swiped his sword across the creature's neck, and as the sword sliced completely through, Levi stood in awe that its head did not detach. Again, Areion lunged into the beast, removing Levi from danger. Another sting to his arm alerted him to an attack to his right. Levi spun into the attack, delivering his sword into where he believed the man's heart was.

"WHY WILL YOU BEASTS NOT DIE?!" Levi shouted in frustration after he removed the sword from the unaffected man without a drop of blood or internal fluid of any kind on it.

The creature lashed out at Levi, shredding the front of his breastplate and penetrating his flesh. Before he could counter, Areion brought the beast to the ground. The heavily-armored horses seemed to be the only saving grace for the Guardians at the moment. Fortunately, the seemingly unbeatable troop of attackers did not seem to have much luck in piercing through the horses' armor.

Levi ducked under another attack, rolled into the barbarian, and used his legs to bring the being to the ground. Levi grabbed his dagger and buried the blade into the top of its head. "You will not bleed," Levi said as the barbarian sprung to its feet. Levi rolled to his side as the tips of four large blades nearly pierced through his chest. Areion took the threat of this beast out of Levi's way as Levi sprung to his feet. There was no time to think. The attack was relentless, and there was no way out of it.

Levi was now using only his blade and shield to protect himself as more creatures dropped out of the sky. As the Guardians' line began to break, Levi turned and reacted quickly to this new attack. A slice to his cheek was nothing compared to what would have happened had he not reacted so swiftly. *"Harrison!"* he mentally called out to his cousin, hoping he was still alive. He turned and saw nothing but the shining sharp edge of four blades being thrust forward toward his heart. At that moment, Harrison shoved Levi back against a tree, pinning him to it as the attacker lunged toward them. Before Levi could blink, the barbarian that had come out of nowhere dropped to the ground after Saracen attacked it from its side. Beyond his greatest fear, Harrison fell forward to the ground as well.

"NO!" Levi growled, knowing Harrison had sacrificed his life for his own. Then without fail, Levi was attacked again. He forced himself to maintain his warrior mindset, despite the shock of what had happened to Harrison, knowing that if he hesitated for a moment, he would be dead.

He reached out to slash his blade into his enemy but gasped when a fiery arrow was plunged into the barbarian's chest from out of nowhere, leaving only a black cloud of dust where the creature once stood. He saw fiery arrows coming from the over the hill behind him, and they were destroying all of the creatures. The dark mist above them thundered loudly, and after a piercing screech the dark mass shattered into black particles that rained down over them.

Levi ran to where Harrison lay on his stomach, face down. "Harrison!" He fell to his knees and turned him over, gripping his lifeless face in an attempt to wake him up. Harrison's didn't respond.

He was alive, but his breathing was dangerously shallow. Memories of what happened to his father in Armedias ripped through him painfully. *I will not lose you!* He inhaled deeply as his body began to tremble. As he stood to assess the rest of the Guardians, he saw a group of foreign warriors quickly approaching each one of his men. They were long, lean, and muscular and wore nothing more than loincloths.

Their hair was long, and their dark-skinned faces and bodies were painted with red and black tribal markings. They soared down from the cliffs with huge wings, and when they landed on the ground, their black feathered wings vanished into their bodies. They carried bows and arrows in their hands, but nothing more.

Two of these men rushed swiftly past where Levi stood and approached Harrison. Levi turned to see that they were rubbing a white paste across the open wound in Harrison's chest.

"What are you doing to him?" Levi growled as he lunged toward them in his cousin's defense.

He was gripped suddenly at his shoulder by Garrett. "Emperor, they saved our lives." Garrett looked at Harrison, and then back to Levi. "This paste is serving to prevent the deaths of dozens of our men." Levi stared at Garrett in disbelief, unable to say anything. He looked past him and saw what appeared to be these winged warriors' leader.

"Who are you?" Levi asked firmly while shoving his sword back into its sheath at his side.

The face-painted warrior said nothing as he reached for Levi's wounded arm. Levi tensed, but when he saw how much blood he was losing due to the severity of his wound, he allowed the warrior to rub the paste on it. As Levi glanced around, he saw the horses and the rest of his men having their wounds attended to.

Levi tried to read into the warrior's mind, but it was empty. The man motioned for Levi to follow him. Levi turned to find the two men that were helping Harrison were now picking him up. Levi ran over to where Harrison remained unconscious in their grips.

"Garrett, help me with Harrison, now," he ordered as he reached out to take Harrison's shoulders in his hands.

The man that held Harrison by his shoulders stepped aside and allowed Levi to carry his cousin. Garrett approached soon after, took Harrison by the legs, and walked with Levi over to where Saracen patiently waited.

Levi looked down at the white paste covering over Harrison's exposed chest and saw that Harrison's wound seemed to be healing. Once Harrison was secured to Saracen, Levi turned and noticed most of his unconscious, wounded men were being helped onto their horses' backs by these people.

Levi turned to face the warrior's leader. The man nodded and gave him a pleasant smile as his massive feathered wings appeared. Areion approached from behind and nudged Levi in his back. Levi turned to his stallion. *"We must find Reece first,"* he mentally ordered. To his surprise Arrow was at his side. He whinnied and aggressively pawed the ground. *Is she safe with these people?* Arrow nodded and began to lead the horses carrying the wounded men up the hillside. One by one, the warriors darted up into the skies above them and flew off in the direction that Arrow was leading the Guardians.

Areion grunted with impatience. Levi hoisted himself up on Areion's back and nodded to the man he believed to be the leader of this group. With that, a gust of wind blew into Levi's face as the winged man shot up into the skies above them. They rode at a slow pace, following Arrow and the men who were casually flying overhead. Levi never took his eyes off Harrison as they rode, desperately hoping that whenever they got to where it was they were going, he would still be alive.

Not long after, a passageway appeared in the side of a mountain. They followed Arrow through as the winged warriors soared above their heads, flying through the entrance. A large wooden door appeared in the trunk of a very wide tree. *What is this place?* Levi thought as they followed Arrow through the tree. He watched in awe when they entered into a large village. Levi looked back, wondering if they crossed into another dimension inside this strange world.

He looked around, seeing small, primitive stone houses situated amongst the trees of the mystical forest. He looked up to see passageways throughout the large trees where small huts were nestled amongst the strong, heavy branches. He wasn't able to study his surroundings for long before a large group of women dressed in sack-cloth clothing walked swiftly out to the wounded men. Before Levi could turn to retrieve Harrison, he was stopped by a young woman who approached him with a wooden bowl in her hand. He looked into her deep brown eyes with concern. She peeked up from under long lashes and smiled reassuringly at him. She brushed her long, black braids of hair over her shoulder and dipped her hand into more of the healing white paste. She reached up to his face, and Levi stepped back from her briskly.

"Do not be wary. This will heal your wounds," she said in a smooth and pleasant voice.

Levi's brow furrowed. "You understand our language?"

She nodded as she reached for Levi's face again, but he caught her hand before she could touch him. "I do not require assistance. How is it you can communicate with me, yet your warrior men are silent?" he asked firmly.

The young woman seemed somewhat intimidated as she looked at Levi. "The woman from your tribe has helped us learn your methods of communicating."

*Reece!* Adrenaline coursed through Levi, and he sighed in utter relief when he saw Reece running out to where he stood. Levi quickly walked past the young woman to meet Reece. She wore a sackcloth robe, and her hair was braided to look like this clan of people. Reece's face was grief-stricken, and her eyes filled with tears as she approached.

"Harrison—" was all she managed through her sobs as she tightly embraced him.

Levi's heart sank. He stepped back from Reece and looked around to see that all of his wounded had been removed from their horses. He gripped Reece's hand while marching forward. "Harrison—" He looked back at Reece. "Where is he? Did you see him?"

"Yes." She sniffed as they walked hurriedly toward a large building. "He's in here," she said as she led Levi into the building.

"Is he alive?"

She nodded. "But I'm not sure if they can save him."

Levi swallowed hard. "He saved my life, Reece," he said in a grave tone.

They walked down a large hallway as people in sackcloth clothing bustled all around them. They turned a corner and found a room with wooden beds placed everywhere. There were roughly two dozen wounded men, and Levi quickly scanned the room for his cousin. He saw Harrison lying in the farthest corner of the room as three women attended to him.

He rushed across the room to his cousin. Harrison was lying on a bed, with only a blanket covering him up to his waist. The wound in the center of his chest was almost entirely healed. He gazed at his cousin, who appeared to be in a peaceful slumber, and he exhaled in relief as he listened to the sound of Harrison's steady heartbeat.

Reece slowly wound her fingers through Levi's, holding his hand tenderly. "He will be fine, Reece."

The women caring for Harrison did not turn to address Levi as he stood at the foot of Harrison's bed. Suddenly, Levi's mind became fuzzy, and he became extremely dizzy. His vision began to blur, and he started to sweat profusely. He shook his head, trying to figure out what was going wrong with him. He tried to walk and nearly stumbled backward to the ground. He reached out for Harrison's bed to steady him, and Reece tightly gripped him at his waist, barely holding him up.

He started gasping for air, and Reece's voice echoed, "Levi!"

\*\*\*

"Bring him to lie down over here at once," a woman said as she darted over to them.

Reece and the women who were attending Harrison shuffled a stumbling Levi over to the empty bed next to his cousin. Reece's heart raced as she tried to figure out why Levi went from being seemingly healthy to violently ill so suddenly. Tears filled her eyes as she watched his body tremble and listened to him as he moaned painfully.

A woman approached him and raised his head up. Levi jerked his head away as she brought a wooden cup to his mouth. "If you can hear me, you must drink this," she told Levi. "The poison has spread throughout your body," the woman said calmly.

Levi tightened his lips as the woman tried numerous times to encourage him to drink from the cup. Reece could bear no more of his fighting. "Levi! DRINK IT!" she yelled as she rushed to the head of the bed. She laced her hands through his hair, cradling the back of his head. Reece reached for the cup that the woman held to Levi's lips, taking it from her. She steadied the cup to his lips and tried not to spill anything as his body's violent trembling shook the bed.

"Drink it, Levi," she said in a calmer tone.

He mumbled something before his eyes rolled back in his head and his body continued to spasm. His eyes closed and lips tightened further as Reece fought to keep the wooden cup to his lips. *Stop fighting me, or I'm going to lose you,* she thought in frustration.

Reece glanced down at his tightened fists and knew she had to find a way to get him to listen to her. "My love," she said warmly. His eyes flicked open, and she stared deeply into his dull blue irises. "You must drink the medicine."

Levi's panting breath slowed, and his lips loosened some. It was just enough for Reece to put the rim of the cup to rest on the inside of his lips. Fighting Levi's constant trembling, she managed to tip the cup, and the fluid was able to seep through his lips. His lips parted more, and his strong hands gripped each side of the cup, pinching her hand between it.

Levi swiftly downed the fluid like a man who was dying of thirst. His grip on her loosened, and he collapsed onto the bed. His eyes remained closed, and his body stopped trembling.

The woman to her right gently placed her hand on Reece's arm. "He will be fine," she said with a reassuring smile, "but we must address his wounds immediately. If we do not rub this paste over every wound, the poison will begin to decay his flesh. Hurry, I will help you to remove his clothing."

Levi suffered wounds to his abdomen, arms, back, and legs. The woman looked at her. "We will attend to the wounds on his back first, and I will leave you to attend to the remaining ones."

Reece's heart ached to see him in this condition, and she wondered what had happened to all of them. As she continued to administer the cream to Levi's arms, she glanced up and shivered with remorse as she took in the images of the other wounded men.

The men looked as though they had been attacked by something with large claws. Their clothing was slashed and ripped nearly to shreds. Levi's left cheek had a long laceration, starting from his temple and extending down to his chin. It looked like a large claw went through his cheek; fortunately, the bleeding stopped once the cream was spread over it.

Once she was finished, Reece glanced around the room to see that all of the warriors were being well cared for. The woman who previously helped her with Levi returned and gathered Levi's warrior attire. "I will have these repaired and will send for clothing to cover him when he wakes."

Reece smiled. "Thank you—all of you." She looked around at the other women who continued working with Harrison. "You and your people saved all of their lives." Her voice cracked.

The woman smiled. "Your men are brave people." She looked at Levi. "He should be waking soon," she said and turned to leave.

"Wait!" Reece called out. "What about my cousin?" She looked back at Harrison, who was alone now. "What about him? Will he be okay?"

The woman nodded. "Your cousin's wounds were extremely severe, and he was very near death; it will take his body longer to recover. We will continually offer him treatment, with the hope that he will regain consciousness."

"Hope?" Reece snapped out of fear of losing Harrison. "Are you saying that he may not survive?"

The woman walked over to Harrison and placed her hands on his forehead. "His mind remains in a healing state. I am unsure at this time."

Reece felt tears well up in her eyes, and she nodded numbly in response to the woman before she left the area.

Reece continued to smear the paste over Levi's wounds, distraught by the reality of their situation. *Levi, what happened to all of you?* she thought. After she tended to all of his wounds, she stood and placed a tender kiss to his lips before she turned to check on Harrison. His breathing was normal, and his flesh a normal temperature. Still unsure if he would pull through this, she leaned over and kissed his forehead. "Don't you die on us, Harrison," she scolded him through her tears.

She turned to leave when another, much older woman approached Harrison. She ran red paste over his forehead that instantly blended in with his skin tone. The next thing Reece noticed, Harrison's skin color was its usual hue, and his expression more peaceful.

"Will he make it?" she asked the older woman.

The woman smiled. "Rest assured, he will survive. However, do not despair if he does not wake soon. His body is healing rapidly, but until it has conquered the poison entirely, he will remain in a sleeping state."

Reece impulsively hugged the woman. "Thank you."

She turned, walked over to Levi, and ran her hands through his hair, wondering when he would wake up as well.

"Reece!" a familiar voice boomed from the doorway, startling her.

She looked up to see that it was King Hamilton who entered. She stood in relief and nearly ran to him. When she reached him, he held his arms open to embrace her.

"King Hamilton, I thought you were with the other Guardian troops? How did you find us here?"

He gently pulled away. "Garrett sent for the rest of us. All of the Guardians are here now." He walked over to Levi. "Garrett informed me about the medicines that are healing our men, but do you know if Levi and Harrison will be okay?" he asked her while looking over at Harrison, and then back to her.

She nodded. "Levi should be waking up soon, but we're not sure when Harrison will wake," she answered him. "Harrison almost didn't make it."

Hamilton gazed somberly at Reece, and then quickly recovered his expression. "Have no fear," he nodded at Harrison, "that boy is as resilient as they come. Although, I am grateful to hear that after Garrett informed me of the wound he suffered." He glanced at the women attending the other wounded men in the room. "Our men are most fortunate that these villagers came to their rescue. We owe them a debt of gratitude that we might never be able to repay."

"I agree." She cleared her throat and stared intensely at King Hamilton. "I have a feeling that Mordegrin may have been behind this attack." She looked over at Levi, hoping to see his eyes had opened, yet he remained in a peaceful slumber.

King Hamilton stared at Levi, and then over to Harrison, and Reece watched his expression go from concerned to determined. He ran his fingers through his auburn, curly hair and exhaled. The formidable man looked at Reece, and his bronze eyes penetrated through her. "We cannot lose any men on this mission. We must learn more about the beings that ambushed the company of men you were in," he commanded in a deep, authoritative tone.

Reece returned his gaze with the same determination. "I haven't had much time to talk to anyone here. As soon as I started feeling better, the wounded began to arrive."

King Hamilton nodded. "It appears that we are safe in this cloaked village—or dimension, perhaps—that we have been brought to. We shall endeavor to learn as much as we can from these people when Levi has recovered."

Reece sighed. "I'm hoping that is very soon."

# Chapter 29

eece sat on the side of Levi's bed, softly brushing a wet cloth over his forehead, cheeks, and through his hair. Since he had been sleeping, she had cleansed the blood from his body, and he appeared to be much healthier. She glanced over at Harrison, who was still peacefully sleeping. It was such an eerie feeling to see both men in this state.

King Hamilton and the other Guardian warriors who were not involved in the ambush were in and out of the room, constantly checking on their wounded men. She brought her attention to Levi's serene face, longing to see his eyes opened again.

*"Open your eyes, Levi,"* she tried to mentally persuade him, with no response.

"Please, my love," she begged him in a soft voice.

Her eyes widened when she saw Levi's lips twitch in response.

"He appears to be waking," King Hamilton said as he approached the other side of Levi's bed.

Suddenly, his eyes slowly began to open.

"Levi?"

Levi brought his attention to her and blinked a few times. His eyes were brilliant in their sapphire blue color, yet extremely glossy. He reached his hand to her face, and in that moment she leaned into his strong hand, covering it with both of her own.

He tilted his head to the side. "Beautiffulll, juuusst beauutiffullll." His eyebrows shot up, and his eyes opened wider. "Thhaatt is what *you* are, my wiffffe," he said, slurring and stammering his words.

Reece looked at King Hamilton, who had an amused expression on his face. *Is he drugged?* she thought as she looked back at Levi, who was trying to prop himself up.

He collapsed against the wall at the head of the bed, slouching over as he reached for her. She scooted closer to him, and as she ran her hand along his cheek, he brought one hand to grip her back and weaved the other one through her hair and clutched the back of her head. Before she could say anything, he forced her lips down onto his, deepening their kiss in that moment. Reece's head spun wildly with this kiss that tasted like pure honey. As much as she wanted to relish in the moment, she had to pull away. King Hamilton was watching everything, and if Levi were in his right mind, he would have never considered doing such a thing.

She brought her hands to his chest, firmly trying to pull back. Levi held her closer, tilting his head to the side and deepening his kiss. Reece couldn't help but chuckle at the way he was acting. He finally withdrew and smiled at her lazily. He released Reece, brought his arms up, and clasped his hands behind his head. He leaned back and gazed seductively at her. "I could spend the ressst of my life kiss—sss—king—" He frowned in desperate concentration, closed his eyes, and then reopened them with purpose. "Kissing you," his eyes widened, "my lady." He gave her a silly grin.

Reece and King Hamilton tried their hardest not to burst into laughter as they listened to Levi's muddled speech.

Levi slowly looked over at the King. "A lobedly woman, is shhhee not?" He cocked an eyebrow at him and pressed his lips together proudly.

Hamilton's eyes glistened in humor. "The loveliest, Your Royal Majesty."

"Levi," Reece giggled softly, "maybe you should—"

Levi brought his attention back to Reece. "The wayyyy," he squinted, "the way in which you speak *my name*," he said in awe as he shook his head gratefully and tightened his lips, "it is so…so soooooothing to my…" He glanced up, searching for words, and then looked back at her with purpose. "To my heart!" he demanded with a firm nod.

"He needs to drink this elixir," a woman said as she approached. "It will help remove the effects from the medicines. His mind is intoxicated with the potent dose that we had to give him," the lady said with a smile.

Reece sighed with relief. "Thank goodness. I was wondering how long it would take for these effects to wear off."

The lady nodded. "He will recover his mental strength soon after he drinks that," she said before she turned to walk over to the other Guardians that were starting to wake.

Reece handed the cup to Levi. "You need to drink this," she ordered him in a humorous tone.

Levi's eyebrows shot up in excitement as he reached for the cup. He took it and studied the contents in it. He brought his brilliant eyes back to hers. He remained silent, staring deeply into her eyes. His lips twisted some. "Havve I everrr told you, Reesh Ahh…Ahhhxsshly—"

"Drink that drink, Levi," she said with a smile. "You can tell me in a couple of minutes."

His eyebrows knit together as he shook his head. "I mussst stell you nnow." He squinted at her. "Your eyes are sooo…sooo very enchantment," he shook his head, "enchantable…no?" He squeezed his eyes closed tightly in concentration.

"Enchanting?" King Hamilton said with a laugh.

Levi's eyes opened widely as he reached his arm out and pointed at King Hamilton. "Thas it! That was thhe word." He smiled sweetly at Reece.

She went to speak, but he brought the hand he held the cup with up. While gripping it, he used his index finger to point at her. "They sparkly—"

"Levi!" she said with a pleading look, "*please*, just drink the drink!"

"I should like a kiss—ifff you want…" he tried, arching his eyebrow at her.

Reece quickly leaned forward and gave him a quick kiss. "Now, drink!" she commanded him.

Levi sluggishly blinked his eyes and raised his cup to her. "Here's to the most beautiffful woman in all," his eyes widened, "in all of the dimmmensssions…in all of the domains…alllll of the worrrrlds," he sung to her.

Reece gently reached for the cup he held in the air and sat closer to him.

"All of the galaxies!" he said as he waved his pointed finger at her.

Reece ran her hands through his hair, and he silenced. His glossy eyes were fixed on hers as she slowly brought the cup to his lips. She nodded to encourage him to drink it. He went to speak, but she used the opportunity to tip the cup and force the liquid into his mouth. His eyes closed as he gulped it down. Reece sat back and sighed in relief as she looked up at King Hamilton.

She shook her head and looked back over at Harrison. "I can only imagine what that one's going to be like when he wakes up on this medicine."

King Hamilton chortled. "There is no telling, but I can say with certainty that my biggest regret on this mission has been not bringing a recording device with us for this moment."

Reece laughed as they brought their attention back to Levi, who sat in silence, staring at Reece with a gaze of wonderment. When her eyes locked onto his, a lazy grin spread across his face. As silly as he was behaving, the expressions that were crossing his face were adorable, and her heart swelled with love for him.

"I am indeed a most fortunate mmm-man," he said, the slurring now starting to fade in his voice. "How is that?" He looked at Reece in confusion. "How is it that I could be so privileged for such a woman to love *me*?" He cocked his head to the side and raised his eyebrows purposefully. "You are mine!" he said proudly. "And I am all of yours." A stiff nod ended the point he was trying to make.

"That's right," she said, watching his personality beginning to change.

King Hamilton had left to assess Harrison and the other men. Reece stayed with Levi, allowing him to run his fingertips across her face now.

She watched as his eyes sluggishly roamed over her face, then without warning his eyes refocused. It was almost like watching him snap out of a daze. She felt the power return to his hands as he caressed her face. "No!" he shouted as he sat up. He went to drop his legs over the side of the bed, but Reece quickly stopped him.

"I must get up. What happened to me? How are our men?" His eyes scanned the room. "Harrison! Where is he?"

King Hamilton approached as he heard the commotion. "Harrison is fine, Levi." He grinned at him. "And it is best to stay under these covers for the moment, as they are in the process of bringing you clothes to wear."

Levi looked down and examined his bare chest. He ran his hands over the fading scars from the wounds he had received in battle. "Where are my clothes?" He stared at Reece in confusion.

"Levi, these wonderful people are mending all of the Guardians' clothing that was torn during the ambush. You nearly died from the poison that was in your body from the lacerations you received."

Levi studied her. "Poison?"

She nodded. "Yes. They had a remedy here for you to drink. It saved your life."

Levi rubbed his forehead. "These people, have you learned anything about them?"

"Very little," she started, "but from what I know, they are a very unique tribe. They are not affected by Mordegrin and the Olteniaus females here. Their dimension in this world is protected the same way that Pemdas is protected from outside forces. Sadly, there is no way they can defeat Mordegrin and the females. They have imprisoned themselves here so they can remain protected."

Levi shook his head. "I must get up. I need to speak with their leaders."

King Hamilton nodded. "Allow me a few moments to see if they have some clothing ready for you."

After King Hamilton left, Levi held his arm out toward Reece, inviting her into his embrace. She immediately reacted and leaned into him. He kissed the top of her head and lifted her chin with his finger. When she looked up, his lips were on hers, giving them a tender kiss. "I am so grateful you are safe. I owe these people more than I can say for caring for you and our men."

Reece laughed as she recalled the previous way he was explaining his love for her when his mind was intoxicated. "It's good to have you thinking and talking normally again."

When she told him about his actions while he was awakening, his face was paralyzed by embarrassment. "You have to be joking," he said as he brought a hand up to cover his face. "You must forgive me. I believed it to be a dream."

Reece held her finger to his lips. "Shh. It was actually adorable, really. I'm just thankful you're awake, safe, and healthy again."

Levi smiled, his cheeks coloring lightly. "I am sure King Hamilton feels the same way as you." He sighed and brought his forearm up on his forehead. "Reece, what are we to do now?" he asked her softly.

Reece gently stroked his arm resting over his abdomen. "What do you mean? We keep pressing on. These people saved our lives, and we will not give up."

He looked over at her, brought his hand from his forehead, and ran it along her hip. "The enemy that mysteriously attacked us—" he grimaced and inhaled deeply, "we could not destroy them. No matter what wound I tried to inflict, they would not bleed, they would not die." His eyes became distant. "I even used my sword to remove one of the beast's head—" His eyebrows shot up, and he softly laughed. "It never detached from its body."

Reece exhaled. "You're all lucky to be alive."

"Before these people came to our rescue, it was the horses that kept us ahead of our enemy in the fight. If we did not have their swift advances coming at the enemy from every side, they would have slaughtered us." He gazed somberly at Reece. "How are we to prepare now?" He looked over at Harrison and shook his head in defeat. "What else is out there that Mordegrin did not tell us about?"

Reece stared at him with sympathy. "We will find a way through this." She looked around the room, watching the people of this land helping the Guardians in their recovery, "They will help us. We will learn more about these people and this world from them. It's obvious that we can trust them after their warriors flew out to save you." She looked at Levi. "How did they manage to get all of you out of there?"

"It happened so quickly, all I could see were fiery arrows coming down from the mountains." He sat up some more and reached for Reece's hands. "Their arrows vaporized our attackers, or so it appeared. The barbarian before me simply turned into a black cloud of dust and was gone. Once they arrived, the creatures immediately fled the area."

King Hamilton returned with neatly folded dark green and cream colored sackcloth clothing. He placed them on the foot of Levi's bed. "Here. I am not sure how comfortable you will be wearing this type of material, but it will have to do until your clothes have been mended," he said in amusement before he turned to bring Harrison's clothes to the foot of his bed.

Levi looked around in speculation. Reece stood up. "I've got this." She grabbed a blanket from the empty bed next to Levi and held it up to conceal him from the rest of the room. King Hamilton walked over and took one side of the blanket, helping Reece.

"Their leaders are willing to speak with you whenever you are prepared to meet with them, Emperor Levi," King Hamilton said. "These are excellent people, and I am sure you will be greatly impressed with the services they have provided to all of us. Their women have been relentlessly preparing fine meals for all of our men."

"You can lower the blanket now," Levi answered.

Reece and Hamilton turned to face Levi, who was tying a drawstring rope at the waist of his loose-fitting pants. "They have impressed me beyond belief so far," he said, leaning over and picking up a cream, gauze-like, long sleeved shirt. He studied it for a moment, and then pulled it over his head.

Reece was pleasantly surprised by how handsome he appeared in such simple clothing. The billowy shirt reached all the way down past his waistline, stopping at his hips. Levi looked down at the slit neckline that was opened all the way down the center of his chest. Tiny leather strings were interlaced and served as a way to close the opening of his shirt. Levi was quiet as he fumbled and tried to figure out the shirt. Once he tightened the laces, he reached to tuck the long shirt into his loose pants. It was all wrong, and he looked ridiculous. Levi looked at Reece, frustration apparent on his face.

She giggled and walked over to where he stood trying to adjust his pants. She untucked his shirt. "From the way I've seen most of the village men dressed here, you're not supposed to tuck this in."

Levi sighed. "I feel as though I am wearing the bedclothes from my childhood."

King Hamilton snickered at Levi's comment. "You will most certainly feel awkward in this type of dress. It is a drastic change from our Pemdai customs and styles."

Reece reached for a dark brown vest and belt. Levi looked down at her and grinned as she handed him the long brown, sackcloth vest and he put it on. She wrapped the wide-banded belt around his abdomen and quickly fastened it.

"You appear to have adjusted to these new styles easily," Levi teased.

She turned and picked up his high boots and handed them to him. She lifted her chin smartly at him. "I've had plenty of practice adapting to other worlds' clothing customs, don't you think?"

Levi laughed. "Indeed, you have."

"We might need to incorporate this into Pemdai culture when we get home. You have no idea how much more comfortable sackcloth is compared to a corset," Reece teased.

"You certainly look like a man who is ready to hunt the land." King Hamilton chuckled.

Levi smirked at him. "Have your laugh, Your Majesty. I will have mine at your expense soon enough."

As Levi said it, a woman approached King Hamilton with neatly folded pieces of clothing in her hands. "Allow us to clean your clothing for you."

King Hamilton glanced down at her, and then back at Levi. Before he could say anything, Levi answered the woman. "Thank you, madam. My dear friend will gladly accept your kind offer."

Reece softly laughed as King Hamilton shook his head. "I shall be back in a moment." He took the clothing from her hands, thanked her, and disappeared from the room.

Levi sat on the bed to pull on his boots, and Reece used the opportunity to go check on Harrison. She ran her fingers through his soft hair. He was peacefully at rest, showing no signs of waking anytime soon. Levi was soon at her side. He pulled the blanket down and placed his hand over the fading wound that should have killed his cousin. He was amazed to discover how all of their wounds were simply vanishing as they healed.

"This is truly amazing. We have something that works very similar to heal wounds in Pemdas; however, our medicine does not remove our scars. This solution they use, I am curious as to what it is."

"It is a paste created from particles from their trees' roots, found deep in the ground," Reece answered. "They combine it with water and rocks that are ground into powder, and it forms this paste." She smiled at Levi's furrowed brow. "They haven't mentioned anything else to me, but it appears as though this place has magical energy within it."

Levi nodded. "It is my hope that they will open up to me and allow me to learn more. When our swords could not kill those beasts, their arrows did. We need to glean as much information as we possibly can from them."

They grew silent as they watched Harrison. Reece hoped he would wake soon. The heartbreak apparent on Levi's face was agonizing to see. Harrison and Levi were more than close cousins; they completed each other in some funny way. Their closeness and companionship was not merely a friendship, it was a relationship that was beyond anything Reece had ever witnessed.

She thought about what he would be like when his eyes did open again. She looked at Levi's attire, knowing Harrison's commentary about it would no doubt be entertaining.

Her roaming thoughts were interrupted when she heard Levi gasp. She looked at Harrison, thinking he may be waking up.

"Reece?" Levi said in a low, breathless whisper.

She turned to face him. His eyes were wide, and his face appeared to be frozen in shock. She brought her hand to his cheek. "Levi, what's wrong? Are you feeling sick again?" she said in concern as his expression remained unchanged.

He stared so intently into her eyes, it made her shiver in response. "Levi?"

He slowly knelt down on one knee, gently wrapping his arms around her waist. He turned his head to the side and rested it against her abdomen. They said nothing, but remained frozen in the moment until she heard Levi let out a breath. He turned his head and brought his lips to her stomach. His hands massaged tenderly along her sides.

After the kiss to her stomach, he looked up at her in amazement. His eyes were mesmerizing in their vivid sapphire blue color. He swallowed hard. "Our child grows within you," he softly informed her. "My love, you are pregnant."

She smiled down at him. "I know," she answered as a tear slipped down her cheek.

# Chapter 30

Levi's body tingled with overwhelming delight. *Is it really so? I am to be a father!* he thought with joy as he slowly stood up. Reece's eyes shimmered as they looked cheerfully into his. He swallowed hard, brought his hand to her face, and caressed her cheek with his thumb. Reece was carrying his child. An heir to Pemdas grew within her. Their sincere and intense love for one another was yielding them the most precious of gifts, worth more to Levi than any sacred treasure in existence.

"Levi—" she started with concern in her voice.

He silenced her by bringing his lips down onto hers. He loved this woman more than anything, and now she was carrying their child. After a few moments of losing himself in the overwhelming feeling of inexplicable joy, the reality of the world they were in forcefully slapped him out of the blissful moment. He was gripped with uncertainty about having his pregnant wife in this dangerous world. He slowly withdrew and brought his forehead to rest against hers.

His hand rested against her neck. "My love, there are no words to express how much I so desperately love you. You have given me so much already, and I am rendered speechless with the knowledge of this precious gift you carry for both of us within you." He pulled his forehead back from hers. He smiled. "My heart and soul are exceedingly overwhelmed with unmatched happiness." He took notice of how healthy she appeared and recalled how she was acting during the journey before they were ambushed. "This must have been why you were feeling so ill and unreasonably famished while we were traveling. You said you knew that you were with child. How long have you known?"

A bright smile stretched across her face. "I was given the news when Arrow brought me to this village. A woman named Ionis greeted us. She is the one who sent the warriors out to save all of you. She told me I was pregnant when she heard the heartbeat." Reece watched him speculatively. "But you? How could you tell I was pregnant?"

"I heard the heartbeat as well." He took her hand. "I was trying to focus on Harrison in order to communicate with him telepathically when I heard it. I had to put my ear to your stomach in order to be certain. Reece, you must know, this changes everything. I must keep you and our child safe.

How are we to rescue my father and battle Mordegrin in your current condition?"

Reece's expression was unyielding. "You will listen to me," she started in a firm tone, "nothing changes. I will be fine. I was fine earlier, wasn't I? I've been through the trauma of opening the portal, and nearly frozen to death. Even with the attack, Arrow brought me to safety. I will not allow you to let this stop us now!"

She didn't understand the burden that weighed upon him. "Reece—"

"Levi, no." She brought her arms around him. "We need to talk to these people first. They will give us the information we need, and then we can decide where we are going from here. You must know that I would never put our child in danger, so you must trust me." She stepped back and stared purposefully into his eyes. "We *will* rescue your father, and in a about nine months he will be holding his grandchild in his arms, telling him or her what a brave man their father was for rescuing him."

Levi grinned. He didn't know how she did it, but she always found a way to win these arguments. She was a strong woman, like his mother, and he greatly admired her bravery.

Harrison's arm moved, prompting Levi and Reece to turn around and see that he was waking up. Reece immediately turned. "I'll be right back. I need to get him that drink that helped you sober up from the medicine."

Levi nodded and turned to Harrison, whose eyes were now starting to open.

"Harrison?"

Harrison stared up at the ceiling, and then over at Levi. His eyes were glassy as he grinned at him. He sat up some, trying to come to. "Mmm—" he mumbled.

Levi laughed. "Harrison, do not speak. Trust me when I say that it is best if you remain silent for now. Reece is coming with something that will help you think clearly."

Reece returned with the drink and handed it to Levi. "They gave him a stronger elixir to help him snap out of this daze quickly."

Levi extended the cup toward Harrison. "Before you say or do anything, drink this. It will help you gather your thoughts and wake up out of the bizarre state you are in at the moment."

Harrison laughed. "Oh?" he said before he slurred some words that made no sense.

Reece chuckled as Levi looked down at her, remembering the embarrassing scene he caused both of them earlier. Harrison gulped the drink and sat back. Relief washed through Levi as he saw his cousin alive and well again. He watched as Harrison slowly ran his hands over the spot where the wound that should have been fatal once was.

"You saved my life, Harrison," he said.

Harrison looked at Levi purposefully. "That I did, my friend, and I would do it again!" His eyes roamed over the outfit Levi was wearing, prompting him to burst into laughter. He sat up some more, still laughing and pointing at his cousin.

*Here we go!* Levi thought.

Harrison cleared his throat. "So 'Robin Hood of *La-Oxley*', do tell me, how are the rest of the *merry men?*" he said between laughs.

Reece couldn't restrain her laughter. "Nice to have you back, Harrison."

Harrison looked over at her, the medicine still fading in his glassy eyes. "Well, if it isn't the lovely Maid Marian as well? What a delight!"

King Hamilton laughed when he approached, and Harrison nearly went into hysterics seeing that he was wearing the same clothing as Reece and Levi.

"Friar Tuck!" he chortled loudly and cleared his throat. Harrison's eyes were wide in humor as he studied the three standing around his bed.

King Hamilton laughed and reached down to the foot of the bed for the clothes Harrison was to wear. He tossed them into Harrison's chest. "Keep laughing, my boy; you shall be just as fashionable as we are as soon as you are well."

Harrison continued to laugh as he held up the shirt. "Ah-ha!" he proclaimed gleefully. "Does this mean I get to be Little John?"

Levi looked over at Reece. "I wonder if he needs another dose of that special remedy? The man is delusional."

Reece's cheeks were red with laughter, and she nodded in agreement.

Harrison frowned. "I am not delusional." He waved his hand at them. "All of you look as though you fell out of Sherwood Forest."

Levi laughed. "I believe your lifelong fascination with the legend of Robin Hood is starting to have an effect on your mind, as it did when you were a young boy."

"You cannot deny that, Robin of Loxley—Levi Oxley..." Harrison's eyes glittered as he laughed again. "It is pretty hilarious!"

Levi gazed down at his cousin, whose eyes were starting to focus now. Levi refrained from answering, knowing Harrison would snap out of his stupor at any moment and realize their current predicament.

A moment later, Harrison's smile died. He looked over at Levi. "Did we lose any of our men?" He sat directly up in bed, as Levi had when he himself snapped out of the strange dream-like state he was in.

"No. Rest easy, cousin, our men are recovering well." He turned to find Reece and King Hamilton holding up a blanket for Harrison. "Get dressed. I will go over what I know when you are ready. First, we must meet with the leaders of the village we are in."

Levi turned away, giving Harrison his privacy. He glanced down at Reece, quietly studying the room. He inwardly laughed at her appearance. She did look like Maid Marian out of the book they read as children. Her hair cascaded down into beautiful waves, reaching the middle of her back. She had two slender strands of braids that started from just behind her ears and then came together in a particular weave and laid neatly with the rest of her hair flowing down her back. Small ivy vines were interweaved into the braids, and a leather band ran along her forehead and was weaved into the small braids of her hair.

"All right, I am okay," Harrison said distractedly.

Levi turned to King Hamilton as Harrison pulled his shirt over his head. "Once Harrison is completely ready, we will take a quick opportunity to check on the men recovering in this room. After that, I am ready to learn more of these people and thank them personally for their help."

Once Levi and Harrison were assured the men were recovering well, they left with King Hamilton and Reece to meet with the leaders of this tribe.

"You have to admit it," Harrison started.

Levi looked over at him, only to find a large smile on Harrison's face. "Admit what?"

Harrison tugged on Levi's billowy sleeves. "You do resemble the 'Prince of Thieves' somewhat, do you not?"

Levi sighed. "Harrison, I do not understand how you are coming up with these absurd resemblances."

"The picture books my father brought us from Earth as children, of course. They wore clothing very similar to what we are wearing now."

"Indeed, but how is it you believe me to resemble Robin Hood?" Levi laughed aloud after he said it.

Reece and King Hamilton softly laughed, listening to both of the men in their exchange.

Harrison shrugged. "You know I have done extensive research on the legend of Robin Hood, which includes various books and cinematics from Earth. Given my expertise on the subject, I think you simply have that distinctive quality about you."

Levi shook his head. "I fear that some of that medicine has not worn off in you yet. It would be best to let me do all of the talking with the leaders of this tribe for now. I am frightened to think of what might come out of your mouth when you see how they may be dressed," Levi said, remembering how their warriors looked when they rescued them in the ambush earlier that day. "You should also be aware that their warriors have large, feathered wings. I am unsure if all residents in this village have the same or not, as their wings disappear once they have no use for them."

"Warriors with wings? Now *that* is something I should like to see."

They walked down a dirt road lined with small stone, hut-like buildings and gigantic trees. Levi glanced up at the enormously wide trees that had thousands of strings of ivy and moss cascading to the ground from their thick branches. He gazed up in wonder, noticing the same buildings built amongst their branches. It appeared as though an entire city existed in the trees alone. Drawstring bridges were used as walkways and strung throughout all of the trees for as far as he could see. Lanterns and torches illuminated everything around the small huts and walkways. The trees were surrounded by dark, lush green foliage that covered the ground beneath them. Taking the sight of this in, Levi couldn't help but see the similarities from Harrison's picture book. *He was right about one thing*, Levi thought as he let out a laugh.

Harrison leaned into him. "Sherwood Forest, am I right?"

Levi bit his lip and refrained himself from shoving Harrison with his arm, like a goofy boy would. People were bustling around the buildings and trees, and Levi could not risk losing his composure in front of them.

They walked toward an open area where a massive, wide-based tree sat, dominating the entire area. Levi looked at Reece. "Have you visited here already?"

"Yes. This is where they gave me some medicine for—" She stopped herself.

*"For me and the baby. I won't say it out loud, I'm not sure if we should let anyone know yet,"* she told him telepathically, hoping he would be able to tune into her.

He smiled and nodded as a confirmation to what she communicated to him. "It is why you are feeling better?"

"It seems it is also why I have control over some of my abilities again. They don't come and go anymore."

He stopped and looked down at her. "Are your abilities as they were before you opened the portal?"

She shook her head. "They aren't as powerful as they were when I had the stone's powers. I have to use them like I did when I was training with Galleta."

"That is relieving to hear." He turned to continue their walk toward the massive tree, and they approached the double door entrance to the tree.

As they walked through the doors, the tree opened into a large meeting room. The only source of illumination came from candles that were placed on a long wooden table in the center of the room and on wooden shelves that lined the walls.

"Are we in the right place?" Levi said, looking around the empty room.

Levi's question was answered when three large men and two women entered the room dressed in the same attire that Levi and the rest of the Pemdai had been given. They all wore pleasant expressions on their faces as they walked over to greet Levi.

Levi nodded and reached his hand out toward them, "My name is Levi Oxley, Emperor of Pemdas, a dimension in the galaxy known as the Milky Way." *Never had to introduce myself that way before,* he thought before continuing. "Please accept my most humble gratitude to you and your people for all that you have done in rescuing and caring for my people."

A man with dark skin and long, stringy silver hair accepted Levi's hand. "You are most welcome, Emperor Levi Oxley. You may call me Shallek. I am the leader of this dimension that you have been brought into. We were more than happy to be of help to your kind." The man turned to introduce the people at his side. He put his arm around an older woman with long, black shiny hair. "This is my mate, Ionis, our two sons, Reinza, Pilazee, and our daughter, Normila."

Levi stepped forward to the woman that Reece told him had helped her. "Ionis, I will be forever grateful for you for helping my wife when she arrived, and for sending your warriors so hastily to save me and my men."

Levi stepped back and gave each one of their children a pleasant smile. "It is an honor to meet you all." He turned to Reece. "I believe you have made her acquaintance already, but this is my wife, Reece Oxley, the Empress of Pemdas." He motioned to King Hamilton. "This is our dear friend, John Hamilton, King of Sandari in Pemdas." He turned to Harrison. "This is the Commander of the Guardian warriors, Harrison Oxley, The Duke of Vinsmonth."

Harrison grinned at Levi, and Levi knew exactly why. It was strange to introduce themselves by their formal titles to unknown people in another galaxy.

*"I don't truly believe they care about our titles, Emperor Levi Oxley of the Dimension of Pemdas, in the Milky Way galaxy, sister to Armedia—"*

*"I get it, Harrison. If you do not mind, I am trying to keep my thoughts straight,"* Levi mentally returned to Harrison.

*My apologies Your Imperial Royal Majesty, previously known as the His Royal Highness, the Prince of Pemdas, son of the great Emperor Navarre, and formerly the most eligible bachelor our realm has ever known,* Harrison responded internally as he stood expressionless.

Levi managed to give Harrison a reproachful glare as Shallek walked over to the table and sat. "Now that the formal introductions are over, please be seated. I have many questions to ask of you, Emperor Levi. The bravery that your kind possesses has amazed me," he said with a smile.

Levi pulled Reece's chair out for her and waited for her to sit. Once seated, Shallek became more casual as he clasped his hands on the table and leaned forward. "If I may, what brings a tribe of people who are not native to this galaxy to travel through this isolated location?"

"We have come to recover my father, Emperor Navarre Oxley. We were informed by a man who goes by the name of Mordegrin that he is being held in a fortress close to a four-day journey from this location."

The man's eyebrows shot up. "The Olteniaus females and Mordegrin have your father imprisoned?" Then the man shook his head disappointedly. "I regret to inform you, but this journey will be futile for you and yours. No one in history has been able to battle such dark powers. Believe me, my people tried at one time, and we nearly lost our entire population as a result."

Levi's heart sank, and he felt Reece place her hand gently on his. *"Levi, there is a way. Don't let this deflate you."*

He looked over at Reece's promising eyes, and then back to the man. "We believe we can recover him. My wife found a way to bring us into this galaxy, and she will help us find a way to defeat them as well."

The man leaned back some and softly chuckled. "I strongly admire the boldness of your kind."

"Thank you, sir," Levi returned.

"Now," he leaned forward inquisitively, "you have my attention. How is it that you found a way to travel into another galaxy?

He looked over at Reece. "My wife is from the planet Earth, in our galaxy. The people of Earth are known as humans. My people, the Pemdai, are known as The Guardians throughout all of the dimensions of Earth. We have sworn to protect this planet for all of our existence. We recently learned that many years ago, an Olteniaus female found a way to create her presence on Earth, and she found love with a human male. My wife's ancestor was born as a result of that union."

The man and his wife's eyes widened simultaneously. "She has Olteniaus powers?" He looked at his wife, and then back to Levi. "Please, go on."

Levi stared at him in speculation. "Her powers are minimal, but enough to help us recover my father and to create a way of travel for me and my men into your galaxy."

"There may be a way to defeat these atrocious creatures after all," Ionis said, smiling warmly at Reece. "Can you alter minds with the powers you possess?"

Reece looked at Levi, and then back to Ionis. "I was told I could possibly do that, yes."

"Will you try with us?" Ionis requested politely.

Levi spoke up. "Forgive me, but—"

"Wait a minute, Levi." Reece gave him a reassuring smile and looked back at the woman. "Who would you like me to try mental persuasion on?"

"There are many people outside walking around," Ionis ruminated, "persuade one of them to bring us some water."

Levi looked at Reece, and her eyes closed. After a few moments of silence, Reece opened her eyes and they all patiently waited. Levi looked back when the doors to the room opened and a young man entered holding a bucket of water.

He looked at everyone in the room meekly before bowing his head and staring at his feet. "I beg your pardon. I have no idea what came over me, but I felt compelled to bring water into this room."

Shallek clapped his hands in joy while Ionis radiated with the same happiness. "Thank you, young man. Please leave the bucket at the door. You may leave now," Shallek said as he looked to Levi. "There may be hope after all. You and your men will require our warriors' assistance to travel to the fortress, and we will gladly offer you those services. However, we must form a plan, and we must prepare all of you and your men."

Levi nodded as great relief washed over him.

"I had all but given up hope that this day would come, but your wife has given us all a hope that we never believed possible," Shallek said gratefully. "We will start tomorrow, and we shall work hard and fast to get you to the fortress of Dresmenia, where you will recover your father, and we will recover our world."

"The enemy that attacked us earlier," Levi asked, "what were those barbaric creatures? Have you ever encountered them before?"

"They are part of the Olteniaus' army of warriors; they are known as the Liesten. Mordegrin," his eyes darkened as he mentioned the man's name, "is referred to as the Shadowy One by our people." His tone grew deeper. "He must want something from you and your people." He scanned the group before him before he gazed fixedly at Reece.

Levi glanced at her and back to Shallek. "You believe he brought us here so that he might take my wife?" Levi asked in confusion.

Shallek nodded. "It is the only reason Mordegrin would send the fiercest ones in his armies after you and your men. You have something he wants. I believe that *something* is the one who carries the genetics and abilities of his kind. They are the only ones left of their kind. I would imagine he would stop at nothing to acquire her."

Levi shook his head. "As I said before, she is entirely human; she only carries a few minor abilities of the Olteniaus within her being."

Ionis smiled. "For her to be able to persuade a mind within our protected domain gives her a talent that Mordegrin and his females do not possess."

Levi thought for a moment. *They want to use Reece to take over this domain?* He stared intensely at Ionis. "There is no way they will take her. We will defend her with our lives, as we have always done." He looked at Shallek. "How were you able to destroy those creatures he sent to attack us? They do not bleed—they would not die."

"That is because they do not live," Reinza returned.

Harrison laughed. "How is that possible?"

"They are a dark creation of Mordegrin's. You might refer to them as clones or something of that nature," Normila answered Harrison.

"Is that why they turned to black smoke before our eyes?" Levi interjected.

"That is what the energy of our land does to the Shadowy One's power," Shallek said. "It incinerates it and reduces it to ashes. If the Liesten were to invade our domain, they would simply turn to ash the moment they came through our barriers. Our energy force is too strong for them to withstand it."

"Then the flames that were on your arrows, it was not fire?" Levi asked.

"No. It was the energy within the rock that the tip of the arrow was fashioned from."

Levi sat back. "That is intriguing."

Shallek and his family chuckled heartily in unison. Shallek crossed his arms. "It is why my warriors will be of excellent assistance to you on this journey. We will sharpen your swords on the same rock, and if your people are comfortable battling with arrows, we will offer more supplies in that manner as well."

"You mentioned that your people tried to destroy Mordegrin and these females before but were unsuccessful," King Hamilton asked. "Why is that? You have the weapons, or so it would seem."

"Their dark force is too great. As you have witnessed, our minds can easily be persuaded, and that is why our people have no chance to destroy these dark ones. We cannot take the risk of the Olteniaus manipulating our minds and persuading us to turn our weapons on each other—or your kind, for that matter."

"Are you certain that you will be able to help us?" Harrison asked.

"We will assist you on your journey. The Liesten army will not be Mordegrin's only attempt to take the Empress of Pemdas and destroy any and all attempts to recover your emperor. For your safety and for ours, we must remain a certain distance away from the fortress so they cannot manipulate our minds to battle your kind."

"My I ask," Ionis said, looking at Reece, "is she able to manipulate a Guardian's mind?"

Levi hadn't thought about that. She was able to impress her thoughts, but manipulate? Levi nodded at Reece when she looked at him in question.

Her eyes closed. *Leave the room, Harrison.*

Levi heard her thoughts. He turned to Harrison, who watched Reece with a grin. Reece's eyes reopened, and she shrugged. "It looks like the Guardian mind is protected; were it not, my cousin would have stood up and rudely left the room."

"Nice try, Reece," Harrison returned.

Levi cleared his throat, trying to remain formal. "Your assistance traveling to the fortress will be greatly appreciated."

"We must meet with your warriors. I want to know what else is out there that we may be up against as we continue on our journey. I must prepare my men," Harrison told Shallek.

Shallek nodded. "I will gladly have you speak with them. But first," he turned to his sons, "go and tell the men to fly to the villages of Grispan and Utan and inform them of our news. Tell them that we need them to gather their armies.

Invite them and their families to our land tonight; for tonight we shall celebrate our unification, and we shall honor our new allies, the Guardians, from Earth's galaxy."

Harrison stood with the men. "I will go as well."

"It is best if you remain, sir," Normila said in response. "These villages are in other dimensions, and you may put yourself in danger once again."

Levi looked up at Harrison, who stood with a grin playing in the corner of his mouth. "I thank you for your concern, my lady; however, after your warriors proved their ability to protect my kind today, I believe I will be perfectly safe amongst them."

Shallek chuckled under his breath. "My daughter is correct, it is best if our men go alone. We need to be able to persuade these armies to join us. They are very fierce people, and very arrogant as well. They will not take kindly to strangers. Even now, I am unsure if they will unite with us."

"If that is the case, then I will gladly remain here to greet them when and if they arrive," Harrison conceded.

Shallek stood, prompting everyone at the table to follow. His sons left the room, and it was obvious this meeting was adjourning.

Ionis looked at her daughter. "Prepare rooms for our guests." She looked back at Levi. "We do not have many places available, as your army is quite large."

Levi nodded. "I am humbly grateful for your kind gesture of hospitality. As for the rest of our men, they have no need for such accommodations."

"If you will excuse me, I must meet with the others to plan our celebrations this evening," Ionis said before turning to leave.

Shallek led the way out of room. He clapped Levi on his shoulder, and Levi was mildly startled by the gesture. They were friendly and outgoing people for certain, but it was something Levi was not accustomed to when meeting with other rulers from other lands. He appreciated the man's friendly nature, yet it was strange to him nonetheless.

"Normila will have your rooms ready soon, and she will return for you when she does," he said with a smile. "For now, I believe you should most likely desire to advise your men of our new plans. And now, I must prepare for the arrival of the other warriors to our domain tonight. So we must part ways for now, and I shall see you when the festivities commence at dusk, my new friends."

Levi nodded, and the man marched swiftly down the dirt road, humming some tune loudly and joyfully.

"I do not wish this to come out wrong, as I greatly appreciate their offer of help," King Hamilton said, "but strange people, are they not?"

Reece laughed aloud, and Levi raised his eyebrows as he looked at King Hamilton in humor. "I could agree with that statement, my friend," Levi answered, "but we must accept that they are from a different culture, far different than any we have ever encountered."

"To be sure," Harrison added with a laugh.

"They are definitely overly friendly, but I like it. I, for one, have never had the fortune of meeting an alien species that wasn't trying to kill me, so I think we hit the jackpot with these natives!" Reece teased.

"Indeed, my love." Levi kissed her head as Harrison and King Hamilton laughed.

The four headed to check on the Guardian warriors who were still recovering from their wounds. Nearly all were up and very well. The Guardians joined each other in a large open area of the forest, and Levi and Harrison began to tell them all about the meeting that had taken place.

# Chapter 31

The Guardians immediately went to work on drills working with the bow and arrow. This tribe's technique on the bow was much different than most were accustomed to. Instead of using quivers to carry their arrows while firing them, they were skilled with holding the arrows with their draw hand. This made their pull faster, and the arrows delivered to their target as swiftly as a bullet.

After conditioning himself somewhat, Levi went to set his bow to the side as Harrison called him out.

"Gentlemen," he proclaimed with a grin, "it is time we put our stealth to good use."

*Give him a chance to play Robin Hood, and Harrison will capitalize upon it.*

"What exactly do you have planned, Commander?" Levi asked, knowing it would most likely be a draw between him and his cousin.

Harrison's eyebrows shot up. "Split the arrow."

Levi wanted to roll his eyes at the dangerous game he and Harrison learned years ago, but this was an excellent drill for the Guardians to run.

Levi positioned himself close to fifty yards from Harrison. Once both men were facing each other, Harrison drew his bow as Levi began calculating the exact location and speed the arrow would travel. Without fail, the instant that Harrison released his arrow, Levi drew his and split Harrison's arrow down the center. The arrows both dropped, and Harrison nodded toward Levi.

"Your turn."

"I almost lost you once today, my friend," Levi taunted.

Harrison shook his head and grinned. "Draw," he returned.

Levi did, and Harrison stopped the arrow with his own as easily as Levi had. The group of Guardians laughed, and it was apparent they were eager to begin the new drills.

Levi and Harrison went back and forth like this for some time before Levi ended their drill. It was invigorating to run such challenging maneuvers, and it took Levi's mind off the night that awaited all of them. In truth, it was slightly frustrating to Levi and his men that they were to join in on the celebration that Shallek and his people were arranging. Being men of valor, celebrations before a battle were not part of their nature, especially now, when there was so much at stake. Their mission had already been compromised by the loss of the majority of Reece's abilities, and by the ambush that nearly took all of their lives. Regardless of Levi's opinions, he couldn't take issue with it. They needed these people so that they would be successful in recovering Navarre.

"Emperor?" Normila said upon her approach.

Levi halted his conversation with King Hamilton, who had just approached, and turned to greet her. "Yes, Normila."

"I have prepared rooms for you and your empress. If you are ready, I will take you to them."

"Allow me to retrieve my wife from the location where our wounded soldiers are."

Levi grinned when he walked into the room. He watched how Reece cared for the last of the brutally wounded Guardians. His heart swelled with pride as she not only continued to help administer medicines, but consoled them as well.

Levi didn't have long to admire Reece before she noticed him standing in the doorway. She brought a basket of white fabric over to a table and walked over to him with a vibrant smile.

"I continue to be awed that these men survived." She looked at the Guardian she was just with. "Mr. Laurent had a wound to his heart. Because of that, the poison spread quickly through his veins. I wasn't sure he would recover."

Levi walked over to the young Guardian who had closed his eyes. "Laurent," he called out, but the man's eyes remained closed.

Reece took his hand. "His body is trying to heal, so he's drifting in and out of sleep. He is quite lethargic, but the poison has left his system."

Levi nodded and turned to Reece. "They have prepared the location that you and I will be residing in for the evening. Normila is here to show us our room."

Reece wound her arm through Levi's as he escorted her from the building.

They followed Normila deeper into the forest and climbed a wooden staircase that spiraled around the trunk of a massive tree. Once at the top, they walked along a drawstring bridge, which led them to a hut. Normila opened the door and gestured for them to walk in.

"There is bread and fruits for you on the table. If there is anything else you and the empress need, please let me know. I will leave you both for now, as I must join my mother to help with the festival arrangements."

"We will be fine. Thank you for everything, Normila," Reece answered with a kind smile.

"You are welcome. I will see you at the celebration tonight."

Levi looked around the small room. All of the furniture was fashioned from carved wood. The hut was small, with barely enough room to place a dining table in one corner and a bench and three chairs in another. At the other end of the room was a doorway that led into a small area where a simple bed was situated.

Reece turned and smiled up at Levi. Even though she was doing very well with the nourishment she had been provided, she looked fatigued. Her face was slightly pale, and she appeared to have lost weight. "Reece, are you using your abilities to overcome your natural exhaustion or hunger at the current moment?"

She nodded. "I have to. I was starving again when you and the Guardians arrived. We haven't really stopped since."

Levi looked over at the table that had four loaves of bread and a variety of fruits on it. "I am only asking because I am concerned for your health and that of our child's. I must request that you refrain yourself from using those abilities to shield yourself from hunger or rest. I do not want to risk you becoming ill in any way. We have been offered a reprieve, and you should indulge yourself in nourishment while you are able to."

"You're right. I don't want to risk hurting the baby either."

Levi followed Reece over to the table and sat adjacent to her. Once seated, Reece reached for the basket of bread and fruits and immediately began eating as if she hadn't eaten in weeks.

"Are you that famished, my love?"

She nodded while chewing the piece of bread she placed in her mouth. She swallowed the bite. "I don't want to seem ungrateful, but this bread tastes awful." She tore off a piece and handed it to him. "Here, taste it."

After Levi swallowed the piece she offered him, he smiled sympathetically at her. "Reece, the bread tastes perfectly fine to me."

She sighed. "Let the strange pregnancy cravings begin. You know what does sound delicious?"

"What is that?"

"The tomato basil soup that the Anders' make at their restaurant in Casititor," she answered.

Levi shook his head and exhaled. He sat back in the chair and looked around at the furnishings in the room.

"Levi?" Reece questioned him.

He turned back to her. "Yes."

"Something's bothering you. What is it?" she said while continuing to eat.

Levi reached for the pitcher of water, poured it into a wooden cup, and offered it to Reece. "I will admit, I am becoming somewhat frustrated by everything at the moment. I am greatly appreciative of these people and everything they have done to help us; however, we do not know much about them. Since we need their assistance, we are at their mercy, and I am uncomfortable with that. Right now, we should be making our plans to recover my father and destroy these Olteniaus females." He rubbed his forehead. "Instead, these people would rather have a festival and celebrate the idea of it. It makes absolutely no sense to me, and it has slowed our mission down even more."

Reece reached for his hand, and her tender touch seemed to relax some of the tension that was building up in him. "I completely agree with you, but we have to keep in mind that without their help, we wouldn't be able to recover your father at all. We have to be patient. Besides, we still have men who are recovering."

"I understand; nevertheless, it is difficult for me to have patience while I watch you sacrifice your well-being as you carry our child in this dangerous galaxy."

Reece softly laughed. "Levi, quit worrying about me; I'm hardly sacrificing anything."

Levi's lips twisted. "I disagree." He looked down at the bread she was forcing herself to eat. "You should be home at the palace, sending for the soup you currently have a great desire to eat." He looked back at the room they were in. "Instead, you are here in this strange place, and I am unable to ensure that your every need is met properly. Not only that, but once these people finally decide to plan our attack on the fortress, we will soon leave, and your and our child's life will be put in great danger once again." He ran his hand aggressively through his hair. "I want this over with, Reece. The longer we sit here doing nothing, the less control I feel I have over any of it."

Reece stood up and walked over to him. Levi extended an arm, inviting her to sit on his lap. When she did, he wound his arms around her waist and leaned his head against her chest. He felt her chin rest on his head, while her fingers ran tenderly through his hair.

"I listened as your mother gave your father excellent advice when he could send no more men to Earth to recover you and Harrison when the Ciatron took you all. He had finally admitted to himself and to her that he failed you, Harrison, and all of Pemdas."

"This is different," He softly argued.

"It may seem that way, yes. But really, it's not. Your mother told your father that she wouldn't allow the one dangerous trait that you seem to have inherited from him take over."

Levi exhaled. "Oh? What is this dangerous mannerism I have?"

Reece kissed the top of his head. "The ability to overreact or become upset in situations you have no control over." She cupped his chin and brought his gaze up to meet hers. "Levi, just as your mother reminded your father that he had to trust you and his men because there was nothing more anyone could do, I shall tell you the same. Quit worrying about me and the baby. Our warriors will take care of us, and you know that. Whether we have to wait to form plans or not, you know very well the Guardians will execute them flawlessly."

"Reece—"

She held a finger to his lips, preventing him from saying any more. "No. Quit stressing yourself out like this. I'm not sacrificing anything. So what if I don't like the food I'm eating? At least I have food to eat. I understand your impatience in wanting to get this over with, but you have to realize that even if you don't have control right now, it will be okay. We will be back on our horses resuming our mission soon enough. If you sit here and concern yourself over unimportant issues like what I want to eat, you will not be able to lead your men properly. I'll be eating a bowl of tomato basil soup before we know it. We are not in a position to be anything but grateful."

Levi stared deeply into her purposeful eyes. "I love you." He brought his hand to her cheek. "And you are correct. I will do my best not to overly concern myself with any discomfort you may have."

She kissed his lips. "When we get back to the palace, you can spoil me all you want. For now, we need to stay focused on why we are here, and that's to recover your father," she said as she covered up a yawn.

"You should lie down for a while," Levi said with concern.

"That sounds wonderful. Go find Harrison. Maybe he's talked to someone and has more information for you."

Levi cradled her in his arms and stood. "I will do that." He said while walking her into the other room. Once Reece was settled under the blankets, he leaned over and kissed her. "I will return for you within a few hours when they are preparing to start their festivities." He sat on the side of the bed and ran his hand over her abdomen. "For now, get some rest."

She gazed up at him with droopy eyelids. "Can you hear the heartbeat right now?"

Reece had lost the battle of trying to keep her eyes open, and she smiled in response. "Even with my ability to hear really well, I haven't heard it yet. You're lucky you get to," she said distantly before curling up on her side and falling fast asleep.

Levi sat there studying her for a moment while he ran his hands through her long, wavy hair that cascaded over the pillow. He leaned over, kissed her softly on her forehead, and then stood to leave the room.

After Levi left Reece to rest, he walked out to where the Guardians continued running various drills with their bows and pulled Harrison off to the side. After Harrison informed him there was no information to give, his frustration began to rise.

"You appear to be quite distressed. Is it Reece?" Harrison asked.

Levi studied him for a moment. "I must inform you of some news, as this information will possibly alter our plans to attack the fortress entirely."

Harrison's brow furrowed. "Very well. What is this news?"

Levi exhaled. "Reece is with child."

Harrison's eyebrows shot up, and his expression radiated excitement. He coughed out a laugh of utter shock and clapped Levi on his shoulder. "Indeed? Congratulations! This most assuredly is wonderful news." He shook his head, and his grin widened. "I should have known you two would waste no time," he teased.

"Of course," Levi grinned slightly, "and thank you. I am overwhelmed with happiness, but my concerns have been elevated for her and the baby's safety on this journey. She should not have ever been required to join us on this mission."

Harrison nodded. "It is understandable that your concern is great, but you know very well there was no way to do this without her. Even at that, we have kept her safe thus far, and we will continue to do so until we return her and the future heir to Pemdas to their home safely."

Levi exhaled, staring past Harrison and out to the Guardian warriors who were relentlessly training for their next battle. "I simply wish she was not subjected to the rigors of such a dangerous world, and in the company of thousands of foreign warriors." He looked down, shook his head, and softly kicked a small rock with the toe of his boot.

Harrison sighed. "Well, if we were not at the mercy of a tribe of festive natives right now, I believe we would be working together tonight to form our plans to leave before sunrise tomorrow."

Levi's lips twisted in defeat. "It is aggravating to me as well. How are our men handling this setback?"

Harrison glanced at the men standing behind him. "The men are anxious to resume our journey, but so long as they keep themselves busy, they seem to cope fairly well."

"I have not had the proper opportunity to thank you—and also to scold you—for saving my life today."

Harrison grinned. "As if I would have made any other decision. Oddly, I was not fast enough in removing us both from harm's way."

Levi shook his head. "That situation was unpredictable in every way. Nonetheless, I did promise a beautiful woman that I would personally see to it that you are returned to her safely," he said with a reproachful gaze.

Harrison chuckled. "And I promised your lovely wife I would keep you safe as well. Do not worry, my friend, I have every intention of making it back to Angie alive. As a matter of fact, I believe it is time I share some excellent news with you."

Levi smiled at Harrison's beaming expression. "Do tell me what agreeable news you have to share."

"Once we return to Pemdas, I plan to ask Angie if she will become my wife."

Levi cocked an eyebrow. "Is this so? I assume the honorable King Hamilton has given you his approval?"

"After mercilessly teasing me, yes, he gave me his consent not one hour ago," Harrison returned smugly.

"You know very well this will not be the end of our teasing. I have waited quite some time for your *theories about love*," Levi said dramatically, "to be proven wrong. I must admit, after all of your arrogant talk about the absurdities of love, it is surprising that you would move so quickly to make Angie your wife."

Harrison nodded with a confident grin. "Very true. Although, I care not what anyone will say or think, this is the only woman I have ever felt this way about, and I will waste no time in securing her as my wife."

Levi reached out and shook his hand while clapping him on the shoulder. "This is excellent news, indeed." He sighed and looked out at their surroundings. He grew somber, and he gazed at Harrison with determination. "We must destroy these dark beings and retrieve my father with haste. We have our own celebrations to be shared with our families."

"Agreed!"

# Chapter 32

Levi and Harrison's conversation was interrupted by the sound of large wings flapping in the air behind them. Both men turned to find Shallek's warriors gracefully landing on their feet, wings instantly concealed behind them. Levi's eyes widened when he noticed the group of warriors following in from behind Shallek's men. Men with harsh expressions on their faces were being carried on the backs of large creatures that resembled lions. The animals were fierce, with horns pointing out of each side of their massive heads. Their bodies were enormous, making these creatures an amazing, yet dangerous sight to behold. Another group of warriors were also amongst them, although they were not as tall or threatening in their appearance. They flew in on birds of prey. Once landed, the black and fearsome birds stood taller than the large, mystical lions.

"What in hell…" Harrison trailed off in disbelief. "They look like mutant lions and hawks!"

"It seems quite obvious that this is their desired method of transportation," Levi responded with the same astonishment as Harrison.

From out of nowhere, hundreds of people in this land came out of the buildings and down from the trees and walked toward the approaching group of warriors.

"Well, I certainly do not remember this part in the legend of Robin Hood," Harrison said in amazement.

"Emperor! Commander!" shouted Shallek. "Come! Come!" He waved his hand out at them, gesturing for them to join him amongst the warriors that had arrived.

Levi and Harrison walked toward the group. "There has to be over four thousand warriors amongst them," Levi said under his breath. "Where will they come up with enough food to feed everyone?"

As soon as he questioned it, he saw enormous wagons filled with food and other supplies.

"And I thought the celebrations at Pasidian were too large," Harrison added in humor.

The large group stopped before Shallek. For the first time since seeing him in the forest, Levi was face-to-face with Shallek's warrior that he saw after they were ambushed. The leaders of the new factions stood on either side of him. The man that dismounted the lion resembled an average human man from Earth. He had blonde hair that fell to his shoulders. He wore only dark pants with braided leather crisscrossing the muscles of his bare chest, with a deep red sash tied around his waist. A crescent shaped sword hung on one side, and a double-bladed axe on the other.

The man who flew in on the large bird was quite the opposite. The warrior's skin was a deep green color, with hair that looked like strands of tiny black ropes, which sat in a knot on the top of his head. His eyes were yellow, and he wore a feathered-like suit with large spikes on his shoulders pointing toward the sky. After Levi familiarized himself with the images of the warriors and their loyal beasts behind them, he was curious as to how they were to communicate.

Shallek proceeded to speak in an odd language, and Levi tried to comprehend the meaning of the words he was speaking. Shallek stepped back and looked at Levi. "Give us a moment." Levi nodded and watched as Shallek and all of the warriors closed their eyes simultaneously.

The leader of Shallek's army approached Levi and extended his hand. "You and your men all seem to be recovering well," he said.

Levi accepted his hand, shook it, and looked at him with confusion. "So you do speak?"

The man smiled. "Of course. I simply needed to learn how your people communicate."

Levi looked over at Harrison, and then back at the man. "I am curious, I was told that my wife was the one to teach your people how we communicate." He cleared his throat. "I know she is a talented woman, but how was that possible? How could you all learn so quickly?"

"When Ionis read into her thoughts, she went into your wife's memories to when your wife first learned how to communicate with those in her world. Ionis assimilated your language rapidly, and we learned from her soon after."

He looked back at the men behind him. "That is what is happening now." He brought his attention back to Levi. "Shallek is transferring your method of communication into Rei and Oble's minds. Once they have fully comprehended your way communication, they will help the rest of their people to learn in the same manner as we did."

"That is intriguing, and quite convenient as well," Harrison said. "So it appears that the people in this galaxy are highly intelligent and have the ability to mentally communicate?"

"Not all, but most." The man smiled. "Please allow me to introduce myself; I am Diexz. I command our armies."

"Diexz, it is an honor for both of us to make your acquaintance. This is Harrison, the Commander of the Guardian warriors, and I am Levi, Emperor of Pemdas. We are exceedingly thankful for you and your men in helping us today."

"We were happy to be of service to such courageous people. I look forward to serving with you and your men to restore peace to our world." He looked out to where the Guardians were training and remained silent as he studied the men continuously running drills with their bows, shields, and swords.

He grinned when he looked back at Levi and Harrison. "Your people are extremely talented in their fighting skills. They use the bow as we do. That intrigues me."

"The Guardian warriors have been raised to fight in any manner we require of them," Levi answered.

The man nodded. "This shall be an interesting journey to the fortress. To align such talented warriors will make for an enjoyable attack."

Levi was unable to respond as Shallek turned back to him. "Emperor, please." He extended his arm out as an invitation to Levi.

Levi stepped forward and became slightly uncomfortable when Shallek brought his arm around his shoulder. Shallek proceeded to make the introductions between the warrior leaders and Levi. Oble, the warrior with the feathered attire, seemed fierce, but accepting of Levi, the Guardians, and their cause. Rei, the man with the human appearance, wasn't so accepting. Levi could sense the tension and reservation within the man, and Harrison's current disposition proved he felt the same as Levi.

"It is a great honor to meet you both," Levi started. "Please accept my and my men's humble gratitude for your willingness to join us to battle Mordegrin and the dark females. To be willing to help in our cause, words of gratitude are not enough."

Rei's black eyes bore into Levi's. He was close to the same height as Levi and Harrison, with a very muscular build. "Do not be misled, Emperor of Pemdas. My people have not come to help you or any cause of yours," the man answered gruffly.

Levi's now fierce gaze did not falter against the man's rigid expression. "Forgive me for suggesting the motives of your people being here to meet with us. I will—"

"What brings you and your people into a foreign galaxy?" the man interrupted Levi. "How did your kind manage such a thing?"

Levi's jaw muscle tightened, and he clenched his fists tightly in response to the man's rude interruption. "Our people are here to retrieve what was taken from us, and that is our emperor. We are here to recover him, destroy the new threat to our world, and return to our home. We are here for nothing more," Levi returned in a grave tone. "As to how we entered your galaxy," Levi spoke deeply, "that is an explanation I do not owe you."

"Oh, but you do owe me the explanation. Do not forget that you are in my world and you require *my* army's assistance. Tell me now, how did you enter our galaxy?"

"Rei!" Shallek said, cutting through the tension. "It would be best to respect the men who have the ability to liberate us from the curse that has been upon our world for thousands of years. You would be wise to find your alliance with them, and soon," he firmly scolded the man.

Levi was somewhat shocked that Shallek could be so commanding with his words. With all of his outgoing, friendly behavior, Levi was beginning to question whether he carried any fierceness within him or not.

Rei looked at Levi, and his eyes narrowed. "I want to meet the female that carries the Olteniaus blood within her veins this instant," he demanded.

Levi was at his personal limits, and any pleasant words he may have had for the man earlier had vanished. "The woman you are referring to is my wife, and I will allow no one to demand anything of her." He stared intensely into the man's eyes. "You will do best, sir, to heed Shallek's words. Your conduct has me concerned about whether I want my men fighting alongside of you or any of your warriors on this mission. It was not my decision to request your help."

The man continued to stare intimidatingly into Levi's eyes. "Do not threaten me, *Emperor,*" he mocked.

"My words were not intended to be taken as a threat, but you can take them any way you like," Levi answered in a deep tone.

Shallek put his hand gently on Levi's arm, and Levi instinctively jerked away from him. He glared at Shallek hostilely, and Shallek nodded in understanding of Levi's agitation.

Shallek looked at Rei. "Tell us, Rei, why have you decided to join us? To cause problems? If so, you and your people may leave at once. It appears that your potential freedoms are not that important to you."

"It is not that at all," Rei answered him.

"Then why do you appear to have taken issue with people that are here to help? They bring no trouble to us," Shallek asked.

Rei looked at Harrison, and then back at Levi. "Because they are not here to help us, Shallek! They are here for themselves."

"We are here to recover Emperor Navarre, yes," Levi returned. "But also to destroy the ones that have taken him, desolated your entire galaxy, and protect ours. If you see that as we being here for ourselves, then so be it. Our warriors are prepared to die for this cause, if yours are not, leave," Levi finished in a low voice.

The man studied Levi for a moment before speaking. "I believe it is best if you allow me time to think. We will remain here and join the celebrations," Rei answered him. "But know this, I am unsettled by you and your men. I believe I will feel better once your wife has proven herself to be no danger to me and my people."

"The empress will be at the festivities later. Once I am assured that your temperament has changed, I will decide whether or not if I will introduce her to you. She owes you nothing."

Rei gave Levi a firm nod in response and spun around toward his men.

After the confrontation, Shallek apologized profusely to Levi and informed him that Rei was a man who did not trust easily, but they needed him and his men. In their own way, his men were much like the Guardians in the way they protected Earth.

Levi and the Guardians remained out and away from the large mass of people who showed for the festivities. Their overjoyed moods were somewhat annoying to the Guardians, and as the hours passed by they were becoming more agitated. Harrison and Levi tried to reach out to Diexz, but it appeared that he was more concerned with the celebrations of the land. Diexz explained to them that it was their tradition to celebrate before a dangerous mission. The people believed it brought them good fortune to prepare in such a way.

As the daylight began to fade into darkness, Levi returned for Reece. He walked into the room and found her sitting at the table, devouring some fruit.

"Did you rest well?" he said as he approached where she sat.

She smiled. "I did, and I'm feeling much better.

"That is refreshing to hear."

Levi informed Reece of the new warrior that came into the land. He told her of the confrontation with Rei and of his demand to meet her, and Reece reassured him that she would be able to hold her own if he became confrontational.

Before they left, Normila returned with Levi and Reece's Guardian attire. They looked at each other in surprise as they noticed how flawlessly the garments were mended.

"It is odd..." Levi said as he tucked his black shirt into his pants.

"What's that?" Reece said as she approached him.

"These people—where do they all hide? How do you repair close to one hundred outfits in such a short amount of time? Where are the people who do this? It is like the people of this land mysteriously appear and disappear from out of nowhere."

Reece laughed. She opted to continue to wear the dress they provided her, given it was lighter in material and more relaxing to be in as opposed to the heavy leather and armor of the Guardian uniform. "I wondered the same thing myself. This place is something else."

"Indeed," Levi answered as he concealed his dagger at his side. "One minute we are conversing with Shallek, and the next minute he leaves to handle a matter and simply vanishes. I believe if I went searching for him, I should never find him." He laughed in disbelief.

Reece ran her hands over the steel pads now covering Levi's shoulders. "I'm pretty sure we're about to meet all of the people that have been hiding amongst these giant trees soon enough," she finished as she brushed along his long black cape.

Levi sighed, noticing it had darkened more outside. "You are most likely correct." He lowered his head to quickly kiss her and rose up. "Let us get this over with, shall we?"

They met the rest of the Guardians in the open area. All of the men had changed back into their Guardian attire, and strangely enough, it brought a sense of relief and reassurance to Levi. Something about seeing his men in their formal uniform gave him the feeling that things were finally starting to move forward.

They walked down toward the large tree they had met Shallek in earlier that day. He and his family patiently waited for Levi, Reece, and his men to arrive, and then they led the way. They walked deeper into the forest to where everyone attending the festivities was already celebrating. Torches lit the pathway to the location, and a large fire in the distance gave Levi the impression that they were close. He could hear the muffled sounds of musical instruments being played, and the squeals and laughter from all of the people present.

"Levi—" Reece quietly called out to him while trying to remove her hand from his grip. "You're going to break every bone in my hand if you don't relax."

Levi instantly loosened his grip on her. "Forgive me! I had no—"

"Don't worry about it, I'm fine. But you need to calm down a bit. This will be over sooner than you think."

When they walked into the large clearing, torches were scattered everywhere, casting an amber glow over the area. People were scattered everywhere. Some were walking in front of the long tables, filling their wooden plates with the variety of food. Others were filling their plates from the animals being cooked over the numerous fire pits that were next to the tables. The loud music came from across the large fire that was in the center of this location, where women dressed in long white dresses danced joyfully around the fire, obviously the entertainment for the evening. Levi looked out past this, and for as far as he could see, there were thousands of people sitting throughout the torch-lit woods, laughing and indulging themselves in the lively entertainment. *So odd,* Levi thought.

Levi sat with Reece, Harrison, and King Hamilton next to Shallek and his family. Oble came over and introduced the family that accompanied him, while Rei sat across the fire from them, in the company of many women. Everything about the man aggravated Levi, and watching him grope the very scantily clad women that surrounded him repulsed Levi even more.

Once they finished their meals, Levi remained quiet. He glanced over to see a brilliant smile on Reece's face as she watched the women in white dance joyfully around the fire. She gave him an encouraging grin, and he forced a smile, feigning his enjoyment in return. When he looked at Harrison and King Hamilton, both men offered Levi expressions of sympathy. It was obvious that they were counting the minutes until the celebration was over as well.

When Levi brought his attention back to the large fire before them, he was stunned to see a woman dancing seductively in front of them. Shallek loudly laughed as he sat on the ground next to Levi. "She dances on our peoples' behalf to celebrate your people and the liberation you will all soon give us."

Levi tilted his head uncomfortably. "Shallek, there is no need for such recognition. There is nothing to be celebrated until we have actually been successful."

Shallek stood up and looked down at Levi. "You are a strange one, my new friend," he said with a laugh before he turned and left.

*I am the strange one?* Levi thought as he looked back at Reece, who was restraining herself from laughter. During the next hour, they were greeted by many different people, and Levi found himself enjoying the festivities more and more. Rei eventually came over and introduced himself and the ten women who were with him. Levi was a bit surprised when the man introduced the women as his wives. He managed to keep his composure when Rei respectfully greeted Reece. The interaction was short, and in Levi's opinion it was more than enough for the man to decide upon whether or not he trusted the Guardians enough to ally with them.

"I'm starving again," Reece said as she looked at Levi with a pitiful expression on her face as they stood in conversation with a few of Shallek's warriors and other Guardians who made their way over to where Levi remained for the evening.

"Allow me to get you a plate. Is there anything that tasted particularly good to you? I noticed you seem to be fond of the cheeses they have available."

"Stay here with the men. I can get it myself." She winked.

Levi's eyes narrowed, and then he scanned the area. "I shall go with you."

Reece chuckled. "No, you won't. Stop worrying about me." With that, she turned and walked over to the tables of food.

As she filled her plate, Levi's hand reflexively clenched into a fist as Rei approached her. He studied them both carefully as Rei spoke to her, and then watched as Reece's eyes grew fierce.

"Emperor, your men—"

"Excuse me," Levi interrupted the man he was pretending to listen to.

Before Levi could take three steps toward where Reece stood in conversation with Rei, the man had clenched his hand around her throat.

"Persuade me, Olteniaus witch! Persuade me not to crush your neck." He spat in Reece's face.

At that moment, the music halted and everyone stood paralyzed at the scene before them. Levi halted his approach when the man spun Reece around and held the sharp blade of his dagger to her neck. "Come any closer, and I will destroy this creature," he growled to Levi.

Levi said nothing as multiple options to attack the man flashed through his mind. He stood calculating as he watched the panicked expression on Reece's face spread. Rei had Reece in too vulnerable of a position. "Take your hands off the woman now, and I will not kill you where you stand," Levi warned him.

Shallek approached. "Rei! Release the woman this moment!"

"This creature is not a woman!" Rei growled. "It is Olteniaus and should be burned in that fire. This creature deserves to burn, and all of the dark powers within it!"

*"Commander, I need a distraction at once,"* Levi mentally called out to Harrison. *Reece is too panicked to get herself out of this position with her abilities.*

Suddenly, Harrison approached Rei from his other side. The closer he got, the closer Rei held the knife to Reece's throat. She gasped in pain as the knife pierced into her throat, causing her to bleed. This was Levi's only opportunity to react, and in that moment he took it.

Levi lunged toward them before Rei could bring his gaze back from Harrison. He brought his hand to Rei's wrist which held the blade and pivoted himself around him, giving him more of an advantage. Shocked by the attack, Rei loosened his hold on Reece and absently pulled the blade away from her neck in an attempt to swipe it at his attacker. Levi promptly gripped Reece and spun her away from the man's strong hold on her. As he did, he pried the blade out of Rei's frozen grip. Levi moved so swiftly that Rei didn't have time to react. He tried to jab at Levi when he got his bearings and swung around, but Levi countered him effortlessly and twisted the arm Rei held out to him high behind his back, sending him directly to the ground. He spun him over on the ground and brought a crushing knee hard into the man's sturdy chest as he knelt down holding the tip of the sharp blade to the man's throat.

"Tell me now why I should spare your life?" he growled viciously through his teeth.

The man stared up at Levi, eyes wide. "I was only trying to see if she truly was Olteniaus. Death should not befall me over my curiosity."

"Do not speak fallacies to me!" Levi ordered him.

"Emperor Levi, I beg of you to spare his life!" Shallek called out. "If you kill this man, his people will exact their vengeance upon all of us."

*Cowards!* Levi inwardly thought. He studied Rei's eyes. "My wife is a human being from Earth. She is not Olteniaus, she possesses no dark powers, and she poses no threat to anyone in any land." He stabbed the dagger into the hard ground so powerfully that it buried the blade up to the handle. "You are the most fortunate being in this galaxy, because I will allow you to live after what you have done to my wife. You and your people should leave this domain this instant, or I will hunt you down and finish this properly where we have no audience."

With that, Levi gripped the man's neck and arm tightly, jerking him up to stand on his feet. He looked over at Shallek. "My men will escort him out and stand guard at any entrance you have into this land." Shallek somberly nodded. Levi continued to grip Rei by his throat, keeping him paralyzed and silent from where they stood. He looked at Harrison. "Remove him and his people, now," he ordered sternly.

The Guardians dominated the entire area now, swords drawn and ready for any order of attack Levi, should give them. Harrison immediately stepped forward and took Rei into his possession.

"Fools! You all are insane to believe they did not bring the Olteniaus female here to destroy your lands!" Rei shouted, and Harrison brought his hand from the man's arm and up to tightly grip the man's neck to quiet him.

Levi's gaze fell on Reece, who stood in shock. She was clinging onto King Hamilton, who had her in his secure embrace. Shallek approached Levi. "Please forgive us, we had no idea he would behave in such a way."

Levi exhaled; the words he wanted to say to the Shallek at this moment were not kind. He needed to gather his thoughts and ensure that Reece was okay before anything else. "Give me a moment," he said in return before he walked over to Reece.

Reece released her tight hold on Hamilton, and with tears streaming down her pale face, she tightly embraced Levi. He closed his eyes, distraught that she was put in such imminent danger in an instant. He stepped back and looked down into her troubled eyes.

He cupped her chin with his hand. "Everything is going to be okay. Please, let me see your neck," he said, lifting her chin and examining the small wound. He ran his finger along the line of blood that was bleeding mildly. The cut was small, but he was still concerned for her. "You will be fine. Are you experiencing any pain?" he asked, trying to contain the rage that was reigniting with in him.

"It burns, but it's not painful," she said meekly.

Normila rushed to their sides and rubbed the white medicinal paste to Reece's neck. "It is a small wound, and it should heal within minutes," she reassured them.

Shallek approached with Diexz. "Emperor," Shallek said, "Diexz has informed me that we must plan our strategy tonight if we want to successfully defeat the Olteniaus now."

*It only took my wife nearly being slaughtered for these people to finally understand the importance of our situation?* Levi thought in annoyance.

"Rei will form armies against all of us and our cause now. I believe he will not rest until he has destroyed your people and your wife. We must take the next few hours to plan our mission, we will rest, and then before the sun rises we will leave."

"I will inform my commander of your intentions. I will not be attending the meetings, as I will not allow my wife to be left alone after what occurred tonight."

"I understand your reservations, Emperor, but please know we will not allow anyone to harm her," Shallek said.

"Please do not take offense to my words, because I mean no disrespect by them; but I can entrust none other than myself or my men with her safety any longer."

Levi took Reece's hand. "My men and their commander will await your warriors out in the location they have remained during our visit." He looked at Shallek. "If I do not see you again before we depart, I wish you well; and once again, I am grateful for the help you and your people have offered us."

"We were honored to help you, Emperor Levi." He looked at Reece. "And you as well, Empress Reece."

Reece said nothing in return, but Levi saw her offer the man a subtle smile in response instead. It was obvious she was in shock, and Levi needed to get her alone to check on her condition. He walked briskly out of the area with King Hamilton at his side.

"Your Majesty," Levi said to King Hamilton. "Inform Harrison that I will not be in attendance as they plan our attack for tomorrow. I will need him to open his thoughts to me and allow me to listen and offer my input in that manner instead. I will not leave Reece," Levi instructed. "And see if any of these people can send some more food for her as well."

Hamilton nodded. "I will see to everything."

"Thank you."

Levi led Reece back to their room, saying nothing along the way. He was reeling with anger, and her current disposition had him greatly concerned. *What did he say to you?* Levi thought. Usually she would have engaged Levi in conversation by now, but she wasn't speaking a word. Something more than the attack was upsetting her, and he needed to find out what it was. After all they had been through so far, he couldn't lose Reece now.

# Chapter 33

When they were back in their room, Reece removed her hand from Levi's and walked numbly to the bed in their room. She climbed onto it, curled up around a pillow, and closed her eyes tightly. She hoped Levi would let her be, but she knew that was not going to happen.

She felt him sit on the bed next to her. "My love, I can tell something is upsetting you greatly. You must talk to me."

She said nothing.

He ran his hand through her hair. "Reece Oxley," he said soft yet, sternly.

"Please, leave me alone right now," she managed.

Before he could respond, there was a soft knock at the door. Reece began to feel that tormenting starvation sensation again. It would be so convenient to use her abilities to shut it off, but she could not.

Levi returned with a plate of a variety of different cheeses and placed it on the bed in front of her. She stared at the plate of cheese; they were so tempting, and the only food that she seemed to like as of late.

"They sent a great amount of food up from the festivities tonight. There are also more cheese platters if this is not enough to satisfy your hunger."

Reece didn't move a muscle. She closed her eyes again, trying to block everything out. "Reece," Levi deeply called her name. Startled, she turned back to him in response.

His expression instantly turned to that of remorse. "My love, tell me what is wrong. You must let me help you."

"That's the problem, Levi," she muttered. "After tonight, and the fact that I could not defend myself against that man, how am I supposed to *help* any of you defeat Mordegrin and those Olteniaus females?"

Levi ran his hand along her back. "Reece," he softly said. "Look at me."

She rolled onto her back, and he took her hand into his. The tender way he caressed the back of her hand was more soothing now than it had ever been. "What happened tonight was an excellent lesson for you in your fight against Mordegrin and those dark creatures."

Reece looked at Levi as if he'd lost his mind. "How is that possible?" She exhaled in frustration. "I was caught off guard. I panicked. I couldn't concentrate if I wanted to. The last thing I thought of was using my abilities to save myself from Rei." She ran her hand along his arm. "If this happens tomorrow—if I panic? Levi, I could get us all killed."

Levi's expression grew somber. "What happened to the confident woman that has been nothing but encouraging throughout this entire situation?"

Reece rolled her eyes. "She was confronted with the fact that she may not be able to do this. If I can't handle myself with a man like Rei, how am I supposed to maintain my focus while we all come face-to-face with the most dangerous part of this journey?"

Levi nodded. "Very well, I admit that you panicked; albeit, you were swiftly removed from the situation."

"Levi—"

"No. I will not allow you to be consumed by fear over this," he interrupted. "You will listen to me, Reece Oxley, as it is my turn to console you now. You are not going into this alone. The Guardians understand that you may be attacked at any given moment, in fact we are expecting it. Our plans are to protect you from any unexpected attacks, so that should be the least of your concerns."

*He's right*, Reece thought with a smile of relief. "I'm sorry for this. The trauma of being attacked by that man, coupled with the fact that I couldn't even think to defend myself, had me doubting my abilities."

Levi traced along her forehead. "Do not let fear consume you. Tomorrow you will be in a different mindset, prepared for danger, and that will prevent your panic. Also, as I said, you are amongst thousands of Guardians that have vowed to protect you and will be armed and prepared to destroy anything that will interfere with your focusing on destroying Mordegrin and the Olteniaus. You must focus on that and know that even though you were near death tonight, you were removed swiftly from that situation. It will be the same when we go to the fortress tomorrow."

Reece nodded. "Thank you for saving me tonight. I'm sorry I let it overwhelm me like this."

"No apologies are needed," Levi returned. "I believe it was an excellent test, even though I still have a strong desire to hunt that man down and kill him for threatening you. But now that you have been in a dire situation, your mind will be prepared and even more focused tomorrow. You will trust the Guardians to protect you, just as we trust you will protect us."

Reece traced her fingers along his jawline. "I'm ready to get this over with."

Levi caught her hand and brought it to his lips. "All of us feel the same." He gazed into her eyes with purpose. "And we *will* defeat them together and recover my father."

A soft kiss to her forehead. "Now that we have cleared this up, I must see to it that you eat." Then his lips curved up into her favorite grin. "Your human body desperately requires nutrition in order to properly nourish the little Pemdai warrior growing within it."

Reece sat up and brought the plate filled with cheeses into her lap. She began eating and smiled at Levi. "You think we have a little *warrior* on the way, huh?"

Levi grinned and kissed her forehead. "Or princess. The prospect of either delights me."

He kissed her once more and stood. "Allow me to change out of this attire, and I will lie down by you while I listen in on Harrison and the men while they plan our mission for tomorrow."

"I forgot about that," she said as she swallowed a bite of the savory cheese. "I'm sorry if you've missed anything."

Levi sat in a chair and pulled his boots off. "They have not begun the meetings yet. And do not apologize; I am grateful that you have taken me into your confidence this evening."

After filling herself completely with the cheese, Reece wanted nothing more than to curl up around Levi and enjoy the security of his strong embrace. He still appeared to be upset over everything that happened with Rei, and she understood why. As frightening as that moment was for her, she found protection in Levi's fierce and calculating eyes as Rei held the knife to her throat. She recalled the memory of when he saved her that day from the men in the park, and even though Rei seemed larger and more powerful than Levi, Reece knew her husband would find a way to keep her safe.

After she changed into a soft white gown, she crawled under the blanket that Levi pulled back for her. Once she was fully relaxed, Levi got onto the bed, lying flat on his back with his head propped up on the pillow. Even though it was obvious he was listening to the meeting through Harrison's mind, he smiled at her and brought his arm out, inviting her into his embrace. She nestled in tightly against his side and placed her face on the warm skin of his bare chest.

She glanced up at Levi, whose eyes were now closed. His lips twitched as if he were about to say something. She inwardly laughed, realizing he was probably communicating something to Harrison within his mind. There were times when he would sigh, seemingly frustrated. It was interesting to watch him, but not much later, with Levi gently stroking his long fingers through her hair, she drifted off to sleep.

Reece had no idea how long she slept before she woke up from a terrifying dream in a panic. Strange as it was, the moment she awoke, she recalled nothing from the dream. All she could remember was the feeling of profound agony due to the loss of Levi. A heavy feeling came over her, a feeling of impending doom, which led her to believe that this may be the last time she would ever be with him. *Another premonition?* she thought, frazzled. "NO!" she nearly screamed as she sat straight up in the bed, trying to calm herself. It couldn't have been a premonition. She could always recall every detail of their content.

"Reece?" Levi sat up. "What is wrong?"

She looked over at him, and her body felt great relief at the sight of his face. She sighed. "I had an awful dream. Even though I can't remember what it was about, I'm left with the emotions of how I was feeling in it." She stared intently into his confused eyes. "I lost you, Levi. I'm afraid it might be part of those premonitions again. The feeling of never being with you again is worse than anything I can imagine."

Levi pulled her down to relax next to her side. "You will not lose me. You may only be feeling this way because of what you have been through today."

Reece closed her eyes. "And the anticipation for tomorrow," she said as she curled up around him.

Levi tightened his embrace. "After our planning tonight, we are more prepared than ever to succeed in this mission. You must relax and rest easy."

"I love you," she said as her mind and body felt the security of him at her side. "I can't lose you, Levi."

Levi kissed the top of her head. "Then you will not," he answered. "Please, rest."

Reece wrapped herself tighter around Levi, and for the first time since entering this galaxy, she imagined they were safely home again. Her tension and negative thoughts faded as she drifted off to a peaceful slumber.

The next morning before daybreak, as Reece was preparing to dress into her Guardian attire, she heard a soft knock on their door. Levi was fully dressed and took long strides across the room to answer it.

"Reece," Levi said as he entered the room, "Ionis is here, and I believe she has an excellent plan to protect you on our mission today."

"Send her in," Reece answered.

Ionis walked in with a warm smile. "First of all, please forgive the actions of Rei at our festivities last night. The man is a great warrior, and it is a shame that he acted in such a way." Her eyes grew distant. "It is most unfortunate that they will not be able to assist all of you on this mission," she said in a low voice.

Reece woke this morning in an extremely confident state of mind. She would not allow anything to shake her. "It may take time, but we will succeed," Reece answered.

Ionis brought her hand to Reece's face. "You are a brave warrior, just as the men you are with. Do not forget this." She stepped back with a bowl filled with black paste. "This may not give you power over all of your abilities, but it will heighten your mind, and you shall be able to mentally battle Mordegrin and the dark ones with him much more easily. Take this and rub it along your forehead, under your eyes, and along your cheeks. After that, to heighten the abilities your child already possesses, you will need to—"

"Wait!" Reece reached for her arm. "How could you know that our child has abilities? Are they like mine?"

Ionis smiled. "The only reason you survived traveling through our lands when you lost your energy from the stone was because of the abilities your child carries within your womb. Of course, the child is new in your womb and will not have full access to these abilities until it is born."

"That's why my ability to mentally overcome things came and went so drastically," Reece said.

"Yes. The child was helping you whenever it was able to."

"Wow." Reece laughed. "That's really amazing."

"That is why I want you to take this paste and smear it over your abdomen as well. It will give strength to the child, and in return help you, should you falter in any way."

"Thank you," Reece answered, "so much."

Ionis embraced her. "We thank you, Empress Oxley." She stepped back and stared purposefully into her eyes. "You are the only one that can defeat them. You are our only hope. The warriors' sole purpose is to keep you safe at all costs while they bring you to the Shadowy One and his evil accomplices." She turned to leave and glanced back. "Destroy them without hesitation," she said in a grave voice before leaving the room.

Levi entered directly after. "Allow me to assist you," he said, taking the bowl from her hands. He began smearing the paste over her forehead. "Do not let her words frighten you. I can hear your heart racing faster than our child's fluttering one."

"You heard what she said about the baby?"

"I did, and I am not surprised. Our child has interesting genetics that reside within him, and I can believe that the child would give you strength in some form."

Reece smiled as Levi continued to rub the paste in lines over her face. "Him?"

Levi grinned. "Or her. We will know for sure in close to eight months."

Once Levi finished administering the paste in the areas that Ionis instructed, he helped her back into the heavy Guardian regalia. He brought her cloak over her head. "From now until we leave this wretched galaxy, you must conceal yourself. Shallek's army consists of both male and female warriors; even so, I do not want your appearance to be noticed."

Reece inhaled and nodded. "Okay. Are we ready to do this?"

Levi nodded. "Yes. We depart as soon as we leave this room."

The dark sky became red as first light greeted the land. The Guardians raced their horses out and away from Shallek's village before daylight, as planned. They sped out of the land from a different location other than the one they entered through. Diexz informed Harrison that the route the Guardians had been taking to the fortress was longer, and the only reason Mordegrin must have informed them of this route was so it would be easier to destroy the Guardians on their journey.

The current terrain they traveled across was eerie, to say the least. The shadowy forest and the black fog that covered the ground gave Reece an odd feeling of darkness and emptiness.

Out of the three thousand Guardians that were with them on this journey, Diexz and Harrison kept to the original plans of only a hundred warriors riding in Levi and Reece's company. The other Guardians remained on the outside lines, traveling with Oble and Diexz's warriors, serving as a protection from any outside forces that may attack them. They were all fully aware that since they had left the protected land they were in, Mordegrin would waste no time sending his armies after them.

They had travelled uneventfully for close to an hour, which was not what was to be expected, and Reece started to become concerned. *This is almost too easy. Something isn't right,* she thought. The horses were pacing at a rapid rate, and suddenly the air became heavy. *What is happening?* she thought as she studied Levi, who traveled in front of her. It seemed that this heavy atmosphere was taking a toll on Areion, as the horse's usual powerful stride seemed to be less aggressive. Arrow slowed down as well, as if he were caught in thick mud. Reece held her chest, struggling to breathe in this air that was rapidly becoming heavier. *Levi, I can hardly breathe!* she mentally cried out to him. The next thing she knew, Levi and Areion were at her side. He looked over at her, and his expression was dark.

"It is difficult for me as well," he said breathlessly. "Do not fear. A shape-shifting dark force has surrounded us. Only Oble's army can battle them, as they are the only ones that can see their true form. They will deliver us soon enough," he managed through long, hard gasps.

Reece was wheezing in pain; it felt like she had a hundred pounds of bricks placed on her chest. "Where...are...they?" she wheezed.

Then everything appeared to move in slow motion. Levi spoke, but she couldn't understand his words. Large creatures flew above their heads, and fiery arrows shot down toward them. Reece was shocked when the large rock that she was passing was hit by the red, glowing dart and the rock turned into a green, monstrous creature. Before she could blink, another fiery dart pierced the beast's scaly flesh, and it turned into a cloud of black smoke and disappeared. All around them, unique shaped trees, rocks, and bushes were being shot with the fiery darts, turning them into their original beast-like form before another arrow incinerated them. Suddenly, the heavy air lightened and the horses regained their speed. Reece inhaled deeply of the light air and looked up to see that Oble and his army were no longer in the sky above them.

Levi changed course. He guided them off the current trail they were traveling on, most likely to throw Mordegrin off. The snowy terrain was disappearing, and bright green grassy hills rolled along the horizon for as far as she could see. They rode through these hillsides for what seemed to be forever before Levi halted, forcing everyone behind him to do the same. He turned Areion back to Reece. "This is where we must go the rest of the way alone," he said somberly.

"Will we be able to do this without Rei's army?" Reece asked him.

Levi nodded. "I believe that man's army would have caused us more danger than help."

"That's what Shallek needed Rei's army for, because they were the only other beings that were able to block their minds from the Olteniaus females," Reece answered. "They were our only help in attacking the fortress."

"We will survive this, but you must remain focused! You must forget about Rei's army and trust our own," Levi said in a commanding tone. "Now, before we go any further, we are at the point where you must use the powers of your mind to block out any bizarre or intruding thoughts you may feel. I have no doubt that the Olteniaus will use their mental powers against you now. Once you feel you are prepared, we will move forward."

Reece exhaled and forced all of her negative and fearful emotions out of her mind. She glanced around, seeing the hundreds of Guardians waiting patiently with fierce expressions on their faces. She allowed her mind to absorb the fearless emotions radiating from the group of warriors. Their craving for this attack fueled her courage, and all doubt was replaced with the longing to destroy Mordegrin and the Olteniaus.

With more confidence than before, Reece turned back to Levi. "I'm already using them, and I am prepared for the Olteniaus," she firmly returned.

Levi studied her eyes intently before he nodded. "Very well. Let us go retrieve the emperor and destroy this dark threat to our world," he instructed.

With that, Levi led the charge. They set out through the grassy meadow at full speed toward the hillside in front of them. The ominous skies above them were a blurry green, and Reece gasped when she noticed a black, swirling mist rolling in from their right. As she noticed it, she looked at Levi, who had dropped Areion's reins, pulled his bow from his shoulder, and instantly started firing arrows toward black creatures flying toward them.

The horses continued to race at full speed as arrows flew from behind Reece and into the long-winged creatures. Reece's eyes widened when she watched the dragon-like beasts explode into particles of black dust in the sky. More and more of these creatures appeared out of the dark mists, and it seemed likely that Levi and the Guardians she rode with would be overpowered soon.

As they maintained their course, arrows flying into the beasts like bullets, the horses charged up the grassy hillside before them. Reece's heart was beating as swiftly as Arrow's hoofs were hammering against the surface of the ground. Levi shot his arrows relentlessly into the skies, this time killing three creatures at once. Reece glanced to her left when she noticed what seemed like thousands of fiery arrows flying from over the hillside. She sighed in relief when she saw the group of men Harrison was leading appear on the mountain range, charging gallantly in their direction. She looked to her right, noticing more Guardians charging in and firing arrows into the air. Under the attack of now thousands of Guardian warriors, the dark mist disappeared.

Levi never once looked back, but continued the charge toward another mountainside. As soon as Levi, Reece, and their group reached the top of the mountains, the Guardian armies coming from both their right and left sides gracefully filtered in with them. Reece rode with two Guardians on each of her sides as they were getting closer.

She looked back, seeing the massive line of Guardian warriors behind them lined up in perfect formation.

They were riding swiftly along the top of the mountain range when Levi turned Areion sharply to his right. Arrow and the rest of the horses followed his lead without breaking their stride. Reece looked out and saw where this world seemed to drop off into nothing. The Guardian horses gained even more speed. She strained her eyes, but the land below seemed nonexistent. She looked forward to see Arrow and the Guardian horses were traveling faster than she had even ridden before. As they neared the end of this mountain peak, she watched Areion gather himself and lunge out into ominous clouds. Arrow gathered himself as well, sending her through the air and across into the red, blurry clouds. The air grew thick. Avoiding panic and trusting Levi's lead and the horse she rode, Reece maintained her calm. She looked down and spotted a valley below them. Areion landed gracefully on another mountainside, as did Arrow and the rest of the war horses. They charged through a peculiar forest until large, jagged rocks surrounded them and a narrow stone bridge came into view.

Levi slowed Areion as he went over the bridge. Three of the four Guardians that rode at Reece's side slowed their horses and fell in behind her, leaving one warrior to travel alongside of her as they stepped onto the bridge. The forest was behind them, and all that was before them was an imposing, eerie stone castle. A swift river flowed beneath the bridge they were traveling over. The river surrounded the mountainous island that this stone castle dominated. It was the fortress, and it was perfectly situated and carved out of the mountain it resided on. As they grew closer, the fortress became even larger and more intimidating.

Reece glanced up, seeing thousands of black birds circle the castle, filling the crimson skies. *Must be notifying them of our arrival,* Reece thought as she remained calm, focusing as Levi instructed her to do. Every now and then, she would feel a strange tingling sensation in her head, and she easily blocked it out. She knew it was Mordegrin and the Olteniaus females already trying to use their mental powers on her.

As soon as they were across the bridge, nine warriors rode up and moved in front of her, riding in threes directly behind Levi, and the two Guardians took their place at Reece's sides again. *This is it,* she thought as the horses slowed to a gentle canter. They traveled along a stone road, leading them directly to the front entrance of the castle. Reece pulled the hood of her cloak over her head, hiding herself even more.

Reece peeked out from under her cloak and noticed the strange people that lined the road. As the Guardians gallantly entered the first part of the fortress, more and more people, who appeared to be starving, filled the area. Their features were that of an average human with distressed looks on their dirty and worn faces, matching the battered clothing they wore. They stared in fear at the Guardians as the horses loudly trotted through the passageway surrounded by stone walls.

Levi didn't falter as he rode Areion regally into the fortress with all of the Guardians following in flawless formation. They traveled under a large stone archway, leading them into another part of the fortress. The passageway opened up more, and they followed through this location for close to ten minutes, passing more people along the way. Everything grew unnervingly silent when, without warning, all of the Guardians halted their horses.

Reece peered around at the Guardians in front of her and noticed that Levi halted the group when he was approached by a group of large, barbaric men. They wore dark metal armor, scraggly beards, and their faces were covered in black dirt. Levi walked Areion out alone, ahead of the group of Guardians. The rest of the horses remained perfectly still. Reece felt a sharp pain jolt through her head, nearly causing her to faint. She inhaled deeply and fought it away. She intently focused on Levi and his imposing nature while a large man approached him and Areion. His commanding disposition gave her the strength she needed to remain focused. She tuned in to the sounds only coming from Levi.

One of the barbarians stepped toward Areion and gazed darkly up at Levi. "You would be wise to turn your horses back and leave this fortress now," the being bellowed. "We don't need any problems from foreigners."

"You will not have a problem with me and my men," Levi returned in a commanding voice, "unless you should choose not to open the gates and let us pass. We are only here for what is ours, and we will not leave until we have him in our possession. Now, *open* these gates," he ordered.

The man's eyes narrowed as he abruptly reached out and grabbed Areion's halter. Arrow's weight shifted beneath Reece. Areion instantly reared up onto his hind feet and whinnied loudly in protest of the man's grip. As swiftly as Areion reacted violently to the man, he brought his front legs down aggressively, using them to knock the man down. Once on the ground, Areion brought his massive hoof onto the barbarian's chest, restraining him on his back. The man's eyes were wide as he looked up at Levi.

Areion's ears lay flat back as he brought his face down to the barbarian's. "It is easy to see that my horse could crush your heart at my command. Believe me, it is his only desire at the moment. But due to his loyalty to me, he awaits my command." Levi looked at the other barbarians, who were watching in amazement at the exchange that had occurred. Areion loudly grunted and whinnied, bringing Levi's attention to the man that Areion was pinning to the stone ground. "If you desire to live, I will only say it once more; open the gates, or you will all die."

"OPEN THEM!" the being pinned beneath Areion's hoof shouted loudly.

The sounds of heavy chains clanking together brought Reece's attention to where a large wooden gate pulled up into the wall above it. Arcion grunted and pressed his hoof once more into the barbarian's chest before releasing his hold on him. Areion whinnied loudly as Levi restrained his agitated horse and led him toward the wooden gate. Areion proceeded toward the entrance, aggressively stomping his powerful hooves against the stone surface. The Guardian line began to move forward, following Levi through the entrance. The barbarians stood back, allowing them to pass, and Reece was distracted by the sounds of a horse's hooves, which were aggressively clattering on the stone road from behind them. Reece turned around and was relieved to see that it was Harrison charging up to the front lines.

Once he reached where the barbarians stood with scowls on their faces, he slowed Saracen to a trot. As he cantered up to the front lines, he guided Saracen over to where the being that Areion had pinned to the ground was. The brute was getting up and seemed to be gathering his senses when Harrison directed his horse into him, shoving the barbarian into the wall behind him, sending the savage back to the ground. Harrison continued past the angered beings, with a smirk. As he trotted Saracen along the Guardian line where Reece was, he glanced over at her and winked. After a reassuring grin, Harrison trotted past her and disappeared into the entryway the line of warriors were following Levi into.

As Reece and the Guardians followed through the gates, they entered into a large courtyard. Reece's head began burning with the Olteniaus mental powers working against hers. She felt herself weakening and reached down into the leather pouch, pulling out more black cream and quickly rubbing it on her forehead and the back of her neck. She felt her strength surge and the burning sensation disappear.

The Guardians filled the large courtyard while Levi brought Areion to a halt in front of steps that led up to two massive wooden doors. The doors opened to reveal a white-haired man wearing a silver robe. He walked down and spoke to Levi, but Reece was unable to hear the conversation. After a nod from Levi, the man stepped back up the steps and waited at the top of them. Levi and Harrison dismounted, prompting Reece to do so as well.

Instead of revealing herself, she waited for Levi to approach her, curious as to what the man said to him. Harrison's gaze was severe, and Levi's expression was unreadable. Harrison called out to some of his men, while Levi pulled Reece off to the side alone with him. He embraced her tightly, and then stood back and stared deeply into her eyes.

"I must go in alone in order to ensure my father's safety."

Reece was flooded with the feelings from her strange dream the previous night. She shook her head and pushed away from him. Tears filled her eyes. "No! Levi, you can't! There's another way, we have to think!"

Levi exhaled. "Reece." His eyes were set with purpose. "Rest assured that Harrison and I will remain mentally connected the entire time. He will see and feel everything I experience. We suspected something like this would happen as the men made our battle plans last evening. Since our predictions proved correct, our plan is for me to enter the location where my father is, alone. When I enter the area where he is, this is when you must start to battle them mentally by impressing into their minds weakness and the urge to die. After you begin forcing your mental persuasion on them, Harrison will wait for me to enter the location where my father is. He will then lead an army of men into the fortress and battle against the trap we know they have set up for me." He lifted her chin with his finger. "It is the only way they will spare my father's life."

"Why you?" Reece said. "I thought they wanted me?"

Levi wiped a tear from her cheek. "Mordegrin wants the stone, and I am the only one who has unlocked the map and knows the location. They need me in that room to capture me and extract the information."

"If we're not fast enough, and if I'm not strong enough, they will kill you and your father." Reece gripped his face with both hands. "You can't go! We have to find another way."

"Reece," he firmly returned, "do not forget the power of my mind. They have to penetrate through my natural defensive barriers, and then figure out a way to get past the protection that Paul created for the map. Have you forgotten that you are unable to persuade my mind to do anything? They can only impress their thoughts into mine. Harrison will see that as well. I will be fine."

"What if their powers are stronger? I'm human, too. What if they can overpower your mind?"

"If that were true, Mordegrin would have done it when he first met me." He smiled confidently at her. "Anyhow, I plan to give them no time to try."

"Once again, I must ask you to remove these fearful thoughts of me from your mind. You and I both know that the fear will weaken your abilities."

Reece wrapped her arms tightly around him, desperately hoping this would not be the last time she did. "I can't help it! I think whatever happened in that dream last night had to be a premonition. I beg you; don't do this, not like this."

Levi brought his lips down onto her forehead. "Your premonitions always stemmed from your visions, not dreams. You know that."

Reece rubbed her forehead. "I don't feel confident about this at all."

"Remove these fearful emotions immediately. We need your abilities," Levi ordered.

"Okay," she answered, giving in to their plans.

Levi nodded. "As I said, Harrison will be watching everything through my mind. When he instructs you, that is when you must do your part."

She wrapped her arms tightly around his neck, securing a passionate kiss. It was too soon when he slowly withdrew from her. He brushed the tip of his finger over her nose. "I'll be right back," he said with a nod. Before she could respond, Levi turned and strode briskly toward the steps that led to the entrance of the fortress.

Reece stood paralyzed, watching Levi disappear into the doors with the white-haired man. She jumped when Harrison unexpectedly brought his arm around her shoulders. "Come," he said in a commanding tone.

She followed him to where a group of Guardians stood with their shields and swords already drawn and waiting. Her legs became weak, even though she was forcing herself to remain calm.

"Kneel with me," Harrison said absently. His eyes were glowing, and she could tell he was watching Levi.

Harrison knelt down on one knee and stared hypnotically at the ground in front of him. Reece slowly knelt at his side, watching him. His eyes moved rapidly back and forth, and his mouth twitched. She sought comfort in knowing that Harrison, even though he was with her, was with Levi, too.

She exhaled, finding her balance and strength within her mind again. Harrison glanced over at her and gave her a reassuring smile. He reached out and gently took her hand into his strong one. "He is perfectly fine," he said. "There have been no attacks against him, and he is almost to his father's location."

Reece gripped Harrison's sturdy hand tighter, seeking comfort in him as she would Levi, and then she closed her eyes. At any moment, they would need her to mentally battle the Olteniaus. Five minutes of silence passed, and it seemed like an eternity.

"What?" Harrison angrily called out. "Where's Mordegrin?" His eyes grew fierce.

He withdrew his hand from Reece and abruptly stood. Reece stood as well. She wanted to ask him what was happening, but his eyes were so severe and distant, she could tell he was studying what Levi was going through.

"He's free," Harrison deeply said aloud, while staring intently at nothing. "Emperor Navarre is free! Excellent work, Levi," he said proudly.

Before Harrison could turn to lead the Guardians into the fortress, he roared in pain. He gripped his head tightly and plummeted onto his knees and elbows.

"Reece!" he loudly growled. "You must stop this, NOW! You are the only one that can save Levi from this!"

So involved with watching Harrison and waiting for his orders, she panicked and couldn't focus on anything but wanting answers to what was happening to Levi.

Harrison was gripping his head tightly and groaning in pain. "Harrison, you have to tell me what to do. What's happening?" she said in a panic, watching Harrison wallow in pain.

"They are destroying his mind!" he groaned in pain. "You have to go into Levi's mind and protect him from this. You must get into his mind like you have done before," he cried out with pain in his voice.

Reece became focused, and with all of her mental power she closed her eyes and forced her thoughts to revolve around Levi, his mind, and whatever pain he was going through. She mentally persuaded his mind to block the intrusion. A sharp pain radiated from between her eyes, and a powerful surge of energy knocked her flat onto her back. She concentrated harder, focusing on nothing but forcing protective thoughts into Levi's mind. Her head felt as if it would explode, and she forced herself up to her knees, gripping her head as tightly as Harrison was. *Leave him!* she thought angrily. In that moment, all pain subsided within her. Her eyes reopened when Harrison stopped moaning in pain.

He leapt to his feet abruptly. His eyes were bloodshot and distant. "Levi!" he called out loudly. "Our minds are no longer connected." He looked at Reece in confusion, and then his eyes widened in panic. "NO!" he bellowed. "NOW!" he ordered Reece fiercely. "You must kill them now!"

Harrison turned to the group of men waiting for him and drew his sword. Without another word, Harrison and the men stormed into the fortress. Reece closed her eyes, sending herself into deep meditation, focusing only on persuading these dark creatures to seek their deaths.

# Chapter 34

Harrison and his men stormed into the fortress, listening for any sign of where Levi, Navarre, and the Olteniaus females might be. Strangely, no one was around to stop their charge, and they continued briskly through the mirrored hallways.

A muffled sound coming from his left alerted Harrison as to where they might find Levi and Navarre. They stepped down a brightly lit hallway that ended with more mirrors in front of them. It seemed to be a dead end until Harrison heard a deep groan that belonged to Levi.

Instantly, Harrison thrust the heel of his boot into the mirror, shattering the glass wall in front of him. The sight before him sent a surge of adrenaline through his veins like he had never experienced. Navarre was pinned against the wall by two large, savage men that resembled those guarding the gates to the fortress when they arrived.

The identical females stood in a circle, their hair wild and eyes white, chanting the same unknown words over and over again. Levi was on his knees in the middle of the circle, blood streaming out of his ears, nose, and eyes while he tightly gripped his head. Harrison tried to lunge forward, but a strange force froze him and the Guardians in their place.

The dark females chanted louder and louder as Levi groaned in agony. The harder Harrison tried to break the hold he was under, the stronger it became until it felt as though his throat was being crushed. Candles were placed around Levi, and Harrison watched in disbelief as they grew brighter when the chanting turned into a bizarre melody.

Harrison's sword fell from his hand as he was starting to lose consciousness, unable to take in air. *Reece, you must stop them,* he thought as the bleak room around him started to fade away. As Harrison felt himself dying, a wave of strength fell over him. The force that was restraining him was revealed in that instant. The black creatures that had ambushed them in the forest had been uncloaked from some spell, and without hesitation Harrison and the warriors with him instantaneously dropped to the ground, gripped their swords, and swept their feet under the black creature's legs. *Yes, Reece! It is working! Do not stop!*

The creatures easily regained their balance and swiped their sword-like claws down at the men. Harrison rolled out of harm's way and flung his dagger into the head of the creature. After the creature erupted into particles of black dust, Harrison spun around and threw his sword as a spear across the room into one of the barbarians restraining Navarre.

The Guardian at Harrison's side followed Harrison's action and was successful in destroying the other barbarian directly after. Navarre was free, and each warrior in the room attempted to turned their attention to the females who were torturing Levi, but they were stopped by an impenetrable force field. Harrison took the sharp edge of his shield and tried piercing through the invisible wall that separated them from Levi and the circle of females surrounding him.

Before anyone could make another move, the walls of the room began to fill with the same black mist they saw when they were ambushed in the forest.

"Use my sword!" Harrison shouted toward Navarre. "This battle is just getting started," he said as he noticed Levi's sword lying on the other side of the room.

Harrison swiftly ran to Levi's sword, and as soon as he retrieved it, the black mist that surrounded the room manifested more dark creatures that immediatcly began to attack the Guardians. Harrison ducked the blades of the beast that swiped his sword-like claws at him, spun around the creature, and thrust his sword into it. Once destroyed, he turned to see that the entire room was filling with these dark entities, and all they could do now was fight and kill each one that came after them, hoping that Reece would find a way to destroy the Olteniaus females before they all met their death.

*** *

Reece continued to maintain her focus of mentally attacking the Olteniaus females, as well as shielding Levi's mind. She sat on her knees, gripping her head tightly, trying to maintain her deep meditation. The excruciating pain in her head would violently come and go as she continued to mentally battle the Olteniaus. She was extremely nauseated and felt her energy rapidly depleting, yet she remained focused.

Over and over, she willed these dark creatures to die, but it was uncertain if she was getting anywhere with it. The only thing that let her believe she was having some form of an effect was the pain and nausea she was experiencing.

A loud screeching in the sky above her distracted her. She opened her eyes and looked up to see large, black, dragon-like creatures blackening the skies above them. The Guardians in the courtyard area immediately drew their swords in response. The Olteniaus were sending their greatest warriors to combat the Guardians, but Reece knew she had to remain focused or they would all be dead.

She gripped her stomach as it wretched in a painful spasm. She closed her eyes, and with bitter anger she continued to mentally battle the Olteniaus. There were deep roars coming from behind her, but she remained undistracted. As she continued to concentrate, she was suddenly interrupted when she was in the grips of Garrett, the Guardian warrior.

"Don't—NO!" she screamed as he pulled her up and led her away.

"I must get you out of here," the man demanded.

She couldn't leave now. Still using her mental abilities, she recalled her training with Harrison. She looked up at the man, and she knew she could take him down. She violently fought against Garrett's strong hold, and to her utter shock a barbaric beast swung his sword across Garrett's neck.

Everything turned into slow motion around her. The Guardians were being brutally slaughtered by these savages. She had to stop it at once, but she couldn't do so unless she was closer to the Olteniaus. Fueled by her shock and outrage by the gravity of their impending demise, her abilities became heightened.

The beast swiped his sword at her, but Reece reacted with stealth. She ducked, rolled, and snagged Garret's sword in the process. She sprang to her feet and thrust the sword into the man's heart, turning him into a black cloud of dust.

She darted up the steps and into the fortress. Loud hooves echoed behind her, alerting her to Arrow following in at her side. Mirrored walls surrounded the hallway she stormed through. As Reece turned down a hallway, following the sound of men and swords clashing together, she was met by black shadow figures.

Without hesitation, Arrow sprung forward from behind her and attacked. Injured, the shadows shifted into men with four heads. Another attack from the side, and Reece rolled and brought the sword into the back of another creature. Reece and Arrow couldn't advance as they were defending themselves against these dark beings. As Reece slashed into another beast, thundering hooves echoed behind them.

Reece tried to run through the corridors when all of the beasts suddenly had arrows delivered into their hearts. She never turned to see who the rider that joined her and Arrow was, but she was abruptly stopped in her fight when she was grabbed from behind. She dropped the sword as the man powerfully hoisted her onto his horse.

"NO!" Reece growled. "I've got to kill them!"

The Guardian on the stallion didn't answer her; instead, he spun his horse around and fled out of the fortress, with Arrow following behind.

As they fled the courtyard, leaving the Guardians to battle alone, Reece realized that this had turned into a suicide mission for all the men. It was over, and she knew that these had to be Levi's orders to the men. If there was no hope left, Reece would be extracted.

The horses charged past hundreds of creatures that the Guardians and their horses were ferociously battling. Once out of the fortress, the horses charged over the stone bridge and back into the forest. They were forced to stop when they came upon another army of warriors. The Guardian swiftly drew out his sword, and the next thing Reece knew, his shield was protectively covering her.

"Rei! Let us pass, NOW!" the Guardian warrior aggressively called out.

The man in copper-colored armor pulled his mask up to the top of his helmet, revealing his face. "Guardian, you are not our enemy. Forgive my lack of trust." Rei looked at Reece. "Forgive my insults."

She stared at the man with trepidation. He sat atop an enormous, lion-type beast that was one of the most frightening things she had ever seen.

"How am I to trust you?" the Guardian responded.

The man grinned. "Because we would not be here to save your men if we chose to destroy you." His face grew fierce. "There is no time to deliberate, all of your men will surely be slaughtered if my warriors do not join in their fight and assist them this instant." Rei looked at Reece. "I will bring you to a location where you will be able to destroy the Olteniaus with your mental powers."

"No," the Guardian answered. "We will not risk her safety anymore. I must return her to our world."

Rei unwrapped a thick black chain from around his shoulder. He held it in his hand, and the long chain fell to the ground. He stared firmly at the Guardian. "If you do not bring her to the location, then there is no hope. You must trust me and my warriors. Once in this location, she will not only be protected, but also successful in destroying the dark ones. She is our only hope, Guardian."

With that, the rest of his army pulled their chains from their shoulders. Rei's lion lunged forward, and in that moment the Guardian turned and followed. As they crossed the bridge, Rei turned directly to the right, and the Guardian following him. Reece looked back, watching the rest of Rei's large army of men use their chains as whips to destroy more of the large creatures that were overtaking the entire area.

A loud crack sounded ahead of them, and Reece turned to see Rei's lion leap high into the air as his chain sliced through one of the dragon-like creature that flew directly at them. *This isn't going to work*, Reece thought, seeing more creatures coming out of the sky toward them. *They know where we are*, Reece thought in fear, seeing how the strange creatures in the sky changed their course and headed in their direction. Rei continued to whip his chain into the creatures upon their attack, but it was getting harder for him to stay ahead of them.

A creature got past him, and all Reece saw were large claws reaching out toward her. The Guardian brought his sword forward to stop it, but he was not quick enough. Reece screamed in fear as its scaly claws gripped each of her shoulders. She was lifted from the horse and out of the Guardian's strong grip. She looked down in fear and watched as a long, fiery arrow plunged into the beast, turning it to black dust at that moment. As she fell helplessly toward the ground beneath her, she was caught by Rei as his lion leaped high into the air. She looked up to see that Oble's army had rejoined them, and they now dominated the skies, attacking and destroying the creatures.

Rei and the Guardian behind them raced swiftly around the backside of the fortress. A dark opening into the fortress came into sight. Rei charged his lion into the opening, bringing them into a dungeon directly under the fortress. They followed a bleak passageway, and then stopped. All grew quiet, except Arrow, who was approaching where Reece was with Rei as the Guardian reached up to help her from the lion's back.

"Empress," the Guardian started, "my name is Caleb. I have been charged to protect your life at any cost. If this plan does not work, we must leave immediately."

She nodded as Arrow walked directly to her, nudging her in the chest.

"Empress," Rei spoke up, "whatever abilities you may have to destroy the dark powers of the Olteniaus, you will be successful, as they are directly above us. They will not be able to sense you from this location, given the reinforced walls in this area. They will be unable to fight the powers you can use against them. You must act quickly, as the females will start manipulating the minds of Shallek and Oble's armies, who have joined the Guardians in their battle. They will turn them against us, if they haven't started to already. When you destroy them, you will destroy everything they have ever created, thereby saving us all."

Reece looked back at Arrow; she held his bridle in both her hands. "Please, Arrow." She placed her forehead against the center of his. "I need your strength, boy. We opened the portal together, and we can do this together, too."

Arrow grunted, and Reece closed her eyes. In some bizarre way, she absorbed the horse's mighty power and used his strength to force all of her energy into manipulating the minds of the Olteniaus.

*You crave death. You wish it. You long for it. The pain and torment of your death will be torturous, and you desire that most of all. You deserve this torture. The darkness within you will be used against you, and it will increase your pain and suffering as you die. This is what you want. This is what you yearn for.*

Reece chanted this thought over and over as she impressed it into the minds of the Olteniaus, waiting for them to die in utter torment.

Everything grew quiet around her. Noises from up above her echoed in the dark chamber they were in. She could hear men shouting and boots scuffling and stomping hard into the floor above her. Everything grew silent again.

Reece continued to focus on her mental persuasion of doom for the dark creatures above them. With her senses heightened, she could hear everything in the room above her.

"It's Reece!" she heard Harrison's voice call out. "She's doing it!" he shouted.

Suddenly, a loud shriek resonated in the room above her. It was so loud, in fact, that Reece covered her ears to ease the pain that this high-pitched screech caused her. Reece maintained her focus as the tormented screams continued. *Just die!* she thought in absolute frustration and profound anger. The screams ceased in that instant, and all grew quiet.

"She did it," Harrison said. "Reece has destroyed them."

Everything silenced.

She heard feet rustling above her. "Levi, my brave son, what have they done to you?" Navarre said repentantly.

Reece's eyes snapped open. She had to get to him. She looked at Caleb. "I have to get to Levi right now! Please, I need your help to get on Arrow."

As soon as he lifted her up into the saddle, Reece turned Arrow and they raced off. Arrow galloped swiftly toward the entrance of the fortress, charging through Oble's army, who stood firmly at attention. Arrow turned and stormed down through the center of the stone walls, leading Reece back into the courtyard. When they arrived, Arrow slowed and Reece took notice of the many Guardian warriors who were lying on the ground, having their wounds attended to by Shallek's army. There were still many Guardian men standing with their swords drawn, and she had no idea if any of the Guardians were slain in the fight that Caleb removed her from.

Once at the front, she dismounted quickly and nearly ran into Oble and Diexz as they approached her. "I have to get in that building." She tried to run past them but froze in her tracks when the doors at the top of the staircase opened and she saw Harrison's back to her. Her legs gave out, and Diexz caught her before she collapsed to the ground. She stared in disbelief as Navarre came into view, watching as he and Harrison carried Levi by his shoulders and legs out of the building. She couldn't move—she forgot how to breathe. *NO! No, not Levi!* It was when they reached the bottom of the steps that Reece was able to move again. Each of the Guardians knelt down on one knee, forcing the rest of the warriors that assisted them to as well, but Reece did the opposite.

"NO!" she screamed, stopping Harrison and Navarre from going any farther. "What happened?"

She ran vigorously to where the men held her lifeless husband in their arms. She brought her hands to Levi's face; it was still warm. Relief washed over her.

"He is still alive, my dear," Navarre said. "They were doing everything possible to extract the map from his mind, but they failed."

"Reece," Harrison spoke up, "you not only saved his life, but all of ours as well."

Reece nodded and glanced back to Levi. She saw traces of blood smeared under his eyes and nose, and it was obvious that one of the men tried to remove any evidence of injury that Levi may have suffered. Even so, the blood stains made her heart wrench with anguish.

She brought her lips to his. *Wake up, Levi,* she strongly mentally persuaded him. *Open your eyes, my love.* Nothing. Levi was unresponsive, and even though he was breathing and his heart was steadily beating, he was gone somehow. She ran her hands through his hair, grieved to see him in such a state. She eased her arm around his neck, cradling it, and slowly knelt down, encouraging Navarre and Harrison to follow as well. Navarre released his grips on Levi, allowing Reece to hold him in her arms.

She wrapped her arms tightly around his shoulders and chest and used a hand to bring his head against her chest. She kissed the top of his head and ran her hand along his cheek. Tears streamed down her cheeks as she began to cry uncontrollably. The dream, the feelings she had...they were a premonition. *I can't lose you. I need you, Levi, our child needs you,* she pleaded with him telepathically.

Everyone remained silent around her. *What did they do to you? Levi, please. PLEASE! I won't let you leave me, you have to wake up!* she impressed into his mind.

She was distracted when Areion approached where she cradled Levi's head in her arms. The horse lowered his head as he slowly stepped closer to Levi, brought his nose into Levi's chest, and softly grunted. He looked at Reece, and the massive stallion brought the side of his face to Levi's cheek. Reece's crying increased when Areion let out a deep and painful groan, showing his anguish as well. If Areion reacted this way, Reece knew that something was horribly wrong with Levi. Areion's head rose up, and he stared down at Reece. He grunted again and stepped back, impatiently raising each hoof one by one.

"We need to bring him back to Shallek's village, Reece," Harrison said while gently running his hand across her back.

Reece held Levi tighter to her and shook her head. "He has to wake up first! Levi, wake up, now!" she commanded as she kissed his forehead. "Levi! Open your eyes!" she demanded him. "I beg you, my love, wake up," she managed through uncontrollable tears.

Levi remained unresponsive to her pleas. Navarre knelt beside her and stared with remorse into her eyes. Immediately entranced by Navarre's sapphire eyes, she suddenly felt as though Levi were staring at her instead of his father. "No!" she shouted through her tears as Navarre gripped Levi and pulled him from her embrace. Harrison knelt alongside of her. He took her shoulders and turned her to face him. In that moment, Reece embraced Harrison powerfully, and Harrison returned the embrace with just as much emotion.

He ran his hand gently over the back of her head. "He will survive, Reece. You must let us get him to where Shallek's people can help him. You must be strong for him," he softly said.

Reece slowly withdrew, sniffed, and pulled herself together. "Okay," she returned, staring somberly into Harrison's promising eyes.

He nodded and stood, helping her to her feet.

"Gentlemen, assist the wounded men and strap the unconscious or fatally wounded to their horses. We must leave in haste for Shallek's village," Navarre ordered as he and Harrison lifted Levi up and walked him over to Areion. Reece raced to their side. "No!" she shouted.

"Reece—" Harrison started.

She gazed at both men sternly. "NO!" she demanded.

She looked at Navarre and gripped his arm tightly. "You can't. I won't let you strap him to Areion like this. Please! I'll hold him up somehow on Arrow with me."

"Reece," Harrison softly called out, "Levi will be perfectly fine. Areion knows how to safely transport a wounded warrior, especially his own master."

"No!" she firmly responded. "I can't watch him be strapped to Areion like that."

"My son will ride with me," Navarre said authoritatively.

Reece exhaled in great relief. Navarre's horse was at his side, and King Hamilton was there taking Levi from his arms. Once Navarre was on his stallion, Harrison and King Hamilton hoisted Levi's limp body up and into Navarre's strong arms. Navarre positioned himself to where he had Levi in a sturdy embrace in front of him.

"Here," Harrison said, approaching where Levi's legs dangled along the side of the horse. "Allow me to secure his legs so they do not interfere with your ride. We must jump over a divide on our return to the village." He looked up at Navarre. "Will you require him to be secured to you?"

Navarre shook his head. "I will be fine."

Once Navarre was ready, Harrison walked over to a disillusioned Reece. "If you are unable to ride, you can join me on Saracen."

Reece brushed her tears away. "I'll be fine," she said distantly.

Harrison nodded and helped her onto Arrow's back. Once settled into the saddle, she continued to stare at the lifeless body of the man she loved being cradled within his father's arms. *This isn't happening,* she thought as she felt Harrison's hand tenderly covering over her own. "You saved his life," he said, bringing her attention down to him. "He will recover, you must know this. Levi is too strong of a man not to." He looked down at her abdomen and back up to her. "He has too much to live for. We will not lose him," he said with tears pooling in his glassy eyes.

She nodded in return. The encouraging words sounded good, but she was afraid to believe them. Once Harrison was on Saracen, Navarre allowed his horse to gently take the lead. The warriors who remained silent were now stepping aside to allow Navarre to pass through. The horses walked past the many warriors within the walls of the fortress. Reece was stunned to find that the strange people from before seemed to have changed in appearance. Their faces were clean and beaming with bright smiles. Their battered clothing was restored and almost new again. Reece couldn't return their smiles, so she brought her attention forward, ignoring everything surrounding them. Instead, she gazed intently at the top of Levi's head, which was resting helplessly against Navarre's shoulder.

After they reached Shallek's village, the injured warriors were immediately attended to. Reece remained in the room, isolated from the others where Levi lay flat on his back, unconscious. Ionis assessed his condition upon their arrival and immediately ordered for a particular type of medication to be put directly into Levi's bloodstream. Then they rubbed a clear cream over his forehead and also massaged it through his hair, rubbing it into his scalp. Ionis looked at Reece with saddened eyes and informed her that Levi was alive; however, his mind was severely wounded. He was in a deep sleep, as his mind was slowly trying to heal itself from the trauma it had suffered from the hostile attack against it. The only hope they had was that the special remedies they gave him would increase his mind's ability to heal faster.

How much time had passed since they arrived back in this village, Reece had no idea.

A soft step from behind her forced her to raise her head up from where she had been laying her head on Levi's chest. The only thing that soothed her was the sound of his steady heartbeat, reassuring her that he would heal soon. She sat up in the chair that was next to the head of Levi's bed and looked over to find Navarre entering the quiet room. She felt horrible. She hadn't said one word to him since his rescue, other than shouting orders at him about how Levi was to be taken care of. She was so relieved to see him again; however, she felt completely numb about everything. She felt empty and alone. Navarre stood at the side of Levi's bed and reached down to softly grip his son's leg. He silently gazed somberly at Levi's face.

Reece reached for Levi's lifeless hand, held it to her lips, and softly kissed the back of it. Tears began forming in her eyes again as she rested her cheek against his hand. She stared at Levi's face. "We're going to have a baby." Her voice cracked. She closed her eyes as tears poured out of them, unable to speak anymore. She felt Navarre's comforting hand on her back. She swallowed hard. "I told Levi when he worried about me and his child on this mission that we would be successful in recovering—" She paused, her crying interrupting her speech. She sniffed and forced herself to continue. "That when we recovered you, in nine months from now you would be holding your grandchild in your arms," she paused again, "telling your grandchild about what a brave warrior their father was in rescuing you—" Her stomach knotted with grief, uncontrollable sobs rendered her incapable of saying anymore.

She managed to look over and see Navarre kneeling at her side, while gently stroking his hand along her back.

Through her sobbing, she managed to smile hopefully at him, while leaning her cheek against Levi's lifeless hand.

His eyes appeared to radiate happiness, and he brought his hand to her cheek. "And I will also tell my precious grandchild the truth of its mother, the brave woman who saved every soul within two whole galaxies."

Reece closed her eyes, and tears streamed down her cheeks. She looked back at Levi. "I can't lose him. He is the love of my life. He is my strength, my happiness, and so much more than I can put into words. I don't know how I survived without him in my life. I don't know how I could live without him now." She sniffed. "I need him; our baby needs him!"

Navarre gently turned her to face him, and he placed a tender kiss on her forehead. "My dearest Reece, my heart swells with love with the knowledge that you and Levi are bringing such a treasured gift into our lives." He glanced at Levi. "My son will wake, and until he does I beg of you to find comfort with our family, knowing we will be at your side, helping you through this."

Reece nodded. "I want to get him out of this galaxy. We need to go home."

"We are bringing him home to Pemdas tonight," Navarre answered.

"Do you believe our doctors in Pemdas can help him recover faster? Possibly with the help of Galleta, maybe she can do something to help him?"

Navarre slowly withdrew. "Yes. That is why I have decided that we shall leave as soon as you feel you are ready."

Reece wiped the tears from her eyes and smiled up at him. "Let's get him home," she said with determination.

Navarre nodded. "Very well."

Even though the situation was devastating, taking Levi back to Pemdas seemed to be their best option. It was time to go home, where they were all safe again. Anticipation filled her entire being, knowing that when they would return to Pemdas, their doctors would know what to do to help Levi. He would wake up, and they would laugh in triumph together that they successfully survived this impossible mission.

# Chapter 35

Harrison had saddled Arrow and led him over to where Saracen waited alongside of the other Guardian horses. Once the horses were fully prepared to leave, he turned to go check on Reece's current state. He knew that Levi would expect him to be a pillar of strength for Reece in this situation. It was heartbreaking to see her in such a condition—emotionless and obviously numb.

"Reece is prepared to leave when the rest of our men are," Navarre said as he approached Harrison.

"Very well. How is she doing?" Harrison asked with concern.

Navarre shook his head. "She is a strong young woman, but I believe we need to get her back to the comforts of Pemdas. Allestaine will be an excellent comfort to her during this time."

"Any changes in Levi?"

"None. I fear for his current condition, and I am uncertain of what trauma his mind has undergone. Our physicians know the Pemdai mind well, and they will know how to treat him."

Harrison nodded. "I agree. I have already sent men ahead in order to prepare for our arrival. They have been dispatched on a quicker route to the portal, and they will have the proper transportation ready to bring the fallen warriors to Pasidian once we have crossed over the protective barriers into Pemdas. I also informed them to notify my father that Queen Galleta and the medical staff need to be onsite to retrieve Levi upon our arrival."

Navarre nodded. "Let us return to our home. Is this shorter route to the portal safe for us to travel through?"

"Yes. Now that the threat has been removed, I have no doubt that we will be safe. It is the best means of travel in order to be out of this galaxy as soon as possible. Also, the men I sent ahead should be arriving in Pemdas at any moment because of it."

"I agree," Navarre answered. "Allow me to give my appreciation to Shallek and his people once more. Tell the men to prepare Levi; as Reece desires, he will continue to travel with me on my horse," Navarre said.

"Very well," Harrison answered. "And Emperor," Harrison called out, forcing Navarre to turn around. "I wish it were under better circumstances, but I am indeed most grateful to see you alive again, and may I be the first to tell you that all of Pemdas eagerly awaits your arrival."

Navarre nodded. "Nephew, I could not be more grateful for all of your bravery. I am overwhelmed with joy to return to Pemdas." He became more serious as he glanced around at their surroundings. "However, I feel that this may come at a higher price than losing our men and nearly losing my son. Mordegrin is nowhere to be found, and if he finds his way to that portal, I fear we all may be doomed."

Harrison returned Navarre's grave expression. "We had reason to believe that he would try to cross through the portal, so we have Guardians standing watch; and the armies that assisted us in your recovery are already searching for him."

Navarre's somber expression never faded. "Let us hope he is found and destroyed. Until then, I will extend my gratitude to Shallek, and we shall be on our way."

As Navarre brushed past him, Harrison turned and walked quickly toward the location where wounded Guardians had fully recovered and were exiting. They had lost close to eighty men in the attack, and as devastating as that was for Harrison and the surviving Guardians, if it weren't for Reece, they all would have surely met their demise.

He walked into the isolated room where Levi remained and saw Reece silently crying while her head rested on Levi's chest. For a man who was not very emotional, this sight made his heart wrench and tears well up in his eyes.

He slowly approached Reece and avoided looking at his cousin in such a helpless state. He softly brushed his hand along Reece's arm. "We are prepared to leave," he softly said.

Reece sat back, wiping the tears from her eyes. Harrison could feel the pain and suffering radiating from her. She stood up, and her lifeless expression was more troubling to him than he could imagine.

He pulled her into his embrace. "Reece, regardless of his current state, he will be okay. Try not to believe the worst."

Reece softly moaned in agony. "I am trying to calm myself because he is alive, and I know he will be better off in Pemdas." She pulled away from Harrison. "But there is an overwhelming feeling within me that makes me believe that I have lost him. I can't explain why or how, it's just how I feel."

Harrison stepped back. "Reece, we all have been through a lot. *You* have been through a lot, and you have experienced far more than anyone should ever have to. Please trust that the trauma you have been through could be contributing to your distress." He pulled her arm into his. "We must leave this place and return you home to Pemdas."

She leaned into his arm as he led her out of the room, holding on to him for support. "Have you eaten anything since we arrived? Even though you are concerned over Levi, you must not forget about your child."

"Yes. Ionis brought me some cheese, and I forced myself to eat it." She sighed. "I can wait until we get home before I need to eat again."

It was close to two hours after they left Shallek's village that they entered the portal and were back into the outer boundaries of Pemdas. Even though the strange curse was lifted from the other galaxy and the appearance of everything was changed back into serene beauty, Harrison was never so relieved to be back in Pemdas once again. Once across the barriers, they halted the horses as Pasidian's imperial guards met them to help with the escort of the fallen warriors. There were four flatbed wagons, each being pulled by six white horses. Harrison immediately dismounted to help with the proper care of his fallen men.

He smoothed his hand over the black, velvety blanket that covered the entirety of the flatbed wagons that the men were to be placed upon. With the help of the imperial guards and Guardians, the fallen warriors were removed from their horses, wrapped in a rich, burgundy material, and positioned honorably upon the wagons. Harrison and the imperial guards each took the folded burial blankets, which were black with a silver arrow embellished onto them, and carefully draped them over each of his fallen warriors' bodies.

With a nod of acceptance from Navarre, Harrison turned and hoisted himself up on Saracen's back. Navarre led the procession to the palace, with Areion to the right of him and Reece riding to his left. The riderless horses of the fallen soldiers were behind Navarre, following in excellent formation. As the commanding officer, Harrison rode behind the group of riderless horses and directly in front of the imperial guards transporting the fallen soldiers. The imperial guards notified Harrison that the families of the lost warriors were grouped alone and prepared for the honorable return of their brave family members. Lady Allestaine and King Nathaniel accompanied them, lending the grieving families support.

A medical staff was positioned to await Levi's arrival to get his condition assessed immediately. As much as Harrison wished to ride his horse directly to where he knew Angeline was waiting alongside of the thousands of other Pemdai people, he had to wait. As the fallen men's commanding officer, he had to give his condolences to each of the family members that were suffering such a profound loss before anything else.

It wasn't long before Navarre reached the top of the hill that overlooked Pasidian Palace. Harrison had just begun to ascend the hill when we heard the cheering of the large crowd from over the mountainside. It was bittersweet; as overjoyed as the Pemdai people were to have their emperor safely returned by their brave and fearless warriors, it was also a time of mourning for those men who gave their lives to bring him home.

Harrison followed the riderless horses up and over the hillside, and the sight below was awe-inspiring. Even more of Pemdas' citizens were there waiting to greet these brave men than the day they left to enter the new galaxy. The crowds grew silent as soon as the riderless horses came into view, along with the wagons carrying the fallen soldiers behind them.

Navarre led his horse directly to where Allestaine stood with Pasidian's large medical staff. The riderless horses stopped along with the convoy and waited for the Guardian soldier that was assigned to take the horses of each fallen soldier to their respective family members. As this took place, Harrison rode Saracen up to where Navarre awaited him. Harrison and King Hamilton were there to help Levi down from the horse and hand him over to the medical staff.

Once Harrison had Levi in his grips, Allestaine walked out to meet them. She glanced up at Navarre with love and longing in her eyes; however, her son's grave condition was first and foremost on her and husband's mind. She brought both hands to Levi's face and gently bent to kiss his forehead. "My valiant son," was all she said before she looked at Harrison and nodded. "The staff is ready, and I will not risk another second not having him in their care."

Harrison knew his aunt would not dare show her grief or distress when there were people around her who depended on her inner strength. Allestaine turned to where Reece stood at Harrison's side and brought her into a tight embrace. "My darling daughter, I cannot put into words how relieved and happy I am to see that you have returned to us safely." She stood back and placed her hand on Reece's cheek. Her eyes were set with purpose as she gazed into Reece's blank expression. "Do not fear for Levi. He is home, and he will recover. You must hold steadfast with that knowledge."

"I understand, thank you," Reece said distantly.

The medical staff brought out a board to transport Levi on into the medical center of the palace. King Hamilton and Harrison gently placed Levi on the board, and immediately after the medical staff was on their way to the palace while Reece traveled quickly alongside of them. The stress and trauma that Reece had endured over the past few days made Harrison increasingly concerned for her and the health of their child. Once he was finished consoling the families of the fallen soldiers, he would search her out to make certain she was mentally and physically stable.

He turned to find Navarre and Allestaine reunited in a strong embrace. They said nothing to each other; only held each other tightly as their separation was finally over.

Before Harrison could walk over and give his condolences to the grieving families, King Nathaniel was there extending his hand to him. Harrison shook his father's hand with a somber nod, and King Nathaniel did the same in return.

"My son, I have never been as proud of you as I am today. Your courageous leadership has brought our emperor and our men home. Pemdas could ask for no better commander for our Guardians."

Harrison sighed and stared into his father's noble eyes. "Father, I appreciate your words; however, I was not entirely successful in leading them or protecting Levi. It grieves me greatly to return to Pemdas with fallen warriors and with Levi in his uncertain condition."

King Nathaniel's gaze became stern. "You know firsthand that as a Pemdai warrior, brave men will fall in battle. To believe you were unsuccessful in fulfilling your duties as their commander only brings our fallen men shame. You must rise above and know that those men gave their lives freely for the emperor's rescue. I stand in awe that only eighty of our three thousand warriors were slain in this mission, as I was unsure that day you left us if any of you would return." He studied Harrison for a moment. "This mission was unpredictable, and everyone knew that our Guardians were on a mission with no certain outcome."

Harrison nodded. "Our fallen men fought courageously; indeed, they are our bravest." Harrison looked past his father and up at the palace. "Levi was the bravest of us all, and if it was not for Reece, we would all surely have been killed."

Nathaniel looked at Harrison with purpose. "That is how you shall console their families. Tell them of their sons' bravery as they gave their lives to bring our emperor home and protect not one galaxy, but two." King Nathaniel nodded. "Now, go. The families await your condolences."

His father's words were exactly what Harrison needed to hear. Being uncertain of Levi's condition was a worrisome distraction, and now he had to engage in the hardest part of being the commanding officer to the Pemdai Guardians. With boldness, Harrison turned to leave his father and approach the families of the fallen.

As he gave his final condolences to the wife of a fallen warrior, he looked over to witness that Allestaine and Navarre were following behind him, offering their condolences to the grieving families as well. He walked back toward the palace after leaving his horse in Javian's care. He scanned the large crowd, looking for Elizabeth and Angeline. As if given a breath of fresh air, his pain subsided when he spotted Angeline. She stood at Elizabeth's side in the front of a large crowd, staring in his direction. They both wore somber expressions, and there was no question as to why. Harrison's heart dropped when he saw the distress on Elizabeth's face with the realization that her brother was severely injured.

She wiped her tears away when he approached her. "Harrison," she sniffed and forced a smile, "it is wonderful to see that you are home safe."

Harrison embraced her. "It is good to be home, sweet one."

Elizabeth held him tighter. "Will my brother survive?" she asked with a shaky voice. "My father assured me a moment ago that he will, now that he is home with our physicians."

Harrison withdrew. "Your father is correct. We believe that having him under our physicians' care will greatly accelerate his recovery."

Elizabeth nodded. "I was not able to speak with Reece, but I am very concerned for her, Harrison. Is she well?"

Harrison exhaled. Reece did not look healthy in any way. "I am concerned for Reece as well. However, just as Levi, she is home and safe in the company of family and friends. Although she is quite distressed, she has proven herself to be stronger than any one of us ever gave her credit for. She saved all of our lives." He bent to kiss her forehead. "Do not fear, Lizzy, we simply must be patient for now."

She smiled up at him. "I understand." She glanced past Harrison. "If you will excuse me. My father is headed this way again, and I have only had an audience with him for a brief moment. I long to embrace him again."

"Go. You have waited long enough," Harrison said as he kindly guided her past where he stood.

He remained silent as he took in the beauty of Angeline again. She smiled up at him, and without hesitation Harrison impulsively brought her into his arms. He brought the back of his hand to cradle her head and buried his face into the side of her neck, absorbing the very essence of her. He said nothing; he only held her, having no desire to let her go.

"I am so thankful you are safe, Harry," she finally said.

"I have longed for this moment since I left you," he said as he pulled away. He gazed down into her eyes. "Allow me to freshen up. There are some other matters of business that require my immediate attention." He glanced around at the crowd of people. "After that, I will return for you. As much as I desire to be back at Pasidian, I cannot bear the chaos of being around all of these people. My only wish is to be in your company alone."

She caressed his cheek. "I understand. I will be with my father until then."

Harrison nodded. "Your father fought bravely today."

She smiled. "He said the same for you. Thank you for keeping him safe."

Harrison nodded and reached for her hand. He brought it to his lips, eyes never leaving hers. "Just as I promised you."

"Go handle your business. I will see you when you have finished."

He bent to kiss her softly, surprised that she would be willing to accept. After their trip abroad, and having been in a horrific battle that morning, there was no telling what he looked like. One more lingering kiss to her forehead, and he released her from his embrace and strode briskly into the palace gardens.

He walked down to the isolated medical center in the lower level of the palace. His heart sank when after all this time the physicians were still assessing Levi's condition. Queen Galleta was in a meditative state, most likely trying to mentally assess the damage he suffered. Reece was in the room, staring somberly at the queen, waiting for any response.

It was obvious that there were no answers, so he decided that once he finished freshening up, he would return with hopes that they would be further along with their assessment.

After Harrison changed into his formal attire, he promptly strode into the command center. He took reports from Vincent and found that nothing out of the ordinary occurred with the rest of the Guardians while they were away. Everything was as it should be, and he left knowing that Vincent was in complete control of everything.

Unable to wait any longer, he went back to the area where Levi was. Once admitted to the room, he found Levi and Reece alone. He noted that there was a tray of food brought in from the servants and that Reece hadn't touched anything on it.

He walked over to where she sat in a chair holding Levi's hand and staring intently at him. When she noticed Harrison, she looked up at him and smiled. He sighed in relief to see that her eyes were much brighter and hopeful now.

"It is good to have you amongst us again, Reece," he said as he glanced over at the untouched tray of food. "I would like to see that you stay that way, so you should try to eat something."

Reece smiled sweetly up at him. "Thank you, but I already have." She softly laughed. "This is the third tray of food that has been delivered to the room for me. Lady Allestaine has informed me that if I insist on staying with Levi, I will not go hungry."

"The *third* tray of food?" Harrison laughed. "Well, I suppose that means you must have informed my dear aunt about her unborn grandchild."

"Yes. She knows and is delighted. I think I'm going to be more spoiled than if Levi was awake and attending to these matters himself." She laughed, and then looked back at Levi's face. "With the remedies they gave him, the physician said he would most likely be waking by tomorrow or within the next few days. It all depends on if his mind has healed enough." She looked at Harrison. "You were right, he will be fine." Reece smiled at him. "Harrison, you need to go and unwind. Like you said before, all that we have been through in recovering Navarre was a lot for anyone to deal with." She squeezed his hand. "Even you, Harrison. Have you had an opportunity to spend time alone with Angeline?"

He exhaled. "No, but I have plans with her later." He rose up and smiled down at her. "I had to come and ensure you were doing better, and learn any news about Levi's condition." He softly laughed when he noticed she was still wearing her Guardian uniform. "Why do you not let me stay with Levi for a while? Go freshen up and change into some comfortable clothing. It will help, believe me."

Reece smiled. "Jasmeen is on her way down as we speak, and she will make sure that I look presentable again." She softly laughed. "Either way, I won't leave this room until he wakes up."

Harrison gazed sympathetically at her. "You will be okay using the showers here in the medical center?"

Reece arched her eyebrow. "Have you already forgotten the wonderful facilities I had the privilege of using in the other galaxy? I am sure a less than elaborate shower will not put me out."

Harrison laughed. "Indeed. It is good to be home, though, is it not?"

"It is. Now, you should go. Finish the rest of your business, and spend your evening alone with Angie. I'm sure she's longing to have time alone with you. Don't forget, she's probably been forced to entertain all of the kings and the families that have been residing at the palace, waiting for the emperor's return since the day we left. Until they all leave, I'm sure she would love to get away from this place."

Harrison softly sighed. "I have every intention of taking her away for a while. Now before I leave, Levi informed me that you have a strong desire to eat tomato basil soup from the Anders' cafe. I will have the palace send for it."

Reece smiled. "That would be wonderful." She stood and embraced him. "Thank you, Harrison—for everything. Now, go and quit wasting time here."

Harrison searched out Angeline and found her in the sitting room with Elizabeth, his parents, and the Hamiltons. He noticed Angeline's face radiate with excitement when he walked in, and he quickly crossed the room to where she and Elizabeth were entertaining Mozart. When he approached them, he rubbed over the top of Mozart's head and chuckled. "It is easy to see Mozart has taken to you nicely, Lizzy."

Elizabeth laughed. "Indeed; however, Angie and I have had the privilege of a cello accompaniment with our music ever since Reece departed. I do believe he misses Reece's company immensely."

Harrison shook his head. "Well, our little zorflak here must be patient, as Reece has no intention of leaving Levi's side until he is awake."

"Do you believe it will be okay for me to go visit her now?" Elizabeth asked.

"I believe that is a most excellent idea." He smiled. "She is doing much better, and I believe Mozart here will help to cheer her up as well."

"Very well, I will leave you and Angie to catch up." She smiled warmly at both of them, and then stood and left the room.

Harrison extended his hand down to Angeline, who was waiting patiently for him to bring his attention to her. She gently placed her hand in his, and he brushed his lips over the top of it. "Would you care to join me for a horseback ride before we lose daylight?"

She slowly stood and gazed at him with concern. "Aren't you hungry by now, Harry? We all took dinner early, and I was surprised not to see you there. I believed you must have been with Levi and Reece."

The room started filling with other guests who were residing in the palace. Navarre and Allestaine retired early, and Harrison had no obligation to stay, as his father and King Hamilton would entertain the guests.

"I took a small dinner in the command center while going over business matters with Vincent," he answered.

Her smile brightened. "Well in that case, I will happily join you. Allow me to go change into my riding habit first."

Harrison escorted Angeline to her rooms, and once she was ready, he walked her down to the stables. "I hope you will be comfortable on Saracen riding with me, as I do not wish to spend another moment without my arms around you," he said as they approached the massive stallion.

Angeline squeezed the inside of his arm tightly. "I will be perfectly comfortable. I never believed I would ever have such an opportunity to ride on one of our Guardian horses," she said with excitement in her voice.

Once they were on Saracen, Harrison led them away from the palace. There were plenty of guests lingering outside in the palace gardens, yet Harrison managed to smoothly avoid them.

As they rode out, Harrison kept the horse at a gentle speed. He used one hand to guide the horse, and the other he held around her waist. He tenderly rubbed along her side as he continued to place kisses along her covered shoulders, her neck, and when she turned to the side, his lips were softly against her cheek without hesitation. He had ached for this moment since she first told him she loved him, and he indulged himself in this moment even more when Angeline seemed to desire their closeness as much as he. She was completely relaxed into his loving embrace while caressing the arm he had protectively wrapped around her.

"I did not expect this would be how you would hold me in your arms upon your return," Angeline said with laughter.

"You will be lucky if I ever allow you out of my arms again, after the week I have been through," he said while continuing to indulge himself tasting the softness of the delicate skin of her slender neck.

"I would not have a problem with that."

Once they were at the meadow where they first spent time alone, Harrison halted his horse. He dismounted and helped Angeline down. Saracen wondered off, and before Angeline could say a word Harrison wound his arms tightly around her waist, abruptly lifting her up as she stared down into his eyes. He spun her around joyfully, so thankful to have her back in his arms and happy that the stress of their mission was all finally over. Angeline shrieked with delight, surprised by the gesture. She brought her hands to each side of his face and leaned down to kiss him. To Harrison's pleasure, she deepened their kiss without any reservation.

As much as Harrison desired the taste of her enticing lips, he slowly brought her feet to the ground. To his surprise, Angeline kissed him with more power, unwilling to separate herself from him. They remained in this state for quite some time until Angeline withdrew, took his hand, and led him out through the tall grass. She slowly turned back to him, and the expression on her face halted his breath for a short moment.

She reached for his other hand and interlaced her fingers through both of the hands that she now held. He was spellbound by her beauty at the moment. All of the stress and unnerving sensations that he and the Guardians had gone through over the last week had simply vanished. All that he felt now was the comfort of this woman who held his heart. Her exquisite, yellow riding habit seemed to enhance the beauty of her bronze eyes and the complexion of her flawless, golden skin. In her eyes, he saw more than beauty now, but also a longing for him and his love.

She looked down to where she held his hands. "Is this really happening?" she asked before her eyes were gazing lovingly back into his and she wrapped her arms around his waist, drawing him closer to her again.

Harrison stared down into her passionate eyes, snaking one arm around the small of her back and the other gently caressing the back of her neck. "I keep asking myself the same question, lovely Angeline." He bent to kiss her, and then took her hand. "Come with me."

Harrison sat, guiding her to sit in front of him. When she did, he wrapped his arms around her, holding her securely in his arms. "I understand very well that I do not deserve such a divine and pure woman as you, Angie."

"Please, do not speak that way—"

"Allow me to finish," he said in humor, while kissing the top of her shoulder. "I must have you know, I never believed that I would ever desire a woman's presence or love, such as I do yours. I prided myself in such things. I was such an ignorant, arrogant man, and I learned that lesson very well in the days following our first kiss." She looked up at him and grinned as he smiled with compassion into her glistening eyes. "All I know now is that I want your love, Angeline, beyond anything else."

As Angeline brought her attention to the meadow in front of them, he reached into his side pocket and pulled out a silver band that he received as an heirloom from his great aunt many years before. It wasn't much, but for now it would have to do. He held it out in front of her and listened as her breathing halted. He softly kissed the side of her neck. "I promised upon my return I would hold you in my arms and prove to you just how profound my love for you most assuredly is." Angeline was frozen as she stared down at the ring he held in front of her. "I plan to start proving my love for you in this manner. I want nothing more than to commit my life only to you, the only one woman who has ever captivated my heart and soul. Become my wife, Angeline Hamilton, as I desire nothing more than to be your husband."

Angeline twisted in his arms, and the expression on her face was so somber that it had Harrison somewhat concerned. She was a young woman, and Harrison knew that committing herself to one man at this point in her life might not be what she wanted. He, himself, had plenty of time to enjoy the luxuries of courting different women, and if Angeline accepted Harrison's request, he was not affording her the same opportunity.

"Angie, I love you so greatly that I will not force this upon you. If you need more time, I will patiently—"

Her lips on his silenced him. She caressed his cheek, tilted her head to the side, and deepened their kiss. After a few moments, she withdrew, her eyes filled with tears. "Harrison, I feel as though I am dreaming. Are you sure that I am *that one woman* who you truly want in such a way—forever?" she softly asked.

He gazed intently at her. "I have never loved anyone as I love you, Angie." He softly exhaled. "On our journey into that galaxy, I was severely injured in an ambush; and for the first time in my life fighting as a warrior, I stared death in the face and nearly lost my life. In that moment, and during my recovery, all I could think about was you and how I would never have the chance to prove how much I ardently loved you." He looked past her, recalling the memory "I promised myself after we survived the attack that if we were to survive the rest of our mission, once I had you in my arms again I would waste no time ensuring that you knew I was willing to commit my life to none other than you. I have wasted enough time already, and in doing that I nearly lost the opportunity to ever have you love me in return." He looked back at her. "I love you, Angeline Hamilton. I never knew the meaning of the word until you and I shared our first kiss together in this location. My outlook on life has indeed changed from that moment on."

Her eyes filled with tears, and she sat back some, still facing him. "Harrison, nothing could possibly make me happier than to accept your proposal. I have loved you since I was a girl. There is no man that I have ever desired to love other than you."

A broad smile stretched across his face as he reached for her hand. "You make me a better man, Angie, more so than I believe you will ever understand," he said as he slipped the ring onto her finger. He softly chuckled. "Accept this token for now, as I have not had time to meet with a jeweler."

She stared down at the silver band. "Having you as my husband will always be more magnificent to me than any extravagant ring I could wear." She looked up at him. "I love this ring, and I want nothing else."

Harrison gripped the back of her neck, gently bringing her to lay her down, and without hesitation he brought his lips down onto hers. Harrison had no desire to pursue more from their kisses; he cherished this woman with all that was in him.

He would patiently wait to show her more of the love that held for her until after their commitment ceremony, which could have easily been done that evening. However, with Levi's current state, he felt it only right to wait for him to recover, as he wanted Levi present in the private ceremony. For now, he would wait and enjoy these treasured moments with Angeline before she became his wife.

***

It had been close to four days, and Levi still lay in his comatose state. Reece was determined to persevere alongside of him, and she had not left his room once. The rest of the family was continually checking on both her and Levi's condition. Reece was doing surprisingly well. Jasmine was giving her a remedy to help nourish her and the baby, and her constant hunger was starting to cease. The doctor that was assigned to care for Reece for the duration of her pregnancy informed her that because she was carrying a child with the genetics of a Pemdai, the baby required more nourishment than her human body could naturally give, and that was what was causing her constant hunger. Now that that issue had been taken care of, she could properly focus on Levi's recovery.

In the last day or so, Levi started to respond somewhat to her voice whenever she was alone in the room with him. She nearly jumped from the chair the previous morning when she told him she loved him and his hand softly gripped hers in response. She knew his eyes would open any time now and she would have him back in her arms again. They would celebrate the news of their child, Navarre's return, and the news of Harrison and Angeline's engagement. All they needed now was for Levi to wake.

In the last hour or so, Levi was beginning to show drastic improvement. Harrison had come in and teased him in his usual manner, and Levi's lips twitched in response. It was obvious his mind was starting to hear all of them, and everyone was waiting. Navarre and Allestaine had just left to have lunch with the rest of the palace guests after stopping by to bring Reece some more tomato basil soup. Reece had finished the last of the soup and nearly dropped the bowl onto the floor when she glanced over and saw two brilliant sapphire blue eyes staring up at the ceiling.

She placed the bowl on the table and looked over at the servant that was sweeping the floor of the room. "Quickly! Let the emperor know his son is awake!" she screeched with excitement.

Levi turned his head abruptly in her direction, seemingly startled by her order to the servant. So overjoyed to see the eyes that she believed she would never see open again, Reece anxiously placed her hands to each side of his face and impulsively kissed his soft lips. So absorbed in feeling the strength in his lips again, she hardly heard the door open, admitting whomever it was to the room.

To her surprise, two strong hands gripped each side of her face, gently but forcefully removing her lips from his. She stared down into Levi's stern sapphire blue eyes, his brow furrowing as he studied her. "Levi?" she questioned.

Levi tilted his head to the side. "Forgive me, madam, there seems to be a misunderstanding," he said in confusion.

Reece softly gasped as she tenderly reached for his face. She paused when his expression darkened, and he moved his head away from her hand. "Levi?" she said softly, "It's me, Reece. I am your wife."

Levi looked past her and stared at Harrison, Angeline, Elizabeth, Navarre, and Allestaine, who stood in astonishment at the scene that had played out before their eyes.

"Please forgive me, but I believe you are very much mistaken. I have never seen you before in my life."

# Epilogue

## Harrison

"Commander," Vincent called out in a deep voice of concern.

Harrison looked up from his notes, finally having time to start catching up on all of his work. "Come in, Vincent," he said as he gestured for Vincent to take the chair across from his desk. "What is wrong?" Harrison asked after Vincent's grave expression darkened.

"The portal," Vincent started, "one of the men assigned to take the next shift has returned with horrific news."

Harrison abruptly stood from his desk, noticing the Guardian standing outside of his office with a petrified expression on his face. *This better not be what I think it is,* Harrison thought, as he never had seen such an expression on a Pemdai warrior's face.

"Mr. Bradley," Harrison approached the man, "tell me what has happened at once."

The Guardian snapped out of his daze. "I have no idea how to explain this, Commander, so I will come out and say what we encountered at the portal."

"Go on," Harrison replied.

"Jeremy and Messac have been turned—" he swallowed, "they are now stone."

"What?" Harrison answered.

"Indeed. We have no idea what has caused this."

Harrison rubbed his forehead in agitation. "Mordegrin," he firmly responded. "Vincent, the command center is yours. Mr. Bradley, come with me immediately."

Once Emperor Navarre was notified of the news, he, Harrison, King Hamilton, and Mr. Bradley walked out of the palace dressed in their Guardian warrior regalia and fully armed. As they walked toward the stables, Harrison's patience grew thinner when their horses were not yet fully armored and dressed to travel to the portal.

"When has it ever taken Javian and his crew this long to prepare our horses?" Harrison growled.

Navarre glanced over at him. "Harrison, we will get to the bottom of this. For now, you must gather yourself so that we can decipher what may have happened when we arrive at Shallek's village to seek answers."

Harrison folded his arms and sighed. "If this is the doing of Mordegrin, Emperor, we must know at once."

At that moment, Javian and the stablemen approached with their horses. The men reacted swiftly and were on their horses and leaving the palace at a rapid pace.

Once at the portal, Harrison swallowed hard at the sight of the two Guardian warriors who had been turned to gray stone. *Impossible,* he thought with anger and grief.

Without dismounting their horses, Harrison turned back. "Bradley, stay at your post. We will return once we have more answers."

The men rode their stallions directly into Shallek's village, and to their surprise Diexz, Oble, and Rei were the first to greet them.

"Guardians, we are most fortunate that you have returned, as we do not know where the portal to your galaxy is located."

"What has happened?" Harrison demanded while jumping from his horse. "Two of our warriors who were positioned to guard the portal have been turned into rock. Something or someone from this galaxy has done this. Is this Mordegrin's doing?"

Shallek approached. "Gentlemen, for fear of upsetting my people with the news we have for you, please follow me into a more private location."

Once in a small meeting room, Navarre placed his hand on Harrison's chest, a gesture offered to politely dismiss him from asking any further questions. Harrison glanced at his uncle and King Hamilton's grave expressions. Navarre silenced him with his stare while King Hamilton nodded in understanding.

They all took their seats around the table. "Guardians, please accept our most sincere apologies. We believed we had finally located Mordegrin after you left our world. As your warriors have been turned to stone, Rei's have also. That was the last location we had any reports of Rei's men nearly capturing the Shadowy One."

"So this is the work of Mordegrin?" Navarre answered. "Now, he is in our galaxy," he answered sternly.

"Yes," Rei answered. "Have you any idea as to whether or not he knows where the location of the powerful stone that protects your galaxy is?"

"No," Harrison answered. "However, the only time we journeyed to that location, he was in our prison chambers. We strategized our journey in such a way that it would keep him from having any idea as to where it was."

"If," Diexz leaned forward, "by any chance the Shadowy One gains control over that stone, your galaxy surely will be destroyed."

Navarre looked at Rei. "When did you first discover your men had been turned to stone?"

"It was only days after you left our world. That was the last contact my men had with him, and they nearly captured him," Rei answered. "We have been searching for him since that time."

"Without knowledge of where the portal to your world was, we could not warn or notify you that this occurred."

"We could not trust anyone with the portal being opened," Harrison answered. "It would seem that we should have placed more trust in your kind, as now our world is in grave danger."

Navarre remained silent as the men continued to discuss the new threat to Earth and how they would search out and capture Mordegrin.

"Harrison," Navarre finally spoke. "Is there a way that we can send Guardians to discreetly guard the stone's location without giving the location away? There may still be time. I do not believe Mordegrin knows where the stone is, or he would have acted by now. We would have already suffered the effects of the stone being altered by such a being."

Harrison exhaled. "I believe we can guard the location. But if Mordegrin does not know where the stone is—and I agree, we would have known by now—we may give the location away by guarding it."

Navarre looked at Shallek. "If this creature seeks to destroy our world, do you believe he would have acted by now if he could access such great power with the stone?"

"Without a doubt," Oble answered. "Before you realized your men were turned into rock, he would have already begun the process of destroying that galaxy."

King Hamilton sighed. "Well, in light of all this tragedy, this is at least some good news."

"Mordegrin must have failed to extract the information from Emperor Levi's mind," Rei answered.

"We have been assessing his mind, and it appears as though it was severely damaged while preventing Mordegrin or the Olteniaus females from extracting the map from it," Navarre said.

"Very interesting," Shallek answered. "Your minds are indeed powerful. Has Emperor Levi made any form of a recovery?"

"Fortunately, he has," Navarre said somberly. "However, he has lost his memories, and we can only wait and be hopeful that they will return."

"Memory loss?" Rei answered. "That is confirmation that Mordegrin was unsuccessful in extracting the map. Although, it does not guarantee that you will be safe."

"How so?" Harrison answered.

"There can only be two reasons Emperor Levi lost his memories when his mind was attacked," Shallek said in a voice of concern.

"The first?" Navarre asked.

"Either Emperor Levi's mind shut off all of his memories during the time his mind was being attacked, or Mordegrin caused the memory loss himself."

"Why would Mordegrin do that?" Harrison asked.

"So that he would become Mordegrin's servant at will. He would have altered Emperor Levi's mind to serve only him by this memory loss," Rei answered.

Harrison shook his head. "Impossible. Reece said herself that she mentally battled against their intrusion."

Shallek exhaled in what seemed to be relief. "This is great news, then. It appears as though Reece protected his mind from the extraction."

"This still does not solve anything," Navarre returned. "How do we hunt down this creature and destroy him?"

"He can only be destroyed if the Empress Reece has her powers fully restored. She is the only one who can destroy him. He cannot be killed by anything other than mental persuasion," Oble answered.

"That is it," Harrison answered. "Mordegrin was unsuccessful in retrieving the map from Levi's mind. He turned our men to stone to make us aware he was in our world." Harrison looked at the men around him. "Do you not see? He knew we would return to this galaxy, learn that Reece was the only answer to his death, and we would have to take her to the stone."

Navarre nodded. "That very well could be his plan. We will not journey to the stone in order to destroy the creature."

"Very wise decision, Emperor Navarre," Rei answered. "Mordegrin's ultimate desire cannot be fulfilled unless he has the stone."

Navarre clasped his hands together and leaned forward on the table. "It appears as though our Guardians will have their hands full on Earth, as I want Mordegrin tracked down and imprisoned. Once this occurs, Reece will return to the stone, gather its powers, and rid this threat to our world."

"Emperor Navarre," Shallek spoke up, "do not be misled into believing it will be as easy as that."

"It is what my Guardians are trained to do," Navarre returned.

"If Mordegrin so much as suspects you have discovered him in any of your worlds, he will shift into a new form."

"Shapeshifting?" King Hamilton answered.

"Yes. That is why we have struggled to find him ourselves," Rei answered. "Until you are certain he is destroyed, do not allow anyone who desires to enter your protected dimension to do so. To do so might be the worst decision you could ever make."

## ABOUT THE AUTHOR

Award-winning author S.L. Morgan was born and raised in California. After 29 years of living in the Sierra Nevada Mountains there, she and her husband began their journeys of moving throughout the United States. She currently lives in California, where she and her husband are raising their three children.

In October of 2011, S.L. Morgan became inspired to write her new novel series, "Ancient Guardians." With her passion and love for Jane Austen and other classic romance novels, she was motivated to write a novel series of her own.

S.L. Morgan is currently anticipating five books in the Ancient Guardians series and is very excited to bring her readers on more adventures and journeys with Levi, Reece and Harrison.

Please follow S.L. Morgan on her social media sites to keep up with the latest updates on the new releases of the upcoming novels in the Ancient Guardians series.

**Sign up for our newsletter for information on new releases:**
http://eepurl.com/7_5I5

**Official Website**: www.slmorganauthor.com

**WordPress Blog**: http://ancientguardiansnovel.wordpress.com/

**Twitter:** https://twitter.com/slmorgan1

**Instagram**: http://instagram.com/slmorganauthor

**Pinterest**: http://www.pinterest.com/slmorganauthor/

**S.L. Morgan Facebook page:**
https://www.facebook.com/slmorganauthor?ref=hl

**Goodreads**: https://www.goodreads.com/slmorgan

**Ancient Guardians Novel Series Facebook Page:**
https://www.facebook.com/AncientGuardiansLegacyOfTheKey?ref=hl

## *From the Author:*

Thank you for taking time to read the third book in the Ancient Guardians series. If you enjoyed *Ancient Guardians: The Awakening*, help spread the word by leaving your review. It is greatly appreciated and always helps other readers decide whether or not this would be a book that they would enjoy, too.

**Happy Reading!**
S.L. Morgan